THE FOXGLOVE PACT

The Dissonant Lineage Series: Book One

By Sen Zhang

 A gift for you

Hope you enjoy my debut novel! Thanks again for checking it out! From Sen Zhang

SPIDER LILY BOOKS

THE FOXGLOVE PACT

WELCOME TO ILLIUM, CITY OF LIES, a home to man, monsters, and magic, where the supernatural hides in plain sight. It lives on your block, runs the PTA, and could trigger a war when it swaps your kid for a Fey Changeling.

Private Investigator Feng Yue "Claire" Giles doesn't mind working with monsters, but kids are another matter. She doesn't get much of a choice though, her influential client claims the Fey stole his baby and he's willing to do a lot to retrieve his real child.

When more cases surface, it becomes obvious that this isn't just a custody spat; it's a political disaster for the Fey Courts and city officials. For some powerful people, it would be better if these children are never found. Claire disagrees, but she'll have to convince her "allies" of that, starting with Dreyson, a monster hunter who lives by "behead everything first, burn it all after."

The Fey Courts are willing to kill to protect their interests – that includes nosy investigators and their own children. Claire needs to survive the purge and find both sets of kids, human and Fey, before someone else solves the problem, permanently.

Published by
Spider Lily Books

This is a work of fiction. Names, characters, places, and incidents either are the product of author imagination or are used fictitiously, and any resemblance to actual persons, living or dead, business establishments, events, or locales is entirely coincidental.

The Foxglove Pact
The Dissonant Lineage Series: Book One

Copyright © 2025 by Sen Zhang

Cover Art by Angry Wolf • www.angrywolf.carrd.co

All rights reserved. This book is licensed to the original purchaser only. Duplication or distribution via any means is illegal and a violation of international copyright law, subject to criminal prosecution and upon conviction, fines, and/or imprisonment. Any eBook format cannot be legally loaned or given to others. No part of this book may be reproduced or transmitted in any form or by any means, electronic or mechanical, including photocopying, recording, or by any information storage and retrieval system, without the written permission of the Publisher, except where permitted by law.

To request permission and all other inquiries, contact Sen Zhang at sen@senzhang.net.

Paperback ISBN: 978-1-967831-99-9

Printed in the United States of America

First Edition

August 2025

Dedication

To the ones who didn't fit: someday you'll shape your own world. Make it a good one.

Acknowledgements

A very heartfelt thanks to Rhys Ford who talked me out of lots of panic cycles and existential meltdowns, while only seeming vaguely perplexed by the ordeal. I also appreciate all the work she put into making this book look good, because that was not me. This would not have happened without her.

I am also grateful to Brian, my editor, for straightening up my delinquent style. I regret to confess, that I will never fully comply with CMOS and I will die on that hill wielding my S-apostrophe combo like a bludgeon. I hope he can forgive me some day.

Thank you to Angry Wolf for making the cover and translating my vague ideas into another medium of art.

A special commendation goes to Daph, Purveyor of Cursed Things, for encouraging me throughout this whole process. Your art made me laugh and go "why" so many times. The psychic damage persists.

Thanks to my beta readers Rebecca Hubery, Alice Lin, Patricia Galvin, Jing Floyd, Jerry Hsieh, Kelly W, Hannah, Becky, and Nik. Your words kept me going and helped shape this novel into a better story.

A very special thanks to J and River, who were very helpful in other ways and somehow managed to make it through this without ever reading a manuscript.

All errors are mine alone.

I also want to thank those of you who bought the book. I know some of you have been supporting me for years, and I'm really glad you decided to continue on this journey with me.

I also need to shout out the "good neighbors" whose interest this garnered: I got you soju; please don't curse my cousin again.

Chapter 1
The Worst First Date

积非成是Trad. 積非成是- Jī fēi chéng shì – This chéng yǔ, or "Chinese proverb," more accurately a Chinese idiom, translates as "a wrong repeated (actively) becomes right." Obviously, it means that if you repeat a lie enough, it becomes "the truth." And here in Illium, a lot of people have an interesting relationship with the truth. In this day and age, you can't exactly go around giving out your actual birth date if you were walking the earth before the reign of Genghis Khan.

I only know of two people with that precise excuse. I'm sure there are probably a couple more, but I'm not in the right circles to regularly encounter truths of that quality.

— *From the Very Personal Journals of FYG*

AS FAR AS bad first dates went, this was one for the records, and it wasn't even the poor guy's fault. I grinned ruefully at him from against the wall, my face pressed hard enough into the brick that I could feel the mealy little indentations deepening in the skin of my cheek.

We had only just met up outside a downtown coffee shop, the warm autumn sunshine casting a golden glow on the morning.

"Stop resisting!" the officer snapped, even though I was holding very still, my hands at my sides. I wasn't trying to talk my way out of it like Dad. I wasn't screaming in anyone's face like Mother. Those tactics would not work well for me, not now.

"I'm not resisting," I said, trying to keep my voice even as I locked eyes with Freddy – I think that's what his name was. He was cute: big brown eyes with long lashes, wide cheekbones, dreadlocks pulled back in a neat ponytail. He fumbled with his phone, holding it up to film. "Am I actually being arrested? Do you have a warrant?"

"Shut up, Giles!" the other officer said, the one with the gun pointed at me. So they knew me and they weren't even going to try with my first name. It was better that they didn't mutilate the Chinese. I went by "Claire" these days, at least with my English-speaking friends. These cops clearly were not my friends.

"Don't know why they let people like you in, since you don't know how to act," the cop behind me hissed.

I gritted my teeth. "I was born h—"

"I don't care!" he snapped, having trouble cuffing me, despite my lack of resistance. It would have been comedic if there wasn't a loaded gun pointed at my head.

"What are your names and badge numbers?" Freddy asked, clearing his throat.

"We aren't required to answer that." The cop with the gun smiled insincerely at him. "You seem like a nice guy. We're arresting her on suspicion of *another* murder. We're doing you a favor. You don't want to get involved with this kind of crazy."

Freddy flinched, his eyes darting to my face, expecting me to loudly protest that I hadn't killed anyone.

"It was self-defense, a couple years ago," I sighed, because he could just google it.

Freddy looked away.

"Oh no, we're not talking about that." The cop behind me laughed darkly as he clicked the handcuffs locked. "This morning—"

"I'd appreciate your names, please," Freddy repeated.

"I'm Officer Ryan and that's Officer Hartford," the cop with the gun said, slowly holstering the weapon. "And I think you should leave before we find a reason to question you. How long have you known her? Do you really think she's worth the trouble?" He flashed poor Freddy a mean smile.

"My lawyer's name is Blake Canaris—"

"Shut up, Giles!" Hartford growled, dragging me toward the patrol car.

"You should stay out of this," Ryan said. "You don't know what this woman is capable of."

"Call Canaris! Sorry about this!" I shouted as Hartford shoved me into the back of the patrol car. "Thanks!"

Ryan took a moment to say something to Freddy, something that made the other man back away. Then the cops hopped in, faces irritatingly smug as they both glanced back at me. Ryan was probably my age, mid-twenties, blonde, in shape, more enthusiastic than intelligent. Hartford was older, in his late forties, red-headed, in a sort of round-ish shape, and watching me with a nasty grin.

"So what am I being accused of?" I asked.

"Shut up," Hartford snapped.

"Because I didn't do it and you know it."

"I know you're cocky because you think that boy is going to call your fancy lawyer, but you're in for a surprise," Ryan said, watching me in the rearview mirror.

"Maybe you did me a favor, then," I said with an extra bright smile. "Can't date anyone who doesn't know how to protect an individual's civil liberties."

"I said shut up!" Hartford shouted, slapping his palm against the cage.

My smile widened, mostly because I could not just shut my mouth, especially in high-pressure situations. Surface thoughts and inappropriate revelations just came out in a sputtering stream of pure verbal diarrhea. "I'm expressing my gratitude for a favor. And that coffee shop? Their lattes are meh anyway. Did you know that every sixteen ounces of coconut milk contains at least two ground-up crab claws? Not little crabs, mind you, but those giant bone-crushing coconut crabs that look like evil Pokemon—"

Honestly, a person absolutely should shut up when arrested so they could not incriminate themselves or give law enforcement any material to use against them, no matter how hypothetical. I was a nervous talker, but I knew how to weaponize it, and I happened to be spiteful, so I kept up a meaningless stream of babble about coffee drinks and other nonsensical trivia that I made up in the moment. Because something was very wrong. Obviously, this "arrest for another murder" was bullshit. But they weren't even trying to do things the right way. No Miranda reading. No warrant. Threatening Freddy. Not even trying to press me for an alibi.

By the time we reached the station, Hartford was shouting profanities at me and Ryan cowered at the wheel.

I expected the usual trip to intake, where someone might recognize me, and that would solve the problem. But instead they hustled in a side entrance and down the stairs, to a very familiar location.

My ears popped as we descended. I shuddered as I passed through the icy cold wards, a high-pitched hum settling in the back of my skull.

The Special Investigations Unit looked hilariously low-tech, and it was: six desks arranged in two rows, surrounded by retro beige metal filing cabinets. Each desk had an actual rotary phone, no computers in sight. There was even an ancient overhead projector set on a metal cart in the corner. The lieutenant's office door was shut, blinds closed. To my surprise, no one else was down here.

"Hurry up." Ryan shoved me, looking around nervously.

Hartford stood in front of the heavy vault door that led to the SIU lockup. Shit.

I stumbled into Detective Minuet's desk, purposefully knocking over her pens and paperwork. She would notice, and in my gut I knew that these guys weren't supposed to be down here. "Oh no, how clumsy of me! It's so hard to balance with my hands behind my back!"

"Goddamnit!" Ryan went down to pick up the mess. I considered knocking over some of the twisted pieces of glass that decorated her desk, but I didn't know what breaking those would do and I was scared to find out.

My phone was still in my pocket. They would confiscate it on discovery. Stretching my arms, I wiggled it loose, dropped it in Detective Mwanje's chair, and then pushed the chair in. At the very least, he would return my phone without frying it.

Hartford finally got the door open. "Stop fucking around!" he snarled.

Ryan hastily climbed to his feet and yanked me over to the door.

Hartford led the way down a narrow corridor to another heavy metal door. I couldn't see what he was doing.

Ryan shoved me against the wall and patted me down, his hands roaming below my waist and between my thighs, his fingers lingering where they had no business being. Rage flared inside my chest, but I bit my tongue, knowing that my protests would only encourage him. He seemed like that kind of power-tripping douchebag. I glanced up accusingly at the camera in the corner, hoping that it actually worked.

"Where's your phone?" he asked as he pulled my keys out of my jacket pocket.

"Fell out at the coffee shop," I said tightly.

"Really?" Ryan yanked hard on my ponytail.

"Doesn't matter," Hartford said with an ugly laugh. "You won't be needing it in here."

We entered the holding area. There were five chambers arranged in a circle—no bars, only glass divider walls and stone exteriors. There were no windows, no other exits. These were the special holding cells, and only two were occupied.

Everyone stopped.

In the nearest chamber on the right was a tall Caucasian man with an overgrown blonde crew cut. He sat on a composite slab bench and looked up when we came in. He had a single moss-green eye; the left one was just gone, a web of jagged pink scar tissue covering the socket.

In the cell to the left of the door were four figures pressed against the glass. They were bipedal and human-sized, but that was where the resemblance to a person stopped. Under the harsh lighting their skins were mottled and maroon, their bellies distended on skeletal bodies with shreds of clothing attached. Their faces were no longer identifiable: eyes filmed over, cheeks sloughing off, wide jaws filled with enormous serrated teeth. They snarled, clawing at the glass.

I took a step backward.

Ryan gripped my arm. "What's he doing here? I thought it was supposed to be clear—"

"Doesn't matter," Hartford said, though his eyes shifted nervously. He went to open the cell containing the Revenants.

"I wouldn't do that if I were you," I said through clenched teeth, kind of hoping he would, because I would get the satisfaction of seeing his face eaten off, right before I died horribly.

"Oh, are you scared of a couple meth heads?" Ryan laughed. "That's not our problem."

It was obvious Ryan couldn't see through the glamour, but Hartford's hands shook as he tried to grasp the door handle, sweat dripping down his doughy forehead.

Even as he started to reach forward, the Revenants screamed in unison and slammed against the glass, blue runes lighting up.

"Fuck!" Hartford wobbled backward.

"You want me to—"

"Forget it. Throw her in there with him. She can piss him off," Hartford said, mustering a weak sneer. He fumbled with the handle—concentric brass rings that folded into a niche in the door. "You stay back!" His voice wavered as he opened it.

Ryan hastily uncuffed me and shoved me inside. The door clanged shut behind me.

I glanced over my shoulder to see Ryan opening the vault door while Hartford lingered in front of the Revenant cell. He reached out, touching something to the glass, and the undead started screeching louder. Then he headed toward the exit, as fast as his stubby legs would carry him.

I looked back at my cellmate, who was still sitting on the gray bench, much...bigger up close than I expected.

My celly was a giant, nearly seven feet tall, and wearing gray pants and a thin white tank top stretched almost transparent across his broad chest. There were more claw-mark scars on his cheeks and neck, disappearing under his shirt. Several intricate tattoos covered his muscled arms, and the rest of him looked pretty solid too. Staring was rude, but a quick glance at his ink told me that he wasn't with any of the local white-power gangs. That was a minor relief, like finding an umbrella in a hurricane. The battle scars made his age difficult to guess. He looked anywhere in his late twenties to mid-forties, but appearances, like certain cops, could not be trusted in Illium.

He watched me stoically, making no move to get up nor any threatening gestures. The green of his eye was a bluer tone than mine, a splash of brilliant color on an otherwise severe palette.

I brushed my bangs out of my face, nodded at him, and then sat down on the other side of the bench, well aware that if he decided to do...anything, there wasn't much I could do to stop him.

That was terrifying, but not as much as the idea of being thrown into the other cell.

I took a deep breath, turning my attention to my surroundings. I was familiar with these cells from the outside: eight by ten, the dividing walls were a crystalline polymer, with sigils etched along the borders. I could read English and Simplified Mandarin and had a passing familiarity with other scripts, but I didn't recognize half of the writing. Given the fonts, the structure, and the patterns, there were multiple languages in play, but I couldn't seem to identify most of them. So I guess there were real-life consequences to sleeping through my historical orthography class. But in my defense, I was tired.

I wasn't tired now. Adrenaline fixed that. And being nervous made me want to talk. The difference from earlier was that I did not want to annoy my celly. It wasn't just how he looked; if he was in this kind of cell, he wasn't a mundane human.

"Are you hungry?" I asked, touching the inside pocket of my jacket. Because that bastard Ryan was so busy groping my ass that he overlooked the protein bar in my pocket. "And do you know what kind of Revenants those are?" Because there were several variants of the restless, corporeal, and uncontrollably hungry undead. Unlike some forms of the undead, Revenants didn't retain the sentience or the personalities they had in life. Fortunately, they weren't popping out of graveyards every night. Here, on average, the incidents occurred quarterly. It was easier to set them all on fire, toss the cremains in a purification tank, and call it a night, than it was to get them to hold still for taxonomic identification: ghuls, craqueuhhes, vrykolakas, vetalas, jiāng shī. There were records of all of them and more within the city.

The man turned that raptor-like gaze on me, his expression hard. It was not a friendly expression, but he remained seated. "There are too many aberrant mutations in this city," he said, his voice deep and rough.

"Oh good, I would have felt bad if you said, 'obviously those are langsuyar, don't you know anything?'"

"Those are obviously not langsuyar, manananggal, or the like," he said, speaking slowly and pronouncing the words with great care. There was a rustiness to his voice, like maybe he wasn't used to carrying on conversations, or maybe his throat was just dry. There were no sinks or toilets in the cell, just a drain in the floor. "Not enough hair left, no identifiable gender—that branch of undead presents as female, and the ones in front of us have full bodies—no levitation or exposed viscera."

I looked at the things, then back at my celly. He was right, and he had not tried to murder me yet. Both were good signs. "I do appreciate how nicely you said, 'obviously those are not langsuyar, don't you know anything?' It was very diplomatic. Hi, I'm Claire," I said and extended one hand.

There was a long pause. He stared at me, giving me a once-over that was less "checking me out" and more "assessing me as a potential threat or liability." Then he cleared his throat.

"Dreyson." His arms stayed at his sides.

"First name, last name, alias?" I asked, trying to keep my tone cheerful as I slowly lowered my hand.

"Dreyson," he repeated, an edge in his voice.

Just Dreyson then, easy enough. I nodded.

"Look—" he began.

And I did, just as the front glass panel of the Revenants' cell shattered and they burst out, shrieking. In seconds, they were pounding on the walls of our cell, their decomposing faces pressed to the glass as they searched for a way inside.

Chapter 2
The Wrong Kind of Gathering

盖棺定论 (Trad. 蓋棺定論)- Gài guān dìng lùn – This chéng yǔ translates as "don't pass judgment on a person's life until the lid is on the coffin." I respect the fair-minded sentiment behind the adage, but I also very much disagree. Here in Illium, you can't assume that a corpse is just going to stay in a coffin. Not without proper precautions, anyway.

But also, if a person has spent most of their life being a saint or being an asshole, you should probably recognize that while they're still alive.

— *From the Very Personal Journals of FYG*

THE GLASS WALLS shuddered with each impact, cracks splintering across the panels of our cell, the faults spreading with growing speed. Fists clenched, I took a deep breath, struggling to keep reins on the fear. Because despite what those asshole cops implied, I wasn't talented in close combat.

Dreyson made a guttural sound in the back of his throat. He slowly rose, rolling his shoulders and tilting his head from side to side. He narrowed his eye, attention on the Revenants.

I stood up too—it seemed like the thing to do—and even with the monsters at the door, I couldn't help but notice how big the man was, how he loomed in this small space. Maybe he wasn't actually seven feet tall, but he was at least a foot taller than me, and I was a respectable five eight.

"I thought these cells were tougher than this," I said, recalling the time I saw a slavering werejaguar throw himself at the walls without any effect.

"They are," Dreyson said. He glanced over at me, his expression verging on accusatory, and I understood what he suspected.

"Do you think that—"

"Yes," he said.

"Oh. Sorry," I said, and I meant it, because I really was sorry that this total stranger got caught up in this situation because someone up top really hated me.

He just rolled his shoulders again.

The glass was holding longer than I expected, blue sigils flashing with each impact, the magic fraying. Those things would break through soon. Where the hell was SIU? I looked around, but there was nothing in the cell I could use as a weapon, and nowhere to hide.

Anything undead was a high-level biohazard. Bites and claw wounds could spread a bunch of unpleasant diseases, but for most, the contagion risk was a lot lower than in popular culture. I was exponentially more likely to get a nasty antibiotic-resistant infection than to catch undead status.

"Are you any good in a fight?" Dreyson asked.

"Not this kind," I said, because I was a mostly normal human with no enhancements and very rudimentary magic skills.

Dreyson nodded, then flicked his right wrist, extending one large fist to me. "Do you know which end to hold?" He clasped a dagger, hilt out, to me.

"Where did you have that hidden?" I asked, reluctant to handle it, given that we were in the Illium Police Department's "special jail," and despite his massive frame, there were a limited number of places that my cellmate could conceal a weapon…

Dreyson snorted and offered no answer.

"You know, 'it's magic,' is a wonderful catch-all explanation," I said out of the corner of my mouth.

"Do you want it or not?"

I clicked my teeth, making the calculations. I wasn't a knife fighter, and he didn't look like a pacifist. "You might be better with it."

"You'll need it more," he said, as one of the things punched a hole in the glass, the walls buckling. The entire facade should have fallen by now, but the protective enchantments were still holding on. "Once they break the glyphs, I won't need it at all."

I took it, the polished hilt cool in my palm. It was a simple piece, bone handle, no cross-guard, and when I drew it from the battered leather sheath, the single-edged blade was eight inches of polished obsidian. "Obsidian is brittle."

"It'll last," Dreyson said without any hesitation. "It's magic."

I laughed, hysteria edging the sound. "Good callback."

"Brace yourself. We have less than a minute."

I gripped the weapon. "I'm not squeamish, but I've never killed a person with a knife."

"You're not killing a person," Dreyson said, disdain sharpening his tone. "These abominations are already dead."

The front wall shattered. The glass hung in the air for half a second, the writing lighting up blue one last time before fading, and then the panel came crashing down. The undead charged forward, their cracked hands oozing black ichor. The stench of mildew and rotting meat hit me an instant before the closest one screeched into my face.

I swung the blade. It cut through the air with uncanny speed, almost moving on its own. When it connected, there was just a little resistance, the softest pushback, and then the obsidian continued through the creature's neck in a gush of black goo and bone fragments. The head dropped off and the body wobbled. I pushed it away, surprised by how solid it felt. Then it went down, bursting like the world's worst meat pinata. It splattered my jeans and I winced, knowing these were going straight into the garbage.

To my left, Dreyson snapped one leg forward, kicking his attacker. It flew backward across the hall, landing in its own broken containment cell. He met the next one with a ball of orange flame in his palm. The sound of moist carrion sizzling was almost louder than the screaming.

The last one lunged face-first at me, jagged teeth clacking. I brought the dagger up, jamming the point into the roof of its mouth. More of that overripe slime leaked from its head. It shrieked. Making sure my own mouth was shut, I yanked the blade back out and cut again at a downward angle, trying to sever the neck. This time the blade slipped lower, going from shoulder to thorax, not quite bisecting the creature. When I pulled the weapon back, it came out clean.

The thing toppled, portions fanning out as it fell, the top slice of the corpse sliding free and across the slippery floor.

I stared mutely at the blade, because I did not have that kind of strength. Dreyson said it would last. He didn't actually say what the dagger could do. "It's magic" was a valid explanation after all.

Dreyson was out of our cell, head thrown back while he laughed maniacally as he stomped the remaining creature, black goo splattering the hall. There was madness in that one eye, all traces of my formerly stoic celly gone under a mask of ichor and blood thirst. He grinned at me wildly, that single green eye bright and wide, his teeth bared.

I didn't like that look at all.

"Two and two," he muttered, his voice harsh. "I don't like ties."

I had two choices: prepare for a fight and probably instant death, or try to defuse the situation and also experience instant death upon failure. Shakily, I lowered the dagger, sheathing it, and carefully tucked it in my waistband. I slowly reached one hand into my jacket pocket and pulled out the protein bar.

Having a snack was the one bright spot in this ordeal. Fishing it out, I maintained eye contact with Dreyson. Jails weren't good about regularly feeding people, and he didn't actually decline my earlier offer. "It's chocolate chip and still wrapped. Do you want it?"

Dreyson blinked, because even with one eye, his gestures were nowhere as whimsical as a wink. Suddenly he loomed in front of me. He plucked the protein bar out of my hands and tore the wrapper open with his teeth. Glowering at me, he sniffed it briefly, like he was checking for poison, and then he devoured it in two bites.

As he chewed, his expression changed, the mad smile and manic energy fading. Seconds later, he was back to being the bored disinterested cellmate.

Then he stared very hard at me and back at the remains of the wrapper, like he couldn't quite believe that he accepted food from a stranger.

"It wasn't poisoned, I was going to eat that, but you seemed like you needed it more," I said, wanting to take a step backward, but unable to will my legs to move. The undead were terrifying, but I was damn certain Dreyson could and would kill me with the twitch of his hand.

He continued to stare at me with that slightly incredulous and vaguely disapproving look.

"Kindergarten rules," I said, panic pushing more words out. "Sharing is caring. Clean up after yourself. Don't try to eat other people. It was vegetarian, but not vegan or gluten-free. Sorry, should have mentioned that first. I hope you don't have any aller—"

"It's fine," he said, voice flat. "But around here, you should be very careful about what you offer and what you accept."

"I appreciate the advice," I said, unsure of how literally to take that warning. What did that imply about him lending me his dagger? And did I want to hand it back to him just yet? I turned my gaze to the oozing remnants of the monsters. If I wanted to stall for time, I should change the subject. "Those teeth, though. I get the rotting and decomp, but how come their teeth change? Everything else goes to shit, but they get a dental upgrade?"

"Their diet changes, and the curse redirects the body's ailing resources. The teeth aren't an uncommon trait in obligate carnivores," Dreyson said. He looked at me funny, like he was bewildered by my line of inquiry. Then he shook his head, staring off at the vault door, his gaze distant.

The heavy metal door swung open, armored cops streaming in, shouting.

I reached backward, making sure my hoodie covered the weapon in my waistband.

Dreyson didn't resist as they threw him against a wall, screaming orders at him. It took them a few seconds to notice me standing there, just an irritated human lady covered in gore.

"Oh no—"

"Why is *she* here?"

"Shit—" someone proclaimed.

"Yup," I nodded with exaggerated cheer. "Mr. Canaris is going to hear all about this."

"What the fuck are you doing in here?" Lieutenant Jon Lawrence, head of the Special Investigations Unit, shouted when the other detectives brought him in. For two whole seconds, he looked shocked, poleaxed even, before he defaulted to his usual twitchy expression of barely constrained violence. In his mid-thirties, with cropped blonde hair, a broken nose, and hard icy eyes ringed in dark circles, he looked, talked, and swaggered like a boxer. He glared at me like I had personally snuck into his home and shit in his cereal bowl this morning.

Or *I* was the metaphorical shit in his metaphorical cereal bowl. Oh, I could see that.

I did not touch the dagger, though I thought about using it. I'd never make it, though. "Oh, you know," I said, crossing my arms so I couldn't reach for the enchanted weapon and give myself away. "Having my civil liberties violated, nearly being eaten alive by Revenants, and cleaning up more IPD messes. Love how you guys always get here *after* the shit hits the fan. In your own basement, even. What the fuck is up with that?"

The lieutenant straightened up, his fair skin turning a vibrant shade of red, those meaty fists clenched at his sides. "Get her out of here, *now*," he said through tightly clenched teeth, as he looked everywhere but at me, surveying the damage. "And find out who the fuck dumped her here!" Real fury sparked in his voice, and several grown men in body armor flinched, drawing up their shoulders and ducking their heads.

Detective Nina Davis, a middle-aged black woman with tight braids and a Tennessee twang in her voice, shook her head and gestured for me to follow. "Come on, Claire. I'll get you some disinfecting wipes, and we can figure out who screwed up this time."

"'Screwed up' implies that this was some kind of accident," I said sharply, because I was too jumped up to be afraid now, and while the lieutenant might hate me from the bottom of his shriveled little heart, he was somewhat professional. I was also emboldened by the fact that he probably wouldn't murder me in front of this many witnesses.

Davis mustered a rueful smile. "Claire—"

"What about him?" I asked, gesturing to the cuffed Dreyson, who was still pressed against a wall by Detective Coronet Mwanje. Mwanje was built like a linebacker and kept his head shaved. He would be intimidating, except he had a baby face and smiled most of the time. They were surrounded by half a dozen cops in SIU riot gear, all pointing their weapons at Dreyson. Oh, I knew how that felt. "We were both attacked."

"You hurt, Dreyson?" Mwanje asked politely.

"I'm fine," Dreyson said coldly. "And I'm not *contagious* either."

Mwanje bristled, his eyes narrowing, the color shifting from brown to muddy green. For a moment, his mahogany skin rippled, but then he just shook his head, rolling his eyes. "Then I'm glad you're OK, asshole. More importantly, I'm glad Claire is OK." Mwanje gave me a good-natured grin. But I caught that little slip. Dreyson got to him. Well, that was a shitty thing to say.

Once the Wergeld figures out where he is, they'll send him a lawyer or post bail. He's a frequent flier," Davis said.

"You good, then, celly?" I asked.

The lieutenant grimaced. "You're worried about him?" He pointed at the berserker. "*Him*? That psychopathic bastard? Do you realize what he could have done to—"

"And whose fault would that have been?" I snapped, because Dreyson didn't lock me in a cell, didn't set up or hurt me. "This is your damn department, Jon. I fucking trusted your people to do things right."

The air went out of the room, or maybe just in the space between me and the lieutenant. He stared at me with a feral blankness that I could not parse into a recognizable emotion. All I knew was that I struck a nerve. Good. There was nothing like telling the truth to *really* hurt someone.

"I'll deal with it," the lieutenant said through gritted teeth as he looked away, something flashing in his eyes. "But don't get the wrong idea about this asshole, Giles. He—"

"I don't hurt little girls," Dreyson sneered. "I couldn't possibly compete with the IPD on that front."

Ooooooh. I grinned at Dreyson, who was glowering at the lieutenant, not even minding that he called me a "little girl." Everyone was little compared to him. "OK, then, see you around, celly."

The lieutenant rested his face in one hand, taking deep angry breaths. "Giles, get the fuck out before I change my mind."

"I'll go contact my lawyer now, since I didn't get that phone call," I said as I walked out there covered in undead goo, followed by a sighing Detective Davis.

Chapter 3
Adjacent Sides

Illium Shadow Law sounds mysterious, but it's really just an extra set of rules for governing the supernatural. It's less of a codified structure, and more of an ad hoc series of addendums to existing laws, from loopholes that allow for specific types of sentence negotiations, to exemptions based on special circumstances, to more permanent solutions for violent nonhuman offenders. It's useful, though not always just. But I think we all know that the courts are meant for punishing crimes, not preventing them.

— From the Case Files of Thomas Remington

MY PHONE WAS still safely tucked in Mwanje's chair. I texted Remington my location. But I needed my keys back or I'd have to change the locks, again. Detective Davis brought me bleach wipes, and I vainly scrubbed at my clothes.

With an antique Bakelite rotary phone cradled between my ear and shoulder, I sat at Detective Davis' desk, explaining the situation to my lawyer. Blake Canaris was a senior partner at Vilkas, Canaris, and Mako. He wore suits that cost more than my car and enjoyed showing off his collection of single malt scotches. He took my case pro bono, for personal reasons. It appeared to be an uncharacteristically altruistic act. But I couldn't afford to decline good legal counsel, even if Canaris had motives that I didn't trust.

"So in summary, the reason I was unable to locate you, ever after that young man contacted me, was because you were imprisoned in a Level Six Containment cell with the Wergeld mercenary known as Dreyson?"

"Yes, Mr. Canaris," I said, trying to keep my answers succinct. Even if I wasn't paying out of pocket, his hourly rate was frightening.

Mwanje came by the desk, holding up my key ring with a grin, which faded when he heard whom I was speaking to. Canaris had that effect on people, especially cops.

"The young man corroborated your account and sent me a video, but is not interested in testifying against them, probably due to the threats Officer Ryan made off-camera."

"Understandable," I said.

"He also asks that you don't contact him again."

"Fair enough," I sighed. Even if the date went to shit, he did the right thing, documented the arrest, and called Canaris. That was a decent guy, and this was a lot for a first date. What a waste. I probably would have liked him.

I relayed the whole story to him, from Ryan's groping to the suspected sabotage. Ryan was surprised to see Dreyson, but that chucklefuck didn't know his ass from a hole in the ground. Hartford was the one calling the shots.

"Your cell was breached by multiple Revenants? As in they lacked basic cognitive function?"

"Yeah, they weren't doing crosswords," I said. "They were pretty far along in the decomposition process. No talking, just ravenous hunger and scary teeth."

"This might be worth discussing with the Wergeld, though they aren't known for being cooperative," Canaris mused, mostly to himself. "Ms. Giles, I will be checking in with you every fifteen minutes, until you leave the premises, and then hourly, till you are situated. I suggest keeping a low profile for the next few weeks."

"Understood. Thanks, Mr. Canaris."

"Keep me informed," he said and hung up.

Mwanje tossed me my keys, a fretful smile on his face.

"In the trash." He nodded at the can by the vault door.

Muttering curses, I reached for the bleach wipes. Aside from just being rude, the implications weren't great. You didn't throw away someone's keys if you thought you would have to account for them later.

And if I died, who would be asking about my keys?

I rubbed my forehead, grim thoughts coming unbidden.

Detective Davis pulled up a chair. "I would normally advise against messing with Beryl's desk," she told me, glancing at Detective Minuet's rumpled workstation. "But in this case, that was smart. She'll know who was touching her things, and she might even overlook your involvement."

I shuddered involuntarily. Detective Minuet was scary. "They pushed me." I paused. "You heard what I told Canaris. I didn't leave out any details."

Detective Davis gave me an awkward smile, unable to deny she was eavesdropping.

"They shouldn't be hard to find, if your cameras are working." I tried to keep my tone even. As much as I disliked the IPD, that grudge did not extend to the Special Investigations Unit, despite my fraught relationship with the lieutenant. After seeing some nasty cases together, I thought we had a friendly understanding, which was why I was so pissed about being tossed into one of their cells and nearly eaten by loose monsters.

Detective Davis gave me an apologetic smile. "Earlier, when I said someone 'screwed up,' I wasn't referring to your arrest. I meant that they really stepped in it by doing it *here* and roping us into it." She sat on her desk, fingers steepled, an odd smile on her face. "The lieutenant is taking this as a personal affront, so he'll go after whoever was responsible with a vengeance. It's a matter of professional pride."

"Glad I can stake my life on a metaphorical dick-measuring contest," I said, not so sure that the lieutenant wouldn't just commiserate with the people who tried to kill me.

"On the bright side, we do take those *very seriously* here," Mwanje said, leaning on the desk. "Not as seriously as a *literal* dick-measuring contest, but close."

Detective Davis pinched the bridge of her nose, but I laughed.

Maybe Lieutenant Lawrence would kick up a stink. Or maybe he would just be salty that those assholes failed to finish their task and dropped the mess in his lap. SIU existed in a bureaucratic gray zone. The lieutenant didn't have the clout to take on the brass; he had enough trouble getting proper funding.

"Can you tell me why you were arrested today?" Detective Davis asked. "Because we don't have any paperwork, Claire. They're denying it ever happened."

"Because I just walked into the special cells, locked myself in that containment unit with Dreyson, and managed to release the Revenants all on my own?"

"They're implying our incompetence led to this," Detective Davis said tightly.

That was one way of putting it. My feelings must have shown on my face, because Detective Davis shut her eyes and sighed.

"Claire, I'm not trying to blame you. I'm asking these questions for our own internal investigation. It might help if you gave us more details on this debacle."

She didn't just come out and say, "help us help you," but I heard it loud and clear.

Detective Davis was a good person, but she was still employed by the IPD, and everyone wanted to cover their asses. Giving them Hartford and Ryan was fine by me, but I was dead certain that this investigation would go like the rest.

"They didn't tell me much," I said. "And I asked. But they accused me of being responsible for a murder that occurred this morning."

Detective Davis straightened up. "Which one?"

"No details. I don't think it mattered, except to get people to stop asking questions." I looked around the office. "It's abnormal for everyone to be gone. They hustled me in like they didn't expect to find anyone else down here."

Detective Davis nodded.

"Hartford was the last person by the Revenant cell, and he was the one accessing doors and giving orders. So nothing about this looks like an accident to me. We all know it wouldn't be the first time someone at the IPD tried to kill me." Or even the second. Saying that to Detective Davis' face felt like a cheap shot, but she wanted my statement.

"Detective Minuet reinforced those wards herself, with help from Detective al-Rashid. They should not have just failed."

Those two were SIU's magical heavy hitters and accomplished in multiple fields. I also had a hard time picturing their work just falling apart like toilet paper. "Surveillance footage?"

"It exists, but it will take some time to acquire."

"I see." I didn't trust that answer: camera footage went missing or got deleted all the time. Or someone trotted out the revelation that "the cameras weren't even on." But I also disliked the idea of Dreyson or myself getting additional charges tacked on for his contraband. Canaris would leverage the situation in my favor, but it was still something to worry about.

"Regular recording equipment doesn't play nice with magic, Claire. We have a reliable system, solid malg-tech, but one trade-off is that we don't have instant access to the records."

Malg-tech was short for "amalgamation tech." A lot of complex electronics malfunctioned around heavy spell usage or even people with a higher affinity for magic. Cell phones, laptops, and other smart devices were especially susceptible. But with the advent of postmodern magic, there was a shift in the Adept community. Several groups were making innovations in the blended field of combined spellcraft and circuitry, but the products were expensive.

"I wish we had that upgrade, but it's not in the budget," Detective Davis continued, a reminder that we were both on the bad side of the IPD brass. She was subtle like that.

"Not doubting you," I said, possibly lying.

"Our system is difficult to tamper with. The idiots who arrested you won't be able to find the recordings, let alone destroy them," she said. "I'll bet they just went and messed with the dummy setup we keep in the main control room with the other security feeds. Won't do a thing, but we can probably figure out who was involved from their attempts to clean up."

"OK," I said, not actually feeling better. I stared up at the ceiling tiles, at the scorch marks over Detective Minuet's desk. Possibly from the last idiot who touched her stuff.

"I have some venison jerky in my desk," Detective Davis said, because she knew how I liked snacks.

I was tempted, but Dreyson's warning echoed in my skull. It didn't matter, I wasn't hungry now, not after smashing through a quartet of reanimated corpses. The smell of rot was still stuck in my nostrils. "No thanks."

"Are you sure?" she asked doubtfully, like she was worried by that answer.

"Can't enjoy anything with this stench," I said, gesturing to my ruined jeans.

"So did Dreyson give you any problems?" Mwanje asked, trying to sound casual. But he was hovering.

"Not really," I said, glossing over that moment. "He's the reason I survived."

Detective Davis winced.

But Mwanje's jaw twitched. He narrowed his eyes at me, like he knew I was holding back. It could be because of his enhanced senses or because we were friends and he knew me.

"So he did *all* the killing?"

I laughed. "Come on, you know Canaris doesn't want me to answer those kinds of questions." I didn't want to make trouble for Dreyson, and if they had the footage, then the truth would come out. Lying would damage my already strained relationship with SIU.

Mwanje frowned. "I see." They both looked me over, clearly picking up what I wasn't saying.

"I know you guys don't do shady shit," I said, because Mwanje and Davis were the most trustworthy SIU detectives. "So I'd really appreciate it if Dreyson doesn't get any additional grief from this."

"The Wergeld lawyers will hammer something out," Detective Davis said, waving one hand. "Don't assume that this isn't going to blow up in *our* faces. With the way things are shaping up, we might end up owing him damages." She tilted her head back, staring up at the ceiling like she regretted getting out of bed today.

Yeah, I felt that.

"This is Shadow Law business," Mwanje said. "We won't be tacking on more petty charges for extenuating circumstances. They won't stick, and it'd be a dick move."

"So where were you guys today?" I asked.

Mwanje and Detective Davis exchanged somber looks. Detective Davis shook her head. Mwanje gave me another apologetic smile.

"That big?" I asked, because I was hoping it was some kind of mandatory work seminar or sensitivity training. But no, having all hands on deck, and keeping mum about why, meant something bad, likely with a high body count.

"The lieutenant is focused on that. Mwanje and I will take the lead on this," she said.

"I know Hartford," Mwanje said. "And the only thing that sounds off base is that he could negate the wards. The man can't even transfer a phone call."

"So he had help," I said, keeping my tone mild. Because of course he did. Because someone up top had it out for me and there were plenty of unscrupulous underlings in the IPD that didn't mind bending the rules to get ahead.

"We're aware of the nuances in this investigation and the potential pitfalls we may encounter," Detective Davis said.

"This bullshit's been dragging on for too long," Mwanje scowled, crossing his arms.

"Because no one here has the clout to stop it," I said.

"We're working on it," Detective Davis said.

I shrugged.

A familiar clacking sound echoed on the tiles as Remington dragged himself into the office, his cane in one hand. "Nina, Claire, sorry I'm late. Oh, didn't see you there, Coronet!" he announced, like the big man was easily overlooked.

Mwanje laughed, a loud joyful sound that cut through the tension.

Detective Davis mustered a warm smile for my employer.

I waved.

The door to the containment area opened. Lieutenant Lawrence nodded at Remington, walked to his office, and shut the door. Oh, he was pretending like he didn't see me, and that was fine. I didn't want to talk to him either.

"Jon's in a mood, then," Remington sighed, gaze drifting toward me.

"It's about to get worse," Detective Davis said with mock cheer. "I better go inform him of...everything. Keep me posted. Go to Paean Hills if you start to feel ill. You know the drill."

"That would make my night: I got to go to jail and the hospital today. Whoopee."

Detective Davis rolled her eyes. "Do you have any questions for me?"

I thought about that for a second. "What was Dreyson in for?" Because it would suck if my helpful celly was actually a sex offender.

Detective Davis paused, then cleared her throat, like she did not like this line of questioning. "Dreyson is an exceptionally dangerous battlemage, Claire. He's a Wergeld enforcer and Mori's bodyguard. You probably realized that he is *very good* at violence. But today he was in on obstruction charges. Looking at the paperwork, he was brought in by the regulars on an unrelated matter, but they didn't have anything they could make stick."

I sat with that for a moment. I was arrested, illegally, on suspicion of murder. The battlemage berserker was in here for obstruction of justice. I began to laugh, a little too hard. My celly, the giant terrifying cyclops, was in here for a goddamn misdemeanor, while I was here for murder.

Remington just patted my back, shaking his head. "Come on, I'll give you a ride home."

"Do you have a Wergeld number that someone will actually answer? My calls go straight to voicemail," I said, putting some towels down in the passenger seat of Remington's car.

Remington slid his cane into the back seat. The black Camaro's footwells were uncharacteristically empty of fast-food wrappers. He must have had a date recently.

He sighed and tossed me his phone.

I put in the unlock code and scrolled through his contacts.

"You sure you're OK?"

"No, but I don't need to go to the hospital."

Remington leaned against the wheel, watching me with a frown. In his mid-forties, with long brown hair and soulful brown eyes, Thomas Remington was a good-looking man. If he didn't dress like a wannabe Sam Spade, he could have passed for an artist or a musician. But Remington really leaned into the noir detective aesthetic. He hadn't gone so far as to don a fedora, but he liked trench coats, cheap suits, and all the accessories of a "hard-boiled private dick." But he owned the look and he knew it.

Working for Remington afforded me some protection. Before his early disability-enforced retirement, he was an SIU detective, with plenty of good ties on the force. But it seemed like that wouldn't be enough now.

Using an encrypted VOIP app on my phone, I typed in the number from his contacts. Running the call through a third-party app while using a VPN was a standard security precaution.

It rang three times and a woman answered, her voice gruff. "Who the hell is this?"

"Dreyson's locked up in the SIU basement at Station 23. He was attacked. Send a lawyer."

"Shit!"

The line cut off.

Remington pulled out of the parking lot, turned a corner, and merged onto a public street. It was only then, safely tucked away in Remington's car, with some distance from the IPD, that I could finally relax. I texted Canaris to let him know I was out and on my way to the office.

Then I stared out the open window, getting a face full of fresh air. Some of the feeling was returning to my body. It was a beautiful fall afternoon now, a little chilly, despite the sunlight. A gnawing discomfort grew in my chest, like a buzzing stone rolling along my sternum, leaving my breathing ragged, my heartbeat off-kilter. My hands started to shake. Now that the adrenaline was receding, I could afford to check in with myself, and what I was feeling wasn't very nice.

"Fuck." I balled my hands into fists, forearms shaking. "Those fucking bastards." It came out now, because I couldn't get mad at them in the moment. I couldn't lash out, couldn't make the wrong kind of scene without risking my safety. I certainly couldn't act scared in a jail cell, not without inviting more problems. All that pressure compounded the core issue. "Those bastards nearly got me killed. You know, if Dreyson wasn't there, or if he was in a nastier mood, I wouldn't fucking be here." I crossed my arms tightly. His motivations were unclear, and they didn't matter. He helped me, I helped him back.

Part of me wanted to go curl up under my bed and wait another three months for the IPD to forget I existed. The question rose again: why didn't I just leave? Why did I stay? Illium was full of monsters and corruption. I could just move, change my name, live a normal life in a mundane place without quarterly undead purges.

But I lived *here*. This was my home. My family and friends were here. Why should *I* be the one to leave?

After I learned about the other side, Illium's peculiar brand of magic permeated my bones. I liked bartering at the Moonlight Market, wanted to see it in all its phases. I liked the exclusive reading rooms in the public libraries, hidden behind glamours but offering grimoires and rare books for perusal. I liked throwing food to the ducks on the river, and if something more monstrous surfaced to feed, that was even better.

The thought of having to leave made me want to go back to the precinct with a sock full of quarters, beat those asshats within an inch of their lives, and then roll them face-first through the undead slime trail so they choked to death on the gunk.

That option was not viable, but thinking about it made me less shaky. Anger dulled the terror, and wonder reminded me why I stayed. This was home, murderers and all.

"It's always a bad sign when Dreyson is the good guy in the story." Remington kept his eyes on the road.

I blinked. "You know him?"

"Had run-ins," he said, clearing his throat, his tone disapproving. There was a history there, and Remington's severe frown told me he would need to ease into that story. The bottle of bourbon in my desk could probably get him there. "Did he tell you to make that call? He didn't threaten you, did he?"

"Nope, no requests or demands," I said, shifting awkwardly with the obsidian dagger pressed against my back. "But since he's the only reason I didn't get eaten, I figured I'd try to help him out."

Remington raised a brow. "How helpful was he?"

I pulled out the dagger and set it on my knee. "He loaned me this."

Remington sucked in a breath and reached out, his fingers hovering over the handle before he drew them back. "He had *that* inside the cell?"

"Yeah." I nodded. "I'm trying not to think too hard about where he was keeping it." I turned it over in my hands. "And whether or not it's evidence that I shouldn't be touching." It was too late to cram that problem back in the box. My fingerprints were all over the handle, and I doubted that he used this thing to cut up fruit for his lunchbox. Did he want it back? Or was it a liability?

"We can figure it out. There are other people in the Wergeld we can consult," Remington said. "So what happened?"

I leaned against the door and gave him the rundown.

"Know Hartford in passing, nothing noteworthy," Remington said.

"Canaris thinks I should lay low. If that shit is starting up again—"

"It hurts me to say it, but he's right," Remington said, wrinkling his nose.

I crossed my arms, wondering if they would start showing up around my place.

"Do you want to go home?" Remington asked. I shook my head. I needed to have an actual conversation with my roommate, Ivy, but I didn't want her to rush home and get upset. She worried too much already.

"Still have work to do around the office," I said, because getting some small tasks done would soothe me. Plus I had extra clothes there, for emergencies like this.

Remington nodded. "We just got a…complicated job, if you're interested. I'll tell you about it over lunch. The usual, my treat." He gave me an awkward smile, like he knew tacos didn't make up for my morning.

"Thanks, I appreciate it." I mustered a lopsided grin. Because no, tacos didn't make up for my morning, but having a friend who would come get me out of jail and then buy me lunch went a long way in making me feel better. Not as much as a change of clothes would, but we were on the right track.

Chapter 4
A Fetch for Iphigenia

Old Town, including Little Italy, is an odd area to police. The reported crime rate is low. The demographic is mostly working class. The population is almost entirely human. Salvatore Mori and the Wergeld hire magic-users, but there are stringent measures set up to repel any obvious "non-humans." This includes therianthropes, the undead, and anything else that isn't easily defined.

No one in Little Italy ever sees a crime.

While the Wergeld's charter predates Salvatore Mori, he was instrumental in raising the organization to its current prominence. He has no official rank, but he does own a majority stake in the business. The Wergeld polices itself and imposes heavy fines on members who get disorderly outside a job. Unless mages are blowing each other up, it is an unusually quiet beat.

Mori's operation has gone from racketeering, forgery, and bootlegging to mostly weapons-dealing. It is suspected that the REDACTED-are laundering funds through his operations, but his connections to Rome make international investigations difficult. It is hard to say if Mori is more interested in turning a profit or conducting a holy war. He is very open in his dislike of the supernatural. The last vampire they caught on their side of the bridge was literally mopped off the streets.

— *SIU Police Reports: Blackout Files*

THE OFFICES OF the Remington Detective Agency were nestled cozily between a tattoo parlor and a small thrift store. The strip mall was floundering, but that made parking easy to find, and there was an amazing *taqueria* just a block away.

Remington unlocked the front door, and I shuffled down the narrow entry hall. To the left of the reception counter was a doorway to the main office, which housed my desk, shelves of reference materials, the snack nook, and a small meeting area. Remington had an office further back for private discussions, weapon storage, and naps.

I grabbed clean clothes out of my desk and changed in the bathroom. When I emerged, Remington waited in the conference area. It was a corner containing a rectangular oak table with four matching chairs and four mismatched rolling chairs.

"What's your plan?" Remington asked.

"Moving or murder," I said, bagging my ruined clothes. "Honestly, one sounds a lot easier than the other. Backing up a U-Haul gives me anxiety."

Remington sighed, glancing up from his phone. "Maybe don't jump to the most extreme options just yet."

Maybe I was doom-spiraling a little. I set the trash by the door and settled down across from Remington.

"Commissioner Porter is shit at his job," I said flatly. "But he's still the police commissioner, and he hasn't gotten over that little incident with his son. To be fair, neither have me and Ivy." Despite two years passing and lots of therapy.

"We might have a solution for this," Remington said, setting his phone down, his smile tired. He traced an "S" curve along the table. "But it involves that difficult job I mentioned."

I frowned, understanding the signal. Every once in a while, he would take a job he couldn't talk about. Sometimes it was a bit part—he would zip out and be done in an afternoon. Sometimes he would disappear for days and return with broken bones and a paycheck big enough to float the business for a couple of months.

"I already accepted the job as a favor. The details are sparse. But it's a priority. I could use the help."

"The IPD?" I asked, because they would complicate matters.

"It's in the Shadow Dunes."

I crossed my arms. Well, the police certainly wouldn't interfere with us there. The exclusive bloodsport arena of the Fey Courts was only partially in our realm of existence and outside the IPD's jurisdiction. It also attracted a certain kind of clientele, and violence broke out both in the ring and around it.

"What is the client mixed up in?" I asked.

Remington shrugged, but kept tracing that same letter, which could have stood for "Secrets," or "Sovereign," or even "STFU." But I knew it meant his sponsor, the silent partner, that secret someone signaled significant situations.

"It's a bad idea," I said.

"It's a big job." Remington leaned back in his chair. "But having a favor would be helpful in dealing with this latest problem."

I blinked. "You think they can make Porter back off? Because he sure as hell isn't going to forgive me for shooting his son." It didn't matter that it was self-defense, or how justified I was, or that the charges were dismissed. If anything, that made the commissioner more vindictive. But then Junior was a chip off the old blockhead.

"We can do more than that, if we handle this right. And I'll push for that, whether you sit this one out or not. But I have clearance to bring in contractors, and I need the help." He gave me a sheepish look.

"I'm more of a liability than an asset right now," I said, rubbing the back of my neck, uncomfortable with the idea of Remington incurring a debt, especially on my behalf, from his sponsor. "But you know I've got your back."

"I appreciate it. The Courts are selective about whom they let in. My name might raise some flags, but if I can't get in, you likely will." He took a deep breath. "It's going to be dangerous, and you won't like it."

"The Courts always are," I said, though I had limited dealings with them. "What's the job, then?"

Remington's smile faded. He told me.

He was right, I didn't like it at all.

Remington went to pick up tacos while I prepared my kit, rummaging through the supply closet. We were low on fairy ointment, but well-stocked on charms and vials of iron filings. It wasn't enough to take on any warriors from the Courts, but with the obscuration and obfuscation charms, if we were lucky, we could squeak by. Getting into fights was not our forte. Guns were not reliable against opponents with lots of magic. The Fey got cagey whenever someone open-carried steel weaponry in their lands. It was certainly done, but it attracted attention.

But Remington and I weren't security. We were going on a fact-finding mission for a paying client. He was *not* Remington's sponsor, but the silent party wanted Remington to take this case, and we would report our findings to them as well. Normally we didn't break confidentiality, but these were extenuating circumstances.

This job was unorthodox in too many ways. The client was searching for his missing baby, possibly taken in a changeling swap. But other than a photo, he offered little information.

And the sponsor? They wanted evidence of the abduction of a human child, whatever we could find. I was not privy to what exactly would satisfy them, and that vagueness was troubling. I preferred tasks with clear objectives.

I sent Ivy an update, letting her know I was laying low and taking a job outside city limits. That would hopefully ease her mind. While not completely unwitting, my roommate didn't want all the gory details about the weird shit. She was one of my best friends, but these days we kept different company. She had a promising career in corporate law; I kept doing improv routines at gunpoint.

I needed to dress up tonight, per Remington's plan, and it meant I needed to pack carefully. Charms were tucked away in a purse. I wore jewelry with attached warding spells. The obsidian dagger could go in my boot.

I was still loading an extra magazine for my gun when Remington returned with a large bag of tacos and a bottle of *horchata*. He set everything down on the conference table.

I was halfway through my second *birria* taco, the goat meat wonderfully seasoned, when Remington broke the comfortable silence.

"Finding evidence is the priority," he said, opening another taco. "And getting out alive. The client and his entourage are secondary."

"Entourage?"

"He's bringing Wergeld protection," Remington said with a tired smile. "Depending on who shows up, we'll have a better idea of how the night will go."

Most of the time, the Wergeld took monster hunting and pest control jobs, with varying degrees of violence. They employed competent mercs, but also a lot of loose cannons and fanatics. Their charter was accepted in the city as a necessity, but the organization was financially liable for their collateral damage, and there were frequent incidents with hefty payouts.

"We can also talk to someone about that dagger," Remington said. I didn't know many members of the Wergeld, but Remington certainly did. Probably through arresting them.

"That reminds me. What's your deal with Dreyson?" I asked, because we didn't have the option of spending the evening sipping bourbon and shooting the shit.

Remington's face scrunched up. "He's a berserker."

"Yeah." I shrugged.

"He's normally just unfriendly, but—" Remington's eyes widened. "When— In the cell?"

I nodded.

Remington's brow furrowed.

"He didn't touch me. Clocked me as a threat, but I played nice, he calmed down, and we were fine."

"Did you mention this to anyone else?"

I just took a bite of my taco, chewing slowly, a pleasant smile on my face. Dreyson did right by me, and I saw no reason to make trouble for him. It wasn't like we were in close quarters anymore, grating on each other's nerves. I would likely see him again at some point, but we didn't run in the same circles.

Remington sighed. "I arrested him a lot—minor incidents, no serious personal grudges. But the first time I met him was on a Revenant hunt in the Sticks."

"During Brewer's tenure?" I asked. Once upon a time, Remington was an SIU detective, and Lieutenant Dickhead was his partner.

"Yes." Remington's mouth twisted in disgust. "When we arrived, there were pieces everywhere. Never did find out what the things used to be, but Dreyson was still going, laughing the entire time. It was a terrible sound, deep and unhinged, and deeply unhinged. He kept it up while swinging an axe, just mowing them down like weeds. It was a bad infestation, but he culled them on his own. We ended up doing nothing, just watched him dice corpses into too many chunks." Remington's stare turned distant, not quite nostalgic nor horrified. "When he finished, he passed by us and slapped the hood of the car. Then he snapped his fingers and the killing grounds went up in flames."

"He just burned it all down?" I wrinkled my nose. That was irresponsible.

"No. He incinerated the remains very fine, as per code. And while there were scorch marks on several graves and a couple pulverized headstones, it wasn't bad. But he left an impression."

"On the stones, the car, or you?"

Remington snorted. "All of it. He did actually dent the car."

"Did you try to arrest him?" I cackled.

"Don't laugh! We were shell-shocked. I've seen many more impressive feats since then, but at that point we were still using football pads and phalanx formations to clear graveyards."

"Under Brewer, though," I said. There were plenty of cautionary tales about him. The lieutenant, despite his many, many faults, was a marked improvement over his predecessor. "I'm glad your survival skills are stronger than your ego, because if you pissed him off, I'm sure he would have crumbled your car into a little cube, with you guys still inside it."

"Thanks." Remington dabbed at his mouth with a napkin. "Dreyson can break out of it and respond to diplomatic overtures from some people. Nina's been able to talk him down. Even with sniper cover, I'm not sure the warded guns would have been enough."

"Detective Davis is good at reading situations," I said, reaching for another taco.

"She really is," Remington said, looking at me thoughtfully.

The client was en route. I took over the bathroom, changing into a little black slip of a dress. It was short enough to run in, if modesty wasn't a concern, and honestly, I didn't care about flashing my underwear to the Fey or some other monster, if it meant I was outpacing them. I donned a pair of warded silver bracelets. My knee-high boots were comfortable, with a low heel.

The fairy ointment went on my eyes, a primer before I applied my actual makeup. I spent a lot of time practicing how to pierce the low-grade illusions of the city, but the Fey glamours were in another class entirely. The ointment ensured that I would be able to see through their tricks and traps. But it would be bad if they figured out I was wearing it. They had a history of reacting poorly when humans counteracted their glamours, blinding offenders because they were sore losers.

Smoky purple shadow went on next, highlighting the green in my eyes. It complemented a darker plum lipstick. A high ponytail kept my hair out of my way. I emerged from the bathroom looking ready for a night out.

Remington glanced up from the conference room table. He gave me a thumbs-up, then went back to packing his own gear.

I slipped on a fitted black trench coat longer than the dress and placed my Glock in the concealed coat holster. Normally I didn't carry, not with the scrutiny I got from the IPD, but it might be necessary tonight.

I tucked the knife into my right boot and put my phone in a lead holster in my purse. Ambient magic could interfere with any electronics I brought. Taking recordings might be a problem, but there wasn't much I could do about that. I carried a pen and notepad in my bag too.

This was not my first trip to the Shadow Dunes, but I wasn't sure what to expect. Halfway in our world, halfway in another, it had its own rules. Technology could work, but magic surges and other eldritch instabilities made it unpredictable. While the combat arena was the main attraction, the Courts housed their other human-facing businesses there. Modern electronics would not function in the heart of the sidhe courts, but could work there. It was in their strategic interest to keep up with developments in human tech.

I made a pot of coffee and poured myself a mug.

Remington looked fine in his khakis, white button-down, and a tan double-breasted trench coat. He wore his hair pulled back in a low ponytail. I looked him over, and even though I knew where he concealed his weapons, I didn't see any sign of them.

"Discreet," I told him, sitting down at my desk.

"Always." He winked. His phone buzzed. "Looks like they're here. I'll let them in." He got up to get the door.

I sipped my coffee, listening to the muffled greetings from the other room.

Remington returned, frowning. A slender young man with red hair and black leather armor followed. Then a middle-aged Asian woman who looked more like an auntie than hired muscle.

The client came next, a "Leonard Armstrong," according to his sparse dossier. He was an average-sized man in his forties, with dark hair, an olive complexion, and sleepy eyes, his thin face dominated by black-framed glasses. He wore a black suit and reportedly worked in IT.

And last, but certainly not least of all, a familiar figure loomed in the doorway. He had to duck to come through, but Dreyson stepped into the office, now dressed in all black—from his long coat to his worn boots, an enormous double-bladed battleaxe strapped to his back. He surveyed the room, his gaze briefly stopping on me, then continuing on. If he was surprised to see me, it didn't show on his face.

Armstrong gave me a nervous nod and shuffled to the conference table. Remington sat beside him, the mercenaries pulling up chairs as well. I snagged a seat beside the woman. She looked like a teacher in her navy blue cardigan with khakis and flats, her glossy black hair in a sensible braid.

"I take my coffee with three sugars, sweetheart," the redhead said, without looking up. He was probably younger than me, in his early twenties, and all wiry muscle.

"Hmm," I said as I sat down.

Remington coughed into his sleeve.

Armstrong looked up, twisting his hands, a slightly paler indentation on his left ring finger. Married then, or recently ringless. Hmm.

"There's fresh coffee on the counter, if you'd like some," I told the woman, taking a drink of my own black coffee.

"No thank you," she said and gave me a sly smile.

"Hey, secretary, I was talking-"

"Be quiet, Liam." Dreyson's voice came out a harsh rumble. He sat with his chair pushed far back from the table for leg room.

Liam looked up at Dreyson, eyes wide. "OK, boss," he said, holding his hands up, his expression genuinely bewildered.

"Hi, Dreyson," I said, inclining my head at him, because greeting him was the only polite thing to do.

"Ms. Giles," he said with a brisk nod, the very embodiment of stoicism.

Hmm.

Liam's eyes grew bigger as he furtively glanced between Dreyson and me, and then hunched down in his seat and squeezed his eyes shut while he mouthed what looked like "Ah shit."

"Would you like some coffee?" I asked Dreyson, because I was a petty bitch.

"That won't be necessary," he said and turned his attention to the woman beside me. "The maps, Naomi?"

The older woman unfurled a large roll of paper on the table.

"How recent?" Remington asked.

"Accurate as of last week," Dreyson said.

The Shadow Dunes were laid out in a rough spiral formation, with the arena at the center, the market in the next ring, and other chambers tunneling outward in numerous branches—mostly offices, petty domains, and other business enterprises. It was as if fairyland opened the facsimile of a mall, threw in several death traps, and fed people to the building itself, as a treat.

About two dozen chambers were labeled. I recognized an apothecary affiliate, two malg-tech companies, and a charm artisan. Did those businesses originate in the Courts, or were they some kind of franchise?

Armstrong cleared his throat. "Thank you all for coming. I uh...appreciate it. Really." He fiddled with his watch, eyes darting around the room. "You already know that I'm looking for my daughter. I don't know when she was taken... I don't know why. Before this, I had no dealings with magic." With shaky hands, he slid a photograph onto the table.

A plump yellow-eyed baby sat on the cushion in a blue shirt and diaper. It had wispy black hair, a round baby belly, and skin in a soft shade of seafoam green. Its mouth was open, exposing a full set of pointed teeth. There was a lavender mark to the left of the bellybutton, a cluster of bell-shaped flowers. Was it a tattoo?

The picture didn't prove a damn thing. The baby wasn't necessarily Court Fey, and that wasn't even taking into account how easy it was to alter images.

"Where's the thing now?" Liam asked.

Remington had warned me already, but my nails dug into my palms, my rigid smile cemented on so hard it felt like it would break my jaw.

"Gone." Armstrong hung his head, refusing to look at anyone. "I...strangled it, thinking they'd bring our daughter back. I didn't mean to. That's how it goes in the stories." He started speaking faster. "They're not always babies. They can change shape, be anyone: an old fairy, a baby one, even an enchanted bundle of sticks! But if you threaten their 'child,' they're *supposed* to come back! You're *supposed* to get your own kid back!" He laughed, the sound edging on hysterical. "But that's not what happened."

I gritted my teeth and looked away.

"My wife thinks it was a crib death. She doesn't know," Armstrong said, twisting his ringless fingers.

"The body?" Dreyson asked.

"Stayed inhuman. Got someone to glamour it normal. Cremated it fast." Armstrong hunched over. "I know, I know. It was dumb. I should've kept it, but I panicked." He shook his head, wiping his eyes.

I kicked Remington under the table. This guy was a mess and unreliable in every which way.

Remington just rubbed his chin, giving me a look. Yeah, the guy wasn't our client, it wasn't our job to vet him, but still... "What are your expectations for tonight?" he asked.

"I need answers," Armstrong said. "I don't know what I'm looking for. I don't understand these Fey Courts and Shadow Laws, and why those things could steal my child. I...understand that we might not get results tonight, but I want to get started. Find information, make contact, get trade offers. I just want my own daughter back."

"Do your contacts have any suggestions on where we should focus our attention?" Dreyson asked.

"Just the obvious ones," Remington said. "Anything prenatal, health-focused, or medically oriented. Were there any fertility treatments, Mr. Armstrong?"

Armstrong blinked. "No, nothing like that."

"What about doulas, birthing classes, or prenatal fitness programs?" Naomi asked.

Armstrong froze. "I-I don't think so. My wife took care of all that stuff." He shrunk down in his seat. "It...wasn't my thing."

Naomi gave a snort of disgust.

I sat with my hand over my lips, like I was cupping my chin. But I was really trying to cover my mouth, partially to stop sarcastic comments, partially because my poker face was awful.

Armstrong painted an unflattering portrait of himself: a man who swung to extremes under pressure, who obsessed over his "own" child, but checked out of parenting decisions. A man who kept his wife in the dark after murdering their child. What were the odds that he strangled his own damn baby? Or worse, what if he was right and just impulsive enough to murder someone else's kid?

"Early on...I knew our baby wasn't normal," Armstrong said quietly. "My wife couldn't see it. She's not superstitious." He gripped the edge of the table. "My wife didn't cheat. The kid wasn't ours, not biologically. It wasn't human."

Without a body or a DNA test, that would be difficult to confirm. Humans interbred with others often enough. But as distasteful as this was, investigating that part was not my job. Someone important found Armstrong's claims credible. Whoever it was put him in touch with the Wergeld and Remington's sponsor.

"That's weird. Didn't think anyone would let *them* in." Liam pointed to a site labeled "HerbAway."

"That's the one that sells organic supplements, knockoff energy drinks, and the gross candles?" I asked. "Where they badger you to come to their shitty 'parties,' pressure you to buy their garbage, and try to get you to 'invest in this great business opportunity'?"

"Yeah, them!" Liam nodded vigorously. "My brother's wife is in it. She's always pushing that bullshit and talking about leadership seminars. It's fucking annoying."

"Multi-level marketing schemes are exploitative and cult-lite," Remington said, glancing at Armstrong. "Is your wife—"

"She had a friend who was," Armstrong said. "But my wife is too smart to get taken in by those scams. She might have bought some products to placate her friend, but she wasn't part of the actual downline."

"We should start with businesses that have ties to the city," Remington said and listed off a few, including HerbAway and a genealogy research service.

"But those people have kings and queens. They understand power. They obviously aren't concerned with bureaucracy and morality. Can't we just go in, offer money or favors, and trade for my kid?"

"There will be a lot of interesting parties there tonight. We can start by making inquiries about business opportunities and sector growth. People like to show off, and sometimes they overshare in those moments, especially our good neighbors," I said.

"But there will be Fey all over, and they will be listening. We can't just barge in, accuse them of violating the Alluvian Treaties, and demand answers about changelings, not without garnering the wrong kind of attention," Remington said.

Armstrong huffed in frustration. "In the stories, they have quests or trials to complete. They can't lie. They can be bribed with milk, or—"

"They don't need to lie to deceive us," Naomi said sharply.

"Think of them as lawyers with *centuries* of experience bending the rules. The inability to outright lie is not as much of a handicap as you might expect," Remington said.

"Any trial or quest they send you on will be near impossible," Naomi said, stern-faced. "The old stories hold some truth, like any cautionary tale. But you are only familiar with the ones where humans win, and those stand out because they're the exception to the rule."

Armstrong gulped.

"Let me make this clear," Dreyson said, crossing his arms. "You don't have the sense or expertise to negotiate with the Courts yet. Consider them a hostile nation. Over there, they don't recognize any governmental authority outside their own. You pitched this job as a networking trip, an investigation. Mr. Mori agreed to render aid on those grounds. Detective Remington was hired as a consultant because he has years of experience and *interesting* connections. My people are here because the Shadow Dunes are not safe. So you need to adhere to those mission parameters and listen to the professionals. Make 'friends.' Pitch ideas. Forge alliances. The Fey are capricious. Offer them something they want and they won't hesitate to turn on each other. Do it wrong, and they will take insult and retaliate, usually in creatively fatal ways."

Armstrong paled, opened his mouth like he was going to argue, but then stopped, clearly thinking better of it. "OK."

"We're testing the waters," Remington said gently. "We might get a bite or two, but we're not diving in yet. It's too murky, and we don't even know where to start looking. But we do know there are sharks under the surface."

"I...understand," Armstrong said. He stood awkwardly. "Bathroom?"

Remington pointed the way. We all waited for the door to click shut.

"If the Courts are stealing human babies, that's a direct violation of the treaties," Remington said softly. "Advertising that we suspect such a thing is going to make our lives much harder or much shorter. We don't need to start a diplomatic incident."

"Politics aren't our priority," Dreyson said bluntly. "Our job is to keep him alive." He stared at the bathroom door. "But I agree. If he brings down the wrath of the Courts on us, our job becomes much more difficult."

That was bad, but so was strangling baby-shaped things. I didn't particularly like baby-shaped things, but that didn't mean I thought that strangling them was acceptable.

"You know this guy is going to be terrible in a fight," I said. "Unless it's against babies. Then he might be the expert."

Liam choked.

Remington rested his face in one hand.

"You're coming as a consultant?" Naomi asked.

"That was the plan."

"And you're the 'date'?" she asked me.

"Potentially," I said. "It might be better if we're clearly on the outs. Fey like drama. He could be looking to trade up. I can be very convincingly not that into him."

Remington nodded. "Whatever you can sell. Court Fey are fractious. We're better off finding fault lines and giving a couple nudges to see who reacts."

"We're providing security, but we aren't on a suicide mission. Don't start trouble," Dreyson said, shooting Remington a pointed look.

We all glanced at the bathroom door, nobody appearing too happy with the situation.

"He needs a better primer," I said. "He doesn't understand what he's getting into."

Dreyson shook his head. "We don't have enough time to give him a real education."

"I'll talk to him on the way over," Remington said. "How are we doing this?"

"We're focused on the principal," Naomi said, passing smaller copies of the maps around the table for everyone. "We'll likely have our hands full, so you shouldn't count on us for intelligence gathering."

I went back to refill my coffee.

Someone cleared their throat. I turned around to see Armstrong fiddling with his watch.

"Can I help you?" I asked, managing to sound polite.

"They're busy...can I ask you some questions?" he said quietly.

I gestured toward my desk, and he pulled up a chair and sat down. At the conference table, Remington and Naomi discussed exit routes while Liam asked questions about security measures. Dreyson studied the map, though his head was angled just right to listen in on whatever Armstrong was saying to me.

"You have misgivings about this, maybe about me."

I grimaced. "You're a client, and we've already signed a contract. Rest assured that my personal feelings won't get in the way of doing the job and I can behave in a professional and ethical manner, which means that as long as you don't start none there won't be none," I said in one breath, like the end of a medication commercial with the narrator rushing through all the gross potential side effects and legal disclaimers at quadrupled speed.

Armstrong sat wide-eyed, clearly needing a moment to process my words.

I steeled myself for his inevitable defensive reaction. I should have just said, "That's silly, mister. I like everybody." That sort of response would have saved me a lot of trouble throughout my life, but I wasn't *that* kind of liar.

But Armstrong just nodded sheepishly. "May I ask why?"

That sounded like a trap if I ever heard one. I pressed my lips together, skepticism turning my polite smile into something crooked and insincere.

"Or I can guess," he said, his face very somber. "It's because I killed the changeling."

I nodded, the smile dropping. "Unless it was trying to eat you or actively harming someone, you don't just murder things." I looked him in the eye. "It wasn't trying to drive a bus off a cliff or do uncanny stuff, was it?"

"No." He adjusted his glasses. "It acted like a normal baby." Armstrong lowered his head, staring at the floor. "Killing it was a shameful thing. I'm not proud of it. And I know there will be consequences." His voice cracked, and his eyes remained downcast. "But my child deserves to know her mother, deserves to know that her parents love her and never wanted to give her up. Maybe the fairies are treating her right, but given what I've heard…I don't think that's the case. So all I want is to give my biological child a chance. If the fairies want to punish me for my sins, I understand. But they're not getting that changeling back. It's a life for a life. They were wrong to take my baby in the first place, and they need to let her go."

The word struck home. The clear regret for his actions and earnest concern for his missing child seemed real. It didn't change what happened, but it gave the situation more nuance. Still, he couldn't look directly at me when he spoke. Was it the shame, or was there something else? Where was his wife in all this? Had he just abandoned her to her grief, or was she harboring her own suspicions?

"I see," I said, though it wasn't my place to offer him absolution. Maybe I hated him a little less for his confession, reluctant as I was to receive it. But I didn't have any comforting words to offer him.

"Throughout this, everyone Mr. Mori introduced me to has been supportive, congratulatory even." He clenched his fists. "It doesn't feel right. That kind of act doesn't deserve praise. I don't understand."

"You're right, but it's a complicated world," I said. Mori had a very obvious stance on what he considered non-humans and how those entities should be treated. The Wergeld followed his lead. My opinions were not the same.

"This isn't how I planned things, but I'm trying to make the best of it. Maybe Mr. Mori doesn't really approve of my actions, maybe he's just being…kind. I don't have any way of knowing, though. I did a terrible thing, but you're the only one who said it to my face."

Because he asked. "You're a distraught parent. I was trying to be polite," I said.

"Thanks for being honest. I'll stop bothering you." Armstrong scratched his face lightly, not making eye contact. "And I'm sorry. I shouldn't have dumped this all on you."

"I'm sorry you're in a bad situation," I said, and that was true. "I…guess I don't know how I would feel if I were in your shoes."

Armstrong finally looked at me, regrets written across his face. He didn't say it, but I understood the sentiment behind that weak half smile. *You wouldn't have made my mistake. You wouldn't have killed the changeling.*

Well, that was true.

"I should, uh, check in with Mr. Dreyson," he murmured, getting to his feet. "Thanks again." He pulled out his phone and began texting as he went to rejoin the others.

We kept the volume low, so maybe our exchange stayed private, but I wasn't counting on it. I was sending an update to Canaris when a shadow fell across my desk.

Dreyson stood in front of me, his gaze expectant.

It was strange to see him in the office. He didn't quite fit, not just because he was a little bigger than scale and had to duck to avoid the light fixtures. Having him in *my* space felt odd, maybe too personal.

"I wasn't sure how to return your knife discreetly. Would you like it back now?" I asked.

"Do you have any other weapons on you?" he asked, looking me over. He did not mention Armstrong or even glance in the client's direction.

"Gun, but I know I can't rely on it."

"Keep it for now, then," Dreyson said, his face grim. "Do you know the rules?"

"Be polite. Don't eat or drink. Don't outright thank anyone. Don't make promises or get entangled in their verbal traps, though I understand that is harder than it sounds…"

"No real names, not if you can help it," he said sternly. "And say less. Don't outright lie if you're bad at it. It's safer to couch your words in truth, and your words will be used against you."

"I'll try," I said, because Canaris also gave me this lecture, and it rarely worked that way because of my penchant for nervous babbling.

"You might be clever, but the Fey aren't like the bumbling cops," Dreyson said. "They're exponentially smarter, and they've had a long time to hone their craft."

"Then I'm really in trouble, because I usually talk my way out of things."

His nostrils flared. "That didn't work so well for you earlier."

"Well enough," I said, holding his gaze. "But I'll pack snacks, just in case." I opened my desk drawer and pulled out two more protein bars, slipping one into my pocket and the other into my purse. "Want one?"

His eye widened, and he frowned down at me, like he wasn't sure how to respond. "Ms. Giles—" he began, sounding exasperated enough that he might be winding up for a real lecture.

"I'll be careful," I added quickly, holding up my right hand. "Thanks for checking in. I appreciate it."

His lips twitched and he nodded; then he abruptly turned and went back to the conference table.

Dreyson did not bring up the call to the Wergeld, which he certainly suspected me of making. But then, if he was delayed in jail, he would not be out here on this fool's errand. Which, now that I thought about it, might have been preferable for him.

Oops.

Chapter 5
Gambling with Fire

The Shadow Dunes is a subjugated domain, held by the Spring and Autumn Courts, the first of many collaborative undertakings by the Vernal Lord and the Autumnal Lady. Unlike most Court domiciles, there is a fixed entry point for the Shadow Dunes on human lands. The realm itself lacks the more deleterious effects that the Courts have on mortals, therefore making it a suitable place for careful visitation and diplomatic meetings. If you must deal with the fairies, the Shadow Dunes is the safest place to do so. It is a crossroads between worlds, and therefore prone to unpredictable passages of time.

The name is likely a bowdlerization of Dún Scáith, the "Fortress of Shadows." The fairies have made it into a raving spectacle: a combination of eastern bazaar, Roman coliseum, and Viking mead hall, where the Seelie and the Unseelie lords sit atop their petty thrones and strike Faustian bargains with rash mortals. Goods, services, and deeds that are outlawed within the city are often permitted here. While the rules of the Courts only apply selectively within this realm, the boundaries between the Courts proper and the Shadow Dunes are not well-defined. Sometimes visitors never leave.

— *An Introduction to Illium by Ann Keyes*

THE WERGELD PROVIDED an armored black SUV. Liam drove with Dreyson sitting shotgun. Naomi and Armstrong were in the middle row, while Remington and I sat in the back.

Tuning out Remington's conversation with Armstrong, I stared out the tinted windows. The sun was already sinking below the horizon, but we were heading out to a state park. There were multiple ways into the Shadow Dunes, and this route had us turning off the main road, going down an easily overlooked gravel path, and then through a dark tree-lined corridor.

I was going into the woods at night with a known axe murderer. As a minority, I already knew how *those* movies ended for people who looked like me. Ugh. I shook my head, trying to banish that intrusive thought.

"So we're dating?" Armstrong asked, not meeting my eye. "You seem nice, but I don't think you're believable as my girlfriend." And there it was, the reminder that the axe murderer was *not* the biggest asshole in this car. In fact, he was my second favorite person here.

I sighed. "Look, whatever your actual taste is, I'm about twenty years younger than you and wearing a short dress. That's enough to be a believable trophy escort for tonight."

Naomi glanced over her shoulder at me with that same sly smile from earlier.

Armstrong's cheeks reddened. "Oh." A look of pure panic froze his face. "No! I meant that yes, you're almost twenty years younger than me and that is...uncomfortable. I'm married, and I love my wife! I didn't mean it as an insult to you! I'm sorry!" He held both hands up, voice shaking.

"OK," I said, some of my irritation fading. "I'm just going to hold onto your arm, and it might be more convincing if we act like this isn't working out."

"Oh." Armstrong gave me a shy smile. "That'll be fine. Umm...how did we meet?"

"Through work. I'm in HR," I said, knowing that would bore the hell out of anyone who asked.

Armstrong nodded.

The gravel road opened up into a field, dozens of expensive vehicles already parked in the grass. There were lanes, solar lights, and attendants directing the cars, which all emerged from different directions. If I thought about it, those routes wouldn't be spatially possible, but I wasn't in the mood for a bigger headache.

We parked, and Liam killed the engine, but the locks remained engaged.

"We're on their lands now, with limited hospitality," Dreyson said sternly. "Assume anything you say will be overheard."

The locks disengaged, and we all climbed out.

Armstrong brushed off his coat, gave me a weak smile, and offered me his arm.

I put one hand on it, surveying the area. Ahead, a glittering stone path led to a large cave mouth. Blue fey lanterns hovered outside the entrance, the orbs of light flickering playfully.

Dreyson took point with Liam. Remington and Naomi brought up the rear.

Pockets of people moved toward the cave.

"So...you're upset?"

"You know what you did," I said with a straight face.

"I didn't mean to leave the toilet seat up?" he said hesitantly.

"And I didn't mean to turn off the router during your big guild raid, but these things happen because actions have consequences."

"Damn, you're vicious," Armstrong choked out, coughing into his shoulder like he was really stunned. "I didn't think you'd be so impossible."

I didn't get a chance to respond because we reached the entrance. There were three tall gatekeepers in filigreed plate armor: a slender blue-skinned man clad in green, a muscular woman with rust-colored skin and copper hair that matched her armor, and a figure in matte black. The elaborate helm hid the mystery man's face; it was shaped like a bird's skull, with angular wings that pointed backward, almost like horns, the beak protruding over his nose, leaving his mouth and chin exposed. He wore a mantle of black feathers, and a sword hung from his belt.

I recognized the colors of the Spring and Autumn Courts; they shared access to the Shadow Dunes. The ceremonial guards watched Dreyson with wary eyes, their long fingers brushing against the hilts of their swords. But Dreyson kept his gaze on the man in black.

"Invitation?" the Spring Court attendant asked.

Armstrong pulled away from me. He made a show of withdrawing the envelope from inside his jacket and offering it up with great flourish.

Three things happened at once:

The attendant accepted the invitation.

The man in black blurred. One moment he was behind the attendant, the next, he was on my left, arm looped around mine.

Dreyson moved, one hand grasping the clasp of the feather cloak, flames bursting from his other palm as he loomed over the man in black. "You overstep," he said coldly.

"And you are *very* fast," the man in black laughed, his accent light and lilting. "Would you care to join me in the ring? I'd be delighted to meet your terms. It could be very fun, for both of us." He tilted his head to the side, smiling under the helmet.

His attention was on Dreyson, so I yanked my arm out of his grasp and side-stepped him, which was only easy because he wasn't interested in me.

The guards had hands on their weapons, but they seemed hesitant to interfere.

"I'm working," Dreyson said, releasing the man, but the fire still burned in his palm.

"That's a shame." The man glanced over at me. "And what about you, dove? Did you not wish for a better escort? One who is charmed by your *vicious* and *impossible* nature?"

I snorted. Dreyson was right, they had ears everywhere. "Sure, but you were clearly trying to get his attention." I gestured to Dreyson. "It was a bold move. Don't ruin it by making a play for anyone else. That's just embarrassing."

Dreyson squinted at me as the fire slowly died in his hand.

But the troublemaker laughed. "Don't be jealous, dove. I can make it up to you, *in many ways*." The purr in his words gave me a good idea of what kind of ways he had in mind.

"How generous. But I'm here with someone," I said, crossing my arms. "If you behave, maybe I'll put in a good word for you with my friend."

I expected Dreyson to protest, but he just gritted his teeth, attention staying on the threat.

"I see," the man in black said with a shrug. "If you change your mind, just ask for the Crow Knight. The Spring Knights will know where to send you." He tossed his head and sauntered into the cave, melting into the shadows.

I pointedly did not look at Dreyson, because even though the Crow Knight faced me, he was clearly talking to the resident badass.

"You are cleared to enter," the Spring attendant said, his voice wobbling.

Without a backward glance, Dreyson stepped into the cave mouth and disappeared.

Armstrong and I followed.

For a second, everything turned dark, the air cold and dry. The world compressed around me and then simultaneously shifted in too many directions, like my mind was bouncing through a pinball machine and my body was locked in full tilt. The pressure in my skull grew and then abated, ears popping as I stepped out of the gate and into a massive chamber.

Blue, green, and lilac globes of light hovered in the air—fey lanterns. Patches of ivy and moss clung to the slate-blue stone walls. There was no ceiling. The walls just terminated into a vast dark, sprinkled with distant stars in a swirling nebula. The constellations here were not familiar, and there was no moon. It was usually night here, though I heard they could paint the sky a perpetual dusk or dawn. The color scheme told me that the Spring Court was ascendant and hosting tonight's events.

"What was that back there?" Armstrong asked, grabbing my arm.

"Which part?" I snapped.

"He approached us, and he seemed import—"

"He was baiting us!"

"I know, but shouldn't we have parleyed?"

"Not with him! That was just pure disrespect. "Let's see what kind of trouble I can start," I said, mimicking the Crow Knight's lilting cadence. "At best, it was unwanted flirtation."

"Enough," Dreyson said, looming over us. "While we're here, we're all on the same side and *nothing is private*. You would be wise to remember that." He stared very hard at me.

I pressed my lips together and nodded.

Armstrong flinched.

"It's...a lead," I said to break the tension. "You know how it is in business. You never accept the first offer, especially not a bad faith one. There will be more offers. We need to remember our own worth."

Armstrong's eyes widened behind those black-framed glasses. "Yes, of course. I...sorry," he mumbled, offering me his arm.

I placed my hand on it, glancing over at Dreyson.

But he was ahead of us now, leading the way to the arena.

We strolled after him, Armstrong's head on swivel as he took in the sights. The swirls of color, the jewel-toned flowers not seen in our world, the faint strains of a haunting melody that echoed in the distance. This place lingered in the imagination, the colors more saturated, the air sweeter.

"It's something else," Armstrong said, wonder in his voice.

I nodded.

He looked around hopefully. "Do you think we'll see any children?"

"I hope not," I said, because we could not trust him to keep it together. "These sorts of events aren't suitable for children, human or otherwise."

The path curved, doors on the right leading to a stadium. On the left were two terraced upper levels housing businesses. We turned right, taking the stairs to our seats, blue fey lanterns casting an ethereal glow.

Dozens of people were already in their seats, overlooking the arena. Thick blue cushions covered the stone benches. Armstrong didn't have a private box, but there were two rows of seats reserved for us.

Some people wore masks for discretion. Others dressed up for the occasion. And one notable pair were still wearing the suits they were in earlier today. Mwanje clocked me first, his eyes getting very big when he saw my group. Detective Davis stared very hard at Remington, like she knew exactly whose fault this excursion was.

I didn't acknowledge them. We were all working. Best not to complicate things.

From a private box, an older man raised his chin in greeting. Armstrong nodded at him. Tall, wiry, and clad in a three-piece suit, Salvatore Mori had steel-gray hair swept back in a loose ponytail, piercing eyes, a sharp hawk-like nose, and a large wooden crucifix around his neck. A trio of suits hung back—security.

Movement in the pit caught my attention. A massive sandy-colored werewolf tore the arms off a screaming man. Well, it looked like a man, but it didn't die like one. It didn't bleed much, it just hissed, unhinging its jaw and unfurling a long barbed tongue that struck the wolf's face, spilling blood in the sand. It was undead, by the feel of it. The werewolf was pure canid right now, though some could pull off humanoid half-forms.

The werewolf didn't seem to notice the flesh wound. It clamped its jaws down around its opponent's head and shook viciously. The body popped off, and a tide of centipedes and rats began to pour from the neck into the sand, the skittering of their tiny feet so much louder than I expected.

On my left, Remington looked queasy. I wasn't too keen on finding out if the werewolf was going to eat the vermin.

"Hey, this is gross. I can't believe you brought me here," I murmured to Armstrong.

He stared at me. "But I— Oooh, we're fighting again, are we?" He cleared his throat. "But I thought you liked — "

"No, I like *babies*, and cakes, and tacos," I said with a straight face and then realized that one of those things was not like the others. Unless maybe you were one of the pit fighters...

Armstrong gaped at me.

"I'm going to take a walk and get some air that isn't all murder-y," I said, ignoring Remington's muffled snorts.

"Oh no, she's really upset," Armstrong said as I left the box. "Was I supposed to get her a baby? Is that something I can buy here? Guys?"

I left before I heard the answer, descending the stairs, and went back into the stone hall with the terraces. Pockets of people mingled out here, having hushed conversations. I headed up to the next level of shops, discreetly checking the map.

Nothing matched. I centered myself on the arena and walked the corridor around it. Some alcoves hung signs, but there were even more unmarked doors. The floor plan was completely different now. This damn place shifted, rendering the maps useless.

Scowling, I looked around, then ducked into the nearest carved stone doorway. Reaching into my bag, I pulled out an obscuration charm. It was a paper packet the size of a teabag, handmade, courtesy of a friend. I crushed it in my hand. A slight mist appeared in the corner of my vision. It was a "don't notice me" spell. I wasn't invisible, but unless I made a lot of noise or got up in front of a crowd, I would just be a piece of background scenery, unimportant and easily overlooked.

I rejoined the groups in the halls.

"Can't believe he actually got in the ring for their entertainment—"

"They have no reputation to trade on. They're absolutely desperate. Isn't it delicious?"

Sticking to the shadows, I walked the circuit again, this time more deliberately. I tried to sketch a new map, but every time I counted the alcoves, the number changed.

"The Vernal Lord is having difficulties. Now would be the time to—"

"*She* is aware. Speak of other things."

A pair of Autumn Knights passed me by, not even glancing in my direction.

"You don't belong here." The voice was very soft, coming from behind me.

I very slowly turned my head, just so I could see a small figure out of the corner of my eye. Whatever obscuration technique they used was strong.

"You *can* see me," she breathed. It sounded like a little girl to my ears.

I nodded once, because not only was her veil stronger, she could see through mine.

A pair of Spring Knights strode by silently, not seeming to notice us either.

"You don't think this is a safe place for children, human or otherwise. But why would there be human children here?" she asked.

"I don't know," I said very quietly. "Why would there be changelings in Illium?"

"You say dangerous things," the child whispered, sounding frightened. Perhaps then, my question answered hers.

"We're just posing questions. We've made no declarations."

"If I heard you, then maybe *she* did too. She might be listening even now, and that would be...bad."

"I don't want to cause you any trouble," I said, wondering who "she" was. "But I am looking for answers. People seek their stolen progeny."

"Don't say that!" she hissed.

"Missing progeny, then." I rested my chin in my hand. Maybe I could get the speaker to reveal herself. "Would it be safer to show me instead of speaking?"

"Maybe. Keep walking. I'll see."

I began another lap around the hall. It was on the fourth circuit that I noticed a new passage in the stone, not a dimple in the walls but a deeper tunnel with a smattering of fey lanterns lighting the way. Definitely not there before.

I pulled my phone out and took a picture. I tried to send it to Remington, but there was no signal.

A small figure waved at me from the shadows, just an outline, and then they faded from view. I couldn't make out the details, but it looked like a kid. Here was my invitation, then. I knew that if I walked away to get someone else, the tunnel wouldn't be there when I returned. I wrote up a quick text, hoping it would send eventually, and then stepped onto the path.

When I glanced over my shoulder, the arena was still visible, so I quietly went forward, looking back occasionally.

It was utterly silent, the air growing cooler as I descended. No creepy laughs, eerie music, or footsteps, even my own. The tunnel emerged in a stone room with shelves and cubbies carved in the walls. When I looked back, the tunnel was gone.

I sucked in a breath, not surprised, but also struggling to stay calm. Just because I expected the bad thing to happen didn't mean I couldn't be upset by it. Well, I couldn't afford to get upset *right now*. I was already in it. Shoving the panic back down, I checked my phone. No signal.

All right, then, where was I?

The room was the size of a studio apartment, with rows and rows of shelves and storage receptacles containing hand-bound books, scrolls, and stone tablets. A single heavy door covered in black ironwork and studs was the only obvious exit. I wanted to open it, but I wasn't supposed to be here. I needed to explore the archive before someone found me.

Some books held curses. I studied the shelves, trying to see if I could pick up anything. If I took the time to focus, I could detect some magic—a numbness in my fingers, a coldness, a glow. I think most people could learn to do that much through constant exposure, but Remington could not, or so he claimed.

The books and scrolls just looked like books and scrolls. I pulled a pair of latex gloves from my bag and slipped them on. The scrolls were not uniform in size or color, and some had a leathery look. I picked one at random; it was fine parchment, maybe vellum. Very carefully, I unrolled it to find that the writing was all dots, lines, and some squares. It didn't look like a code or encryption, more like Ogham script, but I wasn't an expert. I snapped a picture, rolled it back up, and then picked a book from the nearest shelf.

The neat looping handwriting looked like something from a Tolkien novel. I snapped another photo for reference and returned it. I pulled a book from the opposite end of the shelf and it was in German, also handwritten, with heavy block letters.

Shaking my head in frustration, I crossed my arms. Someone beckoned me here for a reason. If it was a trap, I'd already sprung it. But if there was something I was supposed to see, I hadn't found it yet.

I rested my hand on a smooth stone counter. There was no dust on it, but there was some on some of the shelves and cubbies. I inspected the shelves and found three spots without dust on the edges—recently disturbed—and pulled those books. Everything was handwritten. One was an illuminated Latin text, the other a genealogy chart in Ogham-like tree script. But the most interesting one was a thin ledger with onion-skin pages. On the cover was a detailed sketch of a slender stem covered in tubular blossoms. Snapdragons? Columbines? Foxgloves? It took me a moment to recall why it was familiar.

The photo of the alleged changeling baby; it had a similar mark.

I grimaced and opened the book.

There were more Ogham-like symbols with about two dozen entries, maybe three lines each. I snapped pictures from each book. The ledger was mostly empty, easy to photograph in its entirety.

Should I take it? No, theft from the Fey was always a bad idea in the stories. Maybe that was just cunning propaganda, but no sense risking it.

I carefully put the books back where I found them and tucked my phone in my bag. The room was still empty, and the tunnel in the wall was still gone.

"How do I get back?"

If someone answered, I didn't hear them.

I went to the wooden door and carefully pushed on it. It creaked open, and I peeked my head out into another stone corridor. Fey lanterns hovered in the air, glowing red, gold and orange. This was Autumn Court territory then. Shit. As far as I knew, the Courts were mostly the same, hereditary monarchies that looked down on the shorter-lived races. The Spring Court made an effort to come off as more civilized and diplomatic. The Autumn Court reveled in its reputation for brutality and embracing the "old ways."

But I suspected it was just branding. There did not seem to be enough sidhe left for them to wage open warfare on each other, and it allowed them to play good cop/bad cop with the rest of the world.

I looked both ways and shut the door behind me. Which way to the arena?

The lights above me twinkled, oddly sinister in their cheer.

Making a guess from where the tunnel was, I took a right, even though human spatial reasoning didn't apply here.

I walked down the stone hall, the lights flickering as I passed. I wasn't sure how long I walked and if I was actually going anywhere. Worse, my obscuration spell had worn off.

Then I heard a raspy laugh. "There you are, dove."

Shit.

Chapter 6
The Fights We Cannot Win

三十六计，走为上策 Trad. 三十六計，走為上策- Sān shí liù jì, zǒu wéi shàng cè- This proverb simply states, "Of the Thirty-Six Stratagems, fleeing is best." The Thirty-Six Stratagems is another Chinese military-philosophy essay of dubious provenance, numbering, and authorship. But some of the advice is solid, especially Stratagem 36. It says 走为上策- which is generously translated as "if all else fails, retreat." It actually means, "retreating is the best." So the quote, credited to Wáng Jìngzé (王敬则), is both a self-referential play on words and some good life-lengthening advice.

— *From the Very Personal Journals of FYG*

I TURNED AROUND, shoulders squared.

The Crow Knight was right behind me, the beak of his helm nearly touching my forehead. I could not see his eyes under the helmet, only the sharp line of his jaw. He moved closer, and I backed up. I very much wanted to reach for a weapon, but I also knew he could cut me down before I even had it out of the holster.

"Here I am," I said, crossing my arms. "I'm lost."

"You are," he agreed, still advancing.

I stiffened and backed up till I literally hit a stone wall.

He closed the distance immediately, one gloved hand reaching out to grab my shoulder, his grip firm. This time I wouldn't be able to just slip away.

"I took a wrong turn," I said. "When I looked back, the hallway was gone."

"Someone lured you here?" The Crow Knight tilted his head to the side. "How frightening." He gave a low chuckle.

My breath caught, waiting for him to speak in a child's voice or something else creepy.

"Well, you're lucky that you found me, dove."

"Weren't you more interested in my friend?" I asked, wrinkling my nose.

"He's intriguing," the Crow Knight said, leaning in. "You shouldn't fault me for noticing him first. He's very hard to miss. But I think I'd enjoy your clever tongue just as much. You really could do better than that petty man you came with, dove."

"The bird motif is a lot. I don't think there's anything dove-like about me," I said, one hand behind my back, reaching into the cuff of my boot.

"Are you offering me your name?" he asked, the words silky.

"No, but you can come up with a better nickname."

He laughed. "Perhaps you're right. Are you a mink? A fox? A tender little bunny?"

"Something is getting lost in translation," I said with a shudder. "I want to go back to the arena now and rejoin my party."

"And if I do guide you, what will you give me for my services?" he asked.

"What are you after?" I asked. "Because you're probably attractive under that armor, so it's weird that you'd leverage *directions* for flirtations or more."

He reached out, catching a stray lock of my hair between his finger and thumb. "You're so evasive. Dressed like a fragile ornament, a cute distraction, a sweet simpering thing. But you aren't playing that part very convincingly, *hellcat*. And that makes me wonder what you're really after." He smiled broadly at me, licking his lips.

Shit. If I was the kind of person to arrive on some rich guy's arm and get lost, I absolutely would be trying to flirt and seduce my way out of this. I was trying too hard to redirect his attention, and my plan was so cerebral, it was goddamn stupid.

"I'm not...emotionally entangled with my escort," I said carefully. "But there *is* someone I care about." That was true enough; I didn't lie and claim a romantic relationship. "And I don't wish to cause him any emotional distress."

The Crow Knight stepped back, studying my face.

"If you want to judge, just remember that we all have obligations," I said, straightening up. "And if you're going to do something drastic, then let's just get this done." I bared my teeth, gripping the hilt of the knife.

He let go of my hair, laughing softly. "I have no need for unwilling playmates, hellcat." He stepped back, giving me the space to slip by. "Just follow the path. You should reach the arena and your escort."

I nodded slowly. "The directions are helpful."

He clicked his tongue, looking pleased by the fact I did not outright thank him.

I began to walk briskly, feeling his stare between my shoulder blades. Would he cut me down for fun? But I did not turn around, I just walked forward, the fey lanterns blinking overhead. And then they went out, plunging the hall into blackness.

I rolled to the side instinctively, expecting an attack. But I just tumbled through the darkness, the world shifting, my stomach dropping.

And then I was on my knees, my vision spinning.

A hand reached out, steadying me.

"There you are," a familiar deep voice rumbled, even as the lights flickered back on. I blinked, no longer in the hallway, but in a round stone room, a mosaic of a silver tree embedded in the floor. Dreyson crouched over me.

Dark spots floated in the corners of my vision. Pulse racing, I looked around. There were four hallways leading out of the chamber, each lit with solid blue, white, orange, or yellow lanterns. There was no sign of the Autumn Court hall.

"Are you hurt?" he asked, hand on my arm.

"Don't think so," I said shakily.

Dreyson rose, practically lifting me up with him. I gripped his forearm, my balance all wrong. It took me a moment to center myself, because I was trembling.

"Sorry," I muttered. "Sorry, I—"

"It can wait," he said, one hand on my back.

"No, the Crow Knight was behind me!"

Dreyson's eye widened, and then he spun me behind him as the Crow Knight sauntered out of the shadows.

"Well, I can't say I'm entirely surprised, but I am definitely disappointed," he said, drawing his sword. "Maybe even a little jealous. Sneaking off for a tryst with him and not even thinking to invite me? You're a selfish one, hellcat."

It took me a second to realize how this looked, like Dreyson and I purposefully slipped away from the group. And since I just told the Crow Knight that I wasn't attached to Armstrong, well...shit.

Dreyson did not glance back at me or even ask what the hell the Crow Knight was talking about. "Stand back," he said, his voice harsh as he drew his axe.

"You don't have to do this," I said, knowing neither of them would listen to me, but I still felt obligated to try diplomacy, at least as a stalling tactic.

"It'll be fine, hellcat." The Crow Knight glanced in my direction with a smile. "I'll just work off some of my frustrations with the warp warrior. After that, the liaison is back on and we can *all* make up."

"You should go join the others," Dreyson growled. "The blue hall—"

"No, she really should stay. It's dangerous for her to wander off alone. And having her here makes this so much more exciting, don't you think?" The Crow Knight strode forward. "You'll stay, won't you? Who knows what kind of harm will befall him if you don't."

I glared at him. "You—"

"Don't look so upset. Your man can take care of himself. This might even be educational for you."

Dreyson gave an eerie laugh. "She already knows what to expect."

I recognized that tone and backed up more. "Try not to get carried away. I like this dress."

"I can't guarantee anything," Dreyson said, his grin vicious as he glanced at me over his shoulder.

"Oh, you two are adorable." The Crow Knight was smiling, I could hear it in his voice. "Come then, warp warrior. Show me what you can do." He blurred then, zipping forward, the metal of his sword glinting in the low light.

Dreyson spun his axe, and I heard the impact before I saw it.

The Crow Knight's sword slid along the edge of the axe-head, through Dreyson's guard, and glanced off his cheek, claiming first blood.

But Dreyson just laughed, like it didn't matter in the least, and swung the axe. The weapon could easily crush bones, and with his longer arms, he could match the Crow Knight's reach, but not his speed. Unlike the longsword, the double-bladed axe was not a precision weapon.

There was nothing actually stopping me from leaving. Dreyson could clearly fight his own battles. I could just take the blue hall back. But then Dreyson would be alone with the Crow Knight and his threats.

Using my gun would be a mistake. The risk of misfires was higher here, and I did not want to hit Dreyson. So I drew the dagger, watching as the two men went at each other like idiots, Dreyson laughing as he tried his damnedest to smash the Crow Knight, the Crow Knight delighting in taunting him. The Fey had a cat's grace, slipping under Dreyson's guard and darting back just as quickly, staying out of the arc of the axe swing.

Metal clanged. Sparks flew. Dreyson's axe should have smashed that elegant saber, but the Crow Knight was shockingly fast, more bloody gashes appearing across Dreyson's chest and arms.

It was all fun and games to them, these overpowered boys with their oversized toys. Maybe I had weapon envy, but I was mostly tired of being so damn powerless.

The Crow Knight left it half a second too long, and Dreyson's axe slammed into that elaborate black helm.

Fragments of metal scattered across the ground. I forced myself to look, even though I knew I wouldn't like what I saw.

But the Crow Knight did not go down, he just blurred again.

A shadow brushed against Dreyson's back, and then the battlemage dropped to one knee, blood pouring from the back of his leg.

The Crow Knight chuckled as he materialized again and stalked over to the downed man, the point of his sword held to Dreyson's neck.

I circled around and crept forward, knowing I only had one shot at this.

"Do you yield to me, warrior?" the Crow Knight purred, the tip of the blade dimpling the skin of Dreyson's throat as he forced the mage to tilt his head back and look up at him.

Dreyson glared, jaw clenched, blood trickling down his chin.

"Oh, I *like* this view. Even on your knees, you're still a sight to behold," the Crow Knight murmured, his attention on his wounded foe.

Even though I half expected him to reverse his sword and gut me, I reached up, pressing the edge of the obsidian knife to his throat, my other hand gripping his long braid. I had to get very close, my chest pressed to his armored back.

"That's enough," I said.

The Crow Knight stiffened as soon as he felt the blade on his neck. "Are you jealous?"

"No, I just don't like threats."

"'Twas just a little foreplay, hellcat. Don't be angry," the Crow Knight purred. "Or do be angry, but only if you're coming back to my quarters to work out all your frustrations on me. I don't mind." He leaned into me, and I flinched, expecting a headbutt or a counterattack. Instead, his free hand squeezed my thigh. "Relax. I'm at your mercy. You went to all this trouble to put me between your bodies, and I rather like the position."

"Enough," I said coldly, pulling back on his braid, the dagger flush against his skin.

He sucked in a sharp breath and gave a soft groan that didn't quite sound like pain. But he released my leg.

"You OK?" I asked Dreyson, trying to ignore how the Crow Knight rubbed against me.

"Fine," he grunted. Then he pushed the sword aside and stood, axe raised. "Let him go and come over here. If he makes any sudden moves, I'll cut him in half."

"Your man enjoyed himself. If you asked, I bet he would stay too—"

"Are you going to cause us more problems?" I asked sharply. "Am I better off slitting your throat?"

"So ruthless," the Crow Knight said with a laugh. "Don't worry, hellcat. I know when I'm bested."

"That's not actually an admiss—"

Dreyson leaned forward, a manic light in his eye. "*Hellcat*," he growled. "Get away from him. Stop letting him distract you."

I shivered at his tone and released the Crow Knight. Backing out of his reach, I moved behind Dreyson.

The Crow Knight's helm was gone. Under the fey lanterns, his hair was a warm shade of brown, which was a surprisingly normal color. From what I could see, he had elegant sharp features, but it was hard to tell because he was bleeding from a long gash in his forehead. Blood was still pouring down his face.

"I enjoyed the duel, warp warrior. Though I think we both held back, for the lady's sake." He grinned wolfishly at me.

Dreyson tensed. "Leave her out of this."

"That exclusion will only upset her more. Don't worry, warrior. The hellcat showed me her claws. I'll be prepared for you both next time." He winked, blew us a kiss, and then faded from view.

We stood there, watching for any signs of him, but there were no rogue shadows or sudden footprints materializing in the dust.

"I didn't—" I began, unsure of how to explain the Crow Knight's misconception.

"It's not safe," Dreyson said, clasping my arm. "We shouldn't stay here."

"Not arguing," I said, still clutching the dagger. "Status?"

"I'll manage," Dreyson said tightly. He was limping but still upright. He didn't quite lean on me, but he didn't let go of my arm.

"I'm sorry," I said, glancing at his leg.

"Don't apologize," he said gruffly. "*He* isn't the only thing we have to worry about. This isn't friendly territory. We'll discuss it *later*."

He led the way through the blue corridor. I glanced over my shoulder numerous times, aware that we weren't alone but unable to spot a thing, even with my fairy ointment.

We entered another hub where a fountain bubbled up from the rocks, spilling into a basin of white flowers. I didn't recognize them, but the odor was overpoweringly sweet.

"I've been waiting for you." A woman in an ivory ballgown sat on the edge of the fountain, her long pale hair falling in waves across the stone. "You smell delicious," she moaned, her voice melodic, her intonation wrong. "Come closer."

Dreyson froze beside me, and then he released my arm and began to drift toward her.

I reached out, grabbing his calloused hand.

"Celly, you don't want to do that," I said, vainly trying to pull him back.

"Ignore the chittering of the vermin, my warrior," she said, not even deigning to look at me. She was pale, like a vampire, but while she was unsettling and possibly intoxicating, she lacked that aura of coldness I associated with the undead.

Dreyson jerked forward but did not let go of my hand. Instead, he gripped it tighter, almost yanking me off balance. My bones creaked, but I held on. None of the charm hit me, but I wasn't her target.

"Talk to me. Please," he rasped, that polite entreaty tinged with desperation. "Hard truths to counter her false compulsions."

"I don't like how you spoke to the werejaguar today," I said. "I get that you have a problem with cops. I have a problem with cops, but that's no excuse to be a bigot. If you want to insult someone, insult them for something they have control over. Otherwise, you're just being a dick, and in this case, a racist one."

Dreyson turned his head away from the woman, staring at me with faint disbelief.

"Ignore the trash, warrior. She prattles. Why resist me? I only wish to bestow my favors upon you," the woman snarled from her perch.

Dreyson winced, like her words had impact. "Out of everything that's happened today, you're upset over that?"

"It's the only thing I'm unhappy with *you* over," I said. "Right now anyway. But I'll be really sore if you blow me off and go get eaten."

"Put aside the gangly girl—"

"You saw that werewolf in the pit," he huffed.

"Yeah, gruesome shit. But they don't usually get a choice about it. They might be more dangerous than the average human, but innately, they're no better or worse, just more powerful, like a battlemage."

Dreyson scowled at me.

"Also, he's my friend."

"And yet you still ended up in that cell."

"Yes," I said. "I'm upset with a lot of folks today. But don't worry, I have a book of grudges, and I will be going down the list. You're nowhere near the only one to get an earful."

"Put aside the sanctimonious, scrawny bitch!" The woman rose, moving toward us now, a tangle of thorny vines creeping out from under her voluminous white skirts.

Dreyson spun, fire in his free hand, his teeth clenched. "You are interrupting!"

"Mandragora, these are guests." From a far corner, a familiar lilting voice drawled, "The Vernal Lord will be displeased if you break the laws of hospitality."

I flinched as the Crow Knight appeared behind the woman, helmet intact once more.

The flame in Dreyson's hand grew bigger.

"It doesn't matter when he's already bleeding everywhere," Mandragora snapped. "Come to me!" she sang.

He shuddered, the flames sputtering.

I held on. "Celly, I'm getting hungry, but all I've got are these protein bars. Since I brought them, can we eat them here?"

"We should wait," Dreyson said through clenched teeth.

"Want me to save you one?"

"Yes." He was breathing hard now, shuddering with each inhalation.

"Will do. You just have to stick it out with me, OK? And if you're hungry, I know better places to eat. We just need to get home."

"Understood."

"Mandragora, there's plenty of fresh blood in the sand," the Crow Knight said, clearly watching us.

"But I want his," she mewled, her mouth pulled tight in a girlish pout.

"It will end badly for you if you try to take it," the Crow Knight said, tone flippant.

"Mind your own affairs! I don't have to tolerate you! You just like taunting me, you nasty scavenger!" she snapped, slapping a veiny hand against his chest.

The Crow Knight glanced down, and all I heard was a crack before she started screeching angrily.

"*You* don't lay hands on me," he said coldly. "Not if you want to keep them." Then he looked at us pointedly, and even with the helmet, I understood that look: get out of here while you still can.

And perhaps another warning: it would have been very easy to do that to you.

Dreyson's hand in mine, we retreated toward the Shadow Dunes, Mandragora's pained shrieks echoing in our ears.

We emerged from one of the alcoves on the first level to find Remington pacing the floor.

"Where were—" He glanced at Dreyson's injuries and swore. "You OK?"

"I'm fine," Dreyson hissed, looking genuinely offended by the question.

"And you?" Remington looked at me.

"Traumatized, but otherwise uninjured," I said.

"Where's the client?" Dreyson asked, dropping my hand.

Remington's eyes flicked between us. "He got a face-to-face with one of the Vernal gentry. The important one." Remington smiled tightly. "But he didn't want my advice."

"Where?" Dreyson growled.

"Stadium box," Remington said.

Dreyson took off, his limp noticeably better.

I started to follow, but Remington grabbed my arm.

"This won't end well," he said quietly. "He's too compromised. Sent me away. I'm going back in, but maybe you should wait—"

"Let's go," I groaned, not eager to be alone in the Shadow Dunes now.

We ascended another set of stairs, emerging near the top. Remington chewed on his bottom lip, clearly in pain.

Dreyson was already at the box to our right, but I could still hear Armstrong shouting.

"Return my child!" He lunged at the dark-skinned sidhe man who sat before him. Naomi reached out, trying to pull him back. "There's no changeling anymore—"

"Because you murdered it?" the Vernal Lord, lone sovereign of the Spring Court sneered. "Yes, you announced that already."

Thorny vines erupted from Armstrong's body, tendrils coming out of his mouth and eyes. Naomi leapt backward, but Liam was right beside Armstrong. The vines lashed out, coiling around his neck before he drew his knives.

I expected Dreyson to ready his axe or flames, but he leapt over the gate and pressed his palm to Armstrong's face. The man went stiff and then turned gray, vines dropping off.

Liam hit the ground holding his throat, and Naomi was there, paper charms glowing as she raised some kind of shield around the mercenaries and Armstrong's body.

"Stay here," Remington said, already throwing himself forward in a loping run.

The Vernal Lord did not seem remotely alarmed by the mercenaries bunkering down in front of him. He barely glanced up when Remington approached. Tall and slender, he wore a silky emerald tunic embroidered with gold and a green metal diadem shaped like a crown of leaves.

"It would be a shame to cause so much trouble over one lying madman," Remington said, pain tightening his words.

The Vernal Lord inclined his head. "What?"

"One liar disappearing isn't a problem," Remington said. "But three full-bonded Wergeld members? That's bound to cause allegations of inhospitality. After all, the Tithe of Red Sands is supposed to be a diplomatic event, controlled bloodshed only."

"They knew the risks, traveling with such a man," the Vernal Lord said, his smile cruel. "Yet they took his gold."

"Perhaps, but if you kill them, you give credence to his wild claims about changelings in Illium. Of course, that will draw even more attention, don't you think?" Remington asked, his tone breezy. "The man was quite mad, everyone would agree. But the Wergeld members have raised no hand against you, and well, he's stone now. A living statue is an excellent warning to those who would spread lies about the Courts, especially back in Illium."

Armstrong lay on his back, face frozen in agony, his skin petrified and as gray as granite.

"We have no human infants here. Nor could there be infant changelings in Illium. We would not send our children to certain death." The Vernal Lord sniffed in disgust. "Nor should we be forced to endure outrageous slander."

"You are merciful and wise," Remington said in soothing tones. "You have punished the liar but not slain him, and so the Alluvian Treaties are honored."

The Vernal Lord stared down his nose at the scene. "This bores me." He rose, glowering at Dreyson in particular. "Take your employer and get out. This was not even an ill-advised challenge, merely suicidal idiocy. See to it that your people understand that they have plumbed the depths of my mercy and the limits of my patience. Ensure that none repeat these mistakes."

And then he turned in a swirl of green, leaving us with one stone client and two injured mercenaries.

Chapter 7
At Least There Were Waffles

Paean Hills is a place of healing, rejuvenation, and miracles. Many skilled physicians go into private practice, their talents reserved for the service of the rich and powerful. But Paean Hills is a public institution, open to all, with financial aid available to any in need. It is kept afloat with public funding, private donations, and the services of some very talented individuals. If you are suffering from potent curses, preternatural infections, or even just general spell damage, Paean Hills is the place to go. The trauma center is unmatched.

After they cured me of a...condition, I cannot sing their praises enough, but between you and me, dear reader, avoid the cafeteria.

— *An Introduction to Illium by Ann Keyes*

NAOMI PAINTED SIGILS on her hands and carried Armstrong's petrified body back to the car. Dreyson tossed me the keys and picked up an unconscious Liam, his fingers glowing as he closed the wounds on the younger man's neck.

We loaded Armstrong into the cargo area and Liam on the back bench of the SUV.

Remington rubbed his knee as he climbed into the car, his expression grim.

Naomi stayed in the back row with Liam.

Dreyson sat shotgun again, and I buckled up and handed him a protein bar as I cautiously pulled out of the mostly empty field.

"Take that route," Dreyson said, pointing to a path in the woods. He tore the wrapper open with his teeth and finished the bar in three bites.

I followed his directions. Checking the rearview mirror several times, I spotted nothing more than a few will-o'-the-wisps. I handed Dreyson the second bar.

He opened it with his hands this time and held it out to me. "Take it."

I broke off a piece and chewed mechanically, focusing on the road. Fortunately, it led out of the park. Once on the highway, some of the tension evaporated.

In the back, Remington texted furiously.

Dreyson leaned forward in his seat, his gaze distant.

"Are we going to Paean Hills?" I asked, because that was the hospital that specialized in magical ailments.

"Yes, I've called in a guild rep to handle things," he said.

"Cursed clients are bad for business," Naomi said reproachfully.

"Dead clients are worse," Dreyson said.

Naomi clicked her tongue, clearly disapproving of something.

The rest of the drive was quiet until I pulled up to the ER entrance.

"Wait here," Dreyson told me. He got out to help Naomi unload Armstrong and Liam.

"What's going on with you?" Remington asked quietly, glancing at the empty passenger seat, clearly referring to someone else.

"No idea," I said.

"You two seem to be getting along pretty well," he mused. "He's been downright civil."

I shrugged. "I need to eat. My blood sugar is low and I'm wiped."

"Waffle House?"

"Sure, but I need to discuss some things with Dreyson."

Remington raised a brow. "Do you need a wingman?" he asked hesitantly.

"It's not like that," I said, massaging my temples. "Violent stuff happened. I'll give you a rundown later. I'm unhurt, but there's a lot."

"OK, take your time. I have reports to write now. If you want privacy, let's hit the drive-thru, and I'll shut myself in my office." He pressed his palms together, his grin wide. "So is this…?"

"Unlikely." I scowled. "I've gone on two dates today, real and fake, and they both ended in *disaster*."

Remington flashed me a shit-eating grin. "The third time is—"

Dreyson opened the passenger door and climbed in.

Remington shut up.

"We're grabbing food," I said. "Waffle House is still open."

"That's…fine," Dreyson said.

We stopped, though Dreyson made polite noises about not needing anything. Remington just doubled his own order and paid.

We made it back to the office by 4 a.m. Only a few extra hours had passed; we were lucky not to experience any more severe time dilation effects from our visit to the Shadow Dunes. Remington said something about a mountain of paperwork and disappeared into his office.

I plopped down at my desk, and Dreyson pulled up a chair. I stared at the greasy bag. It took some effort to muster the will to move, but slowly I began unpacking things.

"Does this kind of thing happen to you a lot?" I asked.

"It's not rare," Dreyson said.

I shook my head and picked up a piece of bacon. "I normally stick to lower stakes."

"That's probably wise."

I squinted at him. "The Crow Knight likes you."

Dreyson jerked back like I shocked him. "He's bad news."

"Agreed," I said, curious to see his reaction. "But for the record, his attention isn't just competitive, he's attracted to you."

Dreyson gritted his teeth, his face flushed. "Are you forgetting that he propositioned you too?"

"As an afterthought," I said, waving it off. "I'm not the one he kept making sexy eyes at. And all that battlefield innuendo? He wants you so bad, he doesn't care that he looks stupid." I took a bite of waffle as Dreyson flinched. "The only reason he keeps hitting on me is because he thinks we're together. It's to get under your skin." And other places.

"I disagree." Dreyson's jaw twitched. "But I noticed his presumption. Was that your doing?" He looked away briefly. "If so, I would like an explanation."

"When he ran into me earlier, I was lost. He cornered me, made an offer, and I declined, saying there was "someone else." I left it ambiguous, because he already knew I wasn't into Armstrong. Then he saw us together and made an assumption. I didn't correct him, because he was trying to stab you, and so we had other priorities." I paused for a breath and some syrup. "Did I complicate things for you?"

"Not by doing that, no," Dreyson said, taking a bite of his omelette. He made a face but kept eating. "The client got into trouble while I was searching for you. It's his own fault, but the situation reflects poorly on me and my team."

I flinched, recalling exactly what happened to Armstrong. "Sorry, that wasn't my intention."

Dreyson shrugged. "It's done. There were several factors at play. You don't need to apologize."

I ate another piece of bacon because I wasn't sure how to respond to that. Was he saying I had a minority contribution to the fault?

Dreyson dutifully ate his food with no enthusiasm.

"So how did you find me?" I said, instead of what I wanted to ask, because I was done being brave tonight.

"To be fair, you simply fell out of the air in front of me."

"So you were looking for me in random directions?"

"You had my knife," he said, like I was supposed to know that it was magic *and* trackable.

And then I recalled his warning about being careful of what I accepted from others. "I guess that makes sense." I pulled it out of my boot and set it on the desk. "Thanks for the loan."

Dreyson just continued eating his stack of pancakes and foregoing the syrup. I poured the extra on my waffles. Even if it wasn't the good stuff, I needed the sugar.

"Thanks for looking for me and getting me out of there," I said. "I didn't mean to cause problems."

"It's done," he repeated. "Your help was also appreciated, in the Shadow Dunes and earlier." He raised his head, meeting my gaze for a moment, his expression pensive. The exchange was awkward, but he didn't seem upset.

"You're welcome," I said, mustering a small grin. "What was Mandragora?"

"Fey, Spring Court, that's my guess from the plant association. She could be *sluagh*. They're mostly Autumn Court, but usually not capable of strong allure."

"Aren't the *sluagh* undead?" I asked, because while the Fey were mostly known for the beautiful sidhe, the *sluagh* tended to be more like the nightmarish Wild Hunt.

"Some," Dreyson said. "Fey taxonomy isn't an exact science, and Court Fey are mostly from western Europe. They have a few Norse troll-kin and other trooping fairies mixed in, but there are plenty of the solitary sort that don't adhere to the same rules."

"And they probably won't consent to a scholarly review, even if we ask politely."

"I would not advise it. And you should not return to the Shadow Dunes," he said. "They have long memories."

"I don't particularly want to return there." I leaned back in my chair, crossing my arms. "Do you think he'll come looking for you? What about the others?" Because we also ran afoul with Mandragora and the pissy Vernal Lord.

Dreyson shrugged. "I doubt it. Their kind don't do well around so much steel."

"Why do you think he let us go?" Because I did *not* see him crush Mandragora's hand. He was too fast. One moment she was hitting him, the next, she was screaming. If he wanted to, he could have done the same or worse to me in the duel with Dreyson. And Dreyson was aware of it too.

"They like their games," Dreyson said, raising his chin, his mouth drawn tight. "Don't mistake his actions for altruism, Ms. Giles. They're like cats, toying with their prey."

"You can call me Claire, you know," I said on impulse.

"That's not your real name," he said sternly.

Well, there it was. He looked into my background after getting out of jail. Fair enough. I researched him too. "It's the one I use in public. Like how you go by Dreyson. Figured you of all people would understand an alias."

He gave me a sour look.

I just tapped my fingers against the desk, pretending like his expression wasn't scary. "So who do you think was the priority target in the cell today?"

Dreyson opened his mouth, then shut it again, narrowing his eye. He stared thoughtfully at me. "That is a good question. I thought you were, but…" He frowned. "There are easier, more surefire ways to handle a single civilian."

"I think SIU was intended to be collateral damage, but there are easier ways, yes."

He looked me over. "Except they have failed before."

"Yup," I said, forcing a wide and insincere grin. "But I guess they're still trying. Lucky me. It's a good thing they're so bad at their jobs. Otherwise I might actually be worried." The sarcasm tasted bitter.

Dreyson was silent.

"Sorry, that was whiny. I'm just tired." I rubbed the back of my neck. "What will happen to Armstrong?"

"He might live. The petrification spell gives the medical mages time to prepare treatment. He's in stasis. He's not in pain. But once they bring him out of it, the clock starts again. It won't last indefinitely. I only bought them time."

He had vines pouring out of his face, tearing through soft tissue. How did one survive that?

"Will Liam be OK?"

"Yes, he'll be fine," Dreyson said. "You switch topics a lot."

"I panic talk and have…attention span issues. Today's been worse than usual, probably because of the stress." I squinted at him. "You don't have to…"

"It was an observation, not a criticism. I work differently is all," Dreyson said. "But you're right. A lot has happened. I don't have satisfying answers for your questions. I find that I have the same questions, so I need time to think." He plucked a pen and a sticky note off my desk and neatly wrote out a number. "I have some things to take care of." He handed the paper to me. "I may not answer right away."

"Oh," I said and pulled my phone out to input the number. "Is this a landline?" Dreyson had enough magic that he could accidentally fry delicate electronics.

"Hardened mobile," he said. "It's reliable, and I can receive texts."

I raised a brow. Magic-hardened electronics were malg-tech, difficult to make and very expensive. "Can you play games on it?"

He gave a small huff, that familiar twitch of exasperation in his jaw.

"That's a no…"

"Keep gloating and I'll overload your cellphone," he muttered.

"You better not! I'll be very upset with you and retaliate in petty and creative ways," I said sharply.

He tilted his head to the side, lips curving in a faint smile, like he was actually amused. "Ah. Well, I wouldn't want that, now would I."

I stared. It wasn't that smiling made him prettier or made me more comfortable. But seeing him relaxed, maybe even making a joke, that was new. He was teasing me. Was he actually being friendly? I wasn't sure what to think, except maybe I'd like to see more of that from him.

"I have to go now," he said, cleaning up his empty food wrappers. He picked up mine too and took them to the trash can. "But we can talk more later, if you like."

"Yes. Sure. I would like that," I said, standing up. "Thanks for getting that."

He nodded. "Please thank Detective Remington for the food. It was...an experience." His expression turned disgruntled, like he hated the idea of being in Remington's debt. Or maybe that was just the beginning of indigestion.

"Sure, you should try eating in the actual restaurant after a night of drinking," I said cheerfully. "It's also an experience."

"I bet," he said, shaking his head as I walked him to the door and handed him the keys to the car.

"Get some rest, Claire," he said as he walked out.

"Take your own advice!" I shouted back as I locked up. He raised an arm in acknowledgment, but did not turn around. I returned to my desk and found the dagger was still there. I texted him.

You forgot your knife.

The reply came seconds later. *I didn't forget it.*

I stood there for a moment, considering the implications. Then I went back to Remington's office. We had a lot to talk about.

Remington was *still* scrawling his report. The remnants of his meal were in the trash. He looked up when I walked in, eyes immediately darting toward the door.

"He's gone," I said.

"Really gone?" Remington mouthed silently.

"As far as I can tell. I walked him out and locked up. He says thanks for the food, by the way. I think he hated it, though."

Remington gave a little chuckle, like he wasn't surprised. In fact, maybe he chose that food on purpose...

"Really?" I crossed my arms.

"Hey, I nearly had a heart attack when he walked in earlier. I didn't think it was a coincidence then, and I don't know what I think now." He pushed his hair back and rested his chin on his hands, smirking. "So what'd you do to him? Or with him?"

"What?" I scowled, dropping into a chair in front of his desk.

"Claire, you and the Murder Cyclops were holding hands when you came back to the arena."

"That's mean."

"So you do like him," Remington said, his smirk fading, a worried furrow appearing between his eyebrows.

"I don't dislike him," I said with a shrug. "But it's not what you think, gutterbrain. We ran into a monster. She did this thing with her voice and kept trying to lure Dreyson to her because she wanted to drink his blood. And it was working, so I grabbed his hand and distracted him by berating him over…"

Remington's expression grew increasingly perplexed. "Can you start over from the beginning?"

"Yeah, I should. I've had a busy night. But first." I held up my index finger. "Why was SIU there? Don't say 'coincidence' or I'll poison you. Does it haves something to do with whatever had everyone out of the office today?"

Remington gave me a resigned smile. "Yeah. Don't look at me like that. They didn't coordinate with me either. But I know more now." He took a sip from his mug. "Triple homicide today, two adults, one child. Kid was a changeling and an only child. It was pretty brutal. No history of fertility treatments, no adoptions on record."

"Not a murder-suicide?" I asked, thinking of Armstrong.

"No," Remington said. "And it's not the only one. SIU got one last week. Four dead. Both parents, two kids, but only one child was a changeling."

I sat with that, my stomach dropping. "Do they think Dreyson was involved? Was that why he was arrested?"

"No, his alibis are solid. He was picked up today for standing in a doorway and not letting the officers pass."

I could picture that. "Literal obstruction."

"They were allegedly doing a wellness check. Maybe it was related to Armstrong." Remington frowned. "I'll have to ask Jon. Right now, someone is pulling the medical records for 'Armstrong.' Given the nature of his wounds, he should be easy to identify. We'll have a real name by morning."

Apparently, HIPAA violations were not a deterrent for Remington's patron.

"So SIU doesn't like Armstrong or Dreyson as suspects?"

"No, the murderers used a straight blade, probably a sword."

I considered that. A lot of people carried swords, but one in particular stuck out. "How do we know the kids were changelings? Did their bodies change after death?"

"No," Remington said. "And they usually do. The only reason we know is because Niffolm is a sick fuck."

Dr. Niffolm, the chief medical examiner, ran the morgue. And he truly enjoyed his work, at least when he got to cut people up.

"So he recognizes the anatomy because he's dissected them before?" I asked.

"Yes." Remington shuddered. "He also thought it strange that they didn't revert postmortem. Conducted an entire battery of tests. Called in consultants. Gave in-depth anatomical explanations that we don't need."

"But Armstrong said his kid changed after death. Needed someone to glamour the corpse." The discrepancy was minor, but it nagged at me.

"I noticed that too. But it seems we need to verify Armstrong's story first." Remington tapped his fingers on the desk. "What else?"

"Dreyson and I aren't convinced that I was the target today either. It was overkill for me, but good enough for someone who is scared of Dreyson or wants to keep their hands clean," I said, realizing that if that theory panned out, someone still wanted me dead. I just wasn't a priority. That was both a relief and kind of insulting.

Remington groaned. "He's looking into that too? Shit, that could get complicated, Claire."

I shrugged, knowing it could go badly, but at this point, I trusted Dreyson more than the IPD. We had a shared interest in this matter. "After I left the arena, someone found me. It sounded like a little girl." I described the detour, resending the photos on my phone.

"An iron-studded door," Remington mused. "Strange."

Iron burned most of the Fey. Having it in their domain was likely a security measure or a punishment.

Remington looked over the pictures. "The...sponsor can get these translated." He paused, pulling the screen closer to his face. "This flower motif is familiar."

"Yep."

Remington pulled up a picture of Armstrong's changeling baby. The flower marks were very similar. "What the hell is going on?"

"Whatever I spoke to hinted at there being human children in the Courts. It might have just been trying to stir up trouble. I didn't get a good look at it."

Remington nodded absently. "We need more information."

"But we're not going back to the Shadow Dunes any time soon, right?"

"Probably not." Remington took another sip from his mug. "We pushed our luck tonight. That was some stupidly dangerous shit you pulled." He straightened up in his seat, anger tightening his expression. "Don't do that again."

"Just taking a page from your book," I said with a yawn.

Remington deflated a little. "For fuck's sake, Claire. You could at least pretend to be sorry."

"It was unwise. Sorry, I got carried away," I said sheepishly. "But don't pretend like you wouldn't have done the exact same thing."

Remington snorted, because I was right. "Only if you pretend I tore you a new one over it. And you don't do that again, no pretending for that part."

"Heh." I rested my elbows on his desk. "Don't worry, I don't intend to go back to the Shadow Dunes."

Remington examined the pictures. "It's good work, though," he said softly.

"Yup." I preened a little.

"Does Dreyson know about any of this?"

"I didn't mention the kid or the archives. Wait, did you send him after me?"

"No, about fifteen minutes after you left, he just got up and told us to stay put. He didn't say why he was leaving, let alone anything about retrieving you." Remington's frown deepened.

"About that, he can track the dagger. I tried to return it to him before we went to the arena, but he let me hang on to it. In fact, he left it for me again. I don't want him monitoring me, but having an easy-to-use magic weapon might be worth it. Anyway, after I left the archive, I ran right into the Crow Knight…"

"Of course you did." Remington rested his face in his hand.

I gave him the summary of both encounters with the Crow Knight and Mandragora, and it was an honest account, because this was Remington and I made a habit of telling him the whole truth.

"So, just to make sure I understood you, you told the Mur— Dreyson off for making shitty comments about weres? While holding his hand? And he just…took it?" His voice went high.

"He argued, but it worked. We avoided a terminal case of poison ivy, and I guess the Crow Knight…helped us out."

"That one is a person of interest. He's a known Court enforcer, carries a sword, and is trying to get close to you or Dreyson, possibly for intel."

I appreciated the calculating reason behind the Crow Knight's interest. It was less disturbing than the idea that he actually wanted to seduce me. But what if he was also going around slaughtering families in Illium?

"Now I just have more questions. Why are there so many changelings? And how? How many? Who's killing them, and why?"

Remington stared at his notes. "And what side are we on?"

"Not the baby-stranglers or the mass-murderers," I said automatically.

"That much is obvious," Remington nodded. "But I think there are more than two sides to this." He looked back at his phone. "Damn, it's so late, it's early. Let me give you a ride home. We can reconvene tomorrow afternoon…if you want to keep working this case, that is," he said, his smile uneasy.

"Yeah," I said indignantly, especially since Remington wanted to leverage this on my behalf. "I'm already involved."

"I know, but you should be keeping a lower profile, and I don't like the Crow Knight's fixation on you. You have enough trouble as it is." He shook his head, very diplomatically not mentioning Dreyson, though I knew he was dying to do so. "I'll pick you up tomorrow and bring some extra disguise charms. It might be best if you don't look like yourself in some parts of town."

"Sure," I said, because Remington was right. Things were more dangerous for me. I appreciated that he wasn't trying to sideline me, though. We got up to leave his office, my thoughts going back to the dagger on my desk and what I was going to do with it.

Interlude I

THEY ARE CERTAIN that they are dreaming, though the bathroom looks real. It's the same seafoam green tile, the jellyfish shower curtain, the two side-by-side scalloped sinks with their father's razor on one side, their mother's electric toothbrush on the other. But they are drawn to the full-length mirror in the corner of their parents' bathroom, and in it, the girl staring back at them.

They touch their face. Something is wrong, and they can feel it under their skin. One side is human, the face they know, but the other is...other. It is half right, half true, but it doesn't show that in the reflection. Because despite their resemblance, the girl in the mirror isn't them.

"It's you," they say, reaching for the reflection, fingers stopped by the cool glass. It's not real. None of this is. It's a symbol—the only way the two of them can communicate. There are rules at play that they do not understand. But the girl does.

She does not reach back. She just studies them thoughtfully.

They don't like the look in those dark eyes, the sharpness, the greed for things that the girl can see but not touch. Instinctively, they know what she wants. They just don't know what she is willing to do to get it. Just like they don't know what they are willing to do to keep it.

"They're moving now," the girl says. "We're out of time."

They don't know what she is talking about, but they understand the threat. "Are you in danger?"

"None of us are safe," she says. "But you are in more danger than I."

"Do you really care?" they ask, because they have no idea how she feels. They don't even know how they feel about her.

"I don't know," she says, arms crossed over her chest, chin raised defiantly. There is a familiarity to that look. "But I don't want other people to suffer."

They nod. They understand what she isn't saying.

"I don't want them to suffer either," they say, one hand brushing against the handle of their mother's comb.

"Then I guess we're going to have to do something," the girl says, not looking happy about it. "Do try to remember what I'm about to tell you..."

They will try. But like all the other times before, they will only partially succeed.

Chapter 8
The Lies We Tell for Love

LOCAL INESSENTIAL OIL BUSINESS A FOREIGN SPY FRONT!!!!
Our lily-livered lawyerfolk have advised against naming names, because those unfair folk are sue-happy! But that doesn't stop us from pointing the metaphorical finger at those thieving, no-good, muck-daubing spies! And you all know what finger we're talking about! So listen up and listen good! We know everyone is all about burning ethically-sourced sage and bougie aromatherapy induction oil warmers! There's nothing wrong with that; it's a free country! But it's not going to stay that way if you give your money and personal information to those swindlers! They're going around with their fancy athleisure and twelve-dollar nutrition drinks, trying to sell you on a lifestyle! Pay attention to the money trail, sheeple! Their oils are fine and dandy, great quality, but they're selling your personal data to the Eye of Sauron, so maybe be more careful about who you do business with, Janice. Also, stop feeding your kid essential oils! That stuff is not meant to be ingested!
    — *The Trojan Watchtower: April 11, 2018*

"**CONSULTED SOME FOLKS.** This changeling-related activity is a serious diplomatic incident. Someone definitely violated the treaties," Remington told me after I got in the car.

I sipped my coffee and thumbed through the copies of case files. There were *three* known family slayings. Another one, several days old, was discovered this morning. Remington now had the crime scene photos and other documents from SIU.

"So Jon wants us on this one?" I asked.

Remington was silent for half a second too long.

"I mean, he wants you on this one, and he wants me kept as far away from him as possible?"

Remington laughed. "Given the circumstances, we shouldn't mention your involvement, not right now anyway."

"Davis and Mwanje saw us last night."

"Mmm, Jon knows." He stared straight ahead, his smile forced, his eyes tired.

"Hmm." I knew that look; those two got into it again. The lieutenant probably said something shitty and stormed off to berate some other bystander. Remington would just play like nothing happened and his feelings weren't hurt. And then, in a few days, the lieutenant would slink in and buy Remington a beer or a burger and they'd go back to pretending that everything was fine. Because the lieutenant was an asshole and didn't have any other friends.

"Nina says that she and Mwanje are going to be viewing the CCTV footage today."

I just studied the crime scene photos, forcing myself to only look at pieces, not the whole bodies, and definitely not the faces, with their gouged eyes and expressions twisted in agony and terror. It was bad, blood everywhere, bodies arranged gruesomely. The killer posed them, heads in laps or piled on a table like a centerpiece.

According to the reports, the kids were cut down quick. The killer was not so merciful with the adults. They played with them, chasing them down, cutting off bits. They drew it out, like a cat with a wounded bird.

But no one heard a thing. The families lived in the suburbs, houses with some space between them. But with this kind of carnage, I expected someone to hear something, even if they shrugged it off. But there were no noise complaints.

And there was less blood in the bodies than there should have been, even accounting for the copious amounts splattered across the walls. Normally, that would indicate vampires or predatory undead.

Mandragora was Fey, and she desperately wanted Dreyson's blood. But she didn't use a sword, at least not that I saw. It didn't mean there weren't others like her, though.

"Are we expecting retaliation?" I asked.

"Dunno," Remington said, expression troubled. "We'll likely pick up some observers. I grabbed some extra stuff for the office."

"Any luck on Armstrong's real identity?" I asked.

"Yes," Remington said. "We have a name and some basic background. It may come as a shock, but it doesn't match what he told us, and I haven't had a chance to confirm anything yet."

I sighed. Of course it was going to get more complicated. "So what angle are we covering?"

"We're starting with Court financials," Remington said. "That should give us a better picture of their influence and assets. This could be a rogue individual, but that wouldn't explain how the changelings got here."

The Courts were basically a foreign power in Illium, the Shadow Dunes the closest thing they had to an embassy. There might be Fey agents within the city, but we couldn't just show up and question them, not unless we wanted to end up cursed, like Armstrong. SIU would be doing their job: focusing the victims, timelines, security camera footage, and the forensics. Whereas Remington and I could talk to people who didn't care much for cops.

"You called Zareen yet?"

Remington shook his head. "She likes you better than me."

Well, that was true. I was never a cop. I sent her a text.

The response was immediate: *What do you got?*

Looking for a comprehensive financial analysis of the Courts. Rem and I can swing by.

Sorry, can't today! Nephew is staying over. Business line!

I frowned. Her nephews lived in the same building as she did. That wasn't a reason to— Oh.

"We're doing this remote. Something happen between you two?" I asked, giving him the side-eye.

Remington coughed. "I asked her about doing contract work for SIU...over dinner."

I sighed, staring up at the ceiling. "Was it your flirtations or your recruitment spiel?"

"The latter," he said. "I reminded her that I *used* to be a cop and things got awkward."

There were a lot of reasons immigrant communities didn't trust the cops. and even more if you were of a certain look or religious persuasion. Maybe you'd get a fair shake, but given my experiences, I wouldn't count on it. Some people just treated others differently if they thought they could get away with it. And people in positions of authority routinely got away with it.

I didn't bother telling Remington not to flirt with my friends. He was honest about his inability to maintain a long-term monogamous relationship, and for some that was a selling point.

"Back to the office, then," I said, because I would need the work laptop for this.

At my desk, I scanned the document dump, surprised by how much Zareen had available immediately. HerbAway was not a new topic for her. This would have been more fun at her place, drinking potent coffee and eating pastries while spending way too much time gossiping.

HerbAway was a standard multi-level marketing scheme, with the twist of money being a secondary goal. Their actual priority was intelligence gathering, though they still focused on recruitment. Profits did not come from sales, but from adding more suckers to their downline. Each recruit paid for a chance to "buy a share of the company," and the money was funneled to the people above them.

Both pyramid schemes and Ponzi schemes operated on "rob Peter to pay Paul" logic, but Ponzi schemes were limited to fraudulent investments and easier to bust. Pyramid schemes were an entire lifestyle: sell to everyone you know, recruit people, build a social network inside, and if you don't toe the line, they ice you out. If you actively crossed them, they hit you with defamation suits, NDAs, and all kinds of nuisance legal action.

Switching to an encrypted app, I verified the security codes and called Zareen.

"So what do you mean money isn't their objective? They seem to be pretty focused on raking it in."

"Hello to you too," Zareen said. "We're talking about HerbAway specifically. The Courts have a diverse portfolio, but HerbAway stems from the Spring Court. Money is a secondary benefit and the bait. This is an intelligence network. It's a solid cover: multi-level marketing groups -MLMs- always push recruitment. New members profile their connections, which allows the company to tailor their approach. 'Your mother is having health problems? Why don't you try this business opportunity for a chance to make some cash on the side?' Switch that out with a child going to college, a new baby on the way, or an expensive funeral.

Maybe Armstrong's wife didn't join HerbAway. Maybe just being on the periphery was enough."

"So you don't think they're pulling in that much money?" I asked.

"Not from what I could see." She hesitated, letting me know that her research was not entirely above board. "For the amount of work they put into it, it's profitable, but not *that* profitable. Those bastards are in it for the desperate people. When their human members run out of money, sometimes Court reps give the victim a 'chance' to win it back, but it's a rigged game. Sometimes they lose a body part, sometimes they end up as indentured servants in the Courts, sometimes they don't come back at all." She let out a low growl.

"Shit," I said. I didn't know about that, but it wasn't a complete surprise. The Fey had that kind of reputation. HerbAway was just a modern method of implementing their traditional chicanery. "I'm sorry to hear that." Zareen had all this data already, and she was speaking with a lot of emotion. This was personal. "Who did they target?"

She sighed. "My cousin got off easy. I managed to bail her out before she got in too deep. But she signed contracts she didn't understand, spent her life savings on mediocre supplements, and went bankrupt in under a year. The usual scammy shit," Zareen said through clenched teeth. "And no one does anything about it, because they have expensive suits and fancy lawyers. It's all smoke and mirrors. MLMs sell a dream, and the *good neighbors* are better at that than most. They lure people in with promises of stability. They just need to work hard for a year and everything will fall into place. They can even work from home, save money on childcare, have *fun* with it. But it's just another grift. They sell a lie, the poor and desperate mortgage their souls to buy into it, and they lose everything."

Zareen was another mod on a local IRC chat. I was far from the only mundane human who needed to take a crash course on the supernatural. Here, there were a scattering of support groups that offered curated introductions to the weird tailored to mundane folks. Ours masqueraded as a homebrew D&D channel. She was a forensic accountant by trade and managed some Sharia-compliant micro-lending in the local community. But Hawala got a bad rap with law enforcement, so she was very security-conscious.

She stumbled onto the weird while investigating long-term investments and convoluted trusts that the local immortals used. Accounting books made for boring reading, but they were a reliable way to unravel mysteries.

"We're looking into both the Spring and Autumn Courts. They've been doing some shady long-term operations in the city."

Zareen gave a bark of laughter. "Can SIU afford this?"

"We have a private client who prioritizes the accuracy over legality, so we can pass on or leave off certain information at your discretion."

Zareen went silent. "What are you looking for?"

"Missing kids," I said.

Zareen let loose a torrent of Arabic. "They're stealing children again?" she hissed.

"Looks like it."

Another string of guttural curses. "I'll get back to you. Secure channels only. Don't bring this to the IRC."

"Sure," I said. That meant using TOR, Signal, and the malg-tech messenger Tox.IM, which had no central servers and encrypted all connections. This meant we would avoid face-to-face meetings too. So much for baklava and coffee.

Zareen wasn't magically-adept. Just where was she getting her info? She probably wasn't working on this alone. That was something to consider.

"I'll send you what I can, the usual rate. But leave my name off it."

"Check the front door camera," Remington said, emerging from his office.

I pulled it up on my laptop. A small figure in a blue hoodie, jeans, and bright red sneakers stood by the door.

I opened up a new jar of fairy ointment and smeared it on my eyes. Nothing changed.

"Looks like a kid," I said. "How do you want to handle this?"

The kid stared at the camera lens, head tilted sideways, the hood dropping backward, revealing a pair of oversized sunglasses, a mop of dark curls, and brown skin. I couldn't tell age or sex, but given the height, they probably weren't past middle school yet.

"I don't expect an attack in broad daylight, but I don't want to be careless," Remington said. "Do you want to cover me?"

Was I fast enough or even ruthless enough to shoot a kid-shaped thing if it went for Remington's throat?

I didn't know.

"I'm faster on my feet," I said after a moment, not looking at his cane. "You can cover me."

Remington mulled that over. "All right. I'll stay by the counter."

I nodded, heading to the front door, careful not to block his line of sight. Pressing the intercom, I looked out the peephole—still no change. "Can I help you?"

The kid cleared their throat and took off the sunglasses. They looked like a human kid with perfectly normal hazel eyes, a button nose, and a smattering of freckles.

"I'm here to see Ms. Claire Giles," they said.

I tensed. "Why are you looking for Claire?"

The kid blinked, some of that confidence melting away. "My name is Innis Armstrong. My dad is Leonard Armstrong." Their voice wobbled, distress in their eyes. "And he said if anything happened to him, I should find Ms. Giles, because maybe she'd help me." They blinked rapidly. This kid was genuinely distressed, I knew that much. Just like I knew, without any doubt whatsoever, that they were lying to me.

Chapter 9
Sometimes What We Are Not Matters More

The Changeling Swap is the subject of much literary and sociological discussion. This report isn't about the ramifications of false changeling allegations or subsets of Capgras Syndrome, but instead addresses the curious Fey practice of abducting a human infant and leaving an inhuman infant in its place. Consistently, the human parents don't notice when the switch occurs.

The cause is also the subject of speculation. Trollkin believe it is more prestigious for their offspring to be raised in human households. Others claim that the sidhe simply wish for human babies, for whatever reasons, and know that their own children will eventually return to them.

The Fey are very effective at Kirbyan Mimicry or brood parasitism. Such activity is not unheard of in nature. Paper wasps and phengaris rebeli release pheromones to convince the host that the intrusive larvae is their own offspring. The cuckoo bee is more insidious: they infiltrate, kill the queen, and enslave other bee colonies. There is another natural parallel to consider, the slave-making ants. They raid other broods and capture the offspring to work in their colonies. Studies show that some species may have evolved to become permanent social parasites, unable to care for their young on their own.

— *SIU Police Reports: Blackout Files*

REMINGTON LOPED TO my side and gestured for me to open the door.

"Innis" stared at us.

"Can you hold this for me, real quick?" Remington asked, passing them a black metal charm.

"Sure, I guess," the kid said, accepting the item. They studied the coin-sized disc. "What kind of writing is this?"

"Don't you know?" Remington asked.

The kid blinked and shook their head. "No. Looks like hieroglyphics, though."

Remington nodded. "What did you say your name was?"

"Innis Xana Wilder-Ramos." The kid clapped a hand over their mouth, eyes wide. A muffled, "Oh no!" squeaked out.

"Are you here to do harm, Innis Xana Wilder-Ramos?" Remington asked, his elbow shifting as he moved the hand in his pocket.

"No! I'm looking for my dad! And he *did* tell me to find Claire Giles!" the kid shouted.

"Are you working for or under the influence of anyone other than your parents? That includes acts of coercion made to ensure your cooperation," Remington said, speaking quickly as the black charm started to smoke.

"No! Why would you think that?"

"And do you intend to do harm to anyone?"

"No! What the heck?" The kid scowled and dropped the smoldering piece of metal onto the ground. "What did you do to me?"

"Truth spell," Remington said.

"An expensive one," I said, shaking my head. A skilled practitioner could cast a minute-long truth spell without trouble. But imbuing a charm so someone like Remington could use it took a lot of power. And truth spells weren't foolproof; they couldn't force an answer, especially if the subject had no knowledge of the topic. Neither did they differentiate between truth and what the subject *believed* to be true. The most accurate answers came from yes/no questions. A seasoned criminal or Court-operative would not have accepted the charm in the first place.

"It was," Remington sighed.

"Better safe than dead," I said.

The kid flinched.

"Sorry about the rough welcome. Things are complicated. I'm Claire," I said.

Innis stood on the front walk, watching us both with suspicious eyes. They looked me up and down, like they were matching my appearance to a checklist description.

"Are you coming?" Remington asked, not actually issuing an invitation. Because there was still a chance this kid could trigger the defensive wards.

Innis scrunched up their face and glared at Remington. Nostrils flaring, they squared their shoulders and marched into the building.

The wards did not react. No imminent danger, then.

"We good?" I asked.

Remington nodded at me. "Gotta remind you that sometimes two and two is four—"

"And sometimes it's twenty-two." I understood that warning just fine. "Why don't we go sit down in the office and we'll talk about what's going on."

"I don't wanna talk to him." Innis scowled, jabbing their finger in Remington's direction.

He just shrugged. "I understand, but we've had several close calls in the past 24 hours. I'm not taking chances. But if it makes you more comfortable, I'll keep my distance."

Innis blinked at him, suspicion not fading.

"You good taking the lead?" he asked.

"Sure." I pulled my phone out, knowing he would text me anything relevant. I took the kid to the conference table. Their head bobbed as they rapidly looked around the room, motions reminiscent of "Armstrong."

"If you're thirsty, we have water, soda, and juice," I said, gesturing for them to sit.

"Bottled water, please," Innis said with narrowed eyes.

I grabbed two bottles from the snack nook and placed them on the table, letting the kid pick first, before I sat down across from them.

Remington sat on the edge of my desk, one hand rubbing his knee.

"So, you said your father told you to find me? I only met him yesterday, so I'm not sure why he thought I'd be able to help you."

"Dad's missing." Innis' voice was very quiet. They rolled the bottle of water between their hands.

"I see. Since when?" I asked, like I didn't know the answer.

"He never came home yesterday. He was supposed to check in this morning. But he said that if I didn't hear from him, I should find you," Innis said.

"Do you know why?" I asked, with a sinking feeling.

Innis shook their head.

"Do you have a younger sibling?" I asked.

"I'm an only child...sorta." Innis winced.

"Is or was your mother expecting?"

"No?" Innis looked confused.

"Are your parents together?" I asked.

"Yes! But Mom didn't know that Dad was investigating—" Innis hung their head and exhaled loudly. "Let me start over. My name is Innis Xana Wilder-Ramos. My pronouns are they/them. My birth certificate says 'female,' but that's not exactly who I am."

I nodded.

"I'm a changeling."

I opened my mouth and then closed it again, squinting at them, the rest of their words fading.

"-want to hire you to find my dad. He was going by Leonard Armstrong, but his real name is Leonard Wilder." They held up their phone, showing me a recent selfie of them with Leonard, the two of them gazing at the camera with big grins. "I know it sounds outlandish—"

"Goddamnit." I was starting to understand the shape of this family, and I did *not* like the implications.

"You believe me," Innis whispered, shock in their voice. "You really do."

"I wish I didn't," I growled, glaring at the table and rubbing my temples with both hands. I fucking knew Armstrong-Wilder was lying. I fucking knew it! The one time we don't vet a client because he's not really our client... Goddamnit!

Remington rose, phone in hand.

"What does your other form look like?" Remington asked, abandoning all pretenses of not eavesdropping.

The kid looked between Remington and me, took a deep breath, dug their fingers into their hairline and pulled. The tan skin sloughed off, and underneath was a more angular deep green face. The eye went from hazel to bright gold with a serpent's slit pupil. Innis pulled off half their face, the human side moving in tandem with the inhuman portion. "I just learned how to do this," they said, the misaligned lips forming words without any trouble.

"And no younger siblings," I repeated, something else starting to bother me.

"No." Innis slowly shook their head. "There was just me...and her. I don't know when my parents figured it out. I think that's why they didn't have more kids. In case it happened again. But I didn't know, not really, not till this year."

"Is this you?" Remington asked, setting his phone in front of them, showcasing the picture of the green baby.

Innis stared. "I..." They rolled up their hoodie, showing the same flower-shaped birthmark, except now it was a rosy splotch on tan skin. "I guess so. I didn't realize I had—" They reached up and touched their mostly flat teeth. There was a gap between the two front ones, and the incisors were a little long, but they looked human. Did the Fey have the adaptive physiology Dreyson mentioned? "Mom said I had trouble nursing..."

I winced.

"But said I was a good eater." Innis rested their face on the table. "They knew. They knew from the start and never said a thing." Their voice cracked.

"I'm sorry," I said.

"No, they're good parents," Innis sniffled. "I could talk to them about anything. And I did. I told them about me. About *her*. Their real kid. She's alive. I can feel it. But I don't know where she is or how to look. I don't know if my biological parents took her or why. I just want to find my dad, Leonard Wilder."

I glanced at Remington.

He shook his head. Not yet.

"Does your mother know where you are?"

Innis paused, eyes shifting sideways. "Of course!"

"You really have to stop lying to me," I said. "I have enough trust issues."

The kid blinked. "Umm...sorry. But you're a stranger, and well..." They trailed off, clearly not having thought this entire venture through.

I was a stranger all right. One they came to on the off chance I could help them. But coming alone was dangerous.

"Please tell me that *someone* knows where you went," I groaned, resting my face in my hand. Fuck. I could just see the IPD trying to hold me on kidnapping charges.

"We really need to talk to your mother," Remington said.

"But I want to hire you and Claire—"

"No," Remington said.

"But I can pay!" Panic filled Innis voice. "I have money!"

"Can you handle iron?" Remington asked.

Innis stared. "I have metal sensitivities, but I can touch it."

"Can you lie without repercussions? I don't mean when you get caught. I mean, can you lie?"

Innis squirmed. "Yes…I can lie like any person. You heard me. Why?"

That. That was what was bothering me.

Remington's frown deepened. "And you can sense your counterpart? You can tell she's alive somewhere? How long have you been aware of her?"

"I don't know…there's always been a feeling, like an extra limb. But I didn't realize the other me was actually real till this year. But she doesn't matter! Dad—"

Remington nodded at me.

I grimaced. "Innis, you don't need to hire us. We know where your father is."

Innis jumped to their feet. "He's alive?"

"Yes," I said. "But he was badly hurt. He's in the hospital."

Innis' smile collapsed as quickly as it had appeared. "H-how badly?" Their lower lip started to wobble.

"It was serious, but I don't know the specifics," I said. "Hospitals don't release medical information to acquaintances."

"Is he going to die?" Their voice cracked, all the bravado falling away.

"I don't know," I said, because that was the truth.

The kid dropped back into the chair, and I saw that moment of realization that their world was crumbling and I was the herald of that devastation.

Tears rolled down their cheeks, and I sat there dumbly, unable to put it back together again.

"I'm sorry," I said.

"Call your mother," Remington said gently. "We'll take you to see him. But call her now, because there's a lot going on that you don't know about and we could all be in a lot of danger."

Along with the knife, I added my gun, protective wards, and a flashbang to my kit, just in case. I had a few more charms, but it was time to restock.

Innis called their mother, who did not know where they were. There was some yelling on the line, but Remington took the phone and spoke to her in soothing tones.

"We're headed for Paean Hills. That's where your husband is. Your baby is safe. We'll talk more when we get there, ma'am."

"What are you doing?" Innis asked, peering over my shoulder, their human face firmly in place.

"Packing," I said.

"Can I help?"

They could not, but the kid needed something to do. I handed them a notepad and pen. "Can you write down when you started noticing changes, who you told, and what your parents did?"

"I guess." Innis sat down and started half-heartedly scribbling. "So why did Dad tell me to ask for you?" Their tone was so casual, I immediately understood how much they didn't know.

"I have an idea," I said, mind flashing back to last night when some lying fool made a heartfelt confession at my desk.

Innis stared at me expectantly.

"I was honest with him," I said. Though I should not have been. And he was dishonest with me, which was also a mistake.

"About...?" Innis huffed.

"Do you know what your father was doing?" I asked.

"Trying to find the other Innis?" they asked hesitantly, looking at me like I could tell them more.

I shook my head. "I only know part of it, so I'll need to talk to your mother to get the story straight." That was close enough to the truth.

Innis groaned in disappointment. "Is he going to be OK?"

"I don't know," I said. There was a lot of stretching the truth, and I needed to run some things by Remington, but we had little elfin ears around.

And this child could lie, something of a famous inability of the Fey. If the child was lying about their ability to lie, well that was still a lie and proved the point. Maybe they weren't a changeling, weren't even Fey. I didn't know how that would fit in this case, but there was already too much that I didn't know.

"I called Jon," Remington told me as we got in his car. "He'll meet us there."

I valiantly kept my thoughts to myself.

"Who's Jon?" Innis asked.

"You'll meet him," Remington said.

I made a funny snorting noise.

Remington gave me an exasperated look, but dropped a disguise charm in my lap. "In case you need to make a quick exit."

"Thanks," I said. "That fills me with confidence."

Remington just chuckled. Innis was on their phone. I stared out the window, trying to process this new round of information.

Where did Innis fit in this puzzle? Up till now, I'd never knowingly met a changeling. How did I classify the kid? "Human" or "not exactly human" did not equate "safe" or "unsafe." Some categories were too specific to be useful. For example, I was 50 percent Chinese, 25 percent Welsh, 25 percent mixed bag, with an unknown percentage of Jewish heritage that might not count since it was from the paternal line. These were very specific descriptors, but they didn't mean much outside of a genealogy chart.

For work we had other tags: mundane human, magical human, hostile undead, friendly undead, etc. These were more useful for me. Fey skewed neutral at best, but did that apply to modern changelings?

Innis just tapped away at their phone, seemingly oblivious. Like a normal kid.

Back when I was that age, there were times when I really wanted another face, lighter hair, different features. But having the ability to change my face would not have been a good thing, because I would have done it. I didn't have green skin and golden eyes, no, but back then, I would have done *anything* to fit in better.

We parked outside the main hospital entrance, and I spotted the lieutenant standing by the door, arms crossed, jaw clenched. He was clearly fuming. I almost offered to stay in the car.

Remington and I walked with Innis between us.

The lieutenant nodded at Remington and Innis, and pointedly ignored me. "I sent Nina up to talk to the spouse," he said.

"How's my dad?" Innis asked.

"Sorry, I don't know the details," he said, not looking at the kid.

Innis' shoulders tightened. "You think he's going to die, don't you."

The lieutenant flinched.

"Let's go talk to your mom," I said, putting one hand on Innis' shoulder. "She's the only one the doctors are supposed to tell."

The lieutenant bristled when I spoke, but didn't contradict me. That had to be a very painful experience for him.

Leonard Wilder was in the trauma ICU. Paean Hills specialized in supernatural complaints, but was still equipped for mundane ailments. Once we reached the fourth floor, a woman met us by the elevators, tears streaking her face. She rushed at Innis and wrapped her arms around them, speaking rapidly in Spanish.

Sofia Ramos Moreno, Innis' mother, wore a neat gray suit, her dark hair pulled up in a silvery wrap. She was probably at work when she got the call.

Detective Davis stood in the hall, her gaze flat as she studied Innis. "I found nothing."

The lieutenant nodded. Presumably she meant the wife wasn't under any compulsions or spells.

"And Claire," Detective Davis gave me a serious look, "Beryl wants you to write a report of what transpired in that cell."

"I'm kinda busy-"

"Or she could interview you," Detective Davis said sternly.

"Hahaha, that's OK, I'll write the email soon," I said, having no desire to be interrogated by Detective Minuet. She was the scariest person in SIU, no contest.

"Whatever details you can recall. She's already seen the CCTV," Detective Davis said, giving me a sharp look. "And she would also like to caution you about your 'celly.'"

"Yeah, he's a picky eater," I said.

"If you're serious about your family's safety, you need to accept protective custody," the lieutenant told Ms. Ramos Moreno—who stared at him in disbelief.

Detective Davis sighed, held up a finger, and went to rejoin that conversation.

Innis immediately sidled up to me. "I'm going to the vending machines with Claire," they announced.

The lieutenant looked up sharply, but Ms. Ramos Moreno waved them off. Remington and Detective Davis both began talking to her.

"I don't like him," Innis told me, watching my reaction as we headed down the hall. "He's rude."

"Very." I studied the row of vending machines and picked out a guava jelly snack cake that I'd never seen before. Innis got some beef jerky.

We stood in the alcove, not ready to go back.

"You don't like him either," they said.

"Nope, but that doesn't mean he's wrong about the situation," I said, trying not to make things harder for the kid. "We just don't like each other."

"He talks down to people."

I nodded. There was no expiration date on the snack cake, but I ate it anyway, savoring that pop of honey-sweet tropical fruit.

"He smells funny too."

I laughed. "I try not to get that close to him."

"That other detective is strange. But at least she's nice." Innis gave me a gap-toothed smile and offered me some jerky. I took a pinch. "My friend Priya is like me."

I blinked. "What do you mean?"

Innis tilted the jerky bag into their mouth. "I was in this playgroup for kids with serious allergies—the kind that send you to the hospital. I grew out of mine, but Priya didn't. She's...a lot like me. The other kids I'm not so sure of." They nodded to themselves.

"Does your mom know?" It was only a suspicion, but that tip needed to be investigated quickly.

"I just realized it," they said. "Dad asked me for more details recently, but before we didn't talk about it. Don't know if they were scared or ashamed." Innis' breath hitched.

"Do you know why the police are involved?" I asked, changing the subject.

"Because someone kidnapped the original Innis?" they said very quietly.

Fuck, the kid didn't know. And it was likely that no one would tell them. A normal, well-supervised kid wouldn't need to know. But this kid snuck off to find me on their own. This wasn't a "rules and order" kid, this was a "I can do it, so I'm going to" kid, and I knew about being one of those. We weren't the type to take people at their word: we needed to know exactly why we shouldn't do something.

"Do you know what your father's cover story was?"

Innis bit their lip. "He was going to say the changeling died so they couldn't demand me back." Innis voice wobbled. "He did do that, right? Or did he...did he—?"

"Your father was too convincing with his confession," I said carefully. "I wasn't impressed, and the...people he spoke to were even less impressed."

"Is that why they hurt him?" Innis clenched their fists.

"No," I said, and I thought that was the truth. The Vernal Lord was trying to silence the man, though the exact reasons weren't clear. "But he didn't give you up." That awkward man stood at my desk proclaiming "a life for a life." That he would willingly accept the consequences of his actions. That there was no changeling to return, just one of his two kids, and he wasn't willing to lose Innis to the Courts.

Did he really go there to find his biological daughter or to try to ensure that no one came looking for Innis? That noble idiot. That idea probably wouldn't work, and there were smarter ways to do this. But he didn't know, didn't have a goddamn clue. How could he? He just charged in blindly, and everyone who did know better, including me, *let him*. Yes, he was a grown-ass man, but I felt partially responsible.

And the Vernal Lord declared there were no *infant* changelings in Illium. Because this whole switch happened at least a decade ago...which, since he was being so specific, meant he already knew that.

"I don't care if those other things are my *real* parents. I hate them." Innis tossed the empty jerky bag into the trash, their fists hitting the can. "I'm not going with them."

"Yeah, you need to avoid anyone from the Courts right now."

"Will the police actually do something about it?" Innis sniffled.

"Maybe," I said. "But that's not why they're here. There's another problem. Someone is hurting changelings and their parents."

"Hurting them?" Innis asked, face scrunched up. "What do you mean?"

I sighed, not wanting to lie and also really not wanting to answer that question. "I mean it's not safe right now."

"I don't want to be like this," Innis growled. "I wanna be normal. I wanna be like everyone else. I don't wanna be a two-faced pretender!" The words poured out. "But if I don't, bad things'll happen to me and my family. They already have!"

"I know," I said. "It's not fair. You're a part of both worlds. You feel the pull in two very different directions. But you're never going to fit all the way in either, and that sucks because it's double the rejection." That familiar pang of regret turned my gaze downward. I was saying too much to this poor kid.

Innis swallowed loudly. "Yeah...you're not a changeling too, are you?"

I burst into panicked laughter, shaking my head rapidly. "Not that I know of! My life is complicated enough. I don't need *another* dimension added to it." They were growing up in a multicultural home too, but some families balanced it better than others. "Dad's family is very white American. They don't mean any harm, but they don't try to understand me and my brother. Dad is much better, but he doesn't get why certain things bother me. Meanwhile, my mother is...very Chinese. She has expectations that neither my brother nor I could live up to."

"Your parents sound annoying," Innis said gravely.

"Yeah, they are," I said. "But that's parents in a nutshell."

"Mine are great," Innis said, giving me a sidelong look. "Anyway, I thought you would've figured all that out by now."

"I've figured some of it out, but it doesn't happen overnight. I expect it'll take years and lots of therapy."

Innis laughed at me. "That's a letdown."

"Tell me about it."

"So do you think I need to warn Priya? Just in case. I don't really know if she or the others are like me. But I don't think sending the police to them is right either."

I didn't have an easy answer. "Your mom has their numbers, right? She can call. You shouldn't be venturing off alone, not now."

Innis shrugged, obviously not impressed by my advice. "What are *they* like? You've met some, right?"

I thought of the formless child who might have been human, of Mandragora with her sweet voice, tangle of vines, and terrifying hunger, of the Crow Knight, his sword under Dreyson's chin, his hand on my skin, that affectionate mockery in his voice.

"They're different," I said slowly. "It's hard to describe except as 'other.' They're close to us but not, more colorful and beautiful and predatory. Some might have started out as nature deities, but I don't know if that sums it up either. There's something about them that makes me, a mostly normal human, go, 'I'm not the scariest thing in the room.'"

"You're not scary at all," Innis told me with that cheerful, casual brutality that only children seemed to have.

I sighed. "Have you been really close to a lion or a shark at the zoo?"

"I saw the tigers up close for my last birthday," Innis said.

"You know how small you feel, how you look at those huge paws that could smack you down, or the length of those teeth, and you realize how easy it would be for them to hurt you? But they're still beautiful and wild and kind of magical so you can't look away? It's like that."

"That doesn't sound so bad," Innis said wistfully.

"I guess that depends if you're the human or the tiger."

"Or if you're a half-tiger, half-human monster. Like Tony the Tiger," Innis whispered in mock horror.

I snorted, coughing into my hand. "You know weretigers are a thing, right?"

"Really?" Innis perked up. "It's not just…fairies?"

"Yeah, and don't call them that. They get mad."

Innis stroked their chin, eyes alight. "Wait, if there are weretigers, are there wolves, bears, leopards…what else? Koalas? What about emus? And snapping turtles?"

I shrugged. "I have no idea."

"Why not?!"

"Because going around asking people 'what are you' is rude," I said.

Innis blinked. "Oh…yeah."

"Sometimes there are emergencies. You might have to check if the vampire equivalent of a vegetarian only drinks certain kinds of bloo—"

"Vampires are real too?" Innis shouted.

"Let's go find your mother," I sighed. "I think I've done enough damage today…"

Chapter 10
Where the Light Does Not Reach

前门打虎, 后门打狼Trad.前門打虎, 後門打狼- qián mén dǎ hǔ, hòu mén dǎ láng – This idiom translates as "to beat a tiger from the front door, only to have a wolf come in at the back." The meaning is pretty straightforward: there's one problem after another. Now, a person could reasonably argue that people should be locking their doors, especially with multiple types of apex predators in the area. And they would be right, but missing the point. Why the hell are you living in such a dangerous place?

Edit: Metaphorically speaking, I'm an idiot who needs to learn not to leave scraps out for the local wildlife. Also, fuck you, I live here.

— *From the Very Personal Journals of FYG*

I GAVE INNIS my phone number, because they had more questions for me, but Remington needed to leave, and he was my ride. The SIU detectives stayed back with the family. The kid seemed disappointed, but immediately started texting me questions about *everything*.

"So I got some vague warnings about Dreyson," I said, pursing my lips as I climbed into Remington's car.

"If she's not giving you specific warnings, like he needs to regularly sacrifice sneaky woman to his dark god, it's probably fine," Remington said.

"Anything that *you* think I need to know about his rap sheet?"

"I only remember bits and pieces. It's about what you'd expect from a Wergeld hunter. Nina'll get that folder to us eventually."

I shrugged. "It's not my priority, but I am getting annoyed by the nagging. I am very aware of how dangerous Dreyson is. But we're on civil terms, and it's not like I've started a

'Dreyson Did Nothing Wrong' campaign. I'd be more appreciative if they'd show the same concern about other cops' behavior."

Remington winced. "To be fair, with his brawn and your spite, you two are the nightmare team-up for a lot of people."

Specifically, some assholes in the IPD. I grinned at Remington. "Thanks, that's sweet."

Remington shook his head ruefully. "They're trying to be helpful. They're not succeeding, but…"

"It's a waste of everyone's time." I leaned back in the seat. "Innis mentioned another kid that was in their allergy support group. Said they got better, but some of the others didn't. They thought 'Priya' might be like them. Their mother should have the contact information."

Remington's brow furrowed. "I'll pass that on to Jon. But why didn't you mention that in the hospital?"

"Innis is cagey about Jon, and I wanted to ask Ms. Ramos Moreno for details."

Remington nodded. He gave the lieutenant a call before we reached my place, and then he walked me to the door, despite the two flights of stairs.

I watched him get to his car, feeling guilty that the condo wasn't very accessible. Ivy and I moved here with safety in mind, but I still felt bad. She was working late...again. That probably wasn't a coincidence; Canaris knew what was going on.

I was just getting ready for a shower when my phone rang.

"Innis" flashed across the screen. I groaned, not in the mood to answer another dozen questions about who would win in a fight between various supernatural beings. Mostly because I didn't know. The kid made some good points about the undead having an aquatic advantage over terrestrial wereanimals, but I didn't want to reimagine the Shadow Dunes deathmatch exhibit underwater.

The call went to voicemail, but my phone immediately lit up again. They were going to keep calling.

I picked up. "Hey, I was—"

"Claire! I'm at Priya's house and nobody's answering the door. They're normally home right now, but I guess they went out for dinner. Anyway, I thought maybe you could come over and see if she's like me—"

The words spilled out so quickly, it took me a few moments to process what they were saying. I glanced out the living room window; it wasn't that late, but it was already getting dark. "Why are you out? Where's your mom?"

"She's at home with Detective Davis," Innis said cheerfully. "Priya lives just around the corner, and I thought I would—"

My heart sank. "You snuck out?"

"Maybe," Innis said, lowering their voice.

I wanted to tell them to go home right now, but would the kid actually listen? Of course not. Eleven-year-old me would have said, "OK," hung up, and gone and done whatever I wanted to anyway.

"The upstairs lights are on, so they might be home. Maybe the doorbell isn't working. I'll knock." Innis laughed awkwardly. There was a light thudding in the background; Innis had a quiet, polite knock.

"Maybe they aren't home," Innis said, sounding disappointed. "I can wait."

"You really shouldn't," I said. "You should head home."

"I'm right down the street," they said, sounding put out. "Oh, it's getting dark." The words were muffled, like they covered the speaker.

I glanced out the window. There were still gold streaks in the sky, but they were fading fast into a deep navy blue. "I'll stay on the phone, then."

"OK!" Innis said, cheered up by that offer. "I texted Priya earlier. She didn't say they were going out, but sometimes she's forgetful. I'm sure it's fine."

I frowned, drifting toward the door. Why would the kid call me if everything was fine? Kids could be inconsiderate, but... "Wait, you wanted *me* to talk to her?"

"Oh yeah, in case I'm wrong. Priya's my friend. Setting the police on her seems...harsh. But you're— Hey, a bunch of lights just went on. It looks like they *are* home!"

"What?" I picked up my jacket and bag.

"Huh." Innis got quiet. "I'm sure it's nothing."

"What?" I asked.

"I thought I heard Priya, but I don't see anyone. Normally she comes out to meet me. Maybe her parents want her to stay inside. They're overprotective."

I put on my shoes. Something didn't feel right. Maybe it was because I still needed a shower, or maybe it was the hour. At the very least, the kid should not walk home in the dark, not with what was happening right now. Going out was a small aggravation, but it wasn't a huge deal. I could pick them up. "Where are you at?"

Innis rattled off the address. I knew the neighborhood. They were in a Grove Heights suburb very close to me.

"I'm on my way. I need you to go to the end of the driveway and wait for me. Don't go to the house, just wait. I'm leaving now. If anything looks off, or if you have a weird feeling, walk away. I'll call you back in a minute." I raced down the stairs to my car, texting Remington the address, the fact Innis was loose, and that I was en route.

Throwing my bag in the backseat, I started my car so fast it nearly stalled and peeled out of the parking lot.

Unbidden, the crime scene photos resurfaced in my memory. It was the gory little details of slaughter and silence that stuck with me. The bloody maulings, carefully arranged body parts, terror and agony on the faces of the dead; the kills were so messy, but no one heard a goddamn thing. And there was something about the way Innis sounded, just the tiniest thread of uncertainty in their voice, like they were afraid of something but they couldn't see it, because they were too busy rationalizing. Or because they wanted to leave, but they were already ensnared.

Or it was nothing. I was jittery and overreacting. I would get weird looks for barging in on a family of strangers with a kid I met today. That would be supremely uncomfortable, a nightmare of a different sort. But I was just heading over there to give Innis a short ride back to their house so they didn't have to walk home in the dark. That was reasonable. It wasn't my fault the kid snuck out.

And I didn't like how that situation with their father turned out. So maybe I could go a little out of my way for Innis.

I called them back.

They answered after two rings.

"You're at the end of the driveway?"

The patter of rapid footsteps, like someone was running across a hard surface. "Uh-huh!" Innis said, sounding breathless.

Damnit. "Innis..."

"I don't know why you're telling me to leave. I come here all the time. Everything looks fine," Innis said, almost whining. "And Priya's calling me."

"On the phone?"

"No, from the house."

I frowned. "Has she texted you back?"

"No," Innis said. And then in a far quieter voice. "That's not like her."

I bit my lip, focusing on the road.

"You still there?" Innis asked, voice going high.

"Driving," I said.

"You shouldn't talk on the phone and drive," they said with an edge of disapproval.

"That's why I'm so quiet."

Innis snorted. "Oh, I think that's Mrs. Soltani—Priya's mom—waving at me from the window." They paused. "She looks...tired? Never mind, I think it's OK. I can just go. Wait, I see her dad, and Priya, and her sister, Kashi. They're all lined up, smiling big, and waving at me from the living room window."

My blood ran cold. It sounded so small, but the wrongness of it coiled around my throat. "Do they normally do that?" I kept my eyes forward, despite the panic spiking in my chest.

"No, Mr. Soltani isn't friendly. He isn't mean, but he doesn't wave at me. And Kashi is mad at me because last time I was here, we didn't let her make bracelets with us because she tangles the cords... But now she's waving. They want me to go inside..." Innis trailed off, like they knew something wasn't quite right.

"Wait for me!" I shouted.

"But I should go inside, Claire. They're going to think I'm a weirdo if I just stand in their driveway—"

"Then they can come out and see you," I said, realizing that could also be terrible. But the previous crime scenes were indoors... I could decide when I arrived; stall for now. "Are they still waving? The entire family?"

"Yeah," Innis said softly. "But it's fine. They're just trying to get me to come in. It is really weird that I'm standing out here in their driveway."

"I'm almost there," I said, through gritted teeth. "Just wait for me." I left the line open but focused on speed. The streets were empty, the GPS directions simple. It was supposed to be a ten-minute drive. I made it in five.

To my immense relief, Innis stood by the mailbox, seemingly unhurt as they tapped their foot impatiently. But they stared up at a darkened house with a big bay window facing the front yard.

"Wow, you did get here fast," Innis said, sounding more relaxed as I parked at the mouth of the driveway. "Come on! You can explain why I had to wait." They skipped up toward the house, like now that an adult was here, everything would be fine. I jumped out of the car and raced halfway up the driveway.

"Hold on!" I snarled, grabbing the back of their hoodie.

Innis blinked at me in shock.

I stared past them. There were no lights on in that house. This was a quiet residential neighborhood, no bright street lamps, just little glowing posts in each yard with single bulb fixtures by the front doors and garages. Except none of the lights around this property were on. The rear of the house was just swallowed by shadow, the front facade resembling a flat set piece.

"You don't have to be so grumpy!" Innis scowled at me. "I waited, just like you said, and as you can see, everything is fine."

Something moved inside the window. A curtain? A face? Nothing about this looked fine.

"Come on," Innis tugged my hand.

"You said someone was waving," I said out of the corner of my mouth.

"Oh, the lights went out a moment ago. I guess they blew a fuse. Happens at our house all the time." Innis glanced up at a darkened bedroom window. "Priya's waving at me now. I think..."

They waved back at the window, and I couldn't see a damn thing. But I was still wearing fairy ointment, so I knew that whatever Innis was seeing was an illusion. I swallowed, gripping their hand, vainly hoping the kid was pranking me.

"If you're joking," I whispered, "it's not funny."

Innis cocked their head at me. "You can't hear her calling us?"

I took a step toward the house. It was deathly silent. No birds, no insects, no hum of electricity. The stillness only served to amplify the sound of my heartbeat in my ears. I shuddered.

"Come on." Innis traipsed up to the front door. They reached for the knob, even as I put a hand on my gun and quickly walked up behind them.

Before they touched anything, the door creaked open a few inches. The interior was darker, shadows spilling out of the crack in the door.

I shivered, my muscles locking up, terror pooling in my stomach.

"Oh, thanks. I tried to open it earlier, but...," Innis murmured, sounding confused.

I pulled them back. Because even if I could not see what was watching us, I could smell that telltale metallic scent: blood mixed with a pungent, visceral odor. Something tapped against the wood floors, moving around inside. There was a wet sound, not quite a splash but a slurp, then a strangled gurgle. Shapes moved, just over the threshold, not true shadows, rather an absence of light.

"Didn't you hear her? We're good to come in," Innis said, sounding more confident. "They've just blown a fuse."

My heart skipped. I heard nothing that sounded like words. "Of course," I exhaled, putting all my effort into keeping my tone calm, my breathing even. "So let's grab a flashlight from my car. I bet they'd appreciate the extra light."

"Oh," Innis blinked. "I can go inside—"

"I brought some books too," I added hastily, gripping their hand. "Reference materials that I think you and Priya could use. Though some of the pictures are—"

Innis gazed up at me, looking puzzled. But they did not argue as I led them back down the driveway to my car, nattering on about books. I could feel something watching us, feel the pressure of that malevolent gaze drilling right between my shoulder blades. My spine prickled, just waiting for something to attack my exposed back. I wanted to break into a run. I wanted to flee so badly that my knees shook. But if I ran now, it would give chase, and even if I was fast enough to get away, Innis was not.

"Anyway, help me find that flashlight. Can you check under that seat? Then we'll go back in—" I opened the back door. As Innis climbed in, I slammed the door and jumped into the driver's seat.

"Claire, what are you—"

I really wished they would stop saying my name. Keys in hand, I yanked my door shut and hit the autolock.

"Hey!" Innis shouted.

"That's *not* Priya!" I hissed, simultaneously jamming my keys into the ignition and buckling up one-handed. My car sputtered, the engine not turning over.

I glanced up, seeing movement. Then the front picture window shattered, glass exploding everywhere as *something* leapt out and high into the air, disappearing from view.

I tried to start the car again, hand shaking, the engine sputtering weakly.

Then something slammed into the roof of my car and rocked us with its heavy landing. Innis screamed into my ear as something began to scratch at the roof, the metal screeching under its claws.

Swearing, I turned the keys again, and this time the engine rumbled to life.

Then something smashed into the rear windshield, glass spraying the interior of my car, but I was already reversing out of the driveway.

"Get down!" I shouted and turned sharply into the road, before shifting gears and tearing down the street.

Innis ducked as a clawed hand reached through the broken window, trying to grab them.

I slammed on the brakes and would have banged my head on the wheel if my seatbelt didn't catch me.

The thing on the roof lacked that safety measure. It shrieked as it flew forward, limbs flailing as it bounced across the pavement and into a ditch. I didn't bother reaching for my gun. I just pushed down the gas pedal and booked it out of there.

It was dark, and my lights were off, so I didn't see what it was. It looked humanoid, and it was still moving, but I couldn't tell if it was chasing us, so I headed for the nearest main road, aiming for a highway. I did not want to lead that thing to anyone's house.

"Call Remington!" I said, tossing my phone into the back seat.

"It's locked!" Innis shouted, tossing it back to me seconds later.

My gaze zipping between the mirrors and the road, I unlocked my phone and called Remington.

"Where are—"

"Something was in the Soltani house! We're in my car, and I don't know if it's still in pursuit," I said tightly. "The house looked normal to Innis, but I'm wearing the ointment. It stunk of blood. Don't go in there blind."

"Understood," Remington said. "I'll call you back."

I hung up, unsure of where to go. The last time I had Fey problems... I called Dreyson.

It rang once.

"Dreyson." The voice was low, like he was trying to be quiet.

"Something from the Courts is here," I said quickly. "I'm in my car with a kid, and I don't want to lead it anywhere vulnerable. Where should I go?"

"Where are you?" Dreyson asked.

I gave him the location.

"Do you know where the Centerpointe is?"

"Yeah," I said, picturing the swanky downtown restaurant. At the center of the city, it was a well-known neutral meeting ground, something the owner enforced militantly. I went there a few times for work. They took the safety of their paying customers very seriously, not that I needed much incentive to splurge on some good food. It would have been an obvious choice if I wasn't so focused on fleeing in terror. "Oh, duh."

"I'll meet you in the east lot," he told me.

"You don't have to—"

He hung up.

"Thanks," I said to the dead line.

"Who's Dreyson?" Innis asked, popping up from the floor. They were nested down in the footwell diagonal from me.

"You should get in a seat and buckle up," I sighed.

"No, thank you. There's too much glass, and you drive like a maniac," Innis told me primly.

"Yeah, a maniac who doesn't want to die horribly," I muttered under my breath. There was probably a lot of glass on the ground too, but I wasn't going to argue with the kid right now.

"What?"

"Dreyson's an...ally of mine," I said, careful of my wording, because it would certainly get back to other people.

"He doesn't sound very friendly," Innis said hesitantly.

"He's not what anyone would call a 'people-person.' Also, he has some very visible scars on his face. I realize that might be kinda scary or difficult to look at, but I'd appreciate it if you didn't say anything—"

"Ugh, that'd be so rude! I'm not a little kid, Claire!" Innis scoffed, sounding genuinely offended. "So how do you know him?"

I considered lying to them, for convenience. But given the situation, any lies I told would come out and nuke whatever trust Innis had in me. "I met him in jail."

They coughed. "What! Like you were visiting?"

"I was certainly visiting," I said quickly. I did not need to tell a kid my life story.

"Were you arrested?" they asked, lowering their voice. "And did you do it?"

"Yes, I was arrested. No, I didn't do it, and no one filed any charges," I said.

"What about him?"

"Not sure, it's complicated." I took a deep breath. "He was my cellmate, and we fought off man-eating monsters together. We also worked a job together and really helped each other out. That makes us allies." The adrenaline was starting to wear off, and I felt slightly nauseated. "But just to be safe, don't mention your...secrets. The less people know about your situation, the safer you'll be."

Innis stared at me, wide-eyed and shell-shocked.

"Anyway, think about what you want to eat. The Centerpointe is a pretty fancy restaurant, and we might as well get some food while we're there."

Chapter 11
The Restaurant at the Center of the City

The Centerpointe is always worth a visit. A true Illium institution, the restaurant is sacred ground, a neutral location. To take your quarrels there is to invite the wrath of the furies and the rest of the city.

But enough of politics; the food is far more important. The Centerpointe masquerades as a classic steakhouse, but is better known for the revolving menu. One month there might be a medieval European feast with whole roast peacocks, the feathers put back on for dramatic presentation. Another month, it might be a twenty-course sushi omakase, with real leviathan meat. The winter dessert bar is legendary.

Everything from their kitchens is delicious, and the regular changes and limited-time showcases appeal to a broad clientele, offering an irresistible blend of artistry and novelty, something valued greatly by those with longer lifespans.

—*An Introduction to Illium by Ann Keyes*

I PULLED INTO the eastern lot. Dreyson stood on the sidewalk in front of a conveniently empty spot near the building. He wore that menacing black duster, battleaxe strapped to his back. I parked and sat for a moment, taking deep breaths to steady myself.

When I looked up, Dreyson was by my window, surveying the streets. I grabbed my bag and opened the door.

Dreyson offered me his hand.

I took it, knowing I might be shaky on my feet. His calloused palm was warm.

"Are you injured?" he asked, voice low and even as he helped me out of my car.

"No, don't think so." I inhaled the chilly night air and hugged myself.

"Hold still, you have glass in your hair," he said, and carefully plucked a couple pieces off the back of my head. "Doesn't look like you're bleeding."

"Thanks." I reached up to carefully pat the back of my head. My hands came away clean.

He nodded and looked at my car, the center of the roof now slightly concave with scrapes along the edges of the dent. The rear windshield was shattered, broken glass glittering in the backseat. Hopefully, the frame wasn't compromised. Ugh, not *another* thing wrong.

Innis stared at both of us, still crouched on the floor.

"Innis, this is Dreyson. Dreyson, this is Innis. They're a client's kid and a friend."

Dreyson nodded. "Don't move yet," he told them and went around to open the passenger-side door. "With your permission, I'm going to lift you out. There's a lot of broken glass, and I don't want you to cut yourself."

Innis stared up at him, then glanced back at me, lips pressed firmly together in fear. Because even if they had good manners, they just went through something terrifying, and now they were staring up at a very intimidating stranger.

I nodded, trying to be reassuring.

"OK," Innis said and extended their hands.

Dreyson simply lifted them out of the car and set them on the ground. "Hold still," he said, and used his sleeve to brush bits of glass off the kid. "OK, step over there and shake yourself off."

Innis scurried onto the sidewalk and vigorously shook their head, little prisms shimmering as they fell. And then to my surprise, Innis lunged at me, throwing their arms around my waist. On the verge of tears, they stared up at me.

"Let's go inside," I said, patting their back. "We'll be safe in there."

Sniffling, they nodded and grabbed my hand tightly as we walked into the building.

The Centerpointe had a high-end steakhouse aesthetic: dark wood, leather seats, heavy crystal glasses. It was an important meeting place; the refined atmosphere usually reminded everyone to behave themselves. In a green sweater and black jeans, I didn't look awful, but I wasn't quite dressed for a formal dinner either. Fortunately, there was a bar and some discreet seating near it.

Innis gripped my hand as we turned toward the bar, and I thought the stuffy setting might be the only thing keeping them from having a full breakdown.

"You did great," I told them. "Thanks for waiting for me."

They nodded, only half listening to me.

"This will be easier," I told them."

"I know which fork to use," Innis said hesitantly.

"Oh good, I'm glad one of us does." I winked.

Innis squinted at me, like they weren't sure if I was joking.

I caught a glimpse of a familiar hawk-faced man in a tuxedo, at a table with an older woman, her gray hair close-cropped. She wore a lavender skirt suit, her posture uncomfortably proper. I didn't recognize her, but that was Salvatore Mori dining with her.

"Sorry, I didn't mean to interrupt you during work," I said to Dreyson as we stopped at the bar.

"It's fine," he said. "My presence is not required now."

"Good evening, Claire. Are you all right?" Worry tinged that warm smooth voice.

I looked up to see Arcady Primakov standing behind the bar. He was not a tall man, but he was handsome, with dark almond eyes and high cheekbones. People often guessed he was Native American or Inuit, but he told me once, over some very strong mimosas, that he was Chukchi, a Siberian minority. The food wasn't the only reason to stop here. Flirting with Arcady was a pleasure, and waking up at his house for brunch? Definitely a good experience.

"Hey," I said, suddenly self-conscious. A couple minutes ago, I had broken glass in my hair, but I mustered a smile. I was always happy to see Arcady.

He cocked his head to the side, straight black hair artfully framing his face. He wore it long, his beard neatly trimmed. "Your hands are shaking, darling. Let's get you settled." He spun gracefully, plucked an old-fashioned glass from the display, and free poured a couple fingers of whiskey.

He set the glass in front of me. "It's on the house," he murmured, leaning forward, almost close enough to kiss. "Let me know if you need *anything* else."

"You're too good to me," I said with a wink.

He just gave me that slow intimate smile, one that conjured images of rumpled sheets and bedroom voices.

Then he glanced over at Dreyson, hitting him with the exact same smile. "Are you off-duty now? Can I get you anything?"

I blinked, because I knew that look. Arcady was a flirt and by no means monogamous. Dreyson's cheeks seemed to be a faint shade of pink, or was I imagining things?

"No thank you, Arcady. I'm still working," Dreyson said, not quite nervous, but less stoic than I expected. No, I wasn't imagining things. "We could use a booth and some menus, though." He looked at Innis, who was staring awkwardly at the floor.

"Of course," Arcady said brightly, the undertone of lust evaporating. "And for the young gentlethem, can I get you a beverage? Shirley Temple? Hot chocolate? Mulled cider?"

"May I have some hot milk, please?" Innis asked.

Arcady nodded. "But of course. You can take a seat over there." He gestured to a curtained booth a couple yards away. "I'll send someone over." He paused, giving me and Dreyson a lingering look. "You should stop by again soon, Claire. It's been a while. Come over for brunch. I don't mind if you want to bring a friend."

"That sounds fun." My heart stuttered at that invitation. He meant, "Come over for brunch, *the night before.*"

Dreyson coughed into his hand.

"Stop by *any time*." Arcady smiled hungrily at both of us, sinking a lot of feeling into those two words.

I raised my glass to him and took a sip as I led Innis to the C-shaped booth. "Dreyson," I said, a little breathlessly out of the corner of my mouth. "You too?"

"Ms. Giles, I will not have that discussion here," he said quietly through clenched teeth.

"I'm not judging," I said, wondering if Dreyson only preferred men.

"Not here," he said firmly.

"Are you guys fighting?" Innis asked, squinting at us as we slid into the booth. They sat in the middle. Dreyson hovered by the edge of one side, giving the kid space.

"No," we said simultaneously.

I grinned at Dreyson.

He just gave me a slightly exasperated look.

An older man in a crisp uniform appeared with three leather-bound menus. He also set a large steaming mug in front of Innis. "My name is Ferdinand. Please let me know what else you may need tonight."

"Thanks, Ferdinand. It will be a moment," Dreyson said.

Ferdinand nodded, but did not move.

"Do you have any food allergies?" I asked Innis, belatedly remembering they used to have some issues.

"Nope." They shook their head, happily lifting the mug with both hands and slurping the milk. "I'm not hungry, Claire."

"I need to eat something," I said, glancing down at my whiskey. "And they have a lot of interesting dishes here. I promise the desserts are worth it."

Innis begrudgingly picked up a menu.

I wasn't ready to spend a lot on a meal, not when my car was literally bent out of shape. But I needed to buy something, so I flipped to the dessert menu. "Check out the chocolate galleons," I said.

Innis perked up. "They're made of chocolate?"

"With marzipan sails, each both filled with ganache, custard, and mousse. I think I'll get that."

Innis looked at me. "Me too." They glanced at Dreyson. "What about you?"

He sighed. "I'm willing to try them," he said without any enthusiasm.

Innis nodded and cupped their mug in both hands.

"Three orders of chocolate galleons, then, and a refill for the milk," Dreyson said.

I grinned at him.

"He knows about stuff, right?" Innis asked me.

"Even more than I do."

Innis turned to Dreyson. "So a vampire fights a werewolf underwater, who would win?"

Dreyson raised his head, glancing at me in surprise.

"I said vampire, probably, unless it was saltwater, but Innis is full of these kinds of questions."

"Likely a vampire, unless it was saltwater," Dreyson agreed.

"OK, what about—"

My phone buzzed. I pulled it out of my bag, wincing at the dozen missed calls from Remington and other numbers.

"Hey," I answered, taking a gulp of whiskey.

"Where are you?" Remington asked sharply. People shouted in the background, voices harmonizing with car sirens.

"At the Centerpointe. Dreyson met us here. We're uninjured."

Remington exhaled. "You're both safe, good. We'll be there shortly."

"What's the situation?"

"You were right," he said. "It's another one, and it's very…fresh."

"Was everyone…?"

"Yes," Remington said.

I downed the rest of the whiskey. In my other ear, Dreyson explained to Innis why a single werebear was more dangerous than a lone werewolf.

"Is that Giles?" *Someone* shouted in the background. "You tell her to sit her ass down and stay put! She's lucky we don't charge her with—"

The sound abruptly cut off, like Remington muted the call.

"Charming," I said.

"Ignore him. This one is messy," Remington said a few seconds later, the background noise fading. "I'll show you the footage later."

"Footage?" My stomach sank. "I'm not watching a snu—"

"It's not that, but it *is* disturbing," Remington said. "Just…stay where you are. We're bringing Innis' mother with us."

"Your mom's safe," I told them. "She'll join us soon."

Innis blinked, like they didn't realize their mother could possibly be in any danger.

"I have to go. See you soon." Remington hung up.

Innis looked down, their whole body drooping. "Priya's dead, isn't she."

I put my phone away. "I think so."

"I didn't really see her in the window, did I," they sniffled.

"No," I said. "You kept mentioning things that I couldn't see or hear. And I figured something was listening to us, which was why I made up the story about the flashlight and books. If it thought that we had any idea of what was going on, it would have come for us much sooner."

Innis shuddered, scooting closer to me.

Dreyson studied Innis. "What's going on?"

"Something is killing changelings and their families. I...suspect this kid was a changeling. I don't know for sure, though, didn't meet her."

Dreyson sat up straighter. "What attacked you?"

"Not sure. It was too dark. I thought it was humanoid, but it wasn't alone in the house."

"It seemed almost like a person," Innis said. "But I didn't get a good look either...I'm going to have to talk to that jerk detective, aren't I?"

"Not necessarily," I said. "But make sure your mom is with you. The cops shouldn't talk to you without her, and if they get mean or pushy, you can stop. They can't punish you for not talking to them. And if they're being unreasonable, you definitely don't want to talk to them."

"I know," Innis said. "Mom says we don't volunteer information to the police unless we absolutely have to. I think we'll have to. The Soltanis were nice." Their voice wobbled.

"Ask for a forensic interviewer," Dreyson said. "Some law enforcement officers are actually trained on how to question children in a way that doesn't inflict lasting damage. Detective Davis has the certifications."

I looked up, surprised that Dreyson knew that.

"If you want to tell us what happened, we can record it," Dreyson said, looking down at Innis. "Under normal circumstances, people would shout about chain of evidence and tampering with a witness, but these are special circumstances, and it's better to talk about trauma sooner rather than later."

Oh that sneaky bastard. He wasn't wrong. Letting Innis vent now would be better for them, get him the information he wanted, and utterly piss off the cops. OK, as long as he didn't pressure Innis, I wouldn't stop him.

"OK," Innis said as I got my phone out to record. They retold the entire story, from sneaking out their bedroom window to the weird feeling they had at the Soltani's house. They didn't know what to think, so they called me. It was weird that I insisted that they wait for me, but it was a relief too.

"I...was about to shower," I said, feeling queasy. I almost didn't answer their call.

Innis retold the escape with more sound effects, waving, and ducking under the table than I remembered. "And that's how we got away, because Claire is a scary driver! She ran three stop signs in a row! I bet she would've run over that thing too!"

"That is a bad idea. It would likely destroy your suspension or just total your car. Then you'd be stuck on foot," Dreyson said.

Or worse. I rested my face in my hands.

"And you shouldn't be sneaking out," Dreyson said sternly. "Not in this city and certainly not at night."

"I...yeah, that was dumb," Innis murmured, slumping.

"Your fleet of chocolate galleons," Ferdinand said, setting down large dinner plates in front of us and refilling Innis' mug.

The plates were blue with a wave pattern, and on each one was a trio of ships, Spanish galleons, the ones in the pirate movies with multiple masts and billowing sails. The largest was about four inches long. Little squiggles of caramel and whipped cream decorated the plate. The detail was fine: I could make out the names carved into the ships, the shapes of the figureheads, the wood grain, the narrow lines of rigging, and it was all made of chocolate.

"Wow, this is like what that chocolate guy makes in his videos," Innis said, awe in their voice. "I need to take a picture!" They fumbled with their phone.

Dreyson shrugged, picked up his knife, and carefully sliced one of the boats in half. Pink mousse spilled out, and he ate it, expression unchanging.

"Oh no, Mom called...a lot," they murmured.

"She's already on her way," Dreyson said. "Enjoy your chocolate."

"It's almost too pretty to eat," I said.

"Almost!" Innis roared softly and put the entire boat in their mouth.

I snorted and cut into one of mine, revealing creamy bourbon custard. It was divine. "What do you think?"

"It's pleasant," Dreyson said, meeting my gaze. "Do you prefer desserts?"

"I like everything, but it's been a rough couple days, and this chocolate could fix me. What about you?"

"I lean toward more nutritious meals," he said. "Salvatore appreciates fine dining, but my dietary requirements are different."

"Can you eat spicy food?" I asked, taking a bite out of the pink mousse boat. Was that guava? Mmm.

"I *can* eat most things," he said, narrowing his eye at me.

"You don't mean people, do you?" Innis asked, giving him a suspicious look.

I nearly choked on a marzipan sail.

"No. I *could* eat a person. You *could* eat a person," he said sharply. "But that is both morally reprehensible and a way to catch unpleasant diseases."

Innis scrunched up their face. "Eww." They sipped their milk, then glanced at their only remaining ship. I knew what was coming the moment their face lit up.

Dreyson gave me a tired look as Innis placed their last chocolate galleon in the cup of milk and watched it sink slowly, the ship melting.

"The sinking of the S.S. Choccy McBoatface was a national tragedy, but also delicious," Innis said with a newscaster's cadence.

I shook my head and laughed. The chocolate ganache one was almost too much. It was good rich dark chocolate, bittersweet and oh so smooth. I closed my eyes, savoring the mouthfeel and that extra bit of electric joy that surged through my brain, a feeling brought on by eating something decadent.

"Giles, I don't know what the hell you were thinking, but you're lucky we don't charge you with kidnapping!"

I knew exactly who had arrived before I opened my eyes. The asshole lieutenant loomed over me, fists curled at his sides.

"Go away, Jon. I've had a terrible night, so now I'm enjoying my hard-earned chocolate galleon, and you're ruining it by existing."

Innis sputtered beside me and covered their mouth.

"Innis!" Ms. Ramos Moreno stopped in front of the table. "What were you thinking? With everything that's going on—" Her eyes fell on me. "You! How could you lure my child—"

"Mom, that's not what happened!' Innis shouted.

"Giles, you need to—"

"Lieutenant Lawrence." Dreyson stood, not yelling, but his voice carried. "This is not your domain, this is a *civilized* establishment. Mind your manners and stop behaving like a rabid cur."

Innis' eyes widened and filled with sparkly admiration, their smile stretching across their face, and I saw the precise moment when they decided that Dreyson was their new favorite adult.

The lieutenant grimaced, his fair skin turning bright red.

"Is there a problem here?" Another voice cut through the chaos, rich as honey but carrying a steel edge within. The woman stepped between Dreyson and the newcomers, placing one gloved hand on our table. "Are you harassing my customers, Lieutenant? What have I told you about coming here without a warrant?" Her voice stayed low, but there was a whipcrack threat to her words.

The lieutenant actually flinched.

I took another bite of chocolate, savoring the sight of a hot powerful woman taking him down a notch.

As the owner of the Centerpointe, the true center of Illium, Nikita Ragnhildr guarded this neutral ground zealously. A pillar swathed in indigo, she was a striking woman with a Roman nose and bronze skin, her black hair in a complicated updo. It really wasn't fair that she could be so professional in such a pretty lace cocktail dress.

"I don't know what's going on," Ms. Ramos Moreno said sharply. "But she brought my child here without my knowledge. What were you thinking, persuading Innis to leave the house—"

"She didn't!" Innis slammed their palms on the table. "I went to Priya's, but no one was answering the door, so I called Claire." Innis flinched. "But when I went to leave, Priya's whole family was waving at me…or it looked like they were, and Claire told me to wait for her and not go inside." Innis shuddered, their gaze distant. "Claire got me in the car, and something came after us. She didn't kidnap me! It was chasing us, and we didn't want to lead it home, so she came here."

Nikita fixed those amber eyes on me, her expression expectant.

"My apologies for the uproar, Ms. Ragnhildr. It is as Innis says. We needed a safe location to await pickup. It wasn't my intent to disrupt the peace of your establishment." I dipped my chin apologetically.

"Ms. Giles, you're simply here enjoying a dessert among friends. *You* are not the one disrupting the peace of my establishment." She turned those kohl-lined eyes on the lieutenant, who averted his gaze. "And thank you, Dreyson," she said, reaching up to straighten the collar of his jacket, her smile gaining a hint of warmth. "I always appreciate how considerate you are." She actually winked at him.

Dreyson stiffened, that faint pinkness streaking his cheeks. "It's no trouble, Nikita."

She beamed at him, and all that radiance was damn near blinding. It seemed like Arcady wasn't the only person here who knew Dreyson very well. Lucky dog.

I sighed, because Nikita was hot, powerful, and way out of my league.

She shifted, her attention now on Innis. "It seems you have had a distressing night. My sympathies."

Innis stared at her, awestruck, with chocolate smeared around their mouth. "Thanks?"

"And how did you find your dessert?" Nikita leaned in.

"Really good," Innis mumbled, frantically wiping their mouth with a napkin. "I sunk the chocolate-filled one in my milk. It melted like one of those hot cocoa bombs and looked really cool. It might be even better if there was something colorful in the middle, like a sugary shark or kraken!"

Nikita stroked her chin thoughtfully. "That's a marvelous idea. I'll run it by my chocolatier." She turned around, all that charm evaporating as she stared coldly at the lieutenant. "This is a private business, not a public forum. Don't make me warn you again." And then she sauntered off, heels clicking on the wooden floor.

Dreyson sat back down, expression flat.

Ms. Ramos Moreno looked around, now more lost than angry.

"I'm sorry I didn't call you directly," I told her. "Things were hectic, and Innis' safety was my priority. And then I got overwhelmed in the aftermath and needed to fix my blood sugar."

She stared blankly at me for a moment, then back at her kid. "You...snuck out on your own? Again? Oh, Innis..." Disbelief softened the anger into something more fragile, and then she burst into tears.

Innis reached for her.

I grabbed my plate and got up. The lieutenant barely moved far enough back to let me through.

"I'm sorry, Mom," Innis murmured as the woman took my seat and hugged them.

Remington appeared then, looking harried as he emerged from the main dining room. He nodded at me, then took the lieutenant aside.

I sidled up to Dreyson, who scooted over so I could sit beside him. I took my last bite of chocolate, shaking my head.

"Look at them go, like an old married couple." I pointed my chin at Remington and the lieutenant. "Rawr rawr rawr, everything is Giles' fault. She ruined my night on purpose and peed in my shredded wheat!" I used a fake falsetto voice, then shifted to the other side. "Calm down, Jon. Shredded wheat tastes terrible anyway! I'll buy you pancakes. Everyone likes pancakes. Even your grumpy pancake-ass likes pancakes!" I gave Remington a gruff voice, but kept the volume low.

"You do realize you're saying all of this out loud, right?" Dreyson asked.

"Mmm-hmm," I said. "This time, anyway."

Dreyson chuckled softly. "I see why he's always upset with you."

"Because I'm hilarious and I constantly make him the butt of my jokes?" I asked with mock cheer.

"And because he has no sense of humor," Dreyson said agreeably.

"Sometimes I get nervous and all I have are jokes. Wait, you *do* think I'm funny? Huh. You always look kind of incredulous when I go on a tangent."

"I don't always process your comments immediately, because my attention is focused on the task at hand and you are purposefully being distracting. Yes, you're witty, but I think you know that already." He gave me a sidelong look.

I sat with that for a second, unable to stop my smile at the compliment. "Thanks. I'm glad you get it. But I admit I'm envious. Your hardcore focus and no-nonsense demeanor are way more professional than my panic-babbling."

He grunted.

"And also," I lowered my voice. "Nikita too? Wow. Color me impressed."

He stared at me, his one eye getting very big. "How did you — Ms. Giles, we *will not* have that discussion here."

"OK," I said. "But later you're going to have to tell me more."

Dreyson made a growling sound in the back of his throat, but since I was the one sitting on the edge of the booth, he could not politely escape.

Chapter 12
Minding Other People's Business

On the surface, Illium is a modern American city. Its dual nature posits the requirement for a well-stocked underworld. Not all items on the "black markets" are illegal. Denizens with nonconforming appearances require glamour charms to help them blend in. Those with exceptional longevity require paperwork to help them pass unnoticed through society. While false identities are inherently illegal, these are victimless crimes that the city bureaucracy is trained to overlook.

But of course, with its supernatural populace, other problems arise. Most commonly they include magical relics, specialized diets, and ancient grudges. The Italians, the Chinese, and the vampires are the city's oldest established criminal outfits. A variety of two-bit gangs and underground traders fill the gaps.

Any city can have a complex underworld. What makes Illium different is the infrastructure. This city was built to cater to preternatural life wishing to pass as "normal." Witches, sorcerers, vampires, and crime lords all claim to have had a hand in creating it. Some of them are even telling the truth.

—*An Introduction to Illium by Ann Keyes*

THE LIEUTENANT LEFT to take the Ramos Wilder family to a safe house, because we all suspected that once those things finished with the Soltani family, it would swing over a block and visit them next.

Dreyson, Remington, and I remained in the booth, with me in the middle. I had another whiskey. Remington ordered a bourbon. Dreyson stuck to water.

A video played on Remington's phone.

There was more evidence this time. A neighbor's security footage showed our escape, followed by a humanoid blur screaming, "Mommy help me!" after us, sounding like a distressed child. Apparently that was Priya's voice. I didn't want to think about why it was able to mimic her. Then a few minutes later, it showed "me" again, smeared in blood, leaving the scene of the massacre. The thing wearing my face laughed, its mouth opening too wide.

I shuddered, really hating that I had to watch this "not me" disappear into the darkness. That fucker was trying to frame me and possibly going off to commit more murders.

"I don't know what that is, but it doesn't really look like me," I grumbled.

Remington chuckled. "I've seen you make that exact face right before a meal."

I glared at him.

"Only when you're *really* hungry," he said brightly.

"That's a shapeshifter, not illusion magic," Dreyson said. He leaned over my shoulder, studying the screen.

"How can you tell?" Remington asked.

"Look at the way the skin stretches across the bones. It's too thin at points, and in some shots, the face is noticeably asymmetrical. A poor illusion will just lack detail or flicker, but this thing shifted its bones in an attempt to approximate Ms. Giles' visage. If the footage had more color, the tints would probably be off too. This thing could be sloppy, but I'd assume it's nocturnal. It can't replicate the details too closely, but in the dark, it doesn't need to."

The eyes glowed in the dark, like a cat's. Human eyes didn't do that, unless there was something wrong with the person's physiology.

"This is horrifying," I muttered.

"It's not a fetch, is it?" Remington frowned.

"I doubt it's a true doppelganger—if a death curse was put on you, it would be hunting you instead of that family," Dreyson said. "It's likely *sluagh*. Hard to be sure with the shape-shifting, but Redcaps don't move like that. Could be a *mara* or a nighthag, maybe one of the wild hunters or hounds. They come in several forms, but the taxonomy is counterintuitive."

Remington looked at Dreyson thoughtfully, like he couldn't believe the mercenary would say something smart *and* civil. "Could it be the bird guy?"

Dreyson shrugged and looked at me. "What do you think?"

"Different energy," I said. "That guy loves the sound of his own voice. This thing didn't seem capable of conversation."

Remington rubbed his chin. "What do we know?"

"This is a concerted effort." I downed the rest of my whiskey. "The logistics of swapping kids and now hunting them down like this? Too many bodies now to write this off as an isolated incident."

"This violates the treaties," Dreyson said. "Which has significant repercussions for both the Courts and Illium. If certain people can prove breach of contract, they will try to enforce the penalties, and that will get messy."

Politics, ugh. I stared glumly at my empty glass. "I need to drop my car off."

Remington nodded.

"Let's get the check," I said, looking around.

"Don't worry about it," Dreyson said. "It's taken care of."

"By you or your employer?" Remington asked, raising a brow.

Dreyson affected a bored, almost flat look. "You two have...treated me previously. I am simply repaying the favor."

"But I brought the kid—"

"It's already taken care of," Dreyson said, waving his hand.

"But—" I hadn't even seen the check!

"It's inconsequential," he said. "Don't quibble, Ms. Giles. You can try to fight me for it next time. I hear you fight dirty."

I blinked in shock. Who told him about that? "How dare—"

Remington coughed into his fist. "Thanks, Dreyson."

"You're welcome, Detective." Dreyson inclined his head at me pointedly.

"Thank you," I said stiffly, my left eyeball twitching. "I'll remember this." And that definitely sounded more like a threat than gratitude.

"You're welcome," Dreyson said, his expression completely neutral, like this was simply how he did business. But I could feel the smugness rolling off him.

"There you are. I think we're all finished here." The voice was deep and confident with the hint of an accent. Today Salvatore Mori wore a long black coat, his hat in hand. A couple yards away was another bodyguard and that older woman with an imperious bearing. His dinner companion. She watched us with sharp eyes. "How lovely to see you, Detective Remington, Ms. Giles." He smiled brightly at me, eyes crinkling like he was genuinely pleased.

"Good evening, Mr. Mori," I said politely, because how else did you greet an arms-dealing religious fanatic?

"Nice to see you again," Remington said, his tone surprisingly casual.

Dreyson rose, that blank mask firmly in place.

"So good to finally meet you in person," Mori said warmly. "I've heard good things about you."

My eyes darted to Dreyson, who was *not* looking at me.

Mori just winked and gave us a cheeky little wave, which should not have been as charming as it was, coming from a bloodthirsty septuagenarian.

"We can talk later," Dreyson said quietly.

Mori stopped in front of the woman. "Dinner was enlightening as always, my dear." He kissed her hand. "*Buona notte.*" The second Wergeld merc was already getting the door, and Dreyson walked Mori out of the restaurant.

It was then that the older woman approached. She looked to be in her sixties, with cropped gray hair, sharp blue eyes, and a mouth unused to smiling.

"Mrs. Bancroft-Owens," Remington said, actually getting on his feet.

"This is your assistant." She looked me over coolly. I would say with "disapproval," but I got the impression that she looked down her nose at most people, and in her estimation, I wasn't anything special.

"Ma'am," I said carefully, catching Remington's warning glance.

"You recently located rare texts that contained valuable information," she said. "Well done." The words were clipped, perfunctory praise without an ounce of sentiment. "If you continue making progress on this investigation, then we may be able to permanently settle this issue with Commissioner Porter. He is a very tiresome man."

I stared, realizing that this was Remington's sponsor, the secret partner in the agency. I did not recognize her, but here she was, implying that if I did this service for her, she could fix my problems with the IPD. And though I knew nothing about her, I *believed* that she could.

"We're working on it, ma'am," I said.

She turned back to Remington. "I am satisfied with your progress. Salvatore is also looking into the matter." She pursed her lips. "He is surprisingly competent for a blowhard Papist gunrunner. It truly irritates me that such a shortsighted thug holds such a great deal of power."

I assumed she meant his humans-only stance, but maybe she just didn't like Catholics?

"He's a lot more…reasonable in his twilight years," Remington said. "I think some of those views are more lip-service to the Holy See and not something he wants to go to war over."

"Let us hope so," Mrs. Bancroft-Owens said stiffly. "That hulking mercenary of his is still an inconvenience. But we have more important problems to focus on."

My polite smile froze, but she wasn't even looking at me.

"I want evidence that the Alluvian Treaties were broken," she said. "Someone went to a lot of trouble to plant changelings in this city. And now someone is sloppily trying to clean up the mess. We need more of them *alive* if we are to salvage this situation."

Remington nodded.

"And it needs to be done fast," she said. "Because once Ketch gets wind of this it will be out of my hands."

I stiffened, because I knew that name too. How was that kill-happy maniac involved?

"Nobody wants that," Remington said grimly.

"Indeed," she said, her frown deepening. Nodding, the woman turned on her heel and left.

Remington helped me drop my car off at a body shop—the owner was a friend who would at least give us an honest assessment.

"Who was that?" I asked when we were in his car.

"That was Mrs. Harriet-Bancroft-Owens, though I don't think there was ever a Mr. Bancroft-Owens," Remington said. "She's a…civil servant."

I rolled my eyes. "I'm sure that's exactly how she describes herself. I bet she *loves* that term and uses it nonstop. 'I am but a humble civil servant,'" I said, nose in the air. Though something bothered me about our exchange with the woman, something more than the attitude.

"Sorry I was late. I arrived with Jon, but once I got inside, she waved me over for a debrief."

"Hmm," I said.

"She had your photographed documents translated. The foxglove ledger you found is likely a registry of birthdates, all from ten years ago. There were 25 entries." About a quarter of those were accounted for, then.

"It's odd that she singled out Dreyson," I said. Dreyson was one of Mori's assets, and Bancroft-Owens viewed Mori as a threat, but was he worth mentioning?

Remington frowned. "You're right. She and Mori are tentative allies on this matter. Maybe that was a warning for…us?"

"You don't think SIU leaned on her to lecture me too?" I groaned.

"Unlikely," Remington laughed awkwardly. "But it is something to consider. There are a lot of players now, all with ulterior motives."

And I didn't know enough. Mori's angle was easy enough to understand, keeping the Fey out of Illium. As a "civil servant," Bancroft-Owens probably felt the same; their obvious differences would be methodology and politics.

"Speaking of ulterior motives, how's Ketch involved?" I knew him by reputation. Jack Ketch was not exactly a criminal. He held a nebulous position in Shadow Law enforcement because he "solved" bloody messes by making bigger bloodier messes. Detective Davis would mutter darkly whenever he was mentioned. Mwanje would get this pinched look on his face and shake his head. The lieutenant would just go shut himself in his office and break things.

Ketch worked in conjunction with the morgue and their more unsavory practices. Some dangerous things could not be conventionally imprisoned. Ketch had a reputation for being more than happy to find permanent solutions for other monsters, and he occasionally worked with the IPD brass, including Commissioner Porter.

"Ketch is her counterpart, another 'civil servant' in the same way a state executioner is a civil servant. I don't know exactly what he is, but he has a special hatred of the Fey. If he gets involved, the body count could easily quadruple."

"Doesn't Niffolm loan him out of the morgue?"

"Other way around. Niffolm is his subordinate," Remington sighed. "Ketch oversees the morgue system, and he *likes* getting his hands dirty. He's not a fan of SIU, thinks we're encroaching on his territory. But he doesn't actually do much investigating or victim advocacy. He's just in it for the bloodshed."

"Oh, he's much higher up than I thought."

"Yes," Remington sighed. "Ketch is a pillar of the municipal shadow government, one we'd rather not acknowledge. He isn't in Porter's direct chain of command, but he's definitely over the commissioner."

And he wasn't on our side. That cleared some things up. "Do you think he's the one going after changeling kids?" Because Bancroft-Owens seemed to want them alive, if only for political leverage.

"He would," Remington nodded. "I haven't mentioned Innis'...uncommon traits. The kid's safety depends on them appearing as unremarkable as possible."

I nodded. So Remington did not trust Bancroft-Owens completely.

"Report came back on Leonard Wilder. He was geas'd, well compelled to confront the Vernal Lord. He wasn't that stupid all on his own."

"Sabotage? Shit," I said.

"I'm going to count tonight as a win," Remington said, sounding weary. "You got the kid out of that situation, and you both survived. Didn't realize you'd taken a shine to them."

I shrugged. "I don't know, maybe I'm projecting. Maybe it's just a guilty conscience. Maybe I need to pretend that someone will get a happy ending. Selfish, I know."

"That's not selfish at all," Remington said. "We've been in similar positions. We know how bad things can get, and we've paid dearly for that knowledge. It's good that you're trying to make it easier on someone else. Maybe we are trying for a do-over because we don't want someone else's story to have the same bad results we got, even if those better outcomes aren't for us."

Sometimes Remington could be wise, usually when I expected it least. He saw Innis as a lost child thrown into a predatory world, and that struck a chord. I saw a kid undergoing an identity crisis, torn between cultures and values, and I knew from experience that they might never be quite what either side wanted them to be. There was a chance that they would go through life being too "other."

What did Dreyson see?

"They're going to an SIU safehouse. Our part is done," Remington said. "But I still have concerns about what happened at the Shadow Dunes. Who geas'd Wilder?"

"A geas? But he wasn't telling the truth. He didn't kill any changelings."

"It's the other kind. Not the truth-telling oath, the compulsion magic."

The Fey could not outright lie, and one of their more powerful magics was the ability to inflict a geas on someone. It was a compulsion, usually to force a target to speak the truth. But the Fey were not the only ones who could use that kind of magic. Various geas spells were recognized under Shadow Law as reliable methods for getting answers, as long as the right questions were asked. But a geas could also be an oath to commit a certain act, like quitting smoking, slaying a dragon, or talking shit to the goddamn Vernal Lord.

So who set him on that trajectory?

"Maybe he wasn't meant to leave the Shadow Dunes alive," I said. "Even before he encountered the Vernal Lord."

"I think so too," Remington said grimly.

"So was it another Fey or someone closer to home?"

Remington kept his eyes on the road. "That is one of the questions. Claire. And when we find the answer, what are we going to do about it?"

I shrugged and stared out the window at the night sky, starting to realize the shape of things. Too much remained concealed, but we could already see that this was going to be an even bigger mess than we expected.

At home, I did a cursory check on Mrs. Bancroft-Owens, sending a request to Zareen and also rooting through the Trojan Watchtower's archives. It was a local tabloid, one that often used thirty-point font and screaming pun headlines. No one knew exactly who ran it or wrote it, but the weekly papers still showed up at grocery stores and on doorsteps. They had an extensive digital archive in eye-burning color combinations. But the paper was a beloved city-wide joke, full of things like straw-man arguments over whether or not Bigfoot was an alien. It seemed to be an intentional smokescreen, because if you knew enough about the powers in the city, you could glean some useful information from the exaggerated stories.

While I did find an article claiming "plant people" were attacking hikers in the same park used to access the Shadow Dunes, I didn't see much else.

Hopping on TOR, I went to a few specialized marketplaces to make discreet inquiries.

If I was going to work this job, I would have to get more background information, so I set up an appointment with a librarian to find out exactly what those Alluvian Treaties contained. I also contacted a friend who was a graduate researcher in the St. Cassian's linguistic department. It would help to have a trusted source confirm those translations.

With an itinerary in place for tomorrow, I went to bed.

As I began to drowse, an uneasiness spread through my body, like something was in here, watching. I turned the lights back on, but there was nothing actually in the room with me. The wards were up and functioning. Still, I moved Dreyson's knife from my nightstand to under my pillow, and the discomfort faded.

Dreyson loaned me an emotional support dagger. How cute. And then another thought hit me out of the blue, like an Acme anvil.

Arcady invited Dreyson and me to a ménage à trois.

I rubbed my eyes. Why the hell did I put that thought on the backburner? Because Innis was standing right there. Arcady wasn't explicit, but I knew exactly what he meant by "bring a friend." That wasn't something we could discuss in front of a traumatized child.

So I wasn't completely sure that Dreyson did anything with Nikita, but his reaction seemed to corroborate my theory. But I knew Arcady, I had firsthand experience. The idea was intriguing, not just because Arcady had a ridiculous level of sex appeal and a very nice house with a hot tub.

I didn't know exactly how I felt about Dreyson. I liked him, that was true. But I didn't know him very well. While he wasn't conventionally attractive, he wasn't repulsive either. He was in great shape, and his tattoos were interesting. The scars were jarring at first, mostly because I didn't want to stare, but also it was polite to maintain eye contact, so then where else was I supposed to look? I could stare at his chest, since it was at eye level, but that was rude too.

Plus there were his mood swings. One moment he was reserved and as dry as a British comedy, but bring in a threat and then he was cheerfully curb-stomping heads and setting things on fire. There was a lot of pent-up energy in that man; it made me wonder what that experience would be like.

Polite Dreyson seemed to like intelligent conversation, despite trying to appear stoic. I could see him giving a lecture during sex, that rough voice working to stay even throughout all the fun. Berserker Dreyson was another story, though. He was eager, reckless, and competitive. Seeing him unleashed would be equal parts scary and exciting.

I gave as good as I got, so the idea of having Dreyson on his knees, possibly restrained, staring defiantly up at me, just like he had been for the Crow Knight...

I groaned, resting my arm over my eyes. I did not need to have these thoughts about a professional acquaintance who happened to be the *Head of Arcane Security for the Wergeld* and for Salvatore Fucking Mori. This was a "Very Bad Idea."

But...I did call him in a moment of panic tonight. That was a choice I made, even if I didn't want to look too closely at my reasoning. It made sense to call someone who could fight.

He bought me chocolate and whiskey tonight, and I didn't even know if he *liked* women. But even if he didn't, if we went to Arcady's place, there would be something for everyone...

Ugh, I really needed to stop. I pulled a pillow over my face. I had bigger worries to chew on, but this thought was now living rent-free in my head. So I lay there, my monkey-mind wondering what would have happened if either of us accepted Arcady's invitation.

I did not sleep well; my dreams were unpleasant. I woke up too early, my heart beating too fast, my sheets slick with sweat. That sluagh thing was still out there, and I had to concede that it *kind of* knew what I looked like.

Today's appointments were low-risk, just research. I would have to make a couple food pickups—you didn't set up meetings, ask people to take time out of their day to answer your questions, and then show up empty-handed.

My dark web searches netted an offer for information on Mori, but nothing on any of the other subjects. It was pricey, and I wasn't sure if it had anything I couldn't find outside of his SIU file.

Circumstances meant I needed to alter my appearance. I put on khakis, a blue button-down, and a black blazer, knife in the inner pocket, gun concealed in a shoulder holster. I put on sneakers and packed charms in my wallet. Before I opened the front door, I activated the disguise charm.

It was an illusion, an overlay on my body. I "grew" a couple inches, my reflection wider and more masculine. The face was nothing like mine, rounder with a bit of scruff and a weak jaw. I looked like a nondescript young white man with curly brown hair, maybe an IT guy.

Satisfied that I wasn't going to get arrested for being myself, I left the house.

The fox-spirit librarian gave a comprehensive summary of the relevant parts of the Alluvian treaties. (The master documents weighed more than a beagle and were stored in the city archives. Fortunately, someone digitized the text, minus the binding oaths and other magicks infused in the originals.)

Very plainly, the Courts were not allowed to abduct children nor replace them with changelings. The Fey could bargain with the parents, and there were provisions for a variety of convoluted custody agreements, but they were not allowed to simply *take* children.

Most of the penalties were negotiable, and there was an entire section on the topic, ranging from fines to executions. It included estimates of damages to be paid to the families, as well as actuarial charts rating the severity of the offenses and what kind of recompense could be demanded. There were even complex allowances for custody agreements, provided the children wanted to split time between families.

The underlying issue of the Alluvian Treaties related to the guarantors. If the Vernal Lord or Autumnal Lady were party to breaking the rules, that claim needed to be authenticated by a special tribunal, and then the sovereign would be declared *forsworn*. Apparently, being an oath-breaker was a big deal to the Fey, since they couldn't properly lie. Anyone could suffer negative repercussions for breaking oaths, but it was allegedly worse for them. Like the ground opening up and swallowing them or some ancient deity smiting them into a greasy scorch mark, and at the very least, their subjects would cancel them.

The lore was murky about if they could be secretly forsworn without consequences or if they suffered karmic punishment immediately. That ambiguity seemed intentional, to boost their credibility. Given the current circumstances, there needed to be a formal indictment. Obviously, if the sovereigns were involved with this changeling debacle, then they were already forsworn, though nothing seemed to have happened to them yet. The current lord and lady were the same ones who signed the treaties over a century ago.

Upon reaching the university campus, I grabbed donuts and went to Revya's office.

"What the…is there something you wanted to tell me, Clarence?" she asked, lowering her glasses. Revya Tani wore her hair in a sleek black bob, her white sweater dress contrasting with her warm reddish-brown skin.

"I'm incognito," I said, shutting the door behind me. "Cop problems."

"And you chose appropriate camouflage. Smart." She smirked at me. "You know, we'll always accept you, however you choose to identify."

"Thanks," I said, placing the box of donuts on her desk. "They had maple-bacon and honey-glazed peanut butter."

Her smile widened. "You shouldn't have," she sighed happily, pulling the box over to her and embracing it.

"How's Rin?" I asked, because Revya and her older sister were old friends of mine.

"Rin's…you know, I shouldn't tell you." She crossed her arms. "You two will just get into more trouble."

"Too late, but my problem is sluagh," I said. "It jumped on top of my car and later shape-shifted into an uncanny valley version of me."

"Oh fuck." Revya pursed her lips. "Why can't you ever have normal problems?"

"Dunno, but now that you say it, which one of us has normal problems?" I rubbed my chin. Out of everyone, I saw Revya the most. Rin was not always on the right side of the law, but then, neither was I. We were closer in high school, even if she was the tag-along kid sister. But she had a knack for magic, so she garnered an apprenticeship and was now pursuing a graduate degree to complement her studies.

"I looked over the stuff you sent me," she said in lieu of answering my question. "It's a very specific dialect, relegated to a small geographic — OK, I recognize that glazed look, so I won't go into detail." She opened up the donut box, giving me a sour look.

"You know me so well. In my defense, I already went to the library."

"Coincidentally, it's remarkably similar to what the Autumn Court uses in their formal records," she said, narrowing her eyes at me.

"Wow, that is a coincidence," I said brightly.

Revya shook her head, clearly recognizing the provenance of my documents. "The ledger, the flower one, has 25 entries, the dates all from about ten years ago. Ten of those have a second entry, dates all ranging from the past six months."

I raised my head. "What?"

"I don't know what they mean. The other samples are genealogical records, just lineages like 'Claire, daughter of Wayne' or 'Revya, daughter of a no-good grifter.'"

"Oh." I'd hoped for something more useful.

"I sent you the translations. If you get more pieces, I want to see them, and I want to know what you did to get tangled up with the Autumn Court."

"If I survive, I'll tell you the disclosable parts over dinner," I said.

Revya groaned, slapping both hands onto my shoulders. "Don't you dare—"

"And I'll bring Rem, but if you're going to sleep with him, please don't tell me about it."

She snorted, laughing softly. "He's hot, in that distinguished older man way." She leaned in and hugged me. "Come by more often, not just when you have magical problems, you dumb jock."

"Magical intellectual problems that require help from smarter people," I said. "I feel bad bothering you, since you're busy with your thesis and Adept Adder."

"Yes, I suppose we're all busy now." Her gaze drifted to the stack of old books sitting on her desk.

Taking that as my cue to leave, I stood up.

She reached into a drawer and pulled out a dozen charms. "Here. I made them recently. Had the feeling you would need a restock. I'll invoice Remington later."

I blinked as she dropped them into my hands. "Thanks!"

"You're going to need them if you have sluagh hunting you."

"It's not that bad," I laughed. "I was just collateral damage on the periphery. I'm not important enough to warrant that kind of attention."

Revya did not laugh. She just stared at me. "Wow, I didn't think it was possible, but you're even more obnoxious and clueless as a man."

"Huh," I said, tucking the charms into my pocket. "Well…thanks?"

Shaking her head, Revya just took a donut and waved me out.

I caught another bus downtown, taking a detour through Chinatown to grab dumplings and bubble tea. I texted Alice the details of my disguise and my ETA.

The Office of Vital Records had the pillars and moldings of the neoclassical revivalist style customary for fancier government buildings. I took the stairs to the basement, where Alice worked. At least I thought it was Alice; it could have been any one of her four identical sisters and I would be none the wiser.

I walked down a long narrow hall, feeling the buzz of the lights in my back teeth. The door to the record room chimed as I opened it. The basement was an unhealthy shade of green, fluorescent lights enhancing the mood. The décor seemed to be from the 1970s, from the peeling veneer of wood paneling, to the metal furniture, to the unforgivably busy wallpaper, colors faded, but patterns still eye-burning. Was this American government gothic? Bureaucratic urban decay? Or just another example of "interior design crimes"? Truly, it could be everything.

And yet Alice glowed, her crown of natural curls lustrous, her skin a healthy shade of tan. She wore a pretty blue dress, making her a soothing presence in all this harsh lighting. She looked nineteen, and she played the part well, but I knew she was much older. Alice and her sisters, Lacie, Calie, Celia, and Cleia were variations on a theme: notaries, artists, forgers, archivists, and printers. Paper-craft was their passion, and as an original Illium institution, they provided the entire gamut of identity services.

"There's a cop in the record room," she said when I reached the counter.

"SIU?" I asked, because my disguise wouldn't fool any of them. Maybe I should come back later to avoid their questions.

"Beat cop." She wrinkled her nose.

Frowning, I set the food on the counter, and she squealed happily when she looked inside the bag.

"Thanks! I only had time to pack a PB&J, and that's not enough."

"It's the least I can do," I said."

"Let me check and see if he's almost done. I'll grab your stuff if I can. I had to put everything back since he demanded to do the search." Alice buzzed herself in and returned a few minutes later, fuming. "He's making a mess," she growled and gestured for me to come around the counter.

We went back into a cramped little office with one chair and a slim laptop on a single desk. She pointed at the chair and perched on her desk. "Bastard's on the phone with someone. Actually shushed me and shooed me out." She raised both hands in a petulant waving motion, her face twisted in anger.

"And he's pulling some of the same files you requested." She opened the laptop. "So what's going on?"

"Good question," I said carefully. Alice was someone who crafted records for those who needed new identities. She and her sisters specialized in creating thorough, back-stopped, official documents. Some of the work was for the city itself. Her body of knowledge was a valuable resource. "Looking into changelings."

Alice's eyes widened. "From a decade ago?" She stroked her chin, her gaze distant. "Makes sense. Not everyone here likes the Fey, but…" She frowned. "Custody agreement?"

"No, seems to be a traditional swap," I said. "Do you make papers for the Courts?"

She grimaced. "If they're covertly exchanging kids, my services aren't needed. And if I did take on such a job, which I wouldn't, I wouldn't be free to talk about it." She narrowed her eyes. "Is it just you and SIU?"

"We might have run afoul with Ketch."

She snapped her fingers. "That explains it." She pulled up a camera feed on her laptop.

A familiar cop sat on the floor flipping through folders. "Flak from the spook squad. Detective Hayseed won't drop it." Officer Ryan spat in his phone, tossing a folder across the room, scattering papers.

"That bastard," I scowled.

Alice clenched her fists, a flash of rage in her eyes. "You know him?"

"Handsy pervert who likes waving around his gun."

"Hartford pulled the slanty bitch in. I had nothing to do with that. Don't know why Porter's mad. Everyone knows he wants her gone. My partner thought he was doing the old man a favor."

My jaw stiffened.

Alice inclined her head at me.

"So we stuck her in a cell with some bastard that roughed her up a little, not a big deal." He actually laughed.

"Did he now?" Alice asked, her voice silky soft.

"It wasn't my celly—it was the Revenants they released."

Alice folded her hands in her lap. "I'll send you a copy of this video. It best not come back to me. But I expect you to crucify this asshole."

"It's on my to-do list."

"I'm almost done. Porter wanted me to run this errand. Then I'll join you at the bar." He stood up.

Alice scowled as he began to leaf through the papers.

"You should tank his credit rating. Or lure him into Alseides Park at night."

She cracked a smile. "I better go back out. Bet that prick's going to leave a mess."

He did. I watched him on the feed.

"Thanks, doll," Ryan told her. "Things got a little disorganized, and I don't have time to fix it up, but I'm sure you don't mind. It gives you something to do. And how about I take you out to lunch as a treat?"

"I don't go out with pigs who can't clean up their own messes," she said coldly.

Ryan scoffed, muttered something, and slammed the door on his way out. I emerged from the back office. "You could file a complaint."

"Sure, and his bosses wouldn't take it any more seriously than they do yours," she said, rolling her eyes.

Remington texted me when he was outside. I walked out with about thirty dossiers that matched the birthdates on the Fey ledger. Alice didn't give me copies of official documents, but she gave me names, parents, hospitals, and addresses. I knew there were extra subjects, but the birthdates matched, and we would have to do a thorough investigation to exclude them. Actually tracking down the families was a job we could hand off to SIU.

Priya Soltani and Innis Wilder were both in the mix. They were born at different hospitals with the same year. I vaguely recognized a few more surnames from the crime scene files, and one of the secondary dates from the ledger matched the estimated death date.

Revya gave me ten secondary dates. Were there that many undiscovered murdered families?

I also had a copy of the Officer Ryan video. Alice tossed that in for free. I paid for the research, collation, digitization of copies, and a discretionary surcharge, given the illegality of the services she provided. She sent me a neat invoice for the expense account.

Remington's black Camaro sat parked in a handicapped spot. He was staring off into space, dark circles around his eyes. I knocked on the window.

He jumped.

"What's up, hot stuff?" I asked in my voice, even if I wasn't wearing my face.

"That's really disturbing," Remington groaned, unlocking the car doors.

I climbed in, still giggling. We headed back to the office while I updated him. Remington listened, his frown deepening when I explained Commissioner Porter's connection.

Once in the office, Remington went to make some calls. I dispelled the disguise charm and got out my laptop.

"I'll consider us even if you can get me a copy of his calendar for the month. Don't fuck me on this, Kevin," Remington said to "Kevin," who clearly didn't want to be on the phone with him.

My phone buzzed; it was a text from Dreyson. *Let me know when you have time to talk.*

"You're the best, Wendy," Remington said, already on to another call. "Drinks tonight? No? Well, it's my treat."

I rolled my eyes, about to text Dreyson back, but then Remington hung up the phone, no longer smiling. He dropped into a chair in front of my desk and rubbed his face with both hands.

"Did you sleep last night?" I asked.

"Not well," he said. "The Soltani house was…bad. So I put in some time reading through the Alluvian Treaties and other Court-related files."

"Same." I leaned back in my chair.

"How are you holding up?" Remington looked me over.

"Freaked out," I said. "But channeling all that nervous energy into this investigation. I don't want to think about that thing going around with my face." Because I had nightmares about it wearing my skin and eating Innis. Then it started to peel my face off, because once it had more pieces of me, the disguise would be completely convincing and then it would be able to take my place…

I woke up before that happened, but the horror lingered.

"It wasn't a convincing version of you, honest," Remington said with a wince. "I was joking about the expression. You don't actually look like that. Often."

"Thanks." I gave him a tired headshake. My phone buzzed again. This time a text from Innis with more questions about Dreyson. How tall was he? What did he eat for breakfast? Could he beat a werewolf with his bare hands?

"Dreyson?" Remington asked, looking curious.

"Innis," I said. "But Dreyson is their new favorite person."

Remington laughed incredulously. "Seriously? Why?"

"Because he told Jon off," I said. "Well, not just that. He was really good with the kid, talked them through things, actively listened. It was all that responsible stuff you do. You're good with kids too."

Remington blinked.

"I remember what it was like being a kid," I said, trying to explain it better. "The world was big. Everything was new. Adults could fix any problem." I laughed, and it sounded forced. "It's hard, but I do remember what it was like to be small with the stars in your eyes, believing wholeheartedly that the world was full of endless possibilities. But I'm not that person anymore, and I don't know the best way to help someone who sees the world through that lens. I can speak their language, though."

123

"I haven't been that boy for a very long time," Remington said quietly. "And I'm longer removed from it than you are."

It was hard to picture the fragile waif he once was. There were only a few photos from his childhood. Remington was a foster kid who aged out of the system with no real family.

"But you know how to guide that boy," I said. "And that skill might be more useful."

"There's empathy and there's knowing how to handle the obstacles those kids are bound to encounter. Both are important," he said, his smile rueful.

"Whatever happens, Innis is headed for some kind of heartbreak, and that's the best-case scenario."

Remington pushed his hair back. "I know."

"I hate working with kids. In this business, it doesn't spell anything good, least of all for the kid."

Remington nodded absently, slumping in his chair. "But we do our best. You have to hope that someone will get it right, be it the parents, the schools, the courts, the caseworkers…if not them, then someone has to, right?"

I winced. Remington had a penchant for getting too invested when children were involved. Usually I could pull him back, but this time I was probably just making things worse.

"We aren't parents, nor are we small children," he said. "But we remember what it was like, and we both understand the weight of being responsible for another life. We have enough empathy and adjacency that relating to the Wilder-Ramos family isn't a stretch."

What kind of choice would my parents have made? Remington had even more questions about his parents, as he had no memory of them.

"We're doing our best," I said.

Remington sighed heavily. "You're right. No point getting distracted."

"Well, here's Ryan blabbing about some interesting topics." I played the full video, complete with a rant about SIU filing complaints and the union having his back, on my laptop.

Remington groaned. "Coincidentally, Jon let me know that Ryan dropped off a list of fifteen names and said, 'I cracked your case for you.'"

I rolled my eyes. "Clearly someone else handed him the work and he fucked that up too." After all, there were more than fifteen entries in the ledger. But did he choose living or dead changelings?

"He was oh so very gracious about it, said he was doing SIU a favor, and that they should be grateful and just drop the complaint about…well, we can skip the derogatory quotes. There might have been an incident."

"He tripped and fell?" I asked.

Remington shrugged. "Jon didn't say. Nina will update me later. Anyway, I told him we had another fifteen possibilities and more data than just names, if you can send it over a secure connection?"

"Sure. Is looping in SIU going to be a problem for Bancroft-Owens?" I asked, not because it would stop me, but because I wanted to know.

"Shouldn't be," he said. "She wants evidence and the changeling kids kept alive. SIU can do that. She is focused on results. How we work is at our discretion."

"So what were those favors you just called in?"

"Don't you worry about it," Remington said, giving me that easy smile.

"Rem—"

"It could be nothing," he drawled. "I have a hunch who tipped Porter off, since Dreyson seemed to be the primary target."

Because if Ryan was telling the truth, I was an afterthought in the plan. "Was Bancroft-Owens hedging her bets?" That possibility occurred to me; she had the influence and the motives, but I very much doubted that she had any qualms.

Remington's smile faded. He leaned forward, voice low. "I think we must be very circumspect in this investigation, especially regarding how we speak of certain parties. I have some obligations here, as you may already know…"

"So be careful what we share with our *allies*?" I asked.

"Yes," Remington said firmly. "But what I don't know, I can't report. And what others don't know, can't be used against you."

That was not permission, but that was not an objection either. Remington didn't want to upset Bancroft-Owens, but he understood my position. I didn't want to make an enemy of her either, especially if she had even a fraction of the power I thought she did. But I didn't turn my back on my friends, and I didn't like bullies in positions of authority.

"Just how dumb do I have to be to willingly make myself a target in this pissing match between titans?" I asked.

"I guess that depends on how much you like tall, blonde, and scary," Remington said dryly.

Chapter 13
The Offers You Should Not Refuse

杀鸡儆猴 Trad. 殺雞儆猴-Shā jī jǐng hóu translates as "killing the chicken to warn the monkey." It refers to the tactic of publicly punishing an individual to set an example for others. Apparently, if you want to indulge in some animal cruelty and make a really messy show of it, chickens will oblige—flapping, squawking, clouds of feathers flying everywhere. That's not even getting into the gory bits. Allegedly, this saying stems from the practice of killing the less valuable chicken so the more valuable monkey would be intimidated into obedience. (They would teach them to juggle. Who knew?) So there's an unspoken understanding of disparate worth.

Sometimes it's important to understand that the corpse isn't always the target, it's a message. That's no consolation for the chicken, though.

— From the Very Personal Journals of FYG

SIU DID NOT want us to track anyone down in person, but Detective Davis did want our help analyzing the data. Social media was the easiest source to glean information from, and we were still looking for a concrete link among the candidates.

But there were no obvious direct connections. The parents were different ethnicities, went to different schools, and worked in different industries. There were a few common factors, though: they were mostly upper middle class, with steady jobs and the appearance of stability. Most couples were married and predominately heterosexual, though there were two gay couples and a few others who might have used a surrogate. Since they were outliers, it might be best to try to rule them out first so I could get a better grasp of the Courts' baby-swapping methodology.

I texted Dreyson that I was free to talk, but he responded half an hour later to let me know that he was busy.

Innis sent me a slew of messages throughout the day, but fortunately, it seemed they were sticking close to their mom.

The mechanic said that, aside from the windshield, the damage to my car was mostly cosmetic, which was a relief. That sluagh must have been lighter than it looked.

Remington and I worked through dinner, both of us at my desk, going through names, making charts of who knew whom, and isolating mutual friends who were openly involved in HerbAway.

Most of the families remained in Illium.

There were a few whom I strongly suspected of having changelings. I had no solid evidence, just a hunch based on the rough profile I made, but I shortlisted them and checked the social media accounts, paying close attention to anyone who recently went inactive.

Remington passed on the information to Detective Davis, and she replied with an email scan containing Dreyson's laundry list of crimes.

Dutifully, I skimmed it. It was long, violent, and less informative than I expected.

There were many Shadow Law citations against him and the Wergeld for property damages, assault and battery, and the wrongful deaths of bounties. A lot of stories went, "and after a prolonged struggle, instead of taking the rampaging werebear alive, Dreyson chopped her head off." Those events resulted in either the Wergeld taking a reduced bounty or paying damages, but no direct criminal charges for Dreyson alone.

Obviously, I didn't like the use of excessive force, but having seen the damage certain entities could inflict, I understood that stopping them might require more violence. Still, letting a private organization like the Wergeld decide who lived and who died didn't sit right with me. Hell, letting the cops make that call didn't sit right with me.

But I wasn't alone in that sentiment. The Wergeld did not have free rein; judging by the projected numbers, they paid out a lot more in wrongful death suits and civil damages than the police department ever did. Overall, there wasn't a lot of transparency, but weirdly enough it was still more than what the IPD offered.

Dreyson had more mundane instances of "threatening behavior," which ranged from him actually telling someone that he would "tear his head off with his bare hands and shove it down his neck-hole," to mere complaints about the scary glares he gave people. That last one I dismissed; Dreyson could not help how his face looked.

The violence was specific to his Wergeld duties and Mori's outfit. There were no domestic claims, no thefts, very little about what he did outside of work. Of course, he might just live on the job, and he had to be good about not getting caught. The Wergeld also self-policed, which might help him cover up certain crimes, given his own high rank within the organization. So if he was doing reprehensible things in his personal life, there was no guarantee that news would leak.

In the last couple years, most charges against Dreyson ended up dropped. There were plenty of minor nuisance ones like obstruction, trespassing, or loitering, but maybe he learned more self-control, or got a better lawyer...or he was just a lot smarter about not getting caught.

"Are you actually worried about my proximity to Dreyson?" I asked, because clearly SIU was.

Remington shrugged. "It's a complication if things go south, but I'm not losing sleep over it. The others...well, it's the part of the situation they *think* they can control. And what if he poaches you to the dark side?" He gave me a small smile. "The benefits have to be good. I can't match those."

I snorted. "I know it's hard to believe, but I do have *some* ethics."

He laughed. "I wouldn't blame you if Dreyson, maybe on behalf of Mori, takes you out to dinner and says, 'Come work for us, Ms. Giles, and Commissioner Porter will sleep with the fishies.'"

I snorted. "I wouldn't do that to the fishies."

"And Mori was awfully friendly with you," Remington said hesitantly.

Mori did date women with a significant age gap—he showed up to charity events with a certain type of woman on his arm. They were still older than me and more...well-endowed.

"It didn't seem like he was hitting on me." No leers or admiring glances, but then not every creep was obvious about it. "I'm also not his type. Maybe if I was more..." I put my hands in front of my chest and mimed like I was holding cantaloupes in each palm.

"He definitely prefers MILFs," Remington laughed, some of the tension easing. "It probably is business-related. You know how to talk to people. You have a reason to distrust the IPD, but you're professional enough to handle yourself. You're sneaky and you do good work. I'd recruit you... oh wait!"

Laughing, I finished checking my list of people who were absent from social media for more than two days. Remington was going to go over our findings with SIU after he dropped me off at home.

The condo felt empty without Ivy's presence. A work emergency came up while I was dealing with this situation, and I knew Canaris well enough to know it wasn't a coincidence. That was fine; we both wanted to keep Ivy from getting tangled up in my mess.

We had our own lives, but we usually checked in with each other a few times a day and would try to get dinner together at least a few nights a week. Sometimes we would just sit in the living room with snacks, working on our laptops, with the TV on for background noise. And sometimes, when one of us had a hard night, we'd take blankets into the other person's room and sleep there.

I went to bed early. It was kind of sad to just sit around staring at my phone, like I was haunting my own damn home. Throwing on some fuzzy Aggretsuko pajamas, I texted Ivy. *The house is depressing without you.*

She texted back a few minutes later. *Conference is bullshit. They could have sent anyone else. Dinner was good, though.* Attached was a picture of a juicy steak, a glass of red wine, and a Caesar salad. Then another picture of a slice of cherry cheesecake.

That looks good. I sighed. I had a sandwich for dinner. It was… OK.

I'll bring you next time. I'm so bored. What are you doing?

In bed, but thinking about that dessert now. It's taunting me.

She responded with a teary-eyed smiley.

I put my phone aside, checked my weapons, and pulled my blankets up. Then I closed my eyes. Sleep came easier tonight.

Footsteps, soft but steady, woke me. They were slow, measured, and coming toward my bed. It was still dark, but the curtains were open, moonlight streaming in, shadows sliding along my walls.

The intruder was between me and the door. I lay on my side, my right hand creeping to the nightstand. My fingers closed around the cool polymer of the Glock's frame. I inhaled and then rolled onto my back, gun clasped in both hands.

"Freeze!" I shouted, finger on the trigger.

The figure chuckled. "Is that any way to greet me, hellcat?" He sauntered forward, moonlight gleaming on his black armor.

I squeezed the trigger then, but it stuck and nothing happened. Goddamn Fey and their jinxes. Swearing, I dropped the gun and grabbed the knife from under my pillow.

He lunged for me, but I rolled off the bed, dropping into a crouch. He landed on my bed, turning to face me.

I darted around, going for the door, but he was faster, blocking the exit. With no other alternative, I slashed at him.

He hissed as the obsidian blade made contact, scraping through his chestplate.

And then suddenly I was on the ground, flat on my back, air ejected from my lungs, brain struggling to catch up, the Crow Knight looming over me.

I drew my knees up to my chest and kicked him in the abdomen, managing to propel myself backward across the carpet. Knife still in hand, I tried to get back on my feet, but then there was an almost crushing weight on me and I was flat on the ground, the Crow Knight on my chest, the guardplates on his knees digging into my arms, pinning me in place.

He inhaled deeply, plucking the knife from my hand. He turned it over in his metal gauntlets, and I could not see his expression, not in the dark, not under that helm.

130

"Such a nasty thing," he said and dropped it on the floor out of my reach.

I craned my neck, trying to calculate how much movement I needed to reach it, but his body blocked my view. My breaths came in ragged gulps as I thrashed, trying to displace his weight. If I could just get him off balance...

"Shhhh," he murmured, the cold metal talons of his gauntlets lightly tracing my cheek. "This doesn't have to hurt."

My body went cold. I froze in that moment, already knowing the survival calculus. The Crow Knight was a lot stronger than me. If he wanted to hurt me, I couldn't stop him. Any choice I made that got me through this alive was the right choice. Not everyone had the privilege of good choices. Gritting my teeth, I glared up at him.

He tilted my chin up. "Your man was supposed to take better care of you. These wards are pathetic. They can't keep people like me out." He shook his head ruefully. "What was he thinking?"

"Didn't think you wanted unwilling playmates," I coughed, his weight making it difficult to breathe. Comparatively, the thing that landed on my car roof was light and lithe; this man was deceptively solid.

The Crow Knight froze. "Oh, that's why you're so frightened," he murmured, still holding me in place, but his grip softened. He looked away, almost like he was ashamed. "You're right, hellcat. I'm not here for that." He shifted, taking some of the pressure off my chest.

I swallowed roughly, sucking down more air. "Why are you here?"

"Because some reckless mortals are meddling in our affairs," he said sharply. "And so I have been tasked to make an example of the offenders. Regrettably, you're the only one I found."

I blinked.

"I didn't think it would be you," he said. "I would have preferred a rematch with the warp warrior, but he is difficult to track. The crippled lawman—"

I snarled at the mention of Remington. "You stay the fuck away from them, you piece of shit!"

The Crow Knight let out an eerie chuckle. "They're not the ones you should worry about. They're not alone with me. You can scream if you like. No one will hear you."

Just like all the other scenes.

I pressed my lips together, possibilities racing through my mind. Did he want to use me as bait? Or did he intend to turn me into an example? I shuddered at the memory of vines tearing through Wilder's soft tissue. "Showing your true colors now, you sadistic bastard?" I glared up at his shadowed face. Dreyson was right. The Crow Knight was toying with us.

"It gives me no pleasure to threaten you like this," he said quietly, any trace of amusement gone. Worse, he sounded resigned, like he was actually planning on killing me.

"Then why are you doing it?" I growled.

He studied me, like he really was thinking about his answer. "You were raised here in the human world. You don't understand the weight of a vow made in the Courts," he said finally, the words burning with a quiet intensity.

"Help me understand, then," I said immediately, playing for time.

"There are those that I swore to protect," he said. "If you want to judge, just remember that we all have obligations." He released my chin, sighing heavily.

I lay there, processing my own words that he just threw back at me, and the subtle differences between his statement and mine. *If* he wasn't just fucking with me, he was under orders. But he wasn't acting like someone who wanted to kill me. Was he giving me space to find a loophole?

"I don't know what you think I'm meddling in," I said, because that was the truth. I was snooping in a lot of dangerous people's affairs. It could be any reason; he didn't share specifics. "But I'm clearly not high up in anyone's command structure. I'm a freelancer. So if you're trying to make a point to someone, I'm the wrong sacrificial lamb. No one up top will care. Hell, they might not even know it was because of Court business, or worse, they send you a fucking thank-you card instead. Do you really think your boss is the only one who's mad at me?"

He looked around. "A fair point. Your wards were ridiculously easy to shatter."

I winced. I meant to get them refreshed, but I had been busy.

"You're right, you aren't a direct threat," he said, that good old Fey arrogance in his voice, and I tensed. "So I am not in a hurry to do anything drastic. Why don't we just talk?"

Condescending prick- No, don't get distracted. I needed to stay focused. "About?"

"What are you offering me to spare your life?" he asked, one finger lightly poking my cheek.

I grimaced. "I don't think you're hearing me," I said slowly. "I don't know enough to be important in the grand scheme of things. No one in power gives a shit about me, so killing me serves no constructive purpose."

"Is the warp warrior so faithless? What if I just want you to call someone for help? Just a small trade. Give me someone more important, hellcat. You're right, this is *not* your fight," he said, his tone pitying. "You don't have to be the one to pay."

That wasn't going to happen on principle. I bit back that response. Taking a hard noble stance was a great way to end up a martyr. But if Ivy was the one who found me cut up in here...I closed my eyes, hating that I knew exactly how much that would hurt her, how that would reopen old wounds. I didn't want to do that to my friend. But I was grateful that Canaris sent her out of town, that he couldn't use her against me. "Ask for something else," I said, my voice rough.

"What else? What can you give me for my liege? You are striking down the usual bargains and being very careless with your life," he said grimly.

And it clicked then.

"The only person whom my life is truly valuable to is me. Everyone else gets diminishing returns on it." I opened my eyes, smiling sharply at him.

I could feel his surprise. He didn't know how to respond to that.

"You say that you don't want to kill me, that you just need something to satisfy your liege, because they want the investigations to stop. Well, that's not going to happen, no matter what you do to me. That's not a threat, that's just a statement of fact. There are too many bodies now, too many parties involved."

He stiffened. "What do you mean?"

"I'll walk you through it," I said, more confidence in my voice. "The incident at the Shadow Dunes drew more attention than anyone expected. The Vernal Lord wasn't subtle. The Wergeld was involved. And here in the city, the police are investigating multiple murders. They're thick, but even they've figured out that these aren't mundane killings. What with the silencing magic-" I glared at him. "And the shape-shifting, and the nature of the wounds. So I think we both know that certain higher-up city officials, who probably should not be named, are already involved."

"So the *Lares* already know," the Crow Knight said with a grimace. "Both the iron lady and the butcher?"

"It looks that way," I said, because even though I thought I knew whom he was talking about, my bluff depended on me sounding more knowledgeable than I was. "Anyway, how could they not notice when some asshole is going around killing entire families *and* leaving their bodies on gruesome display? You really think that was the best way to handle it?"

The Crow Knight released a long breath, his shoulders tensed. How involved was he? Was it just the sluagh participating in the murders? "Hellcat, if you really think that of me, perhaps you shouldn't taunt me so," he said, his voice gravelly, talons pricking at my throat.

I clenched my fists, trying to stay calm. He wasn't exactly denying involvement, but I thought he might be offended by the implication. "I don't know this for certain, but if a specific person was already involved, the body count would be higher."

Though perhaps we had yet to find all the victims.

Another realization blindsided me: maybe what was killing the changelings wasn't just from the Courts. Maybe Ketch was hunting too. Wholesale slaughter was on brand for him.

"You have made your point," the Crow Knight said somberly. "Perhaps the situation is not what we believed it to be. And so I find it necessary to report back immediately. I will likely receive more specific orders on how I must deal with you later. It would be unwise for you to be here when I return. It would be even more foolish for you to continue looking into this 'changeling' issue."

I nodded in acknowledgment, not agreement.

He pressed one hand to his chest. "You cut me, hellcat." A hint of the old playfulness warmed his voice.

"You let me," I said, not the least bit sorry.

He reached out, those metal talons smoothing back my hair. "Don't let me find you again." And then the weight on my chest was gone and so was he. I lay on my floor, staring up at the ceiling, because even if vague threats were an effective interrogation tactic, I knew that he wasn't joking. He came here prepared to kill me.

I drew in a shaky breath and then picked up the knife and grabbed my phone. I called Remington first. He didn't answer. I hoped it was because it was after two in the morning and he was asleep.

"Wherever you are, make sure it's warded. The Crow Knight was just here. He asked after you. Someone wants to make an example of us."

After stuffing my computer and Wu, my stuffed tortoise, into my go-bag, I realized that I didn't have a fucking car right now. Goddamnit!

I sent Mwanje a warning, letting him know that the Courts were starting to take things seriously.

I sent Ivy a message, telling her not to come home.

And then I called Dreyson.

Chapter 14
Confidential Kitchen Conferences

投桃报李Trad.投桃報李 - Tóu táo bào lǐ – This one is easy enough. "Toss a peach, get back a plum." "Scratch my back, and I'll scratch yours." That's a lot less exciting than a random fruit-trading station, but I can't argue with the efficacy. One of the most important life lessons I learned wasn't on any school curriculum: bribery or social capital will make just about any encounter run a whole lot smoother.

— From the Very Personal Journals of FYG

DREYSON ANSWERED ON the second ring.

"The Crow Knight was here. Broke the wards and had orders to kill us. I don't know if he's actually gone, but I thought you should know."

"Are you under any compulsions?" he asked, voice gruff.

"Not that I know of."

"Where are you?"

"My place." I rattled off the address.

"I'll be there in a moment." He hung up.

I stared at the phone. Well, good for him? I was getting the fuck out, even if I had to call a taxi.

There was a knock at the front door. I stared, my left eye starting to twitch. That couldn't be him. Unless he was just hanging out around my place at night, which was a disturbing thought.

My phone buzzed; it was Dreyson. *I'm outside.*

I didn't hear any vehicles. I went to the door and checked the peephole.

Dreyson stood there in that long black duster, battleaxe on his back.

I opened the door.

He studied my face, like he was trying to gauge if this was a trap. "Would you be safer out here?"

"I have no idea." I shrugged.

"Your wards are demolished."

"I found that out the hard way," I said, stepping back so he could get through the door.

Dreyson ducked inside, looking around. He pointed to a chair in the living room. "Go sit over there." He tossed me a charm.

I caught the small piece of metal, shaped like a well-worn dog tag, the writing long faded. The magic was thick, something defensive.

I went over to the chair, pulled a blanket off the couch, and wrapped myself in it. I was shaking now. How embarrassing. Dreyson was in my house and he saw me in my fuzzy Sanrio pajamas. I pulled the blanket over my head, forcing myself to take deep slow breaths.

I could hear Dreyson walking through the halls, opening doors and checking rooms. Curled up in the chair, I stared at my phone, willing someone to answer me. But there was nothing.

"He's gone, Claire. I locked up."

I lowered the blanket, alarmed to find Dreyson standing in front of me. I didn't even realize he was in the room.

"Are you hurt?" he asked.

"I don't think so. He just knocked me down a few times."

"There's blood on your carpet."

"It's his. Used your knife. My gun jammed."

Dreyson looked at me for a long moment, his expression stark. "You're not safe here."

"He said as much. He said a lot, actually. And Remington's still not answering me."

"SIU found another scene," Dreyson said. "He's back on-site as a consultant."

That was a relief, well, not entirely. But I had an explanation for Remington's silence.

"Get your coat, your shoes, and whatever else you need. Pets?"

"No, my roommate is out of town." I shook my head, got up, grabbed my shoes, and trudged back to my bedroom, Dreyson following close behind.

There was a small bloodstain on my carpet. I grabbed my coat and picked up my bag.

"I should change-"

"We need to hurry," Dreyson said. "You have clothes in the bag?"

"Yeah."

He offered me his hand. "This won't be comfortable, but we'll be harder to follow. It's likely something is watching your house. Are you ready?"

I nodded. It was a lie. I was not ready.

He grasped my hand in his, and then the world folded in on itself.

Cold. Airless. Too bright for too long. Like being frozen in a flashbang. I fell, unable to scream or even move.

And then I was back on solid ground. I dropped onto my butt, my stomach in my throat. A wave of crippling nausea made me tuck my head between my knees and hyperventilate. My eyes watered. I dry heaved a few times, the world still spinning. It was almost as bad as that time I was hungover with major food poisoning. Doing all those shots and then eating the tuna salad at the all-night diner nearly obliterated me.

It took a moment for me to notice that I was sitting on a wood floor, Dreyson standing over me.

"This is awful," I groaned. "Dreyson, how could you do this to me? I thought we were friends. At least the Crow Knight promised to kill me quickly."

"First time with a teleport spell?" he asked, sounding amused.

"Are you sure you didn't mix that up with a projectile vomiting spell? Because I'm about to puke on your floor," I muttered. "Come closer, I'll get your shoes too."

"I can carry you to the bathroom," he said, and I could hear the smirk.

I glared up at him blearily. "If you touch me, I will puke on you."

"It will pass in a few minutes," he said. "If you haven't thrown up by now, you won't."

My stomach was pretty empty. No steak or fancy cake. I rested my head on my knees. "Where are we?"

"My house."

I raised my head in curiosity. We were at the foot of a staircase. In front of me was a long hallway with a couple open doors. The overhead lights were exposed fluorescent tubes. The stone walls held little recessed alcoves every few feet. It wasn't laid out like a house. Were we in a school or a church basement? Oh shit, did he pack me off to a nunnery? That seemed like a Catholic thing to do.

Another wave of nausea cut through me, but it was milder than before. Now that the sickness was receding, I could feel the prickle of ambient magic crawling along my skin. The air practically buzzed with energy. The Wergeld's Head of Arcane Security would have a ton of active defensive magic.

"Is my laptop safe?" I rubbed my eyes.

"I have a shielded room for electronics. If you have a protective case for your phone, leave it in there for now."

I nodded and instantly regretted it.

"We can put your computer in there." Dreyson gestured to the first door on the left.

I handed him the laptop bag, a brief flash of paranoia almost yanking my hand back. If he fried my electronics, I wouldn't have a way of contacting anyone. And no one knew I was with Dreyson. Fuck. I forced myself upright, slowly climbing to my feet, the world still swimming.

"Come to the kitchen," Dreyson said when he turned back to me. "I'll make you a cup of tea, and you can call Detective Remington in there. Do you need me to take your other bag?"

"No thanks," I said, reluctant to let it go. I leaned against the wall. "How bad was your first teleport?"

"Never had a problem myself, but it's a very common side effect." Dreyson had the nerve to chuckle.

"Ugh," I grumbled. He was tall, magical, and didn't get motion sickness. I *hated* him so much. Staggering forward, one hand on the wall, I followed him down the hall to a small cheery kitchen. It wasn't fancy, but it was clean and painted yellow. It contained an old gas range, a separate wall oven, and an ancient fridge. A blue metal kettle sat on the stovetop.

Dreyson snapped his fingers and the burner lit up.

I stumbled over to a wooden table with two chairs. One was handmade for a taller person, the other was mass-produced, the burgundy faux leather cracked and worn. I plunked down into it and rested my face on the cool wood of the table.

"I need to eat. I'm going to make egg sandwiches. Do you want one?"

"Sure," I said. "Once my insides stop trying to escape through my face."

Dreyson retrieved a frying pan from the cupboard and dropped a small pat of butter in. He did a perfectly decent job of frying up four eggs. There was a homemade loaf of bread on the counter that he cut into thick slices. He buttered each piece and cut up a tomato. The eggs were over easy. He salted the tomatoes, but he didn't add anything else, not pepper, or hot sauce, or even cheese…

Dreyson made a plate of sandwiches and set them on the table. The kettle began to whistle. He went to the cupboard and got out mugs. After filling two ceramic tea balls, he poured in the hot water.

It was relaxing to watch him work in the kitchen. The room was a little small for him, but he moved smoothly, like this was his normal routine.

"Chamomile and peppermint," he said, setting the steaming mug in front of me, along with a plate.

I inhaled the fragrant blend, cupping the warm ceramic. The steam was soothing. I was starting to feel better. "Thank you."

"How come every time I see you, something bad has happened or is about to happen?" he asked, sipping his tea.

I squinted at him over the rim of the mug. "How do I know it's not your fault?" Actually, I did know. "Because, for the record, you were the actual target in jail. I was only a bonus body."

Dreyson raised a brow. "You've confirmed it?"

"Yeah, did some digging yesterday." I sipped my tea and glanced at the sandwiches. "Is it safe to use my phone?"

He nodded.

I texted Remington the update, though I had limited signal and no new messages. Then I pulled up the video of Officer Ryan and turned my phone so Dreyson could watch it.

"Just a content warning, he's universally offensive," I said.

"Where did you get this?" he asked with a frown.

"Friend. We had serendipitous timing."

He watched it twice, jaw twitching at Ryan's accusation about his conduct. Then he took an egg sandwich. "I would like a copy."

"Can do," I said. "Though I'm going to have to share with SIU later."

Dreyson nodded, looking disgruntled. "So Hartford was calling the shots."

"Sounds like it," I said. "But I haven't been tracking him, not with everything else that's going on."

"There are other ways of getting answers," he said without any emotion, taking a drink of his tea.

I smiled, maybe too pleased by the prospect of comeuppance. "Just remember that I have to share this with SIU, so give yourself plausible deniability."

"Are you going to tell them that you sent me a copy?"

"Nope," I said. "But at the very least, they'll suspect."

Dreyson did not seem bothered by this. "Anything else relevant to the IPD issue?"

I sipped my tea. "Is there a reason why Bancroft-Owens has it out for you?"

Dreyson was mid-bite when I asked. He stared very hard at me, chewing slowly. "You think she's behind it?" he asked finally.

"Dunno. I have no evidence, but last night she expressed personal...irritation with you."

He nodded, like he wasn't surprised.

"Also, if I did think that she was trying to kill you, it would be very unwise of me to say so outright, because she's my boss's boss, and if we do a good job with this changeling problem, she's going to fix my situation with Commissioner Porter."

Dreyson remained stoic. "I don't think she's the one who ordered the hit. If she wanted me dead, it would have been handled competently, and we most likely would not be here."

"OK," I said, unsure if I believed him. But for the moment, I was glad that I didn't have to worry about split loyalties. "I heard they originally brought you up on obstruction charges."

"Someone requested a welfare check on Armstrong. It wasn't his wife. We're still not certain who exactly called it in." His voice wavered. "My people got him out, I stayed behind to stall. Usually they wouldn't bother detaining me over something so trivial. And when the regulars bring me in for something nonviolent, they usually put me in the general lockup."

I nodded. "How long were you in there before I arrived?"

"About two hours."

"Did you ask for a lawyer?"

"I did." He shrugged. "I wasn't worried. It's no surprise when cops aren't quick to do their jobs."

"Yeah." I clenched my fists. "Was the Wergeld actively looking for you?"

"Not yet, as there was no record of my arrest. They weren't concerned until they received your phone call." He tilted his head back. "I was out soon after you left. Detectives noted how quickly the word spread." He cleared his throat. "Did that cause problems for you?"

I shrugged, not wanting to broach that topic. "Some people have opinions, but if those people weren't there to handle my situation, their opinions don't matter as much, you know?" The edges of my smile were sharp enough to hurt.

Dreyson nodded solemnly.

"So given the fact Hartford doesn't know a wingding from an Enochian sigil, we can both agree that someone else helped him break the cellblock wards. Since he was working on behalf of Porter, and Porter isn't magically-talented, I'm thinking Ketch might be the one who ordered the hit, if it wasn't Bancroft-Owens."

Dreyson rubbed his chin. "Ketch has closer ties to the police brass than Bancroft-Owens does, so your reasoning is sound. But his motives for doing so aren't clear."

"No grudges?"

"I didn't say that," Dreyson said with a sigh. "But I wouldn't expect him to involve the IPD. That being said, imprisonment, mutilation, or death would make it difficult for me to continue this job."

"That tracks. I'm also wondering if he's behind the changeling murders too. No evidence, but he could." I took a sandwich. The bread was thick and fluffy with a crisp crust. It was plainer than I liked but not unsatisfying. "The bread is really good. Did you make it?"

He paused, his eye widening, like he was surprised I would ask. "Yes."

"Nice," I said. The bread soaked up the egg yolk. The tomato added a pleasant sharpness. The sandwich would have been elevated by hot sauce or cheese, but pointing that out would be rude.

"You heard that Armstrong was geas'd to confront the Vernal Lord." His voice grew rough.

"Rem mentioned it." I glanced up at him, unsure of why the mood shifted.

Dreyson glowered at the table, shoulder tensing, his anger practically vibrating in the air.

I fought the urge to scoot backward.

"Detective Al-Rashid did the workup on Armstrong's afflictions. It wasn't Fey magic." Dreyson looked at me. "In the post-mission reports, no one mentioned any third parties getting near Armstrong. Detective Remington confirmed that with Salvatore last night."

Dreyson missed the lead-up to the confrontation because he was with me. I tapped my foot, understanding what he was so reluctant to say. "Was one of your team responsible, then?"

"Liam doesn't have the skillset. It was Naomi," he said, making a guttural sound of disgust. "She's a veteran. I've worked with her for years. Never would have expected this."

I nodded sympathetically. Naomi also provided the maps in the Shadow Dunes. Maybe it was no accident they were useless. "Why would she do that?"

"Don't know." Dreyson rubbed his temples. "She's gone to ground."

"What now?" I asked, picturing some kind of medieval punishment or violent manhunt.

"If she's lucky, she'll get half her pension, but the penalties for this many contract breaches are high. No one in the guild will ever work with her again. Armstrong's family also has the option of seeking retribution."

I blinked. That wasn't what I expected. "What about you and Liam?"

"The family has priority. We're abstaining for now." Dreyson shook his head. "I'm displeased to say the least, but I'd like to hear her explanation first."

"I'm sorry," I said.

"We weren't friends," Dreyson said stiffly.

"Sure, but it sounds like you depended on her at times, so that still sucks." Dreyson nodded curtly.

"More tea?" I asked, getting up to refill my cup.

"Please."

I took his mug and poured us both more hot water.

"Are you going to tell me about the Crow Knight's...visit?" he asked as I set the cup down in front of him.

I froze, then exhaled slowly. "Sure." I pulled my feet up into the chair, knees tucked against my chest. "I woke up, tried to fight, lost pretty quickly. Then instead of killing me, he started a sad conversation about how he needed to make an example of someone and gave a stupid apology about how he didn't *actually* want to hurt me, how he was looking for you or Remington instead." I glared at the table. "That fucking pissed me off, you know? 'I'm not a bad guy, I don't want to hurt you. I was just planning on killing your other best friend, *the crippled lawman*. Look what a nice guy I am.' Ugh." I vented the disgust from the back of my throat.

Dreyson made a cautious "hmm" noise.

"He couldn't resist telling me how hard things were for him, but he also very obviously gave me an opening to convince him not to kill me. I don't know if that was just a ploy for information, but I think the Courts were trying to avoid the attention of Ketch and Bancroft-Owens. I pointed out that it was too late for that. He called them the *Lares*."

"Pretentious titles," Dreyson said with a scowl. "But yes, that's their role."

"The Crow Knight said he was going to report back to his boss, and that I should be harder to find, and the obvious warning to stop working this case."

Dreyson nodded, dropping his gaze. "Do you need to see a medical professional tonight?"

"What do you mean? I'm not inj— *Oh.*" I coughed. "No, nothing like that happened. He says he's not into rape, plus breaking into my room and threatening my friends doesn't put me in the mood. Shocking, I know!" The words spilled out rapidly.

Dreyson watched me with that careful gaze, like he was looking for holes in my story or cracks in my facade. I didn't have a good poker face, so I didn't think I was hard to read at all.

"It is worth considering why he let you go."

"So he could follow me back to you, Remington, or a higher-value target, obviously," I said, because I wasn't an idiot. "And even if that's not the case, this visit demonstrated that it's best to assume he's hostile. I know he let me cut him, I don't know why, but he seems like he's into that." I gave a tired shrug. "I do believe he was told to kill me and that he really was reluctant to do so, for whatever reason. Don't care, though. The information he got about the *Lares* seemed to be news to him."

Dreyson nodded.

I rubbed my hands together, letting my legs drop back down. "You said there was another killing tonight? How does the timing line up?"

"Not sure yet." He leaned back in his chair, crossing his arms. "There are a lot of changelings in Illium. Do you know why?"

"I do not." I rested my elbows on the table, chin in my hands. "But I am dying to find out. Nearly have a couple times already."

Dreyson rolled his eye at me, but gave me that faint sardonic smile. "Really, Claire?"

I liked this, I realized. We were sitting here, drinking tea and talking, trading information in his kitchen. I usually did this with better food, but here we were again, in the wee hours of the morning, having snacks and conversation. Sure, it was mostly shop talk, but I liked it.

"Over a decade ago, there was a malg-tech company that paired with the Courts to address their fertility issues."

Many of the Fey lived for a very long time, partially because of time dilation between their realm and ours, partially because they had magical longevity. But the trade-off was that their birthrates were extremely low.

"They tried all kinds of treatments, with a malg-tech twist. IVF backed up with growth and probability charms, the use of homunculi for genetic testing, IUI processes tailored to sidhe physiology. They even used a variety of volunteer surrogates from other species."

"Oh," I said, wrinkling my nose.

"In the tales, the Fey didn't have a problem interbreeding with humans and other things. Had a lot more luck, in fact. But in the interest of…preserving the species or maintaining old bloodlines, that's not exactly what they wanted."

"They were trying to produce purebred Fey test-tube babies."

"Yes, but it wasn't working, or at least they weren't getting the results at the rates they wanted. The Courts were about to pull the plug on the project when one of the founders hit upon something different. Something that got them excited. And that's where my details dry up, because six months later, everyone working on the project was dead or in hiding."

"Yikes," I said, not expecting that. Six months wasn't even a full gestation period for humans. Maybe it was for Fey? What happened?

"The project was called the Foxglove Pact," Dreyson said. "I can't find anything else about it."

My mind flashed back to the mark on Innis' stomach and the ledger. *Oh.*

"You know something," he said, leaning forward.

"Maybe," I said. "That name just connected some dots." I did not want to lie to Dreyson, not here and not now. But in my book, lies of omission had more leeway. "You saw the picture of Armstrong's baby and the birthmark."

He nodded.

I showed him pictures of the ledger I found in the Fey archive. "They were birthdates, from ten years ago." I bit my lip and added what Bancroft-Owens left out. "There were some with a second date, all within the last six months. But I don't know what that second date means."

"Death or retrieval?" Dreyson frowned. "And with these changeling murders, are they tying up loose ends, or is something else going on?"

"Don't know, but we're looking closer at HerbAway right now."

"Yes, if you want to compare notes—"

My phone lit up. It was Remington. "I need to take this!" I picked up immediately. "Rem?"

"Hey." His familiar voice was a welcome relief, even though he sounded exhausted. "You good?"

"Yeah, you?"

"Long night. Sorry I didn't see your message sooner. Was working with Jon. It got messy." He blew out a long breath. "So they're onto us now and they're going to be homicidal about it?"

"Looks like it," I said.

"We'll reinforce the office wards tonight and look into fixing up your place later." He cleared his throat. "Are you still with Dreyson?"

"Yup."

"How do you feel?" he asked softly.

"Terrible, I must've gone to bed sober," I said, quoting the safety passphrase to him.

He chuckled with obvious relief at the stupid quote. "Yeah, sounds about right. You're not hurt?"

"Nope, mad as hell, though."

"Me too," he said, and I could hear his smile. "Do you need a pickup? It'll be a bit, but I can get Jon to—"

"Is it OK if I hang out here longer?" I asked Dreyson, not in the mood to deal with the lieutenant.

He nodded.

"No, I'm good," I said cheerfully.

There was a long pause.

I waited for him to say something dumb.

"I'm glad you're OK," Remington said in a tone that let me know that other people were now listening in. "Call me or Mwanje if you need anything. We've turned up the ringers on our phones."

"Thanks," I said.

"Be *safe*."

I hung up, rolling my eyes. To be fair, I said the same thing when he went out on hookups, but clearly the circumstances were different. He was going places with the intent of having sex. I just had to leave my comfy bed because the Fey Court sucked. I took a sip of my tea.

"Detective Remington is a Dashiell Hammett fan?"

I set my mug down, a little surprised that he knew the quote. "Yeah, doesn't he look like one?"

"Sure, but I didn't realize he enjoyed reading," Dreyson said with just a little bit of derision.

"He prefers the movies," I said, wanting to defend my friend, but alas, I could not. Remington was perfectly literate and kept numerous reference volumes around the office, but he did not read for fun. Sometimes he listened to audio dramas, mostly because I checked them out of the library for him.

Dreyson gave me a thoughtful look.

I yawned then. "Do you mind if I crash on your couch or something? I'm starting to lose steam" I picked up my mug and the empty plates, and carried them to the sink. "Should I—"

"Leave them," he said, bringing his mug over. "Follow me. I'll show you where you can rest."

144

Chapter 15
Slumber Party Confessions

妙在不言中- Miào zài bù yán zhōng. The charm lies in what is left unsaid I guess this is true. Things that aren't said can be great mysteries, which are interesting by default. And sure, oversharing can be a real ordeal. Both my parents have said this to me in the vain hope that I would talk less. When my dad says it, he smiles. When my mother says it, what she means is "shut up."

— *From the Very Personal Journals of FYG*

DREYSON'S BATHROOM WAS tidy with a big tub. I valiantly resisted the urge to snoop in the medicine cabinet. My go-bag held all the toiletries I needed.

Dreyson waited in the hall and showed me to another room a little farther in. It was a large bedroom with spring-green walls, several bookshelves, a large weapon rack, and an abundance of plants placed all over. There were no windows, but there were a few UV lamps, so it didn't feel too oppressive. The bed was huge, with a dove-gray comforter. I took off my shoes. The gray carpet was soft and thick, and the entire chamber felt surprisingly cozy.

"Is this your bedroom?" I asked, studying the bed.

"I...don't often have guests," he said, clearing his throat. "It's the only comfortable sleeping quarters."

I glanced at him, but Dreyson was looking away.

"You can have the bed," he said. "I already have a sleeping roll—"

"I can take the floor. It's *your* bed."

"You're the guest," he said. "And if the Crow Knight manages to track us down, I'll be up faster."

Was that actually a valid argument? I wasn't sure. But I didn't point out that the bed was big enough for both of us and maybe two more people. He had to know that already.

"If you're uncomfortable with my presence, I can go—" he added quickly.

"No, I just feel bad displacing you." I winced, realizing that he was being considerate. Why did good manners kick in now of all times? "Are you sure—"

"There is also a pest animal on the loose, and the bed is warded against such things," Dreyson said.

"A what?"

Dreyson sighed. "You took your shoes off—"

"Like a civilized person!" I said sharply. "I would've done so when I got in, but I was distracted by trying not to throw up all over your floor!"

"You'll threaten to throw up all over my floor, but think it's rude to leave your shoes on?" he asked, deadpan.

"Yes!" I said. "They're unrelated, and you know it!"

He stared at me like he didn't know it. Then he cleared his throat. "If you have to use the facilities, put your shoes back on."

"OK, but what's on the loose in your house that *you* can't catch?"

"A...larger-than-natural Brazilian wandering spider," he said, looking embarrassed.

"Is it a pet? Or an assassination attempt?" I asked, my voice going high, because *spiders*. Did not want. Also, would he have mentioned it if it was nonvenomous?

"An unwanted guest," he said, averting his eyes. "It's a long story and also why you shouldn't explore the building unaccompanied."

Would I do that? Absolutely. But I was a guest, and straight-up snooping would be rude. So I looked around, checking the ceiling and peering at the plants. I marched up to the bed and pulled back the blankets, half expecting something to scuttle out. The sheets looked clean. I shook the pillows. Nothing fell out.

"It's probably not there," he said. "It can't hide very well in here. It's too big."

I slowly turned my head to stare at him incredulously.

"It doesn't like light, and it's the size of a rabbit, but it doesn't hop. It's just very venomous."

What the fuck? What the actual fuck? I covered my face with both hands. "That's awful. I think I'm going to take my chances with the Courts."

"Oh come on, the fangs aren't that big, maybe half a finger-length."

I looked up in horror to see Dreyson chuckling to himself.

"Oh, you *asshole*," I growled as I realized he was just fucking with me. "Did you make that whole story up?"

"No, there really is some kind of tropical spider loose, but I don't know if it's venomous, and it is within a normal size range." He smirked.

I set my bag on his dresser and plugged in my phone, because I couldn't tell if he was *still* joking. What was the normal size for a tropical spider anyway?

"Don't wander off, though. I wasn't joking about the security protocols. It's especially dangerous for the kind of woman who explores the Autumn Court on a whim. Normal people have stronger self-preservation instincts."

"I was working," I said, even if he had a point.

He just shook his head and went to the closet to get out a sleeping bag. He shut the bedroom door as he passed by.

"Did the spider come in your plants?" I asked, suddenly suspicious of Trojan houseplants concealing their treacherous bounty of arachnid hordes.

"After a fashion," he said. "You'll be safe in the bed. I'll show you the thing in the morning."

I gave a huff of annoyance and climbed into the bed. Still in my pajamas, I pulled the comforter up, frowning at how light it was.

"Will you need another blanket?" Dreyson asked as he unrolled his sleeping bag.

"Maybe," I said.

Dreyson went back to the closet and brought out a blue quilt. He placed it beside me and set his sleeping bag a couple feet to the right of the bed, closer to the door.

"Pillows?"

"Please," he said.

I tossed him two.

He caught them with ease.

"More?" I asked, though there were only four on the bed.

"I'll be fine."

I spread out the quilt and nestled under the blankets, lying on my side to face him.

Dreyson was on his back. He had enough room to stretch out on his floor. "Lights off?" he asked, glancing over at me.

"Sure."

The lights faded slowly, something that could be done with a remote, but I felt that frisson of power from him.

"Show-off."

His laugh in the dark was low and rich.

There was a faint gleam under the door, hall lights. I could find my way out if necessary. I lay there in that big bed, again very conscious of the fact that Dreyson and I could easily fit in here together, with divider pillows even. But instead, he was on the floor.

But mentioning that in the dark seemed more...significant than it should. It was still just the two of us here, but now it felt different. The atmosphere was suddenly heavier. I was very aware of him, only a few feet away. I rolled onto my back and stared up at the ceiling, though I couldn't see much. I lay there for awhile, unable to close my eyes or even relax. The weight of that discomfort continued to bear down on my chest. I rolled onto my other side; it was no better. I ended up on my back again, the pressure still growing.

"Hey." I kept my voice low, in case Dreyson was already asleep, oblivious to my anxieties. "You awake?"

"Yes." He was quiet, but he didn't sound like he had been sleeping either.

I had questions for him, a lot of them. And we had privacy now. We had privacy in his kitchen, but that felt different. Sitting at the table in the light was not the same as lying here in the dark. This was the time to ask: Why did he almost attack me in the jail? Why did he come looking for me in the Shadow Dunes? Why did he bail me out tonight?

But I couldn't quite bring myself to start with the important ones. "So...you and Nikita?"

He gave a sharp exhalation. "Really? You want to ask about that?"

"Well, we both know how Arcady is. We can talk about him too," I said, laughing awkwardly.

He fell silent. I wished I could see his face, but I was glad he couldn't see mine. He *might* have magical night vision, but I had one arm over my eyes and the illusion of privacy.

"It was a long time ago," Dreyson said, clearing his throat. "She initiated. It was pleasant. We kept it professional thereafter."

So Nikita seduced Dreyson? I considered that for a moment. Well, it seemed he did like women. Or Nikita was just that powerful.

"I meant to ask." He cleared his throat. "When you told the Crow Knight that you were interested in someone else, who were you referring to?" There was a rustle from the sleeping bag.

I exhaled slowly. "I didn't actually say I was dating anyone, because I'm not. I just said there was someone that I 'cared about,' to put him off. It's true. I care deeply about Remington, but we're not like that. Never have been."

"Ah." There was a lot of weight in that syllable. "The detective has a...reputation."

"Oh yeah, he's very popular. But we couldn't work together if we did. Good boundaries, and I think we're too much alike."

"How so?"

"He's my friend and my work partner: I put him first in certain situations, and he does the same for me. But if we dated, that would get tangled up, and I think we would start to resent the job or each other. It would happen specifically with us, because we're so similar." I laughed awkwardly. "Not to mention the age gap. He's about twenty years older than me. It's not a deal-breaker, but it's not something I pursue either."

"Nikita and Arcady are much older than that."

"I know," I said, rolling my eyes. "That's different. Arcady isn't looking for anything long-term. We just...enjoy each other's company on occasion. He's cordial and fun. We keep it light." And Arcady invited us both to visit him, at the same time. That thought did not leave my head. "Is it different for you?"

"Claire, given my current employment, that sort of relationship with Arcady would be frowned upon."

That didn't answer my question, but it wasn't a denial either. "Is it just Mori, or is the Wergeld homophobic too? Damn, Dreyson. Why do you work for—"

"It's complicated," he said sharply. "Like your relationship with SIU."

My words stopped. Objectively, we both knew that we investigated each other. It was a matter of practicality, something you did when you worked a high-stakes job with another entity. But thus far, we were able to avoid talking about it and our potentially conflicting sides.

There was another kind of tension between us now.

"I'm a contractor at best. You're the Head of Arcane Security. You're an integral part of the operation."

"Doesn't mean it's not complicated."

I didn't know exactly what he meant, but I could believe it. He was high up in the Wergeld, but maybe the reasons he stayed were complex ones. They paid his legal fees. Maybe there was some kind of debt.

"Do you want to talk about it?" I asked.

"Later," he said, after a couple seconds of silence. "It's a conversation for later."

"OK," I said. Part of me wanted to press, to demand more answers, but we didn't know each other *that* well. And if he tried to make me talk about things I wasn't ready for, I certainly wouldn't take it gracefully. The least I could do was respect that boundary. I groped for another subject. "So, what's your take on the Crow Knight?"

Dreyson sighed heavily. "Really, Claire?"

"Because you two have insane tension; I know it's probably just the bloodthirst on your end, but is there history there?"

"No. I was aware of him before this, but we never interacted. His reputation seemed…grimmer."

"Aww, you bring out his playful side."

"That was clearly my intent," Dreyson said dryly. "Who doesn't want to court the homicidal flirtations of a manipulative Fey assassin with an avian fixation?"

"Some people like that sort of thing," I said with a laugh.

"Do you?"

"I could take it or leave it," I said, shaking one hand from side to side. "Mostly leave it, because while I like banter, I don't like worrying about being murdered by whoever is in my bed. Though it is fascinating to watch other people with that urge." Remington had an unhealthy weakness for women who could, and would, obliterate him.

"I'm glad you find this so entertaining," Dreyson muttered, his bedding crinkling as he shifted inside the sleeping bag. "But I agree with you. I dislike the idea of being murdered by whoever is in my bed."

I wanted to ask more about the Crow Knight's reputation, but then I realized something. "I know you meant 'in my bed' in the metaphorical sense, but as I'm literally borrowing your bed, I want to assure you that I have no intention of trying to murder you, even as foreplay, as that would be extraordinarily rude, beyond the pale even."

"I appreciate that," Dreyson said, not sounding especially worried.

"I also realize that this declaration is not actually comforting, now that I've said it aloud, but honestly it's a catch-22. If I don't say something, it's suspicious. If I protest, it's possibly disingenuous. Honestly, the smart thing to do would be to shut my mouth, but we both know how terrible I am at that."

Dreyson laughed softly. "You make it work."

My lips quirked upward at the compliment. "Yeah, I do."

"I suspect the Crow Knight has a soft spot for you because you're so clever."

I snorted. "I wouldn't call—"

"I didn't say that he isn't a danger to you or that he has treated you courteously, but for whatever reason, he hasn't used the full extent of his abilities against you. But I don't think you can count on things staying that way."

"Yeah, I figured. But I don't think he's that interested in me. He's just using me as an extension of his power games with you."

"Possibly," Dreyson said. "But I don't enjoy those kinds of games."

"Same," I grumbled. "So is he actually attractive? I haven't seen his face. The one time I saw him without the helmet, there was way too much blood."

"He isn't bad to look at," Dreyson said, his voice steady and painfully disinterested. "The armor is ridiculously impractical and overly dramatic. But he's fast, strong, and good in a fight, which are all attractive features. But I don't make a habit of flirting with the enemy."

"Probably wise," I said, though I would absolutely flirt with someone to lower their guard, but that was for survival, not fun.

"When we run into him again, don't worry about it," Dreyson said, his voice going gravelly. "I can handle him. I misjudged the situation last time. It won't happen again."

"OK," I said, unsure of what to say to that. "He's damn fast."

"I know," Dreyson said. "But last time I held back. That was a miscalculation. I didn't want to cause an incident, and I didn't think you would get involved like you did. But circumstances have clearly changed."

"What do you mean about my involvement?" I asked.

"This isn't a condemnation," he said. "I thought you would leave once the fighting started, because that would have been the smart thing to do. But you did not. And he did not behave how I expected either. I thought he would draw the match out, given how hard he pressed for the fight. But he was more interested in bringing you into the mix, and he baited you into staying."

I pursed my lips. "That was the rudest way to ask for a threesome. Arcady did it way better, don't you think?"

Dreyson made a strangled sound and started to cough.

"Anyway, if I ran, he would have tried to use me as a hostage," I said quickly, realizing what I blurted out.

"I think you're right," Dreyson said after a moment.

"About being a hostage or—"

"About being a hostage," he said quickly. "I've considered the different ways that scenario could have gone, and I am grateful that you made the choices you did, even if they drew the wrong kind of attention."

"I…you're welcome. I'm pretty grateful to you too. Wondering what you told Mori, though."

"I recounted the events that transpired. Salvatore pays attention to what goes on in the Wergeld," Dreyson said carefully. "I think your impromptu involvement piqued his curiosity. He might try to recruit you, but you can decline without fear of repercussions."

"Good to know." I lay there, wondering if he really meant that. Dreyson might, but did Mori? "It's your turn for a question."

"If you don't want to talk about it, I understand. But why did you choose to work with SIU, given what happened a few years ago?"

I thought about playing tit for tat. He kept his story to himself, so I would keep mine. But it was not the same situation. My story was in the papers. Nothing about Dreyson's outward demeanor hinted that he had reservations about being the Wergeld berserker. There was different weight to things done in secrecy.

"If you're tired, or if you'd prefer to keep it light," he began, his voice softer, conciliatory.

"You probably already know most of it. It's no secret." I adjusted the pillows, turning to face him in the dark.

"I'd still like to hear it from you," he said, his tone gentle. "Unless it makes you uncomfortable."

I snorted. "No. It's old hat, and I don't have trouble talking about the past. You probably know that I still live with Ivy Beaumont, though I haven't seen much of her lately. We were college roommates."

Dreyson made a "hmm" sound, encouragement to continue.

"I wanted to go to law school. Ivy was already working for her godfather, Blake Canaris. She wanted to do criminal law and play for the defense. Canaris and her WASP family didn't like this, but Ivy does what Ivy wants."

"Sounds familiar," Dreyson said.

I smiled. "Anyway, she's working for Evelyn Vilkas, and they're handling defense for this big scandal coming out of the comptroller's office. The old bastard is guilty as hell, but he's got an imperial ton of dirt to spread around. So Ivy does her due diligence, passing out subpoenas like Halloween candy. She gets the fucking police commissioner and decimates him on the stand for the shit he pulled during his tenure as a DA investigator. By the time Vilkas's crew is done, everyone looks bad, and the comptroller walks away, looking no worse than everybody else. Those revelations launched more investigations. Don't think they went anywhere, but everyone was outraged for at least a week."

Dreyson coughed.

"Now Commissioner Porter has a son who's about to enter the police academy. And he's pissed about how Ivy wrecked his papa's shit. This asshole shows up at our apartment. I hear him yelling, and then..." I gritted my teeth. "I come out to see him beating her bloody. He says some bullshit to me, like, 'Do you know who my dad is?' and other sexist, racist tripe that doesn't need to be repeated. But he broke Ivy's jaw and wasn't about to stop. I shot him five times in the chest. It was a good grouping. Dad was proud."

There was a lot more screaming and crying than I wanted to describe, so I didn't. It was bloody and ugly, and Ivy and I both remembered it in vivid detail.

"He wasn't actually a cop, but he was close enough." I smiled tightly. "They arrested me immediately. Tried to spin it as a domestic dispute. Detained me for hours. Turned the cameras off." I blew out a breath. "Ivy was out of it, and I wasn't allowed to call anyone. They kept at me, hoping to get me to incriminate myself. But I'm no idiot. I knew better than to give them the time of day. I just asked for a lawyer. Repeatedly. Said it, chanted it, maybe sang it too.

"It took hours, but Canaris himself got me out. I couldn't afford him, still can't. But Ivy made a deal. He wanted her to switch fields, to go to the corporate side. It's safer and more lucrative. In exchange, he takes care of my ongoing issues. And he's kept the bargain. He just made one of my best friends give up her dream in exchange. She was already working for him. Why the fuck would he make her do that?" I sniffled. "I hate it, you know? She worked so damn hard, and for what? She says she likes the new job, that it's interesting and fulfilling. Like I can't tell when she's lying."

"I'm sorry," Dreyson said.

"Me too. But anyway, Porter Junior had a history of sexual assault and violence. Daddy covered it up, but Canaris had enough to smear them with. They spent a lot of time trying to link Junior and Ivy romantically, but it didn't work, and proving self-defense was easy. Ivy's face was enough evidence. So

I never went to court, but that's when the real harassment began. By then I'd seen enough of the law's failures. Lost my taste for it."

"Hypocrisy is a bitter pill,' Dreyson said. "And the system is rife with it."

I sighed. "I know. But I met Remington in jail. I think that's where I've met a lot of my favorite people. But that's another story. He wasn't a cop anymore, but he got Detective Mwanje to let me out, and well… Working with Rem afforded me another layer of protection, but he has enemies too. And surprise, surprise, they overlap with mine."

"You're the one who broke open that occultist judge case for SIU," Dreyson said. And I wondered who told.

"I guess. It was more that SIU was busy, so Rem and I got called in as auxiliaries. He's a magical null, so I did the dowsing, much to the chagrin of the asshole detective in charge. It was less formal ritualism and more hellhole murder dungeon." I closed my eyes. That was another nightmare day, descending into that blood-soaked basement, only to have that girl die on the table in front of me.

"Who taught you about Illium's underworld?" Dreyson asked.

"Canaris and Rem. I didn't have an education on the preternatural before I killed Porter Junior. Afterward I started seeing things, and they filled in some of the blanks. I've been digging ever since. Canaris has offered me a job, but…I don't really want to play more of his games. I'm too enmeshed already." I squeezed a pillow. "So here I am, playing these games instead… This is not the life I thought I would have."

Dreyson was quiet, though I didn't think he had fallen asleep.

I'd definitely earned more answers from him. "So why are you in the modern version of the Inquisition? Maybe not why you stayed, but why you joined in the first place. How does one become an axe-wielding battlemage? I did not see the option for that educational track in high school."

Dreyson sighed. "I didn't grow up in Illium. The monsters here are different…more human I guess."

"Ready access to support services and specialized care makes it easier to survive, thereby reducing the need for violence," I said brightly. It was something Remington like to remind SIU of. "If you treat someone like a monster, don't be surprised if they behave like one."

"That too," Dreyson said, reluctantly. "But it is *not* like that everywhere."

"Makes sense," I said, though I was a lifelong resident of Illium.

"My skills manifested young. I was sent to exclusive boarding schools that handled occult education, mostly in Europe. They were a combination of upper-crust British institutions and penal military academies. The common thread in these establishments was to put a bunch of younger boys in the care of older boys, with the expectation that this would toughen them up and teach them how to be men."

"Oh, not good," I said, because I had read *Lord of the Flies* and I had an older brother. Though Lee was never a bully.

"Part of the education was how to hunt monsters. Often because they were causing serious problems: *upirs*, *púcaí*, night hags, werewolves. Our instructors were capable, but there were still casualties."

"That's not right. How old were you?" I asked, voice going high.

"I was thirteen when I went on my first hunt," Dreyson said. He had a plainspoken tone, one that allowed no sympathy. Some people who went through bad things had a certain way of speaking about the trauma, both detached and viscerally honest. I recognized it well enough; sometimes I used it too. "When I was sixteen, a coven set up near our school. We thought they were harmless. Later that year, we went on a hunt in a forest nearby. Something was killing livestock. We suspected a werewolf. Fifteen people went in, a dozen students and three instructors. Only two students stumbled out. Gregory did not survive his injuries." Dreyson's voice remained cool, his words precise.

I wanted to ask for more information, but I just listened to Dreyson's irregular breathing.

"I'll tell you more, if you want to know," he said after a very long pause. "But I'll ask that you wait till later. It is not a story for the dark."

"OK." I wanted to hear more, but Dreyson's palpable discomfort filled the space between us.

"It's different outside Illium," he said, his voice a bare rumble. "Some places are similar, but not many. I think you agree that a preternatural being has the potential to cause much more damage than a mundane human. I came out of school very good at two pursuits: killing things and doing research. Monster hunting pays more than academia and is only slightly more violent."

I laughed. "I can't afford to be a grad student in this economy!"

"Exactly!"

I yawned, wearing out, but not wanting to sleep just yet. "Are you sure you're comfortable down there?"

"Don't tease, Claire," he growled. "I'm staying on the floor tonight."

"Oh," I said, breath catching as my heart rate spiked. "I wasn't trying to—"

"I know," Dreyson said. "But we've had a stressful couple of days. Things keep trying to kill you. That affects people."

"I'm dealing," I said, squinting at his silhouette. Which one of us did he think was "affected"? And what did that entail? "People are trying to kill you too."

"I'm used to it," he said. "It doesn't change how I do things."

"I'm not," I muttered. "Even if I should be."

"You're holding up, given the circumstances. You're a survivor. You'll find a way through this," he told me with a shocking amount of confidence.

That was nice to hear from a guy who won fights against monsters. "Thanks." I smiled. I *was* a survivor. I *could* be brave. I could just ask a simple question. "Why did you come looking for me in the Shadow Dunes?"

Dreyson exhaled slowly.

"I'm not complaining, and I'm certainly not ungrateful—"

"I thought you were in trouble," Dreyson said, voice steady. "And it turned out that I was right."

He answered the question, but then he actually didn't. Or maybe I just didn't ask the correct question. "Dreyson—"

"It's getting late," he said. "We have work to do tomorrow. I need some sleep."

"Yeah. OK," I said.

"Good night, Claire," Dreyson said firmly.

"Good night, Dreyson," I said, understanding that this conversation was over, though not *why*. I certainly didn't believe he was suddenly that tired.

And even if he was, I lay there wide-awake, for a very long time.

Chapter 16
Where Everyone Fits

<RogueRunner> Keep any kids and pets away. Call the emergency animal control number. Specify this is about an unknown preternatural predator. Tell them everything. There will be a $50 fee for coming out. Pay it. Best/cheapest resource to identify your problem. If it's something small, they can remove it. If it's something bigger or smarter, they might not be able to, and then you should look into negotiating. Or call the Wergeld. If it's flat-out committing violent crimes, call the Special Investigations Unit of the IPD.

<farmerjojo> I could try to fix it myself first.

<RogueRunner> If you don't even know what it is, then you don't know how to get rid of it. Do not pick up "quick remedies" from anyone in the Sticks. You can go to the Medicine House in Chinatown. The proprietor might be able to give you another solution, but it will cost a lot more.

<farmerjojo> It can't be that tough if it's only taking ducks.

<RogueRunner> Lol, if you want to presume on the unconfirmed good nature of an unidentified cryptid, that's your mistake to make.

<farmerjojo> Can't I just dump cement or dynamite into the pond?

<RogueRunner> You could. And maybe that would work, or maybe that would just piss it off and get your household cursed for seven generations. I know someone who has a very old kelpie in her pond. Those things run faster than a race car and devour human flesh. If she tried to kill it, it would probably do that curse thing. Instead, she made a deal. She gets it slabs of beef, and it keeps other monsters off her property and away from her livestock.

<farmerjojo> oh. Can I get those numbers?

— *From the Very Personal Journals of FYG*

IT HAD BEEN a while since I woke up alone in an unfamiliar bed. The room was dark, and I had no idea what time it was. I groped for my phone; it was only nine in the morning, but Dreyson's room didn't have windows. I had texts from Remington, Mwanje, and Ivy. I responded with a generic "Alive, will check in after coffee" message and lay there for a moment...in Dreyson's bed.

I sat up straight, flicked on my phone light, and rolled out of bed, putting on my shoes before I opened the door, because *rogue tropical spider*.

I squinted under the hall lights. The bathroom door was open. There was another open door around the corner. I shuffled to the bathroom first, to do my morning routine and change clothes.

There was dried blood on my pajamas – I somehow missed it last night. Ugh. I could clean up blood, as anyone who menstruated and did their own laundry could. But it was the principle of the matter. That asshole attacked me in my own bedroom, threatened Remington, and then had the nerve to bleed on my stuff. Yeah, there were bigger things to worry about, but those feelings were daunting. It was much easier to be mad about having to clean up after the Crow Knight.

Once I looked presentable—or at least like I wasn't attacked in the middle of the night in my bed, I headed around the corner to the other open door. Spiders? I could handle. In theory. Dreyson's draconian security? Maybe not.

Something grunted.

I peeked around the door frame.

It was a gym, with a weight bench, a variety of exercise machines, and mirrored walls. In the far corner, Dreyson hung from a bar, knees bent as he did pull-ups. He grunted again, muscles rippling as he performed textbook-perfect sets. He wore a thin white tank top and gray sweatpants, and judging by how damp his shirt was, he had been at it for awhile now.

It would be a lie to say that I didn't notice how well-built he was. It would also be a lie to say I was looking *respectfully*.

But it was not OK to just gawk at him, even if I suspected that he already knew I was here. So I knocked on the open door before going in.

Dreyson dropped from the bar and grabbed a towel off the bench. Wiping his flushed face, he came to the door. "You're up early."

I wasn't sure what he meant by that, considering he was up longer than me and we lay down around the same time. "I guess. I need coffee."

He drew back, startled. "I don't have any."

I stared at him. It took me longer than I wanted to admit to process that. "Huh."

"I have tea," he said.

"OK, I'll go make tea," I said. "You don't keep poisons incorrectly labeled in your cupboard, do you? You know, it says rosemary, but it's really arsenic."

"No," he said slowly. "Who does that?"

"Some people," I said. "Which is why I asked. I'm going to go make caffeine and food."

"I can—"

"You're doing Dreyson stuff," I said, waving a hand. "Don't worry, I can make egg sandwiches or something."

He regarded me, jaw twitching, like he was trying to conceal his alarm. "I'm about done. I'll go shower. Then I can—"

"It's just egg sandwiches." I scowled. "I'll even leave off the poison."

"How generous," he said, one corner of his mouth lifting. "What about fires?"

"No promises," I said with a shrug. "You're not the only one who can cause rampant flaming destruction."

"I'll make it a quick shower, then," Dreyson said, brushing by me with a chuckle.

Bag slung over my shoulder, I made my way back down the hall to the kitchen. I turned on the lights and started the kettle.

Rifling through Dreyson's cupboard netted me a nice Earl Grey. He had quite a lot of tea, but not a lot of spices, which wasn't really a surprise. I got out the salt and pepper, then went through his fridge. There wasn't much in it: a jug of milk, protein shakes, and eggs. The drawers had tomatoes, wilting green onions, and a salad. I found a little container of unopened packages of cayenne and parmesan with the "Sal's" label on it. That was Salvatore Mori's family restaurant in Old Town. He probably ate there regularly. Finding some chili crisps or a good hot sauce would have been the jackpot, but I could make do.

I washed the pan from last night, heated it up, and slapped some butter in it. Using a glass, I cut little circles in the bread, then dropped the slices and the cutouts into the pan, cracking eggs to fill the centers. I sprinkled the slices with cayenne, parmesan, and salt, but made a few plain ones, because maybe Dreyson *liked* bland food. Which was sad, but he was sequestered at a boys' school in England, so there were a lot of tragedies in his background.

I stacked the "eggs in a basket" and the little fried bread rounds on a plate, sliced up the tomato, and made two cups of tea. I took it black, because sometimes when I added milk to Earl Grey, the bergamot oil, the temperature, or some fairy curse curdled it, and I was too groggy to fuck around with that.

The tea was good quality. I sipped it and took an egg-filled toast slice, happily eating it with my hands. Dipping the crispy little buttered bread round in the yolk was even better.

Dreyson entered the kitchen, now wearing black compression gear, his hair damp, another towel around his shoulders. His gaze went to the stove first. When it was apparent that there was no fire and the burners were off, he sat down at the table with me.

"Want?" I pushed the plate toward him.

"Thank you for cooking. You didn't have to." He studied the cooling mug of tea and the golden-brown fried egg-bread. Sighing, he gave me a disgruntled look and took a gulp of tea. Then he lifted a slice off the plate. He held it at eye level, looking over the bread, structurally impacted by the addition of the egg, and then he took a bite. His eye widened briefly, and he set it down on his own plate. "What did you add?"

"Parmesan and cayenne pepper from your fridge," I said, taking another slice. "The ones on the bottom are only salted, if it's not to your taste."

"So not the arsenic-rosemary mix." He picked it back up and took another bite.

"If you're not careful, I'm going to leave here believing that you have a sense of humor."

He just gave me that faint crooked smile.

"It's not too spicy?"

"No," he said, finishing it off. "It's good. I'm not picky. I just stick to a strict diet when I'm working."

"Mmm-hmm," I said diplomatically.

Dreyson snorted.

My phone lit up. *Come to the office? Z has updates.*

Everything all right?" Dreyson asked.

"Rem wants me to come in and sort through some files." I yawned and drank my tea. I would have to use more secure channels for her updates. "But I want to see your magical plant room first."

Blotting at his mouth, Dreyson nodded agreeably and reached for another serving.

"I hate this," I moan, crouching on the ground outside the office, Dreyson holding my bags as I cradled my face.

"I hear you get used to it," Dreyson said, having the audacity to chuckle as I hyperventilated, motion sick from another teleportation spell.

"I'm about to reconstitute egg on your shoes, Dreyson. I'll fucking do it!"

"What will the sloth think?" he asked, tone light.

Damnit, he had a point. And a sloth. In fact, Dreyson had a slice of Amazonian rainforest inhabiting the sanctuary of his defunct church-turned-lair. It was a magical greenhouse experiment that went out of control, and it was better than the zoo. I had to stay friends with him for that reason alone.

It took me a few minutes to wobble to my feet, the nausea slowly dissipating. Wincing, I opened the door and shuffled into the office, surprised to see Remington reading at the chair by my desk.

He glanced at me, then slightly past me. "Hey, Claire, Dreyson. Coffee's brewing." His gaze returned to me. "Are you OK?"

"Teleport spell," I muttered, plunking down in my chair. "It's like being thrown in a blender on a molecular level. I'm just one shaken bag of sick, held together by homeostasis. The pressure from the resulting migraine is the only thing keeping the force of the projectile vomit down."

"That's…very descriptive," Remington said. "I've got some leftover calzones if you're—"

"Fuck you."

Remington laughed.

Dreyson pulled up a chair beside me. "She keeps threatening to throw up on my shoes."

"Oh, she only does that to the people she really likes," Remington said cheerfully.

"I'll remember this," I said, putting my head down on my desk.

"So were you planning on sticking around?" Remington asked, his smile easy, belying the wariness in his eyes.

"We have matters to discuss," Dreyson said, his tone polite but firm.

"Hmm," Remington said. "I suppose we do."

I raised my head to see them both staring intently at each other. Dreyson wasn't doing anything threatening, but that focused look from his scarred visage meant business. Remington's smile held a sharp edge, one hand in his pocket, like he was just daring Dreyson to try something.

I extended one hand between them and waved it a few times. "Hey, I get that you two like looking at each other, but we have work to do."

Remington blinked, then gave me a crooked smile. "So do you want tacos for lunch, then?"

"I hate you," I said, stomach still churning.

"Sheesh, we don't have to order tacos if you don't want any." Remington laughed.

"I'm going to see what the accountant sent," I said, opening up my laptop, now managing to get upright because my aggravation was overcoming the nausea. They were annoying me into feeling better. Ugh. "What happened last night? More of the same? What's the progress on finding and warning potential victims? Also, if anyone knows where the Crow Knight will be, I would like a heads-up so I can pick a good vantage point and borrow my dad's best rifle."

Remington crossed his arms. "Last night was more of the same, only we showed up while the killers were still in the house. That's family number five," he said, the humor gone. "There were three children. Niffolm confirmed that the ten-year-old was a changeling. It was…messy." He pinched the bridge of his nose. "SIU finished tracking down all the families from the lists. The ones still in Illium are in protective custody, and they're sorting out which kids are actually changelings. But we've hit another problem."

"The families that left town?" I asked.

"Not responding or not interested, so not in our scope of influence," Remington said grimly. "But no, from our list, there are ten families with a *missing* kid in the target age range. Some were scared stiff, and a few didn't *remember* the missing child."

"Oh," I winced. "Geas'd and glamoured?"

"Exactly," Remington said. "It's taking time to unravel the magic correctly, high level sidhe stuff. Though…" He shook his head. "The dates roughly line up with the ledger and school attendance. But Nina questioned one family. They admitted *something* demanded their son, claimed he would be cared for, but if they kicked up a fuss, everyone would be killed."

"So they just…gave up their kid?" I asked.

"He was the oldest of four," Remington said, shaking his head. "They said he went willingly. But between the lines, Nina thinks they *encouraged* it, especially after the 'adoption' reveal."

I stared at him incredulously.

"Morality aside, it was the smart choice," Dreyson said. "They couldn't protect themselves or the other children."

"Right, why bother with a kid that wasn't really theirs? Even if they raised him?" I stared at my desk. Those people made silly Leonard look like a saint.

"They were in hiding?" Dreyson asked.

"Yeah," Remington said. "No, they weren't looking for him."

"Making the choice to put off the fight, that makes sense," I said, because I understood survival calculus. "Not even reporting him missing? Fuck, at least Leonard *tried*."

"We don't know if the boy is even alive," Dreyson said. "Changeling or original."

"We don't know if *any* of the human counterparts are alive," Remington said.

But that family? They didn't even try. It was the opposite of Leonard Wilder. For all his faults, he was willing to step up for his kids. "That's the fucking worst."

Startled, both men looked up at me.

"I know we all have different backgrounds, but you have to remember what it was like, getting the rug pulled out from under you. How devastating it was to be little and helpless and faced with the realization that not everything was going to be OK."

"I didn't have parents to be disappointed in," Remington said with a wry look.

Dreyson's face went blank.

"It's not necessarily about parents," I said. "I guess it's the loss of innocence, which is less of a loss and more of a betrayal. I'm pretty sure that's a universal concept. There are entire literary genres devoted to it. I remember going through it, and I'll probably spend the rest of my life getting over it."

Remington's smile wavered. "In that kid's case, it's likely. But now he doesn't have any choice but to grow up fast, though with a family like that, maybe he was already on that path."

Dreyson remained silent.

I took a deep breath. Innis was different. But their story could be just as tragic. I rubbed my eyes, nerves raw from the last couple days. "Sorry, I know ranting about it doesn't change anything. I'm just mad."

"I get it," Remington said. "I know our lives didn't turn out how we expected." He paused, glancing thoughtfully at Dreyson, like he wasn't sure if that statement applied.

"I would agree with that," Dreyson said.

"I...appreciate the validation," I said, taking a deep breath. "Thanks for the group therapy session. We should do it again sometime. I'll get back to work now."

Focusing on my computer, I found a large file dump from Zareen. Still on an encrypted connection, I switched to a more discreet account to check my other messages. No marketplace hits on the Lares, but the broker with info on Mori sent a sample for perusal. I would check that later, when Dreyson wasn't in the room.

Zareen came through though with a file on Bancroft-Owens, with a simple warning: *Be very careful.*

Opening up my IRC client, I jumped onto our server. §D&D Solutions as +RogueRunner. +WizardWadiah was not on, but +Pally-Flux pinged me immediately, opening a new channel with a private message.

<+Pally-Flux> hi RR, got a newbie today, irl friend. Trouble with their pond oneshot. Know how you like river monsters.

<+RogueRunner> Got a few minutes to critique their campaign.

Moments later another window flashed and <farmerjojo> had an entire story typed out for me. I read it and decided to poll the office.

"So it's avoiding cameras and eating ducks. Looks like it lives in the pond, but it's going inside the duck house and dragging them into the water to eat."

Remington wrinkled his nose. "That could be anything."

"There are many *púcaí* variants, a myriad of other water fey, nagas, those cursed fire-breathing turtles—" Dreyson stared off into space.

"Oh, I remember those," Remington said. "Those were nasty. Whatever happened to them anyway?"

"Found the guy making them," Dreyson said. "Made him unmake them."

Remington raised a brow.

Dreyson sat there stoically, mouth firmly closed.

"I see," Remington said.

"So probably not a ghost, though, yeah?" I asked.

"Unlikely, if it's taking the prey back to the water. Despite the amphibious predation, it's probably an aquatic species," Dreyson said. "Who are you talking to?"

"Dunno," I said. "People pop up on our chat when they need help, but they don't know how things work yet. Anyone in the Wergeld you recommend for water monster removal?"

"Liam is good at it," Dreyson said.

I typed up the numbers and recommended Liam by name. With that handled, I closed the channel windows. When I looked up, Dreyson was reading through some HerbAway documents that Remington elected to share.

"This is thorough," he said. "Can you cross-reference Lydia Vine? Her name cropped up often in my investigation."

"Sure." I ran the search. "So Lydia Vine was an outspoken critic of HerbAway. She was a member once, spent a few years working at the corporate office, and swiped a hard drive before quitting." It seemed much of Zareen's intel came from that drive. Unfortunately, her former employers took their corporate *omertà* seriously. "After she lambasted HerbAway, they sued the shit out of her for 'breach of contract' and 'theft of intellectual property.' She disappeared shortly after."

"I knew she went missing," Dreyson said, narrowing his eye. "I didn't know about the hard drive."

"I'm sure that's not something HerbAway wanted publicized," I said, because that did not seem to be common knowledge, but I knew better than to press Zareen about her sources. There was a lot of data to sort through. Zareen prioritized financial documentation, but I ran a search for "Leonard Wilder" and "Sofia Ramos Moreno."

The resulting file was called "Foxglove Candidates." I opened it immediately; it contained dossiers that included the Wilder-Ramos family, the Soltanis, and other names I knew from crime scene documentation and yesterday's research.

I sent it straight to Remington. "Forwarding stuff that SIU is going to want to see. Have you seen anything on the Foxglove Pact?"

"No," Remington said, frowning. "What's that?"

I glanced at Dreyson.

He leaned back in his seat. "About a decade ago, a malg-tech company was tasked to help the Fey solve their fertility problem. They eventually hit on a mysterious solution, but then everyone involved turned up dead. The project was called the Foxglove Pact. I don't have much more detail than that."

"Who killed them?" Remington asked.

"A rogue element within the Fey was blamed," Dreyson said.

"No confirmation, though?" Remington asked.

"Who else would it be?" Dreyson said with a shrug. "The Fey are prone to petty in-fighting and tend to be their own worst enemy."

He had a point, though it was only speculation.

But the Fey weren't the only mass-murderers in the vicinity. I sent Zareen a message on Tox.IM asking more about Lydia Vine.

Wizdiah *Don't think she's alive. But a friend passed this on.*

RoRu *Can you see if they know anything about foxgloves? The plant?*

Wizdiah *OK*

Remington passed some folders to Dreyson, crime scene photos from the changeling murders. Dreyson scanned them, his expression flat.

"There was a change in methodology at the Soltani household," he said.

"What do you mean?" I asked, because I had not seen those photos yet. I wasn't sure if I wanted to. Especially since Innis and I were so close to that scene. Proximity made it all too real.

"There were multiple killers," Remington said. "Last night was the same. There were hunting beasts, hellhounds, and probably more of those shape-changing sluagh."

"Why are they killing some and kidnapping others?" I asked. "They have the power to do either. What's the deciding factor?"

"Maybe they don't take rejection well," Remington said.

"Or maybe it's another rogue faction," Dreyson said. "The inter-Court rivalry is strong. They'll unite against us, but they can't keep it together."

Maybe one Court wanted to keep the kids, but the other was killing them so they couldn't be claimed? Shit. That made sense.

The messenger client flashed.

Wizdiah *wtf. Foxglove? You really freaked him out.*

Roru *I'm freaked out by this double-digit body count. Will he talk to me?*

Wizdiah *He's willing to answer some questions. Make sure you're secure. Check your bridge-mojis. No fairy ones!*

I triple-checked my suite of privacy connections and confirmed the bridges. "You two shush. Accountant's source is calling me."

Remington sat on my desk so he could watch.

Dreyson got up, standing off to the right so he could see my screen.

Minutes later, "Fleance" added me and began a voice call, no video.

I started recording.

"Rogue?" The voice was androgynous: hesitant, soft-spoken, and definitely put through some kind of distortion for anonymity.

"That's me," I said.

"You sound young." And even with the filtering, I could hear the frown.

"We're on the internet. I could be using a vocoder too. But I assume you're talking to me because Wadiah vouched for me and because of the Foxglove Pact. I'm talking to you because I'm tired of seeing pictures of cut-up kids."

A sharp intake of breath. "Changelings?"

"So I'm told, along with their human families as collateral damage."

Fleance groaned. "That wasn't supposed to happen. I burned our records"

I blinked, realizing that Fleance was an original member of the Foxglove Pact Team. "Didn't do any good, because HerbAway already had them on file. Why would you not expect the Courts to know who has their kids?"

"The Courts?" Fleance sounded genuinely startled. "You think the Courts are behind this?"

"Yeah, since I had a threatening visit from a known Fey enforcer last night."

"Damnit," Fleance ground out. "If you know about the Pact, then you know that most of us who were doing the research and the bond-work are dead."

"Allegedly at the hands of a rogue Court faction," I said.

Fleance let out a garbled sound, and it took me a moment to recognize it as hysterical laughter. "No, not at all."

Dreyson leaned closer.

"How do you know?" I asked.

"I didn't see it. I wouldn't be here if I was around to witness it," Fleance said haltingly. "But Eugene was on speaker phone when it happened, and Maria was with him." My speakers crackled from hard breathing. "I heard her death-curse. Don't know if it did any good, but she named her murderer."

It clicked. "And his name was Jack Ketch?"

Fleance choked. "Damnit, Rogue! Don't just say it aloud!"

"My location is heavily warded," I said. "And he doesn't seem like the tech-savvy type."

"Still," Fleance huffed. "You'll excuse me if sole-survivorship taught me to err on the side of caution."

"You're right. Don't want that freak crawling out of a mirror or whatever monsters like him do," I muttered. "I have a lot of questions about the project. My boss and I have spent the last few days digging through records to find these kids so we can keep them and their families alive. We're not fans of Ketch, and we're definitely not allied with the Courts."

Fleance sighed. "Rogue, I know you do good work on the IRC, but I haven't survived this long by being careless. That bastard wiped us from the city. You can't mention my former employer's name without triggering an alert."

"That's high-tier magic. Why didn't you go to the Courts for asylum?" I asked.

"Because I wasn't born yesterday. You can't trust them either," Fleance said sharply. "The participants were *supposed* to be volunteers. There wasn't *supposed* to be any kidnapping or deception. There was *supposed* to be full disclosure. At least that's what the Vernal Lord said. But that Fall Bitch had other ideas. Look, I did lab work. I didn't know the plan changed till it was too late, and I *left* in protest. That choice saved my life."

Dreyson slid a piece of paper to me. I read his question.

"What exactly did you do to those kids?" I asked.

"The alterations weren't unethical. At least we thought they weren't," he said, voice softening. "The sidhe are at an evolutionary bottleneck. Their fertility rates are so low, and they have trouble surviving in our modern industrial world. We had to find a way to work around their weakness to cold iron. This experiment made a generation of full-blooded Fey more like us."

"How?"

"You've met the Five."

"They have names," I said.

"Yes, and they call themselves sisters, but they're not five separate people, Rogue. Alice, Celia, Lacie, Calie, and Cleia are one person separated into five identical bodies. They're attuned to each other. They can split their attention or pour resources into a single body. That was a messed-up thing to do to a kid, and we were *not* trying to replicate their situation. But their tethering-bond was...unique. The one calling herself Cleia agreed to show us how it worked." Which meant all five were in agreement to cooperate.

I wondered how much Alice knew about this case. She told me what she was willing to share. Pushing harder wouldn't have helped. "What happened next?"

"We already had success in increasing fertility rates. It was less pronounced for the sidhe, and the Vernal Lord also sought to strengthen the next generation, so we tethered each Fey baby to a human one."

Dreyson slid me another slip of paper.

"How closely tied are they?" I read his question. "How...parasitic is the relationship?" I added.

"I know it sounds bad," Fleance said. "But we weren't monsters. It was meant to benefit both children. The changeling gains access to human traits like iron-tolerance. The human gains a boost in magical aptitude. We couldn't guarantee results, but we could tilt probability toward those outcomes. They cannot drain each other, and if one dies, it shouldn't cause harm to the bondmate."

Innis said they could sense their counterpart.

"Do they have an awareness of each other?" I asked.

"I have no idea," Fleance said. "In theory, yes. As long as one had innate magical talent, that would be enough, I assume. We were supposed to have regular checkups with the parents of both sets of children so we could monitor growth. But obviously, that didn't happen."

"Fuck," I said.

Fleance coughed. "The Fey, not that...mass-murderer, they are killing their own kids?"

"Yes," I said.

Fleance was silent for a moment. "They take the Alluvian Treaties seriously. Well, the consequences anyway. But I never thought the Vernal Lord would go that far to cover his tracks. The Fall Bitch, sure. But he seemed genuinely invested in this project. His own consort—" Fleance sighed heavily. "But what do I know?"

"A lot," I said.

It was Remington's turn to pass me a note. I had to reread it.

"What if I can connect you to someone who can guarantee your safety? Would you be willing to come in?"

Fleance made a strange noise, like a warbling hiccup. Choking over voice filtration was a fascinating auditory experience.

"We can send over geas'd contracts for your amendments," I said. "My boss's boss is open to negotiations."

"Who?" Fleance asked tightly. "Because there aren't many people who can offer protection from *him*."

That was fair. I could think of four, and at least half of them weren't good options. "Would the other *Lares* be convincing enough?"

Remington sat with his eyes closed, arms crossed, chin tucked against his chest as he waited for the answer.

Dreyson stood straight with his hands behind his back, staring intently at my screen.

The silence dragged on.

Static crackled along my speakers, and I flinched, expecting him to cut the connection.

"Send me the paperwork," an older man's voice said shakily, the distortion gone. "I'll have someone look it over."

Chapter 17
Lines in the Sand and the Palm of Her Hand

针锋相对 Trad. 針鋒相對-Zhēn fēng xiāng duì – "The needle and the tip of the spear oppose each other." It means to wage a tit for tat struggle. A needle and a spearhead don't seem to be evenly matched, but they are for this idiom. Honestly, this just makes me question what kind of needles people were using back then.

— *From the Very Personal Journals of FYG*

AFTER I FORWARDED the documents to Fleance, Remington went to his office, probably to have a private discussion with Bancroft-Owens or the lieutenant. Dreyson sat down, watching me work. I drank my glorious coffee, basking in caffeine-fueled motivation.

"What's on your mind?" I asked.

"What SIU fought and what you and Innis encountered were likely *not* from Ketch. He prefers to do his own killing, and he doesn't usually bother with glamours. But there is a difference in the mutilations. I'm certain at least one of the Courts is responsible for some of the kills, but Ketch isn't a stranger to false flags."

I nodded. "That occurred to me, but I have no evidence and didn't want to spook Fleance."

Dreyson leaned forward. "Can you track Fleance?"

"Oh no," I laughed. "My tech skills are basic. I'm no hacker, but sometimes I'm a social engineer."

"You're friends with the Five," he said.

"I know them. Everyone knows them," I said. "But yes, we're friendly."

"That video you showed me. It was in the Office of Vital Records. One of them works there. Is that who gave you the video?"

"Does it matter?" I asked.

"Their favors don't come cheap, Claire."

I tilted my head to the side, wondering what he *thought* I did to get the video. "Favors aren't cheap if you're *rude*. But if you're friendly, some things are freely given."

Dreyson folded his hands in his lap. "Do they like protein bars, then?"

"Bubble tea and potstickers, actually. Sometimes we do karaoke and hotpot. Plus there's conversation, courtesy, and being treated like a person, which, now that you mention it, are big things. Priceless, really."

Dreyson huffed and looked away.

"Look, I wasn't planning on charging you for the video, Dreyson. It was gifted to me, and so I passed it along to you. Please keep the source confidential, but don't overthink it."

Dreyson sighed. "You work very differently from me."

"We can't all be badass warriors with giant battleaxes and cool scars," I said. "My life would be easier if I had your skills, but alas."

Dreyson shook his head, face drawn. "I suspect you would be disappointed."

Recalling the cautious way he almost confided in me last night, I thought I understood his point. "Do you want to do karaoke and hotpot with us?"

He gave me a small, tolerant smile. "It's amazing how often you seem to miss the point, then ricochet back and hit another target entirely."

I grinned at the compliment. "You think in arcs and angles too. You have to when you swing an axe or throw fire, right?"

Remington emerged from the office. "Jon's on his way over. Bancroft-Owens is pleased. Hopefully, Fleance doesn't keep her waiting. She's liable to use other channels to hunt him down." He turned to Dreyson. "Any developments on your side?"

"No updates on Naomi," he said. "But if you want to track down Fleance, the Wergeld has a cybersecurity team. They could—"

"No," I said. "If he doesn't want to come in, I won't force him. Especially not at the risk of exposing my other contacts."

Dreyson regarded me thoughtfully. "Ah, my mistake." His gaze turned to my computer.

I quashed the urge to shut it down and lock it away.

Remington chuckled. "Do you want to pick up lunch since Jon's stopping in?"

"Am I supposed to get him something?" I asked archly.

"Nah, he's not going to eat or be reasonable," Remington said, mustering a halfhearted smile. "I just figured you two would rather not deal with him."

How thoughtful. And perhaps Remington wanted to have a private talk with the lieutenant.

"What do you want?" I asked, even though I knew the answer.

"Tacos?" Remington said hopefully.

I almost lied and said I didn't want tacos, since he was taunting me earlier. But I did love tacos. And while I was a petty bitch, I wasn't going to martyr myself on the wholly respectable altar of spite, not with tacos on the line.

"Dreyson, what are you in the mood for?" I asked.

"I'm not picky," he said without any enthusiasm.

"Tacos it is," Remington said gleefully, rubbing his hands together. "Make sure to get extra goat, tripe, and tongue!" His eyes darted to Dreyson.

Dreyson stared stoically at the wall.

"They're really good. You'll have to try some," Remington continued.

The door alarm chimed. Dreyson turned toward the entryway.

The lieutenant limped in, clothes stained and rumpled, his fists raw. There were bruise-like circles around his bloodshot eyes. His head snapped back when he saw Dreyson.

"I guess I could grab him something too," I said quietly to Remington, because the lieutenant looked rough.

"Don't do me any favors, Giles," he said, upper lip curling in disgust.

"No favors for ungrateful bastards," I said cheerfully. "Just charity."

The lieutenant's nostrils flared. He jabbed a finger at me. "I don't need your charity either, Giles. And neither does the Wilder kid. Just because you feel guilty about what happened to the dad—"

Dreyson's head snapped up.

"—doesn't mean you're qualified to handle a changeling!"

Dreyson slowly turned to me, his expression severe. "Innis is a changeling? And they're Leonard Wilder's kid?"

I clenched my teeth. Yes, he knew Leonard Armstrong was a fake name, and he didn't share that. "Yes."

Dreyson inhaled sharply. "And you didn't think to mention this to me?"

I glared at the lieutenant, who blinked slowly, like he was only now realizing what he said aloud. "What the fuck are you doing outing kids?"

The lieutenant flinched.

"Ms. Giles," Dreyson said my name like a warning, demanding my full attention. He was on his feet now, towering over me and my desk.

"Jon," Remington said, gesturing for the lieutenant to go into his office.

"But—" The lieutenant stared at Dreyson.

"Jon," Remington repeated firmly and shot me a questioning glance.

I glared at the lieutenant and waved them off.

The lieutenant hesitantly walked toward Remington's office, glancing back over his shoulder at me.

"Why would you keep that from me?" Dreyson asked, louder this time, palms flat on my desk.

"Why would you not share Wilder's real identity?" I asked crossing my legs.

"Client privilege. He was out of the picture anyway—"

"So you could have shared it," I said, palms outstretched. "Just like you could have done more digging and discovered Innis all by yourself."

Dreyson's chin jerked up, lips drawing back in a snarl. "Why wouldn't you tell me that that child is Wilder's? He was my client. We've been cooperating just fine."

"The kid's safety is my priority. I wasn't spreading their identity around, period," I said, already getting a crick in my neck from staring up at him. He wanted to hide behind his "connection" to Wilder? Fine. "Why didn't *you* vet him? He was *your* client. *You* should have done a more thorough check. You dropped the ball."

Dreyson grimaced. "That... That's not the point. I thought we were working together. You certainly had no problem running to me for protection when the Fey Courts came for you." The bitterness of his tone left a bad taste in my mouth.

"Yeah, I'm human." I stood up, because otherwise he would be hovering over me, dominating my field of vision. "The Wergeld doesn't have a problem with me. But the kid...?" I leaned closer. "You gonna try to tell me that the Wergeld would be just fine with them?" I met his gaze, daring him to try to sell me that lie.

Dreyson gritted his teeth. "That's not the point. Why didn't you tell *me*?"

I wasn't keen on sharing Innis' identity with anyone, for their own safety. In fact, I wished it wasn't necessary to tell SIU, and by extension that blabbermouth lieutenant, but what was done was done.

"No smart answer for me?" he sneered. "Can't talk your way out of this one? Did you realize how big of a mistake—"

"I didn't tell you, because I didn't know how you would react!" I shouted back.

Dreyson jerked away from me, the momentary shock on his face morphing into something harder and more aggressive. "Oh," he said through clenched teeth, real anger sparking along his skin. "I see."

My heartbeat thundered in my ears.

"You think I'm a danger to the child." Dreyson lowered his voice, a cold fury hardening that accusation. He shuddered, expression remaining the same, but there was a sharper intensity to his face, a jerkiness in his movement.

"I didn't say that," I growled. "Don't put words—"

"Claire, you're a *social engineer*. You didn't have to say it," he snapped. "Your actions are far more honest than your words."

"Infer what you like," I snarled. "When Wilder came through and said he murdered his changeling kid, everyone seemed A-OK with that bullshit. I was not." My arm slashed through the air between us. "It wasn't human, so who cares? We won't bring it up. So when Innis actually turns up alive and well, they came in asking for me by name. Do you know why? Because your client told them that they could trust me. He sent them to *me*! How desperate was he? We only just met. So you're damn straight I'm not telling people, given what's happening to changelings!" My breathing was ragged. Maybe because I spat all that out so quickly. But this sentiment had been fomenting for awhile.

"We both know Wilder was a fool. But I didn't realize that you thought so little of me," Dreyson said, the words dropping an octave.

"*It wasn't about you,*" I growled back, mad that he was so much taller than me, that he kept missing the point, and that I could not pick him up and shake him to fully express my frustration. Not that I ever picked up anyone and shook them, but it was a thought. "I didn't know who to trust with the kid. I'm *still* not sure. I mean, look at your own team, Dreyson! Naomi—"

"That isn't your concern! I'm not her!" Dreyson shouted, slapping his palm down and rattling the desk.

I blinked, shocked by his reaction. I'd hit a sore spot, but I was very good at that. "Isn't it? I was at the Shadow Dunes too! Naomi could have gotten us all killed!"

"I'm not Naomi," he bristled, baring his teeth.

"No, but you're both Wergeld, and the track record isn't great. Naomi sabotaged us. Mori doesn't tolerate preternaturals. You've said stuff that's made me wonder—"

"Enough." Dreyson stepped back, fists at his sides. He glowered at me, cheeks flushed, "This *is* a job, Ms. Giles. Say what you want about my character, but don't impugn my professionalism. Unlike you, I can separate the job from my personal feelings."

My ears rang. I had to take a second to process what he just said. Oh, that conceited prick. He wanted to pretend like I was the irrational one? Mr. Crazy-Laugh Berserker-Pants? "Now you want to talk about feelings?" I shouted. "*Oh, this is complicated, oh, that's off-limits! Oh, you don't understand what's going on, but I'm not going to tell you relevant information either!* That's all you, Dreyson! You had legitimate reasons to withhold information? Well, so did I! Don't pretend like I'm wrong to be cautious!"

"That's unrelated—"

"No, it isn't! This is a two-way street!" I pointed between us. "Be a good ally, I return the favor. Insult me like that? I return the goddamn favor! Trust, cooperation, insults, it all goes both ways!"

Dreyson drew in a deep shuddering breath. "All right. Fine. You don't have to say any more." He kept his fists at his sides, his cheeks now bloodless. "You barely know me. You can't tell if I'm trustworthy. You disagree with my standards, and you made a judgment call because you didn't know how I would react. Do I have it right so far?" he asked, his voice flat.

"Sure, but my actions with Innis were not about—"

"You don't owe me anything, Ms. Giles. My favors were freely given," he said, the words taut and vicious. "But neither of us should be working with someone we can't trust."

"I'm the untrustworthy one? You've kept plenty of things from me! Of course I had to do research on Wilder. You didn't volunteer it, nor explain just what your employer's angle is!"

"So if I'd just spilled my secrets, you would have returned the favor? You decided to explore the Autumn Court alone. You were at a dead changeling's house at the time of the murder. You keep very questionable contacts." Dreyson's voice grew harsher. "Don't start on me about keeping secrets."

"Oh, *now* you want to talk about it." I threw my hands in the air. "Because last night—"

Dreyson's eye got very big, lips drawing back, but then his expression shuttered. He took a step back, his voice deadly calm.

"That's enough, Ms. Giles."

"Oh no, I'm just getting warmed up," I said, no longer feeling any inclination to hold back.

Something flashed across Dreyson's face, a strange light in his eye. Heat poured off his skin. In that moment, I expected fire to bloom from his fists.

"You've got a great handle on those personal feelings," I sneered. "Real professional. Like how you vetted your client."

He shuddered and shut his eye, cracking his neck from side to side. Biting his lower lip, he looked at me, the red-hot anger evaporating, leaving only icy disdain. "We have nothing useful to say to each other. So I'm going to leave, and Detective Remington can contact the Wergeld through the usual channels."

Turning his back to me, Dreyson made a gesture, the air around him fluctuating. A small vortex blew across my desk, lifting papers and knocking back my coffee mug. It shattered as it hit the floor, and he disappeared.

"Fuck!" I slammed my fists on the desk and then backhanded a pile of folders off the side, watching the papers fly into the air and then flutter down around me.

When I looked to my left, Remington and the lieutenant were still in the doorway, watching me with big eyes.

"I'm going out," I said, grabbing my bag.

Hunched over the gray-specked Formica table, my booth closest to the kitchen, I slurped my extra-sour mangonada, a wax-paper-lined red plastic basket of fish tacos in front of me. There were only a couple other people in the dining room. The restaurant was a small standalone building with a cheerful patio outside. Strains of cumbia music played over the speakers.

Miguel, Valeria's husband, shook his head as he set down a serving of goat tacos. He was a short balding man at an avuncular level of paunchy. Despite his deceptively friendly smile, he was a little too salty to ever be mistaken for jolly.

"Are you just ordering food to look at it?" he asked.

"It cheers me up," I muttered.

"It'll cheer you up more if you eat it," he said, crossing his arms.

"I'm getting there," I said, clasping my drink in both hands, the sides and the lid dimpling under the pressure. It was a wonderful partially frozen mix of mango, lime juice, chili sauce, and tamarind. "Can I get another mangonada?"

"You're going to get a brain freeze," he said. "And then you'll cry, 'Oh, Miguel, my poor head. How could this happen to me?'" His voice went high and falsetto. "And I'll tell you then what I'm telling you now. Eat your lunch and stop pouting."

"I don't sound like that," I said, squinting at him.

"Eat your lunch and stop pouting."

Grumbling, I picked up a fish taco and took half of it in one big bite. He told me to eat, so I would.

The flour tortilla was still warm and soft. The fried fish was crispy and spiced with chilies and lime. The cabbage was fresh and had just the right amount of sauce. There was no cheese. It didn't need it. It was that good.

"Delicious," I said with my mouth full, bits of cabbage falling out.

"You're a monster," Miguel told me.

"More mangonada," I said, finishing the taco in another bite. I reached for a goat taco.

Miguel rolled his eyes at me. "I'll get you another mangonada. Try not to scare away my customers."

"You're the best," I called after him, and consoled myself with the goat taco.

There was a rustling sound, and a figure in a gray hoodie shuffled into my booth and sat down across from me. But I recognized that unwelcome face immediately.

"I apologize for the rude interruption," Naomi said, her head tilted to the side, her eyes staring forward, unseeing.

"You—"

"If you scream, I will kill everyone in here, starting with the old man," Naomi said, her voice deeper and raspier than I remembered.

I swallowed and picked up my mangonada in one hand, drinking it quietly to keep my mouth busy. With my other hand, I reached into my bag.

Naomi, or whatever was wearing her body, smiled at me. "I have questions for you."

I bit the straw, keeping my smart-ass comments in my mouth while I studied her face. Naomi didn't look dead, she was breathing, but there was a jerkiness to her motions, like a marionette tripping across a stage.

"Who do I have the dubious pleasure of addressing?" I asked, setting my drink down.

She laughed, a throaty sound, her features viciously expressive, so unlike the subtle auntie I met a few days ago. "I think you already know."

"Maybe, but the pronouns of possession are confusing. I wouldn't want to get them wrong."

Not-Naomi stared blankly at me. She raised her arms, sleeves sliding down to reveal sigils carved in her hands, angry open wounds in her skin that disappeared under the fabric. Those were not there before.

Fire tore through my veins. I lurched forward, back arching as my body spasmed. My jaw snapped shut as my burning nerves locked me in place. My limbs shook, tensed hard enough to start cramping. The pain held me paralyzed, unable to breathe or scream, my lungs bursting, my eyes watering.

And then that flare of agony was gone and I dropped back in my seat, gasping for breath. My right hand fell into my bag, fingers brushing against a familiar bone handle.

Not-Naomi smiled sweetly at me. "Go on, waste my time, girl. I'll break you—" She shuddered, her face shifting into a snarl. "Ungh— Stay quiet!"

For mere seconds, the woman in front of me lost that glaze of casual cruelty. She opened her mouth, trying to force words out, her eyes darting down to her hands.

And then the mask snapped back into place.

"Now I really am going to kill—" Not-Naomi hissed, eyes unfocused.

I struck then, swinging my arm forward, the obsidian knife drilling down into Naomi's left hand, slicing through the sigil lines.

Not-Naomi screeched as I pinned her hand to the table, her eyes on the dagger. "That's—"

And then Naomi blinked, her face pale, her breathing rapid. "Kill me now, before he regains control."

I dug through my bag, seeking the right charm. Tearing open the packet, I threw the powder in her face.

Naomi gasped, stiffened, and slumped back in her seat.

Paralysis charms were nonlethal, but who knew if it would hold her. I called Remington immediately. "I'm at Valeria's. Naomi attacked me, but I think it's Ketch puppeting her."

"Fuck." I could hear him scrambling. "We're on our way."

I put down a protective charm, knowing it was not nearly enough to stop Ketch if he decided to stroll in, but it was all I had. The other patrons in the dining room were groaning and holding their heads, but they didn't have a good view of my table.

Ketch clearly didn't care about subtlety or collateral damage.

Blood spattered the dishes, the tip of the knife embedded in the tabletop. I picked up my napkin, blotting at the small trickle of blood coming from my nose.

My tacos were ruined.

Shaking my head, I picked up my mangonada and took a long drink, like it was a replacement for all the serotonin I was losing to this case. The sweet-sour spicy slushie felt nice on my throat, but then I winced as a bolt of jagged cold cut through my skull. On top of the lingering pain from Ketch's attack, I got a brain freeze.

Miguel staggered out of the kitchen, holding his head. He looked around the dining room and flinched when his gaze landed on Naomi, her impaled hand, and our bloodied table.

"Rem and SIU are on the way," I said. "Sorry about the mess."

"Not again, Claire." Miguel shook his head at me like a disappointed dad. "Can't you just stay calm when someone tries to take your tacos?"

Chapter 18
No Safety in Numbers

After crossing a river, you should get far away from it.
    — Sun Zi, The Art of War

Later scholars expand on this with practical advice about terrain and battle formations. My take is simple: if you've cleared an obstacle, GTFO. Don't stick around for a rematch.
    — From the Very Personal Journals of FYG

JON AND REMINGTON arrived in minutes. Detectives Al-Rashid and Davis were close behind. I stayed at the bloody table with Naomi's unconscious body. She didn't stir, and I was grateful for it. I really didn't like the idea of Ketch being able to springboard back into her with me right across the table.

Remington took Miguel aside. He and Valeria were not strangers to magic, but our bullshit did not normally spill into their place of business.

The lieutenant took one look at Naomi and swore. I waited for him to make the predictable turn and shout at me, but instead he sat down in the booth across the aisle. Hunched over, he rested his elbows on his knees and didn't say a word to me.

That's when I started to worry.

Detective Davis rolled up Naomi's sleeves, displaying elaborate carvings, deep red lines in her ivory skin that went all the way to her elbows.

"Yes, that's Ketch's work," she said grimly.

Al-Rashid hummed to himself, appearing as a middle-aged olive-skinned man with dark curls, a bushy beard, and a touch of gray around the temples. He wore a rumpled gray suit and murmured in a language I did not recognize. He gestured to the knife.

"You want me to remove it?" I asked.

He nodded.

I glanced at Detective Davis, who also nodded. Al-Rashid knew ritual magic like few alive did, but Detective Davis was the one who understood that what was safe for them was *not* always safe for anyone else.

I pulled the knife out.

Blood welled from the wound. Detective Davis wrapped Naomi's hand.

I wiped the knife with a napkin, but it came away clean. A little confused, I slipped it back in the sheath.

"What exorcised Ketch?" I asked. The dagger or the pain were likely causes.

"Hard to say, but you disrupted his flow by mangling the sigils," Detective Davis said. "Enough of a pathway remains that he could still get in, but you made it harder for him to stay."

"She fought him." I picked up my cup, but it was empty. Boo.

"He targeted you." Detective Davis frowned.

"I guess. I just wanted tacos," I muttered, pointedly ignoring the lieutenant as I stood. "I'm going back to the office now."

"Giles, wait," the lieutenant said quietly. He didn't bark. He didn't yell. He didn't even have that taut-angry tone that strangled his voice on the rare occasion where he was *trying* to be polite to me.

He remained sitting, one arm propping his head up. His shirt was torn, sleeves rolled up to his burly elbows. From this angle, I could see the dark bruises along his neck and arms. But those pale blue eyes were still sharp, bold, and tired. His shoulders sagged. He took a deep breath, wincing midway.

I crossed my arms. I had a lot of things to say to the lieutenant, none of them very nice. But in that moment, he looked beaten. I wasn't above kicking someone when they were down, especially someone who was as big of a bastard as he was, but right now that seemed like the wrong thing to do.

"Ketch is a serious problem," the lieutenant said, rubbing his face with both hands, like he could hide behind them. "And so is the Crow Knight."

"I noticed," I said, one arm out, gesturing to the table still covered in blood and ruined tacos.

The lieutenant flinched as he straightened up. Yeah, he was in a fight recently, and he was still feeling it.

"Remington is meeting with his…contact," he said, jaw twitching. "That *might* make Ketch back off." He stared at the wall just slightly to the left of my head. "But even if that pays off, the Courts are still a problem."

"Jon, what are you actually trying to say?" I asked, failing to blunt the edge in my voice.

Irritation flashed across his face, but he looked away for a moment, clearly struggling to compose himself. "You should shelter in an SIU safehouse."

Because I couldn't go home. Both Ketch and the Crow Knight could track me anywhere without strong wards.

"Nice offer, but—"

"I shouldn't have outed the kid and said all that other shit. It wasn't right," the lieutenant said, head tilted back as he stared up at the ceiling, avoiding eye contact. "I'm not on guard duty, so you don't have to worry about being around me."

It took me a second to process the words coming out of his mouth. The lieutenant said a lot of shitty things, and I usually responded with equally cutting comments. This change, this *almost* apology was both shocking *and* underwhelming. He must be seriously concussed.

"Does he need medical treatment?" I asked the others.

"Oh, fuck you, Giles," he growled.

Detective Davis gave me a thin smile. "Stop baiting him, Claire. It's excessive and in bad taste, as he *obviously* needs medical attention and is too stubborn to get it."

"Nina," the lieutenant groaned, closing his eyes.

"Mmm," I said, nodding slowly, always impressed by Detective Davis's ability to bring us all down a notch.

"And you should accept his offer," she continued. "Ketch is going to be madder than a boiled owl, and he'll lash out, as he's a spiteful creature with more power than control."

"Sounds familiar," I said, massaging the spot between my eyebrows. And while I was actually surprised, I was unimpressed by the lieutenant's almost apology. I resolved to do him one better. "Thanks for the generous offer, Jon. Your concern for my safety is very altruistic."

His head snapped up, and he squinted at me.

"And what do you say to that appropriately civil declaration of gratitude, Lieutenant?" Detective Davis asked, clearly enjoying this.

"You're welcome," the lieutenant muttered.

Al-Rashid chuckled.

"I'm going to order more lunch," I said, trying to salvage my afternoon.

Miguel and Valeria planned to close the restaurant for the day, because of the "gas leak" that left everyone with splitting headaches. In a shocking display of humanity, the lieutenant put in a catering order for whatever else they needed to use up.

I went to pay my bill and apologize, but Miguel let me know that he added it to SIU's tab. He also gave me another mangonada and a bag of tacos.

He was the best.

Remington waited by the front door, checking his phone. "Fleance took the deal. I'm going to the extraction. Mrs. Bancroft-Owens should arrive soon. She would like to talk to you."

"If that's what she wants," I said with a shrug.

Remington leaned on his cane. "We were worried, you know. Thought you were going to rip his throat out with your teeth."

"Really?" I asked, skepticism drawing out the word.

"Worried that we'd have to separate you two," he said.

"With what? A spray bottle? Jon's barely standing on two legs," I snorted.

"Yeah." Remington nodded. "Last night was bad. Showed up too late to save anyone, and it wasn't an easy fight."

"Didn't realize it was *that* bad," I said.

Remington mustered a lopsided smile. "I'm fine. I think Dreyson's in worse shape. You really let him have it."

"What?" I put my hands on my hips. "He got mad at me."

"I didn't say you were wrong," Remington said. "But you do have a disarmingly cheerful way of saying incredibly insensitive things, and despite his martial prowess, I don't know if he can defend against that kind of attack."

"Is that your way of saying that I periodically hurt your feelings?"

"Me?" he laughed. "Oh, just a little." He held his thumb and forefinger about an inch apart. "But I know you. It's different."

"He heard what he wanted to hear. There's a difference between 'I legitimately don't know how you would react and didn't feel like opening that can of worms' and 'I think you're an untrustworthy psycho.' I can't help that he can't see that."

"Hmm," Remington said, lips pressed firmly together.

I knew that look. "You have thoughts."

"I do, but…" He held up his hands. "First, you're not wrong. Second, do you want my thoughts? Or would you rather I remain unflinching moral support? Because I am definitely more comfortable on the 'fuck that guy' bandwagon."

I rolled my eyes. Ugh. I had other worries now. Might as well wrap this up. "Go on, then."

"In the moment, you weren't that clear about the difference. You did start off hot, holding him personally responsible for some things. Honestly, you were both zipping in and out of personal territory. I think some wires got crossed. It was uncomfortable. I was acutely aware of our lack of popcorn."

"OK," I said, annoyed again.

"What you want to make of that is your own business." Remington checked his phone. "I'll admit, I was surprised by his reaction."

"The part where he stormed off or the part where he got his feelings hurt?" I asked.

"Remington chuckled. "The part where he didn't squish you."

"He's not like that." I rolled my eyes. "Don't make me defend his ass when I'm mad at him, OK? I already had to be nice to Jon today, and that was terrible."

Remington made a small noncommittal noise, avoiding my gaze.

"Oh, you coached him, did you? That explains it. Well, he didn't deliver an actual apology, but it was quite close...for him."

Remington closed his eyes, not denying any of it. "Mrs. Bancroft-Owens is outside. Please behave."

We headed out to a large black SUV idling in the parking lot. The windows were too tinted to see who was driving. Remington opened the rear passenger door and climbed in.

The front passenger window dropped down for Mrs. Bancroft-Owens. Behind her, the driver was a slender blonde man in an expensive suit and sunglasses.

"Ma'am," I said.

"Tell me about your encounter with Ketch," she said.

I gave her the rundown of my impromptu lunch date.

"That impulsive fool," Bancroft-Owens said, clicking her tongue. "I will be having stern words with him, given what occurred today and what he pulled with the Foxglove Pact. We could have solved this *years* ago, but instead he was overzealous and drove everyone into hiding." She shook her head. "I will handle him, Ms. Giles. However, you would be wise to keep a lower profile for the near future. He is a petty, vindictive thing, and he nurses grudges like his own offspring."

"Great," I said. Because that's what I needed. *Another* feud with an immoral man in a position of power.

"But you did well to track down a survivor of his rampage. I suspect that is why he wanted to question you. It is good that you exorcised him from the mercenary. His interrogations are very unpleasant. It would have been unwise and unhealthy to remain in his company."

Chapter 19
What a Bird in the Hand Is Worth

李代桃僵-Lǐ dài táo jiāng — Number Eleven of the Thirty Six Stratagems says, "sacrifice the plum tree to preserve the peach tree." It means that sometimes short-term objectives must be forsaken to reach a long-term goal. Plums and peaches turn up a lot in metaphors, like they will make the underlying idea more palatable.

— From the Very Personal Journals of FYG

"WHEN DID YOU become such an overachiever?" Mwanje asked. He handed me a milkshake as we left the drive-thru. "First the Commissioner, then the Fey Courts, and now Jackass Ketch? Can you settle for not pissing off every petty tyrant in the area?"

"I thought I should cut the lieutenant a break." I sat in the back of his Jeep. Detective Davis was in the front seat, nursing a fresh coffee. She had bags under her eyes, her hair frizzing free of its braids. She looked exhausted from unraveling Ketch's spellwork.

"You're hilarious," Mwanje said with a chuckle, elbowing Detective Davis. "Do you hear this?"

"I am here, in the car, with you both," she said, like she would rather be almost anywhere else. Yawning, she set her coffee in the cup holder, tucked her chin to her chest, and crossed her arms. "Make sure you turn off anything with location services, especially your phone."

I complied, slurping my milkshake. Normally I didn't binge this many sweet dessert beverages, but it was that kind of day. We headed west toward the University District. Since Ketch was hunting me, Mrs. Bancroft-Owens did not bring me along to the meeting with Fleance.

Naomi was admitted to Paean Hills. Hopefully, she would be safe there.

"You doing OK?" Mwanje asked, using his rare inside voice, because Detective Davis dozed off.

"Been better," I said, trying to fix my problems with ice cream.

He bobbed his head. "So about the lockup cock-up..."

I groaned.

"We have Hartford and Ryan on camera, both in our facility and the cafe. The footage is safe. We've pushed the complaint to Internal Affairs. But the Union is trying to block it, and we're already seeing pushback."

"How bad?" I asked.

"We didn't get the backup we needed for yesterday's extractions," he said. "That slowed everything down...a lot." He gritted his teeth, his normally cheerful voice turning guttural.

I inhaled deeply. Everyone from SIU looked rough. They probably pulled double or triple shifts. And because they didn't turn a blind eye to what Hartford and Ryan did, they were getting shafted when they required serious support. Worse, maybe those people, the ones wiped out by Court hunters, would have survived if SIU had the manpower they needed.

It wasn't my fault, but I didn't feel good about it.

"I'm sorry to pull all this heat down on you," I said.

"It's not on you," Mwanje said sharply. "We're documenting everything, and we're not letting it go, Claire. If someone up top tries to quash this investigation, a copy of my files will *somehow* reach you or your evil lawyer."

"I have a funny little video of Ryan," I said.

"Remington told me. You should avoid him and—"

"I wasn't trying to find him," I said, because if I was, maybe Ryan wouldn't be out walking around. But I knew better than to say that to the cops, friends or not.

Mwanje's smile was crooked in the rearview mirror, like he knew what I was thinking. "No, Claire..."

"Dude, I have way bigger problems than a handsy fuckwit manchild who is obviously compensating for his atrocious personality."

"Brutal, I like it," Mwanje laughed. "So what's this rumor I hear about you joining the dark side?"

"I wasn't aware that I ever left." I shrugged.

"Well, transferred over to Wergeld management."

I crossed my arms, my left eye twitching. "That's news to me."

"Not even as a professional liaison?"

"No," I said. Dreyson's offhand comment about recruitment wasn't anything to bank on.

"So if it's not professional, then this thing with Dreyson is personal?" Mwanje asked innocently.

I glared at him in the rearview mirror. "You're not smooth."

He just patted his bald head with a chuckle. "As a baby's bottom."

I laughed, in spite of myself.

"So then, what *is* going on with tall, blonde, and homicidal?" he asked.

I rolled my eyes. He knew the scope of our investigation, knew I was working with Dreyson. Part of me was tempted to make up something salacious, but that would probably backfire. The truest answer was one I wasn't going to tell the cops. Someone tried to kill us both, and neither one of us were inclined to let that go. "What is everyone's fixation on Dreyson?"

"Hey, he was spotted with you at the Centerpointe eating a truly decadent dessert. That casts him in a totally different light. So inquiring minds want to know. You've put a mystery in front of us. Is the Wergeld's most fearsome berserker also its most eligible bachelor? Like and subscribe to find out."

I snorted.

"Don't be jealous. We still like you better. For now." Mwanje briefly lifted his hands up in a surrender pose.

"Keep your hands on the wheel, Coronet!" Detective Davis snapped out of her repose. "Some of us don't have accelerated regeneration!"

"I'm using my knees, Nina!" he said quickly, reaching for the steering wheel.

"Hands. On. The. Wheel."

"Sorry, Nina," Mwanje said awkwardly.

Detective Davis glowered at him, before curling up and going back to sleep.

"Sorry, we're all a little rough right now," Mwanje said. "I guess I'm not as coherent as I thought."

"What are you actually saying?"

"Look, just...be careful with that one. Objectively, he's not the worst of the worst, and if he were on the IPD, most of the shit he's done to criminal bounties wouldn't even get a real investigation."

"Sounds like a procedural and moral failure on the IPD's part," I said.

"I don't disagree," Mwanje said.

"Is he a big problem like Mira Silver is a big problem? Because if he is..."

Mwanje laughed. "I don't know. If I did, I would say something. The whole situation with the Wergeld is complicated, and I wish I had better answers. But I'm trying to be open-minded. I do trust your judgment. Sorta. Just, proceed cautiously. The Wergeld has fewer rules than we do, and that's saying something."

"Thanks," I said. "I think."

We pulled up to one of the cookie-cutter apartment buildings that populated the University District. There was an abundance of cheap housing, but this building had a buzzer, a security guard, and sharp wards that glittered like glass panes in the sunlight, provided you knew how to look.

"We have a few rooms here. Do you want to share a suite with the Wilder kid and their mom?"

"What?" I blinked.

"Kid's been asking about you, wouldn't stop pestering us about it." Mwanje chuckled.

"If that's a problem, we can move you," Detective Davis said.

"If they get annoying, I can shut my door," I said, not minding a chance to check in with Innis. We took the stairs to the third floor.

Detective Davis used a badge to open the doors. Magic crackled as I entered the tan hall with fluorescent lights and faded maroon carpet. I opened my mouth, nearly tasting the potency of the protective wards in the air. It felt like licking a battery.

"Use a landline if you need to make calls," Detective Davis said, like she knew I had Remington's number memorized. She knocked on a maroon door before opening it.

We entered a small common area with a tiny kitchenette. A small television sat on an old entertainment center in front of a worn plaid couch. The lights were dimmed; the blinds stayed closed.

"Claaaaaaaaire!" Innis shouted, bursting out of one of the bedrooms.

Mwanje winced. Sometimes enhanced hearing had drawbacks.

Innis bounced up to me and grabbed my hands. "They said you were coming! I brought Super Smash Brothers if you want to play! Or we can play cards! I saw some board games here too—"

Their mother, Sofia Ramos Moreno, emerged from the bedroom, weary and resigned in a cream sweater and jeans. She regarded the police thoughtfully before giving me a tired smile. "It's good to see you, Ms. Giles. Innis has been like this since Lieutenant Lawrence asked if we wanted to share a suite."

I grinned down at the kid. "Super Smash Brothers sounds awesome."

"We brought burgers, but if you need something else, just give the front desk a call," Detective Davis said.

"Come on!" Innis tugged on my hands.

Shaking my head, I let the kid drag me off to the sofa.

In the background, the others conferred.

"What happened?" Innis whispered as they handed me a controller.

"I ran into even more unfriendly people. There are a lot of those around," I said.

"Human or fairy people?" Innis asked.

"Fey and...I don't know what the other guy is," I said, keeping my voice low. "But if you come across anyone who acts possessed? Jerky and dazed, like they're not awake? You need to get away. Fast."

Innis' eyes grew very big. "What happened?"

I groaned, unsure of what to tell the kid. The Crow Knight was a threat. But maybe I should check with their mother first. "I'll tell you about it later."

"OK, but was Dreyson there?" Innis asked eagerly. "Did you see him use that axe?"

"Dreyson arrived after," I said stiffly. "He did not use the axe."

"Boooooo," Innis said. "Did he get you more fancy food?"

"No, we had egg sandwiches."

"Oh," Innis said. "Nothing special?"

I shrugged. "I thought the ones I made were good, a little more flavorful than his."

"He made you a sandwich? You made him a sandwich?" Innis asked. "Where were you?"

"His house," I said, trying to look casual and probably failing.

Innis' eyes widened. "Is Dreyson your—"

"No," I said quickly. "There was an emergency. I had to leave my house too. Look, I'll tell you that story when your mom gets here."

"But—"

"Do you want me to whip you as Samus or what?" I asked.

Innis scrunched up their face. "You wish, old lady."

"Old lady?" I squinted at them, and they broke out in a gap-toothed grin. "I see how it is. Prepare for an epic beatdown, maggot."

After the detectives left, Ms. Ramos Moreno settled on the couch with a cup of tea. We sat on the floor, Innis chattering nonstop, asking about the supernatural, Dreyson, my family, and of course, the Fey Courts. I did my best to answer the simple questions and redirect the more complicated ones.

"Claire says she has a story to tell us if you're ready, Mom," Innis said after losing another round to me. I wasn't particularly proud of beating a child at a video game…but I damn well wasn't going to lose to one either.

"I can keep it pretty…clean," I said, looking up at her.

She cupped her mug, expression pensive. She was a slender woman in her late thirties, with brown skin and black curls. Now that she wasn't in the middle of yet another family crisis, there was a calm confidence to her.

"We do need to talk, Ms. Giles," she said, with just the trace of an accent. "But first, I'd like to apologize for going off on you the other night. That was very unfair. I am so grateful that you went when Innis called you, even though I am very displeased about what they've been doing behind my back. *Me vas a sacar canas verdes!*"

Innis laughed sheepishly. "I'm really sorry, Mom. Your hair isn't green yet, and I barely see any gray!"

"Hmph," Ms. Ramos Moreno said, not sounding impressed by that apology. "That's because I touch it up regularly."

"Hey, I'm glad it worked out," I said, holding my hands up. "How much do you know about the situation?"

"The lieutenant explained the HerbAway connection, the threat from the Fey, and part of what my husband was doing." She pressed her lips together firmly.

I got up and sat on the couch. This was not a discussion I should have sitting on the floor. "I can tell you what I know, but some of this gets heavy, Ms. Ramos Moreno."

"Please, just call me Sofia."

"Sure, and I'm Claire."

She nodded.

"What should I start with? Your husband?"

"I think that would be easiest," she said. "I hate to admit it, but I did *not* know what he was doing. If I did, I would have stopped him."

I gave her a summary of the story he told us before we went to the Shadow Dunes, our mission there, and the fact he was compelled to confront the Vernal Lord. I did not describe the injuries. I did not mention my adventures. "How did he know to go to Salvatore Mori?"

Sofia groaned. "He had a network security contract for some of Mr. Mori's businesses. But if I knew he was asking around, I would have gone elsewhere." Her gaze drifted to Innis, confirming that she knew about the Wergeld's reputation. She seemed to be better informed than her husband.

"Do you trust the men you work with?"

"That question is too vague," I said. "I trust Thomas Remington with my life and much higher value things. I, personally, have no reason to distrust Dreyson, specifically with my life. And SIU has good intentions, but limited resources."

Sofia's brows went up. "What about Mrs. Bancroft-Owens?"

"She wants the changeling kids alive, for political reasons. It's not...ideal, but I trust that motive over 'the goodness of her heart.' She's the type that might not have one, but she's better than her counterpart."

"I've heard." Sofia shuddered. "He attacked you?"

"Earlier today," I said. "And someone from the Courts broke into my house last night. He's called the Crow Knight. Has recognizable armor, and he's inhumanly fast. He's also...whimsical, which is why I'm still alive."

"Can he beat Dreyson?" Innis asked.

"Yes," I said. "If Dreyson isn't careful."

"Oh." Innis sat back on their haunches, their eyes wide. "Is he really big?"

"No, but he's fast. He's allegedly under orders from a VIP. I think he prefers to make deals, but he doesn't shy away from violence. If you come up against him, you *might* be able to talk your way out of it," I told Innis. "But unless you're hiding superhuman speed or strength, you can't outrun or outfight him."

"The regular Fey can't lie, right?" Innis asked.

"Not like we can," I said.

Sofia stiffened.

"Which is something you need to keep to yourselves," I told them. "As far as I know, Remington hasn't told anyone else, and I'm not going to."

"It's that big of a deal?" Innis asked.

"You can do something that the rest of them cannot, so yes. We're not spreading it around because that would make you a bigger target."

"Oh," Innis said.

"You've given me a lot to think about," Sofia said, her worried gaze on Innis. "Can I talk to you more later?" It wasn't really a question. This discussion was drifting into uncomfortable territory, and there were subjects she did not want brought up in front of Innis.

"Sure, I'm not going anywhere," I said.

"Hey, I'm hungry," Innis said, tugging on my sleeve. "Want to make tater tots in the oven?"

"Sure, if it's OK with your mom," I added quickly.

Sofia waved us off.

Innis did most of the cooking, to prove that they could. It was just preheating the oven and lining stuff up on trays, but I wasn't going to complain. We had a fun dinner of tater tots, mozzarella sticks, and soft pretzels with spinach artichoke dip. Dreyson could take hosting tips from the kid.

Eventually, Sofia sent the kid off to bed and firmly shut the bedroom door. I doubted that would stop the kid from eavesdropping, but we couldn't make it too easy.

"We're going to need something stiffer for this conversation," Sofia told me as she brought out a mostly full bottle of Glenlivet single malt scotch. She poured us both a couple fingers. That definitely did *not* come with the room. She returned to the couch, her face hard.

I took a sip of the smooth smoky spirit. Nope, not in SIU's budget.

"I want to thank you again for risking your life to save my child." Sofia inhaled deeply, staring at the floor. "I've been so busy at work. I didn't think things had gotten so bad." Her voice cracked. A week ago, she was a normal human, with a normal husband, a mostly normal child, and an enviable life.

I took another drink, knowing this was just the warm-up.

"I feel awful. If I had been paying attention, this wouldn't have happened." She rested her face in one hand. "But I was so busy, so sure everything was under control. I missed the signs."

"Your husband should have just talked to you first, instead of concocting a wild story, appealing to an infamous fanatic arms dealer, and rushing off to the Shadow Dunes," I said. "It doesn't matter how noble his intentions were."

She nodded. "I...know that. I know he was doing his best to protect us. But that's a cold comfort when he's dying in that hospital bed." She took a swig of scotch, squeezing her eyes shut. "All right, let's get this out of the way. Yes, I knew Innis wasn't like other kids. We both did. The difference was, I thought it was my fault."

"Why?" I blinked. Was there something extramarital going on? I almost said that aloud, but bit my tongue in time.

Sofia groaned, not looking up from her lap. "Please understand, Claire. I oversee a fairly large R&D lab. I consider myself modern, with a scientific-focus. But my family is different. I have an aunt with a reputation as a *bruja*. Before her, it was my great-grandmother and her twin brother. In the family lore, we have an extra...spark of something. I thought, when we first saw the teeth and the green skin, I thought it was from me."

"Oh," I said, because I would not have thought that at all.

"Initially, the illusion was sporadic. It stopped flickering by the time they were eleven months. Leonard and I canceled so many things on the days when Innis couldn't blend in. It was so stressful, but thankfully, 'the baby is sick' is a very convincing excuse. Eventually I worked up the nerve to consult my aunt, and she told me that the child was not mine, not biologically. But by then, Innis was a toddler. They were happy, healthy, and so sweet. We loved them so much, and both Leonard and I agreed that we did not want to lose them. They were our child, no matter what."

"Didn't you worry that whoever swapped the kids would return for Innis?"

"Of course," Sofia said, biting her lip. "But we didn't know what to do about it. We didn't even know if our biological child was alive. We knew that one day Innis might see...different changes in their body, so we resolved to be the kind of parents that they could always come to. We needed them to trust us. It was...very different from our own upbringings." She laughed awkwardly. "So much time in therapy, so many fights with my mother about my parenting choices. Leonard had similar problems. Our parents love us, but the older generation has its own idea about how things work. Still, I think we succeeded, because in the past year, when Innis began to develop new abilities, they came to us."

I rubbed the back of my neck. I knew people with parents whom they trusted with every detail, who held open channels of communication with them. But that was all alien to me. Mother was a mystery unto herself, full of judgment and righteous fury. Dad was easier to get along with, but he was the type to agree with you to your face, then go do whatever he wanted anyway. I had to learn it somewhere.

"How did you come into this line of work?" Sofia asked.

"Learned about it a few years back. I was already going through some stuff, so it was less of a world-shattering event and more of a paradigm shift."

"No one prepared us for this mess," Sofia said, shaking her head. "Do you talk to your family about this?"

I laughed. It was the only polite response, though maybe disruptive: a loud burst of hysteria tapering off into hiccupping convulsions.

"I'm sorry. Should I not have asked?" Sofia gave me a sympathetic look.

"No, no, you're fine. I've just spent a lot of time hiding *everything* from them," I said, wiping my eyes. "There were some really close calls…" Like the time I had to conceal Mwanje's furry form under a too-small afghan. "But 'internet stunt' and 'LARPing group' are excellent cover stories."

Sofia winced. That was exactly what she was trying to avoid.

"You're a good parent," I said, because even if I didn't know exactly what that entailed, I liked to think I recognized it when I saw it.

"Am I, though?" she murmured. "Innis might think so, but my…other daughter might disagree."

"That's more about philosophy than methodology," I said, briefly wondering how things could have been if my parents were like Sofia and Leonard. It was too alien. "Innis is the one you raised. You looked into the future, predicted you would have to take extra steps to keep the rapport strong and build a good foundation. You put in the work, and they trust you, so it looks like your efforts paid off."

"Maybe," Sofia murmured, finishing off her scotch. "Or maybe I was just *pretending* that this fairy tale would have a happy ending." She blew out a long breath. "I tried to raise Innis to be more independent. Just in case. They took outdoor survival classes. Leonard read them all the folklore books we could find. I took them to the library, showed them how to do their own research, how to use public transit, and let them do it on their own. All the things I thought I would be too overprotective to teach a normal child at that age, I *encouraged* them to do." She sighed heavily.

That explained a lot.

"You gave them an advantage," I said.

"They love the freedom. I raised a sensible child," she said, smiling softly. "But children's brains are still developing, specifically the frontal cortex. Over time, I grew too comfortable, because Innis *rarely* had any problems. I was too overconfident, thinking my precocious child was as capable of rationality as any adult. They are extraordinary, but they are also still a child. It was naive to think they could match the same standard as an adult."

"Innis is a confident and clever kid, and they know it." The frontal cortex was the part of the brain that dealt with rational thought and promoted impulse control. Arguably, mine wasn't working correctly either, but I didn't have the excuse of being a child.

"I love who they are," Sofia said, misty-eyed. "But I don't think that will be enough to keep them safe."

I nodded sympathetically.

"Why do they want the children now? Why are they killing them?"

"I don't know," I said. "The prevailing theory is that they're cleaning up evidence. It doesn't matter if they leave behind changeling bodies, because they can claim the kids killed their families and the Courts dealt with the lawbreakers. But kidnapping human babies broke the Alluvian Treaties, making some very important people into oath-breakers. This has major cultural significance to the Fey. The original point of this project was to produce more Fey children, but along the way, the priorities changed." I sank back into the couch. "As for Ketch, he just hates the Fey and loves violence."

"Can you tell me about Dreyson?" Sofia asked hesitantly.

I groaned. "Maybe."

Sofia coughed into her hand. "Innis seems to think you two are good friends. And they keep comparing him to different superheroes."

"You mean they ask, 'who would win, Dreyson or Batman?' And then immediately give their answer and defend the argument with lots of exclamation points."

Sofia winced. "That is exactly right. How much has my child been texting you?"

"Often," I laughed.

"I'm sorry—"

"I don't mind," I said. "But I can't answer all the questions at the speed they're sent."

"You should have seen them when they got into dinosaurs..." Sofia rubbed her forehead. "It was an obsession. You would think I would be proud that my child was rattling off six and seven syllable scientific names, and I was, but it was dinosaurs all day, every day, for *months*."

I chuckled. "Dinosaurs are cool. I love them. My favorite is the Achillobator, one of the biggest in the raptor family. What's yours?"

"Don't you start," she said sternly. "And it's the pachychephalosaurus."

"Hard heads," I nodded approvingly.

"Little Innis went through a headbutting phase, specifically because of them," Sofia sighed. "It was annoying at the time, but now I miss those days." She shook her head. "I'm sorry. I'm getting distracted. Do you think we're better off trying to leave? I have family in Medellin. Leonard has relatives in Catania..."

"I don't know," I said. "The Courts are established here, but they're not in the same dimensional plane as we are. It might confuse them for a bit. It might not."

"That's what Detective Davis said. And I don't want to leave Leonard." She stared at her empty glass. "Innis didn't tell me, not till after what happened to Leonard. Didn't tell me that my other child could be alive, that they can feel her presence. I don't know how to think about that. I...I was a good mother to

Innis, but in doing so, I have utterly failed my biological child. Do you really think she's still alive?"

"It's possible," I said.

"That's happy news." She drew in a shaky breath, not looking reassured at all. "I'm sorry, can we talk later? I want to check on Innis."

"Sure," I said. "I'm going to hop in the shower, then, if you don't mind."

"Not at all." Sofia went to Innis' room and shut the door.

I used the facilities and went to my own room and opened my laptop, ensuring security measures were on for the work profile.

I opened Zareen's small file on Bancroft-Owens. She was firmly rooted in the city's financial structure and was one of the names that approved funding for SIU's inception over two decades ago. She, or someone with her surname, had been at this for nearly a century. She seemed very spry, but that was Illium for you.

As far as Zareen could tell, there was never a Mr. or another Mrs. Bancroft, Owens, or Bancroft-Owens on record. No known family. Some aliases sent personal funds to a variety of European institutions like museums, schools, and charitable foundations. Zareen thought they were actual donations and not money laundering fronts.

She was a respected Adept, though Zareen wasn't sure what flavor. Witches and mages were born with their own reservoir of magic. As far as I could tell, there wasn't a big difference. Witches tended to specialize in slower magic like charms and alchemy, whereas mages gravitated toward flashier, faster, and more combat-oriented spells. If one had the interest and the talent, one could do both.

Sorcerers were different. They used more rituals and often had to tap into something else for their magic pool, be it a patron deity, a location, or an item. Theoretically, anyone could learn sorcery, if they had access to magic. A lot of weaker witches studied sorcery to supplement their skills with good results. Revya was one of those; Naomi was likely one too.

An odd thud came from the common room. Was someone knocking? I shut my laptop, wondering if Sofia was ready for another conversation. Hopefully, Innis was already asleep.

I got up and opened my door.

He stood by the couch, in that terribly distinctive armor. Sofia lay facedown at his feet, unmoving.

He raised his head, that obnoxious helmet obscuring his eyes, and sighed heavily. "Hellcat, why are you here?"

"Innis, run!" I shouted, backing into my room and slamming the door shut. The knife came out of my bag.

Bits of the door exploded inward as he smashed through, those metal gauntlets shredding the particleboard. And then he was inside the small bedroom, blocking the only exit.

I didn't think, I just slashed, the upward arc of the blade slicing his chest and glancing across his throat. Reversing my trajectory, I went for a downward pass, knowing that the first cut was too shallow.

I never stood a chance.

He caught my wrist, gripping it with crushing force in one hand. With the other, he simply plucked the dagger from my fingers and threw it to the side, embedding it in the glass of the window. Then he grabbed me by the throat, lifting me off my feet. I kicked at him, but it felt futile and weak, even as I tried to pry his hands off my neck.

"Hellcat, you shouldn't be here," he said, his voice very soft. "You should have left when you had the chance."

"Go fuck yourself," I wheezed, hoping Innis took the distraction and ran.

The fingers around my neck tightened. Blood roared in my ears as I stared at the Crow Knight, my field of vision starting to shrink into blackness.

"Leave Claire alone!" Something thwacked against the Crow Knight, and he spun, still holding me aloft. The pressure on my throat briefly subsided.

Innis stood in the hall, a baseball bat in their hands.

"Run!" I rasped.

Innis backed up, their eyes wide with fright. But they shook the bat, like they were winding up for a home run.

"If you flee," the Crow Knight said in a shockingly pleasant voice. "I will kill her. Next, I will kill the woman you call 'mother.' And then I will catch you anyway, but they will still be dead. If you stay, perhaps we can come to an understanding."

"Don't listen to him, get out of here!" I snarled, even as he shoved me against a wall, knocking the wind out of me, his hand tightening around my neck again. Squaring my shoulders on the flat surface, I tried to use the extra leverage to push him away from me.

"Claire." The Crow Knight said my name like he was tasting it. He smiled with an inappropriate gentleness as he leaned in, the cool metal of his helmet pressed to my forehead. "If you don't be quiet, I really will have to kill you. I don't want to, but I have orders to do so."

"Innis, don't listen to him, just run—"

He squeezed, and the words died in my throat. I gasped, spots flickering in my vision.

"Shh, this is for your own good," he said. "Innis, child, I mean you no harm. My lord simply requires your return home, for your own safety."

"This city, with my parents, is my home," Innis snapped. "And put Claire down! You're choking her!"

The Crow Knight chuckled, even as he lowered me a couple inches so that my feet were touching the ground, but he did not let go. "I am sorry, but I have my orders. If you won't cooperate, then I must simply—"

I slammed my hand into his wrist, breaking the grip on my neck. Grabbing his shoulder, the metal plate slicing my hands, I drove my knee into his solar plexus. Hitting his armor hurt, but it didn't completely shield him from impact. He grunted, dragging me to the ground.

I wrapped my arms around his neck and locked my legs around his waist, trying to hold him in place. "Innis, I swear to Guanying, you better RUN!"

Instead, Innis charged forward, swinging that bat, smashing it into the Crow Knight's back. The strike echoed, as the bludgeon cracked in half on impact.

The Crow Knight winced, broke my limb-lock, and turned to Innis.

Innis' eyes widened, and they backed up.

"One last chance," the Crow Knight said gravely, even as he knelt over me, those metal fingers closing around my neck. "You alone can save Claire and your mother. You have my word."

"Don't belie—"

He pressed his other hand over my mouth, shaking his head. The metal bit into my lip, and I tasted blood. If I tried to chomp his gauntlets in retaliation, I would break my teeth.

"I heard that you can't lie, that if you do, you're forsworn and that ends badly for you," Innis said, their voice shaky but defiant.

"Close enough," the Crow Knight said, smiling. "So make me an offer, Innis of Illium. Swear that you will return to the Courts with me, in exchange for the safety of your family and friends."

Innis inhaled sharply, their eyes flashing gold. "You have to swear too."

"I will," the Crow Knight said solemnly.

"I swear I will willingly go with you to the Courts, if you swear that you will not hurt or kill Claire and my parents, and that any of them who were harmed should be restored to good health."

I blinked, oh that clever little shit.

"I will admit that I have already hurt Claire. But the injury isn't too severe."

Innis was silent for a second. "You will cause no further harm to Claire—"

"What if she attacks me?"

"You deserve it," Innis said sharply.

The Crow Knight glanced down at me, his smile widening at my glare. "She will try to kill me."

"You can have self-defense," Innis said reluctantly.

I made a growl in protest.

The Crow Knight laughed. "I find your terms agreeable. Let's hear it then, Innis of Illium."

"I swear that I will go with you willingly, to the Courts, if you swear that you will cause no further harm to my parents or Claire, except in self-defense, though killing is not allowed, and any of them who were harmed should be restored to good health."

"I, Corwin of the Spring Court, the Crow Knight of Skye, acting emissary of the Vernal Lord, so swear that if you willingly accompany me to the Courts, I shall cause no further harm to your parents, nor to Claire the Hellcat, except in self-defense, should it be necessary. I will not kill them, and any who were seriously harmed shall be restored to good health."

Innis nodded, even as the Crow Knight released me and stood, reaching a hand out for them.

"Come along now," he said.

"Don't—" I said, even as the child took the Crow Knight's hand and they both vanished.

Staggering to my feet, I lurched into the common area where Sofia stirred. I made my way to the phone and called it in.

"We're alive, but he took the kid," I said and hung up.

Chapter 20
Breathing Room

Subject: The Crow Knight

Aliases: Corwin of Skye, the Blackbird, the Crowfucker

Affiliations: ~~*The Courts*~~ *Most likely the Spring Court, formerly of the Blackbirds*

Species: Unknown

There is little point in including detailed descriptions of the Crow Knight's physical appearance, Fey are too adept at glamour. He appears as a humanoid white male, with long brown hair and black crow-themed armor. He possesses all the hallmarks of a sidhe warrior, making him dangerous in both melee and magical combat. He utilizes swords, favoring the saber over heavier varieties of blades.

His interactions with us have mostly been confined to brawls at the Shadow Dunes, violence due to intra-Court disputes, and a plethora of minor traffic violations.

— *H.B. for The City Archives*

I SAT WITH Sofia, trying to coax her awake. I wasn't sure if he hit her with blunt force or magic, but I didn't try to move her. She groaned, mumbling incoherently to herself.

The door rattled, seconds before it burst open. The lieutenant came in first, Detective Davis and Mwanje close behind.

I straightened up and waved. My throat hurt. I was lightheaded. And now that I had time to sit, I was starting to ache. But that did nothing to distract me from the terrible mistake I made.

Why did I ever tell Innis to bargain with that bastard? I should have told them to run. I did tell them to! Maybe they could have made it. No, that was unlikely, especially in a solo encounter. I gave them the advice on the assumption that there wouldn't be anyone else around to distract the Crow Knight. Not that I did a good job of that. Damn that precocious brat for listening to me. Damn that precocious brat for repeatedly blowing me off.

The lieutenant stared at me, a blaze of pale fury in his eyes—nothing new, then. I just didn't have the capacity to yell back at him, which was a real shame. Guess he could win this argument by default. To my surprise, Detective Davis whispered something in his ear, and he turned away, pointedly not looking at me. In fact, he stepped out into the hall.

Detective Davis knelt beside me, checking Sofia's pulse. "Can you tell me what happened?" she asked briskly, calm and businesslike.

"Crow Knight came alone. Didn't see what he did to her," I rasped.

"You're bleeding, and your neck is starting to bruise."

I shrugged, wincing as I swallowed. "I'll survive."

Mwanje returned from clearing the apartment. "If you didn't like the room, you could have said something. You didn't have to trash it," he told me with a lopsided smile, his breathing shaky.

I gave him two thumbs down.

He just laughed and stepped into the hall.

Remington walked in then, breathing hard. He took one look at me and came over, crouching down and steadying himself with his cane. "Sorry I took so long." He hugged me then, two arms carefully wrapping around my shoulders, the faint scent of his cologne soothing my nerves. He was warm, and he was someone I trusted. Having him here was a comfort I didn't realize I needed.

I hugged him back, shaking as some of the tension started to bleed out of me. "He took Innis."

"I know. You can tell us all about it later. Let's get you checked out."

"Bargained," I said, wincing. "Innis agreed to go."

"Otherwise he would kill you and Sofia," Remington said, always quick on the uptake.

"My fault, told the kid to—"

"Shh," Remington said, helping me up.

Dizziness rocked my balance. Ugh.

"I mean this in the nicest way possible, but stop talking, you're just making it worse."

"She hears that all the time." Mwanje chuckled, peeking back in. "And not in the nicest way possible."

This time I gave him both middle fingers, only to see that the cut on my palm was *still* oozing blood.

"Let's get you fixed up, and maybe you can type your report after," Remington said.

I started to nod, but the motion hurt.

The lieutenant stood in the doorway, watching us with a scowl.

Returning to the bedroom, I grabbed my stuff. My computer was undamaged, but there was a dent in the wall where the Crow Knight pinned me. I went to the window and pulled the knife out of the glass, surprised by how easily it slid free.

Detective Davis followed me in, surveying the damage.

"Tried to keep him busy. Innis hit him with a bat," I said. "Did nothing."

"Broke the bat," Detective Davis said. "Wouldn't call that nothing."

Was the wood weakened? Or did the kid have hidden strength? I hope so. They needed it.

I sheathed the knife, my mind looping back to the kid reaching out and taking the Crow Knight's hand. I should not have told them to bargain. I should have told them to run. I made the wrong call, and now Innis was paying for it.

I awoke curled in a ball and swaddled in blankets, my throat swollen and raw. Grimacing, I clawed my way out of the tangle. I was on the couch in Remington's office. He was awake at his desk sipping something in a mug. His gun was out on the desk. Between the bleary eyes and five o'clock shadow, it looked like he spent the night in his chair.

"Oh." He winced. "That looks even worse now."

I grumbled.

"I have painkillers, hold on." He grabbed me a couple ibuprofen, a two-pack of saltines, and a bottle of water.

"Coffee," I rasped, taking the pills.

"Water," he said firmly.

"Not my dad."

"Nor a barista," he said with a wink.

I scowled, but drank the water, even if swallowing stung.

"It's about ten in the morning. I'm going to find some breakfast."

I was hungry, but I wasn't sure how eating would work today. I was running perilously low on extra clothes, now down to a dark green oversized Saint Cassian's University hoodie and ripped jeans.

Cleaning up in the bathroom was another shock. I looked rough. My neck was a purplish-blue mess of fingermark bruises and angry red scratches left by metal gauntlets. My eyes were bloodshot. The cut on my hand didn't need stitches, but it was big. I had more bruises on my trunk, which I could conceal under my shirt. A lot of people were much worse off after encountering the Fey. Overall, I got off easy.

It just cost us Innis.

I shuddered, wiping my eyes. I was wallowing. I needed to stop. There wasn't time for it right now.

Last night, we went to the ER. I typed out a statement on my phone, which the lieutenant accepted grimly. He avoided talking to me, which meant he missed out on his only opportunity to have the last word.

It was magic that incapacitated Sofia, but the doctors said that there should not be any permanent damage. They still kept her overnight.

Remington and I crashed here, because the office wards were freshly reinforced and we had security measures that SIU could not use.

"Bancroft-Owens will be here at noon. She's calling in everyone," Remington said when I emerged. "Last night was the provocation she needed."

"Ketch?" I asked.

"She didn't say," Remington said. "Doubt it, though."

"Here?"

"Yeah, it's a neutral downtown location."

Was it, though? She was funding us.

Some of the pain started to dull. Taking ibuprofen on an empty stomach was unwise. I needed more food. I found a can of soup in the snack nook, heated it up, and drank down the too-salty yellow chicken broth and limp noodles. It hurt, but I was too hungry to care.

"If Valeria's is open, I'll grab you some soup," Remington said as we cleaned up the meeting area and put down more folding chairs.

SIU would be here, maybe Fleance, and of course, Dreyson. Well, maybe he wouldn't come. Mori could send any number of people. It didn't have to be Dreyson.

Remington watched me down more coffee. "You know, you weren't wrong to tell the kid to bargain."

My head snapped up, and I glared at him. He would do this when I couldn't argue back efficiently.

"I said it." Remington leaned on his cane. "You, Sofia, and the kid all walked away from the fight alive. That result was better than the others. I'm not saying that him taking the kid was ideal. But now we know exactly who kidnapped Innis and where they went, so we have a chance to regroup and get them back. We wouldn't know any of that if you and Sofia were dead."

I stared at him grimly. "Told them to run."

"You can be mad at me for it, but I'm glad they didn't. I'm glad that Cullen Crowfucker didn't get to kill you."

"Eww," I said.

"I know, right? Can you believe he does that to birds? It's absolutely sick, criminal even." Remington beamed at me.

I let out a wheezing laugh, then grimaced. This wasn't the first time Remington started a malicious rumor against someone he didn't like. He might be able to make this one stick. "Stop. Laughing hurts."

Remington gave me a crooked grin. "I'm serious, Claire. I know how you think. I do the same thing. And you have to remember that your advice got Innis and Sofia out alive. You didn't abandon the kid. You didn't trade them. The kid stepped up and bought us all time to save you and themselves."

"Shouldn't have had to."

"I know," Remington said gravely. "But they did, and now we have to do our part. So don't waste energy feeling guilty. That fixes nothing. Our focus is solutions."

He was right. That was obvious. But I still needed to hear it.

"Thanks," I said, my eyes watering a little.

"You can thank the kid for being brave, and then yell at them for being stubborn once we get them back," he said, patting my shoulder. "And after your throat heals up."

I nodded and regretted the motion immediately.

Remington went to get the door for some early arrivals, and then he stepped out to pick up some lunch.

The warning text arrived as a large familiar shadow appeared in the office doorway. I started to pull my hood back up, but it was too late, he was looking right at me.

He's back.

Dreyson wore a black duster, a blackened chainmail tunic underneath, cinched with a pouch-laden leather belt. He didn't clink when he walked, so there was magic involved. Tapered black pants and knee-high leather boots finished off his monochrome outfit. All he needed was a big fur cape and horns, and then he could step into any generic dark lord position.

I looked up, lips pressed firmly together as I raised my chin.

That single eye focused on my throat, then flicked back up to meet my gaze. I didn't know if it was just because of the scars or his ironclad willpower, but he had a grade A poker face. He stopped in front of my desk, looming, as was his way, and even though I couldn't read his face, there was an intensity to him that made me want to back up.

But I didn't. This was my territory. I wasn't going to give him a goddamn inch. I pulled my collar up, not keen on showing off my injuries.

"It's a healing poultice," he said flatly and set a Ziploc bag on my desk. "The same kind they're using on Liam. It should speed up recovery."

Silently, I debated how wise it was to take another unsolicited magic item from him. On the upside, maybe I would be able to talk by the end of the day. Or I could be really unlucky and it could turn into a snake-construct and bite my face off. One outcome was a lot more likely than the other, though.

"It will help, and the ingredients are all ethically sourced," Dreyson said, his tone civil.

I did not miss the implication that he made it. And I was, briefly, tempted to ignore him and the offer of help. But my throat hurt, and I was meaner (and more effective) when I could talk, so I opened the bag. Inside was a cheesecloth poultice, filled with crushed plants and what looked like cotton balls, it smelled faintly of astringent herbs mixed with a hint of vanilla: warm, spiced, and floral. The poultice was damp, but not dripping, and I wound it around my neck like a scarf. A cool, almost minty burn ran along my skin.

I sat back in my chair, watching him not fidget. He was statue-still. It was kind of eerie. I silently bounced my knee.

Dreyson finally sat down, now looking me over again. His gaze stopped on a few things, my bandaged hand, my cut lip, and my bloodshot eyes.

Maybe it was polite that he was waiting for my throat to heal before we started Round Two. But I wasn't in the mood to hold back now. Seeing him brought back my bad mood. After everything, I was grumpy, in pain, and certainly not ready to hear *him* critique my decisions, especially when I was still in the midst of doing so myself. If he pushed me, well...Dreyson was a grown-ass man. He could take it. He was even wearing armor.

"So this was all from the Crow Knight?" Dreyson asked. "Not Ketch?"

"Yeah," I said, my voice still raspy, but the scraping pressure in my throat was already subsiding. So he knew about yesterday's encounters.

"And he kidnapped Innis," Dreyson's voice was calm. He spoke hesitantly, the sentence starting even, but Innis' name came out heavy and gravelly. Dreyson flinched and looked down, avoiding my gaze.

It wasn't much, but it wasn't what I expected either. I realized then that he was worried about the kid too.

Now it didn't seem so fun to lash out at him. Some of that anger drained away, because I also recognized that note of regret in his voice. Or maybe I was just projecting. What did I know?

I rubbed my eyes, wincing as I moved my head. "Yeah, he took Innis." It hurt less than it should have to say those words. "You can say it. I royally fucked up trying to protect the kid. I did the exact opposite. I got them taken instead. You would have done a better job."

Dreyson jerked back like I had slapped him. A minute ago, I would have found that hilarious. Now it was just awkward.

"I'm sorry," he said.

"It wasn't—"

"No, I'm sorry I lost my temper yesterday," Dreyson said plainly. "Cooperation goes both ways. You weren't wrong to be cautious or to question my motives." He took a deep breath. "Naomi vetted Wilder. I took her word for it. It's not an excuse, it's an explanation. The responsibility was mine. You were...not out of line to question my professionalism." He gritted his teeth.

"I know," I said, because I was an asshole.

He gave me a sharp look.

"But people make mistakes, and if they're good, then they try to fix them. I do it all the goddamn time," I said, shaking my head. "It's not the end of the world...till it is."

Dreyson snorted. "Yeah."

I tapped my desk. "To my knowledge, you didn't have an obligation to me or the kid."

"To your knowledge," Dreyson said.

"Yeah, and I can only make decisions based on the information I have, and I only have that information if it is *shared* with me." The words came out terse.

Dreyson crossed his arms. "Wilder was injured in my care, by one of my teammates. I have a professional and personal obligation to his interests now."

"You didn't say that yesterday."

"You didn't give me a chance."

"I did!" I scowled. "You were too busy being mad and telling me to mind my own business."

"All right." Dreyson rubbed his forehead. "But you were aggressive too. I was upset about Naomi. I...wasn't as rational as I should have been."

"Yeah, you came at me—verbally," I said. "And when that happens, I hit back and uh...sometimes get under people's skin and escalate."

"You don't say," Dreyson said, expression deadpan.

"Immovable object meet unstoppable force," I said, waving my hand. "Rem said I made some of it about you while saying it wasn't about you, so sorry for the confusion. Innis was the priority, and me not sharing their info had nothing to do with you. Even if there were concerns about operations, I wasn't planning on saying anything too anyone. Too many people knew, and you saw what happened. But then you kept demanding to know why...and I decided to answer 'why not' instead. I probably should have just stopped talking. Don't say it."

Dreyson sighed. "The way you said it sounded like you think me especially untrustworthy."

I rested one hand over my eyes. "Rem also said that I was unclear. I meant that 'I didn't know how you would react, and didn't want to deal with that can of worms then,' as opposed to 'I think you're a psychopathic child-murderer who can't be trusted.' To be fair, if I actually thought that, I would have said so yesterday, unwise as that might be."

"I know," Dreyson said dryly. "That occurred to me later." He paused. "The detective and the lieutenant witnessed our entire exchange." He exhaled slowly, wincing, like he only just remembered that part.

"Yeah. I'd be mortified too, but I was too mad at you. And they were so shocked and embarrassed that they didn't say much in the aftermath." And then Ketch attacked, so we didn't have to address it. Now that I thought about it, maybe I should send Ketch a fruit basket and a card in gratitude. That would go over splendidly. Yeah, bad idea. Stop that train of thought.

"I think I'm mortified enough for the both of us," Dreyson said, shaking his head.

"Yeah, you broke my coffee mug in your exit too," I said, sprinkling a soupçon of artisanal salt in the wound.

Dreyson closed his eye, nostrils flaring, lips pressed firmly together for a moment. "My apologies. That was unintentional. I will replace it."

"Don't worry about it," I said, more satisfied by his offer and his clear discomfort than any need for another mug. I had a whole cupboard of expendable thrift store mugs. Sometimes things got messy here. Sometimes you had to bust a cup on someone's head. "And don't feel too bad. I am *very good* at upsetting people. Jon can vouch for that."

Dreyson looked away. "A little too good, given recent events."

"Ketch had it coming," I said. "I'm a big fan of bodily autonomy, and he violated that on a disturbing level." I assumed that was a big reason why Dreyson was behaving so civilly today. Because I kept Naomi alive. But it was hard to tell how much of this good will was out of obligation and personal pride, and how much was…anything else.

Dreyson gave me a faint smile. "Ketch has had it coming for a very long time."

"Yeah." I took a breath, because it was my turn to finish squaring things. This part was less fun. "I get Innis, maybe a little too well, and that *is* making me attached. But if you say anything about 'maternal tendencies,' I will shoot you."

"I would not accuse you of demonstrating that particular trait."

"Thanks," I said. "And I know that you genuinely like Innis, so I don't think you'd hurt them. But…they really look up to you. Not just because you're tall. They think you're a superhero. They text me to ask about your exploits. They think you're the best. If you'd been even a little cold to them after finding out they were a changeling, it would have crushed them." I looked down at the bandage around my hand. I would need to change it soon. "I didn't want to risk that, not right now. They're going through enough grappling with their identity, the state of their father, and the fact things are trying to kill them."

"That is…more understandable," Dreyson said. "But I didn't realize that the child thought so highly of me."

"When you ripped into the lieutenant at the Centerpointe, their face just lit up. They were very impressed. They don't like him either," I said, smiling at the memory. "Anyway, I'm sorry I hurt your feelings. That was rude of me."

Dreyson stiffened, jaw twitching. "You didn't— You were offensive, Ms. Giles."

"Sure, that too, but you're *offended* by someone farting in church, or taking aim at your rep. I wouldn't have pissed you off as much if you were just offended. I know a lot of people say shit about you, and you don't seem bothered at all. But yesterday maybe you expected differently from me, and that probably stung. I know I was fuming, because we did get personal. And even if you were being unreasonable, I shouldn't have behaved that way either. I feel bad, and I'm sorry."

Dreyson sighed. "This is a lot harder when you can just come out and say things like that, Claire."

"You should have gotten your speech in before I started recovering." I shrugged.

"It didn't seem fair," Dreyson said.

"I don't play fair," I said.

Dreyson leaned back and crossed his arms. "I'll keep that in mind."

"We good, then?" I asked.

"Yes," Dreyson said. "Now do you want to tell me what happened last night?"

I did not want to tell him. I did not want to think about it. But I still did, because it was necessary, from the ambush by Naomi/Ketch, to the talk with Sofia, to the fight with the Crow Knight.

"He says his name is Corwin, from the Spring Court, blah blah blah Crowfucker of Skye or some shit." I clenched my fists. "Also, he ruined breath play for me."

Dreyson coughed.

"Kidding," I muttered, touching my neck. "Shit, this thing is potent." The pain was still there, but it was fading fast. "I know I told them to bargain with the Crow Knight. But when he showed up, I also told the kid to run—"

"People usually do the first thing you tell them to," Dreyson said. "And in this case, that wasn't a mistake. Innis was very clever, but I think the Crow Knight might have guided them."

"Yeah." I clenched my teeth, knowing he was right.

"He made Innis drive a hard bargain to countermand his alleged orders. He could have killed you, incapacitated the mother, and taken Innis anyway. He played it this way intentionally." Dreyson stroked his chin.

"So what, I'm Crowbait? Because I know my limits, and I'd rather take him out with a long-range weapon."

"He's sworn not to harm you," Dreyson said. "Except in self-defense, and even then there's a 'no killing' clause. I do find it interesting that he'd let himself be maneuvered into that position."

"Some things live too long and get really weird," I said. "Maybe he has a death wish."

"Or maybe he has less violent intentions toward you. That can't be so hard to imagine," Dreyson said, tilting his head to the side.

"I *only* have violent intentions toward him," I said. "He broke into my house, roughed me up, kidnapped Innis, and I'm not the least bit interested in him, except as target practice. Maybe he didn't kill those other families, but—" I bristled, biting my lip. "He doesn't matter. This entire week sucked, and I don't have the emotional bandwidth to process everything that's happened. Being semi-respectable for Innis and apologizing to you like a grownup wiped me out completely." The words poured out of me. I put my hands flat on the desk with enough force to sting. "I just want to get the kid back, eat some delicious food, and take a very long nap, without anyone trying to kill me."

Dreyson reached out, his massive hand covering mine.

The contact shocked me. I stared at it for a moment. His rough palm was very warm, but I didn't pull away.

"Do you want to take care of him yourself? Or may I?" he asked, watching my face, his tone careful.

It took me a second to realize that he was *asking* my permission to deal with the Crow Knight. "I wouldn't mind a shot at him," I said with a half smile. "If I can get a warded gun that'll work in the Fey domains. But I won't be mad if you end up getting him. The goal is rescuing Innis. The Crow Knight is incidental at best."

Dreyson chuckled. "He would be offended to hear that."

"Good," I said. "Feel free to repeat it to him. Exaggerate if you like." I studied his hand for a moment. Scars crisscrossed all along the exposed skin. He had blunt short nails, but they were clean. I lifted one finger, slowly stroking the inside of his palm. He did not move, but his eye flicked down to our hands. "You know, most people just get me flowers."

Dreyson regarded me thoughtfully. "Do you want flowers?"

My breath caught, but I didn't look away. "Sometimes," I said. "Are you offering?"

"I'm not most people, Claire," Dreyson said, but he did not move his hand.

Interlude II

THE CROW KNIGHT deposited them in a coral stone room. Veins of gold gleamed in the walls, and vines grew up along the pillars, their pale star-shaped blossoms fragrant. Several brightly-colored cushions were placed around a low table covered in fruit and vibrant pink and green cakes.

Innis knew better than to eat or drink here. Even if it looked wonderful, even if it smelled wonderful, even if they were starving to death. If they took anything from this place, they might not be able to leave. And they were counting on escaping, just as soon as they figured out how things worked.

"Are you hungry?" The girl — *that girl* — walked into the room.

Innis did not bother with an answer.

They were a similar height, the girl wearing a bright yellow dress that was more robe than ballgown. Her dark curly hair was in a single braid. Her skin was lighter than theirs, her bone structure more delicate, more like their mother's. They were not identical, but they could have been siblings.

"We finally meet," Innis said.

The girl nodded solemnly.

They were being watched.

"What's the point of this?" Innis asked.

"I don't know," the girl said, and Innis knew that she was lying. "Aren't you hungry?"

Innis snorted. "It doesn't matter. I won't accept food or drink from here."

"Because then you would belong to this place?" the girl asked, her smile cruel. "Are you so certain that you don't already?"

"I am," Innis said with more confidence than they felt. "Illium is my home. I don't want to stay here. I don't want to give them up. I didn't choose any of this." They looked around, but did not spot any watchers.

"Do you really think they would still want you if they knew?" the girl asked, like she didn't already know.

"Yes," Innis said. Their parents did know.

"What if I want to return? Are you afraid that they will love me more?" There was a sharp light in her eyes, an unsheathed viciousness to the question.

"A little," Innis said after a long pause, because they knew not to lie here, not to lie unless they absolutely had to.

The two children faced each other. Innis knew the girl was human. Even if she had special knowledge, Innis was probably stronger. They could remove their rival. Innis' own position would be secure, if only they got rid of this girl. Their parents *never* had to know.

But that wasn't the person Leonard and Sofia raised. Innis felt their face go hot with shame for even considering the idea.

"Do you want to come with me?" Innis asked.

The girl frowned.

"Our parents have enough love for the both of us," Innis said. "They always wanted more kids. They would love to meet you."

The girl's smile tightened as she took a step back, an animal show of fear. She was not expecting that response.

"Do you hate me for stealing your life?" Innis asked flatly. They had always wondered.

"No," the girl said, and Innis couldn't tell if she was lying. "But I am mad at you."

Innis nodded. "I'm mad at you too. But we're tied together in this, and I don't hate you enough to want to punish myself or our parents."

The Crow Knight returned, waving the girl out. He was smiling. Innis did not trust that smile.

"Hold this for me, will you?" The Crow Knight extended one arm, a small black orb the size of a ping pong ball in his bare hand.

"Not falling for that again," Innis said, shoving their hands into their pockets.

The Crow Knight laughed. "It will be unpleasant if you force our hands, Innis of Illium. This object is not magical, and while it may cause you some discomfort, I'd ask that you hold it for as long as you can."

Innis sighed, suspecting the Crow Knight of lying. They were pretty sure he could lie too, but that was only a hunch.

"If it hurts, just drop it. I promise it is not magical, poisoned, nor prone to growing spikes."

"What is it?" Innis asked.

"Cold iron," the Crow Knight said.

Aware that this could get worse, Innis complied.

The metal burned too cold, like ice ratcheted up to another level. It sat in their palm, much heavier than it looked. Innis groaned, that alien cold sapping their strength. Regular iron, or whatever they used around the house, didn't bother them as much. After almost a minute they dropped the ball, and the Crow Knight caught it before it could hit the ground.

The skin on their palm was peeling and angry like a burn.

Nodding, the Crow Knight gripped Innis' wrist, holding up the hand so someone just out of sight could see the results. "Does it hurt?"

"Duh," Innis hissed.

"I'm sorry," the Crow Knight said, still holding that ball in his hand. "Tell me, you live in a busy part of the city, full of metal and 'normal' human houses."

Innis nodded hesitantly.

"Do you get burned like that often?"

"Enough."

The Crow Knight gave an exasperated sigh but did not lose that relaxed stance. "How often are you burned by metal that is not at an extreme temperature? Once a day? Once a week?"

Innis shrugged. "Dunno."

The Crow Knight's lips twitched. "Interesting. One boy couldn't handle it at all. Said the pain was *excruciating*. But if you don't recall" — the Crow Knight tossed the ball into the air and caught it—"perhaps your reaction isn't so severe."

Innis said nothing, realizing the trap.

"That's very lucky," the Crow Knight said. "You're a clever kid."

Innis bit their lip, aware that this reveal was not good. Claire said it would be bad if the Fey learned that they could do something the rest could not. It might make them too interesting so then the Fey might never let them go.

"Now, let's talk about magic," the Crow Knight said.

With Dreyson or Claire, Innis would have been exuberant. But when they looked at the Crow Knight, despite his friendly smile and pleasant words, all they felt was dread.

Chapter 21
The Fellowship of Necessity

SIU has three heavy hitter Adept-Detectives with vastly different specialties, which is helpful because neither the Wergeld, nor the Sorcerer's Council, nor any of the major Covens like working with the police.

Detective Nina Davis specializes in folk magic, mostly of the defensive type. While this tradition has been derided as "backwoods hedgecraft" or "low-magic," Nina gets the job done quickly, affordably, and ethically. Her explanations of the arcane are the only ones that kind of make sense to me.

— From the Case Files of Thomas Remington

FROM OUTSIDE, REMINGTON texted to ask if it was safe to return. I rolled my eyes, but gave the assent.

Dreyson sat in his seat, legs in a figure four, his left arm draped over the back of his chair, his right hand in his lap. His thumb curled against his palm in the spot where my hand had been.

My right hand was still very warm.

Remington stopped in the doorway, brow arching when he saw my neck. "Fixed?"

"Mostly," I said, with minimal pain.

"Aww, I liked the three-packs-a-day voice. It was very sinister," he said, shaking his head in mock disappointment as he set a bag of tacos on my desk. "Just so we're all on the same page, we *are* going to the seat of the Spring Court to confront the Vernal Lord for violating the treaties and to retrieve the kid?"

"Yes," Dreyson nodded.

"And Mori is OK with the kid and the entire mission?" I asked cautiously.

"Whatever allegiances the changelings have, their ability to do real damage evaporated when their cover was blown," Dreyson said. "My assessment is that Innis poses no innate threat to humanity. Mrs. Bancroft-Owens gave a similar report on the Foxglove Pact changelings, but I can only speak from personal experience."

"So Mori is OK with this?" I repeated.

Dreyson sighed. "He agreed to the terms."

Those were two different things, but they were close enough for now.

Remington coughed. "SIU is splitting their forces between this run and protecting the remaining families. Mrs. Bancroft-Owens is coming. She'll probably bring Samuel."

"The driver?"

"Yes," Remington said. "I assume he's a fighter."

"He can take care of himself," Dreyson said. "He mixes melee and magic. But Mrs. Bancroft-Owens doesn't need his protection. She's a perfectly capable mage with extensive training." He glanced at Remington. "Is SIU providing weapons for you?"

Remington nodded. "Warded guns, enchanted ammo, and riot armor, though we'll pass on the latter. Too cumbersome, not enough protection. There's still some debate over who's coming and who's staying back, in case Ketch tries something."

Dreyson frowned.

"I'll try not to start any fights," I said.

"That's a relief. You're definitely the one I'm worried about," Remington said without missing a beat as he reached for a taco.

Mrs. Bancroft-Owens walked into the office two minutes before noon. She wore a dusty rose pantsuit, with a conservative cut and lots of jewelry. Her driver, Samuel, followed with Sofia. Sofia was in a sage green pantsuit, alert and ready, like she was about to give a presentation to a boardroom.

I wasn't expecting her.

Sofia narrowed her eyes at me, a flash of fury on her face.

I nodded back, knowing she was probably mad that I told Innis to bargain. Understandable.

She bit her lip as Samuel whispered something to her and guided her to the conference area.

The lieutenant came next, carrying three large metal gun cases, his expression hard. He tensed when he saw Dreyson.

Dreyson stared right back.

Huffing in irritation, the lieutenant silently went to the conference area and set the cases down in a corner.

Detective Davis and Mwanje arrived last. Detective Davis was in old jeans and an inside-out blue flannel shirt, some errant red thread sewn into the hem. Gray-blue glass bottles hung from her belt. A pair of aviator sunglasses rested atop her head. She carried a battered brown leather messenger bag. Mwanje had the matching one and a large military rucksack on his back. He wore gray sweats—disposable clothes that did not quite cover the rune-etched metal vambraces on his arms.

Dreyson and I took our chairs to the conference area.

I took the space between Dreyson and Mwanje, to act as a buffer.

Mrs. Bancroft-Owens surveyed the room, her gaze sharp. She wore gold jewelry and a lot of rings and bracelets adorned with big rocks. Looking at all that ostentatiousness gave me a headache, but not because it was a fashion faux-pas. Each piece was infused with magic. Packing all that power meant that a punch from her could literally knock someone into the astral plane. She was armored for a fight, and she was not to be trifled with.

Sofia wore a blue stone pendant that also gleamed with magic.

Samuel was harder to read: gray suit, gray eyes behind rimless glasses, platinum blonde hair slicked back. The lack of color made him look anemic, but he was handsome and maybe just a little older than me. Younger than I thought. He smiled politely at me.

I nodded back.

"You already know why we're here," Mrs. Bancroft-Owens began. Her voice carried, cool and crisp. "The Spring Court is in violation of the Alluvian Treaties. Last night, they came into Illium and abducted a child under Ms. Ramos Moreno's care. So we will be traveling to the domain of the Vernal Lord to lodge a formal complaint and demand the return of the 25 human children taken a decade ago, as well as the return of the changeling children, if that is what they want."

Sofia ground her teeth.

"This is a diplomatic mission to the Fey Courts, so we will have to travel heavily armed." Mrs. Bancroft-Owens gave us a frosty smile. "I don't expect them to make it easy, but I know their tricks. I can shorten the route and ensure we have an exit. Ms. Ramos Moreno, the complainant, will accompany us to state her case for the return of *both* of her children."

Sofia nodded, shoulders relaxing a little at that acknowledgment.

"The Fey Courts are not friendly territory, and the journey is dangerous." Mrs. Bancroft-Owens looked at me. Good to know whom she thought was the biggest liability. "I will be focused on greater magicks, diplomatic negotiations, and Ms. Ramos Moreno's safety."

No guarantees for the rest of us. Got it.

Lieutenant Lawrence, your service has been satisfactory. The Special Investigations Unit performed well, despite departmental hindrances." Mrs. Bancroft-Owens raised her chin. "Who will accompany me?"

The lieutenant exhaled slowly. "Detective Davis and Detective Mwanje will escort you."

"Understood, thank you," she said, though her voice held no warmth. "You and your mages are better suited to deal with my counterpart, should he try something foolish in my absence."

Like going after the surviving changelings or their families. I glanced at the grimacing lieutenant; he was not happy about staying behind. I had theories about why he landed the job as head of the squad when both Detective Davis and Detective Minuet were more qualified. What did he bring to a fight besides muscles and a gun?

Detective Davis opened her bag, pulling out packets of dried plants, ropes, and more bottles. "I have experience with the land. Mrs. Bancroft-Owens' guidance will shave time off our travel, but we'll still be traipsing through the woods of the Spring Court. Those are old trees and older magic. That place is nothing like our forests, so stay on the path," she said, her drawl heavier than before. "I'll be handling defense. I have my kit, so before we go, I'll fix you up with workings that guard against haints, curses, and our not-so-good neighbors." She didn't look at us while she spoke. Deftly, she slipped three long iron nails into a leather pouch embroidered with a red five-point star. She added coins, salt, a scrap of fabric, and dried herbs. Then she closed the drawstrings and looped a red cord through, tying it on with specific knots. She repeated the process, making her conjure bags while talking. "I have the sight, and I've walked those roads before, so when I tell you not to step somewhere, you best listen."

Dreyson leaned over, watching with interest.

"She's the brains, I'm the muscle," Mwanje said with an easy smile, and that was his speech.

"I will also be on security," Dreyson said, his tone neutral. He was *trying* to be civil. "If you have a moment to coordinate, Detective?"

Mwanje blinked, brows going up, but he didn't lose that smile. "Of course."

"Claire and I will handle sharpshooting," Remington said.

"We have warded guns to loan out for this trip," the lieutenant said, giving me a hard look. "And special ammunition for the Fey."

I smiled at that. You could load shotgun shells with rock salt and iron bearings, but shotguns required you to be kind of close to the target. SIU had custom cartridges made with iron, salt, silver, and sometimes spells etched on the bullets or the casings. They were *expensive*. But they were effective.

"All you need to do is escort us to the Vernal Lord. Any questions?" Mrs. Bancroft-Owens asked.

Plenty, but none that I wanted to ask in front of the group.

"Finish up preparations and then we'll move out."

The lieutenant opened the cases, looking displeased when Remington selected a shotgun. "You shouldn't get that close to anything over there," he told him.

"I can't move like I used to, Jon," Remington said with a shrug. "I'm just accounting for the fact that maybe something will get close to me. But I'll take a revolver too, if that'll ease your mind."

The lieutenant sighed. "Giles?"

"Can I take two too?" I asked, eyeing a black polymer rifle with a nice little aftermarket sight on it. Semiautomatics had a better rate of fire, but they also had a higher chance of jamming, misfiring, or complications due to bad luck hexes. A revolver would be good backup.

"Sure," the lieutenant rested his face in one hand. "Why not?"

"Yes," I said pumping my fist. "I take back all the terrible things I said about you today!"

He scowled at me.

"Which is actually nothing, because she just recovered her voice," Remington said with a grin.

That was true. and I saved the really awful things to say to his face.

"Giles…" The lieutenant unpacked more ammo for us. Everything was 9mm—the caliber mattered less than interchangeability. "I'm sorry about last night. You and the Wilder-Ramos family should have been safe. I take full responsibility."

I snorted, because of course he was apologizing for something that wasn't his fault. He really didn't understand how apologies worked. "I'm not blaming you for that. That's all on the Courts, especially that Crowfucker." I lowered my voice. "Can you believe he does that to birds?"

The lieutenant stared awkwardly at the floor, like he actually did know what kind of depraved acts the Crow Knight inflicted on birds. "Be careful. Both of you."

"Because the guns are expensive and your funding is tight. understood." I happily checked the sights. They looked good, but I wouldn't know till I got to test fire the gun. Then I began loading spare magazines.

Remington cleared his throat.

"You should also come back so we can deal with Hartford and Ryan," the lieutenant said. "Without you, the complaint disappears."

I paused, suddenly realizing that the lieutenant was trying to be civil. I had a smartass response on the tip of my tongue, but he was trying to bury the hatchet. There was no need to dig up a rusty spoon to shank him with. "Excellent reminder. I am too spiteful to be trapped in fairyland. I need to come back, wreck their shit, and make them regret ever laying eyes on me."

"You're good at that," the lieutenant said.

Remington laughed.

Someone tapped my shoulder. "Ms. Giles, I need to speak with you," Sofia said, her expression stony.

I was "Ms. Giles" again. Uh-oh. My good humor withered. I nodded and set the magazine down. "Hey, Rem, can we borrow your office?"

"Yes," he said, eyes darting between us. He raised his chin questioningly.

I shook my head and led her back. My mess of blankets was still on the couch. I hastily folded them so she could sit.

She just crossed her arms, hugging herself tightly, her dark eyes accusing. "How could you let him take them?"

I tilted my head back, staring up at the ceiling, my hand going to my throat, slightly regretting letting Dreyson fix me up. Looking more beat up might assuage her anger. Oh well. "I didn't let him take them. I couldn't stop him, and I tried. But that's not the same as letting him. Still, I'm sorry."

"You—" She clenched her fists. "Innis trusted you! My husband trusted you!"

"Yeah," I said, feeling like an absolute shithead. What could I say? That they were silly for doing so? That wouldn't help. "Sofia, I'm one human. I did what I could. I still got my ass handed to me in a takeout box. And then Innis saved us both." I touched the poultice on my neck. "I'm grateful that they did that, but I don't feel good about it."

Sofia sniffled. She started pacing. "One moment I was getting ready to come talk to you…and then I woke up in the hospital. I never got a look at him."

"He's really fast," I said.

"Would he have caught Innis?" she asked, half to herself.

I bit my lip. Saying that felt like making an excuse, even if it was the truth. "You're right to be upset, but I don't know what you think happened."

Sofia stopped pacing, her eyes going from my face to the bandage on my neck, and then my hands. She groaned and finally dropped down on the couch. "The detectives told me some of it, but—" She clenched her fists. "It's fuzzy. I was upset. Maybe I misunderstood. What actually happened, Claire?"

I sat down, leaving some space between us, and recounted the events. From discovery, to the too-short fight, to Innis breaking the bat. "That kid is going to be a hell of a teenager."

Sofia's bark of laughter turned into a strangled sob.

"Crowfucker kicked my ass embarrassingly fast and told Innis if they didn't agree to come with him, he'd kill us and take them anyway. So they stayed and bargained. Innis really did some clever wording. There terms were that they would leave willingly. In return, he could not hurt or kill us and 'any who were harmed shall be restored to good health.' They agreed to go. But they didn't agree to *stay* in the Courts. So there's that."

Sofia exhaled slowly. "You didn't just let him take them." The statement seemed like more of a reassurance to herself and not a question for me.

"Of course not, but I am kind of responsible. You were there when I told Innis to bargain with him. But it was a contingency plan, in case Innis met him alone; I wasn't setting them up."

Sofia stared at the floor.

"I really didn't expect or want the kid to sacrifice themselves to save us."

"I didn't raise a coward!" Sofia snapped, glaring at me, her eyes watering.

"No, you didn't," I said carefully.

"But maybe I should have." Sofia started sobbing into her hands, tears leaking down her face as she covered her eyes. I retrieved a box of tissues from Remington's desk, placed there specifically for crying clients.

"I'm sorry," I said again, feeling useless.

"Why? I'm the one who couldn't protect them!" she wailed. "Not Innis, not their sister, not Leonard! And now I'm losing them all!"

I sat with her, letting her cry it out, because she needed to. Some things should not be bottled up and left to fester. "We're going after Innis," I reminded her as the hiccupping gasps began to subside. "They were very smart about their terms. They think carefully about how to talk to the Fey, and it shows. You taught them well. They gave us wiggle room."

Sofia blew her nose. "You don't think he hurt them, do you?"

"No, he's not the type," I said. But who knew what would happen to Innis in the Courts. "I don't think he's the one killing families. I think he's the one taking kids alive, if that's any consolation." I rested my forehead in my hands. "Sofia, I feel like garbage about last night. I can't say anything that's going to make it better, but I'm coming along to help get Innis back."

She nodded weakly, wiping her eyes. "I know. Thank you." She got up, turning her back to me. Her shoulders trembled. "I'm ready to go back." She started to take a step forward, then burst into tears again and sat back down. She hugged me then, not because she forgave me, but because I was there. I gently patted her back.

"It's going to be OK," I said, knowing that I might be wrong and also knowing that *if* that was the case, my white lies would be the least of her worries.

She clung to me, breathing deeply and blotting at her face with more tissues. I let her, because it was all I could do.

"I'm sorry," she said, blowing her nose again. "I should be handling this better-"

"You're doing amazing. I can't imagine how awful this is," I said, trying to muster an encouraging smile. It felt wrong.

When Sofia was really ready, I followed her back out.

Dreyson sat beside Detective Davis, examining one of her conjure bags. "This is well-crafted," he said.

"Of course it is," she said, not looking up from her pouches. "We don't all get to go to continental academies to learn how to perform a working."

Dreyson just studied the red cord. "Never thought the trip necessary. I'm familiar with some of the elements, but not the nuances of this tradition. I'm simply curious."

She squinted at him, like she didn't quite buy his sincerity.

"I understand the use of the carpentry nails, the silver coins, and the salt. But the witchmark, the rag, and the knots are unfamiliar. I also meant to ask about the herbs. I have extra rowan twigs if you need any."

"Dried yarrow and powdered ivy root," she said after a moment. "Maybe to the rowan."

"Hey, you got a minute?" Mwanje marched toward Remington's office, grabbed my arm, and practically dragged me in there before I could answer.

Mwanje shut the door. "What did you do to Dreyson?"

"What?" I asked.

"Like, did you blackmail him? Did you bribe him? Did you...threaten him?"

"What?" I asked again, louder this time, completely lost.

"You use that word a lot," he told me.

"Because you are *terrible* at explanations."

Mwanje chuckled. "Yeah, OK. Let me start over. While you were busy with the angry mama bear—good job calming her down by the way, she didn't want nothing to do with any of us—Dreyson asks me to step out to the front room. I figure we're going to have to sort out dominance, maybe make some oblique threats. Best to get the pissing match over with. Instead, we have a civil conversation about our respective strategies and ideal formations. Fair enough, he's a professional. That's great. I love working with professionals. And *then*..." Mwanje grabbed my shoulders, shaking me with each word. "*And then*," he repeated, with heavy neck-flopping emphasis. "He *apologized* to me for making a disparaging remark about my 'condition,' and explained that it was wrong of him to insult me for something I could not control."

I blinked, brain rattled from Mwanje's emotional exhibition.

"It was that flat deadpan delivery, but those were the words coming out of his mouth." Mwanje was bent over, his face inches from mine, his eyes enormous. "He apologized! To my face! Mori's personal berserker, the head of Arcane Security for the Wergeld! He apologized to me! What did you do to the mercenary, Claire? How did you break him? Did he lose a bet? Can you do it to the lieutenant?" He paused. "Because you absolutely *should not*!"

"I told him off for being a bigot," I said with a shrug. "That was ages ago."

"Claire, you met him less than a week ago."

He was right. Huh. Felt like longer, honestly. "When has that ever stopped me?"

Mwanje released my shoulders. "Oh, good point." He rubbed his chin. "I guess that's part of your charm." He stared off to the side. "Yeah, I can see that. I'm immune, but weaker-minded men..."

I rolled my eyes.

"So you didn't threaten him, or use mind control or any other form of coercion. And even if you did, you wouldn't confess it to an officer of the law..." Mwanje squinted. "OK, well, thanks, Claire. I'm officially weirded out, and we're planning on going to an aspect of fairyland filled with ambulatory trees and men who have inappropriate relationships with birds, so that's saying something..." He trailed off. "You know, the next time you decide to brainwash a Wergeld berserker, can you warn me in advance? As a professional courtesy. Please. I can only take so many surprises."

"Mwanje, I'm going to go talk to Detective Davis about her conjure bottles now."

"Sure, leave me alone to sort through these overwhelming feelings of confusion," he said sullenly. "I'll be fine."

"Glad to hear it," I said, opening the door.

"My therapist is going to want a word with you!" He shook a fist at me.

"Tell them to get in line!" I came out to see Samuel sitting on one side of Detective Davis, Dreyson on the other, and both of them staring into a blue-gray glass bottle filled with nails.

"Oh, there you are, Claire," she said. "You're just in time to spit into the witch bottle."

"What?" I blinked.

"Spit," she told me, pointing at the bottle. "Everyone is doing it."

Both Samuel and Dreyson looked at me expectantly, and suddenly I was eight, back on the playground with Rin Tani and Jake Stevens, right about to eat a live worm on a dare.

I made a very rude noise in the back of my throat and hocked a loogie into the bottle.

Detective Davis nodded approvingly.

I just stared, wondering if they'd convinced Mrs. Bancroft-Owens to do something so pedestrian. I understood the basic theoretical principles behind connective sympathy and the powerful associations of bodily fluids. But looking into that bottle, a mishmash of saliva dripping down the insides on the nails and bits of twisted metal, I was left pondering the most obvious truth: magic was really weird.

Chapter 22
The Expedition

Travel between Illium and the Courts is not recommended for novices. There are a plethora of dangers, not limited to the mercurial Fey and their peculiar cultural norms. The land itself possesses a level of awareness: the flora, the fauna, the very rocks themselves. And the Fey lands do not welcome trespassers. The concentration of arcane energies within Court biomes can have a variety of deleterious effects on the human body. Prolonged exposure can be fatal. Plan accordingly.

It is impossible to accurately map the layout of the Courts. Land masses move. There are numerous iterations of Court sovereign bodies: Seelie and Unseelie, Winter and Summer, Spring and Autumn. As the Spring and Autumn Courts are ascendant, their most common land masses are forests and grasslands, however the Autumn Court has seen increased desertification, with shrublands, deserts, and lava fields becoming more common. Whether this transition is an unconscious reflection of the Autumnal Lady's condition or the direct result of her will or whims, is unclear.

— *An Introduction to Illium by Ann Keyes*

WE WENT TO a Metropark north of Alluvia that bordered the Anian River. Remington and I had already set up the messages that needed to be sent in case we didn't return. Mine were notices for my parents, Ivy, and other close friends, as well as incriminating documents for Canaris. At Remington's recommendation, I had everything prepared ahead of time. It was easier that way.

We regrouped on a walking trail, Mrs. Bancroft-Owens leading the way. The revolver was in a holster under my jacket, the rifle slung over my shoulder with a carrying strap. I had a selection of charms in my pockets, spare magazines and Dreyson's knife clipped to my belt. Detective Davis' conjure bag hung on a leather thong around my neck, tucked under my shirt. This was me at my most heavily-armed, but I didn't feel anywhere near ready.

Remington wore his usual trench coat, cane in one hand, shotgun case in the other.

Weapon strapped on his back, Dreyson was already prepped to go.

Samuel carried a long wrapped bundle that looked like a sword.

Detective Davis had a lot of items on her belt: pouches, more of those gray-blue glass bottles in specially-sized holsters, her gun, and most strikingly, a two-foot-long bone-handled hunting dagger. She slid her sunglasses onto her face and pulled on a pair of latex gloves.

Poor Mwanje looked the silliest by far. He was in gray sweats, a loose oddly-fitting spiked leather harness over his clothes. It went around his neck, across his back and chest, and down around his thighs. It was very hardcore leather-daddy meets couch-potato in the most unflattering way.

"Not a word," he muttered to me.

"You're very brave," I told him.

"Just to remind you, I can fit your whole head in my mouth," he said, like I wasn't the one who stuck my face in there just to look around.

"Yeah," I said with a shrug. "What does that have to do with anything?"

Mwanje snorted.

We walked a trail for about ten minutes, then veered off into the brush. The leaves were starting to turn, a spectacle of red, gold, and orange.

"Poison ivy," Detective Davis warned, pointing to clusters of plants with reddening leaves. "Leaves of three, let it be."

"I'm immune," Mwanje said smugly as he marched through a patch of it.

I sighed. The stuff was *everywhere*. We spent another five minutes walking through a damn field of it. That couldn't be a coincidence. It was likely placed here as a deterrent. Not a bad idea for a natural barrier. Thankfully, I wore long pants and boots.

Finally we reached a large circle of gray mushrooms, barely poking out from under the leaves. It took me a moment to realize they were stone.

"If you need ointment, now is the time to apply it. If you have defensive charms, now is the time to activate them," Mrs. Bancroft-Owens told us. "Remember, do not accept gifts or make promises. Do not eat or drink anything offered to you. Do not attack anything unprovoked. Do not be rude. Do not thank anyone not in this party."

I twisted a few paper packets open to activate Revya's charms: an all-purpose warding spell, a sound-dampener so gunshots didn't blow out my hearing, and a little something for luck. They went back in my pocket, and the air seemed to shift around me.

I glanced over to Dreyson, whose gaze seemed distant.

"Solid spellwork," he said. "Do you have spares?"

I patted my pocket.

"Form a single-file line. Hold onto the person in front of you," Mrs. Bancroft-Owens ordered, like we were a crowd of unruly second-graders.

I grabbed Remington's hand and Dreyson's sleeves, even as we began to walk into the circle. Belatedly, I realized what was going to happen and gripped Dreyson's wrist. "Oh no."

The world cracked open, releasing a blinding white tornado, so loud and bright, it was like being right on top of a flashbang. I shut my eyes, but my eyelids didn't protect me, and I didn't have free hands to cover my face. There wasn't enough air or time to scream. But somehow those moments without air stretched on far too long.

I slid sideways through reality, suffocating in the light and yearning for solid ground.

And then I hit the dirt, going down hard with Remington, gulping in deep breaths of sweet air and dry dust. Coughing, I winced as I opened my eyes, bracing myself for the nausea. As feeling returned to my body, it surfaced too. But I held still, letting my soul settle back in my bones.

Remington sat on the ground, wincing as he rubbed his knee. "Sorry. Didn't mean to pull you down."

"No," I said, rubbing my head. "I can't stay on my feet after a teleport." This wasn't as bad as the first two times, but the world was still quaking and unfocused.

Dreyson crouched beside me, one hand still wrapped in mine. His skin burned hot. There was a predatory sharpness to his gaze now. He cracked his neck from side to side and rose, helping me up too.

"Thanks," I said, wobbling.

"I've got you," he murmured in my ear, his breath warm against my skin, one hand steadying me.

I took deep shuddering breaths, locking my legs so my knees wouldn't buckle. The nausea wasn't as bad this time. I could power through it.

"That's it. You're a quick study."

"Oh, good tactic. I like praise," I said, closing my eyes and trying to center myself better.

"I'll keep that in mind," Dreyson said, his voice low.

My breath caught. I opened my eyes.

Dreyson surveyed the area, shoulders squared, one hand curled for spellwork, the layers of his magic swirling around him. In that moment, he was absolutely focused, and his veneer of careful reserve was gone. Dreyson had power, and he wasn't afraid to use it. He closed his eye, head tilted like he just caught the strains of a song in the distance. His blonde hair was growing out, and it looked downy soft. He was very masculine, with a square jaw and strong stark lines to his face. The scars added character.

I liked looking at him, I realized.

He opened his eye and looked down at me, the corner of his mouth curving upward. "Yes?"

He totally caught me staring.

"The change of scenery agrees with you," I said, clearing my throat.

"I removed my dampening charms before we went through the portal," he said. "I wear them so I don't disrupt electronics. That isn't necessary here."

I didn't realize his magic was that potent. I turned to check on the others.

Remington slowly climbed to his feet. Sophia was bent over, loudly retching. But everyone else looked annoyingly unfazed.

The world was subtly alien.

We were in another fairy circle in a clearing, this one formed by three-foot-tall spongy lavender toadstools. The sun was high in the sky, but the light was different, stronger, with a deeper saturation of orange. It threw off the colors. The air was sharp—purer than back home, but thinner, maybe at a higher altitude. It felt wrong in my lungs and smelled too strongly of flowers. I could practically taste them. Prolonged unshielded exposure to the ambient energy of this place would do strange, often destructive things to human bodies. Fortunately, both Mrs. Bancroft-Owens' magic and Detective Davis' wards were supposed to counteract that.

Outside the mushroom circle were trees, clusters of them as far as the eye could see. They came in an array of colors: many with brown trunks, but some were silvery white, others gleamed gold, bronze, crimson, or violet. Several were thick enough to build a house inside.

The sky was a deeper blue than our own and the world lush with an abundance of plants.

Detective Davis placed her hand on the bark of a pale tree that I didn't recognize, but I was a city kid. She gritted her teeth. "The land does not welcome us. We are trespassing. I can ease the way, keep us on the path, but the forest will not make this journey easier."

"That's the reception we were expecting," Remington said, leaning on his cane.

Samuel unwrapped a gleaming silver rapier with a gorgeous intricate basket hilt.

Mrs. Bancroft-Owens didn't seem quite as old as I remembered. Magic leaked from under her skin, though nothing about her appearance looked different.

Mwanje said something to Detective Davis, and then he changed. Fur erupted from his body, and he dropped to the ground, writhing as his bones cracked and his joints realigned. I didn't like watching the transformation. Mwanje claimed it didn't hurt that much, but other shifters I knew said otherwise. But unlike most of them, Mwanje was born into it. When he was done, he was an unnaturally large leopard with beautiful rosettes and a well-fitted spiked leather harness that protected his neck and other regions. On all fours, he came up to my chest and was easily nine feet long, not counting the tail. He lightly headbutted Detective Davis, who rolled her eyes.

"Does the harness need adjusting?" she asked.

Mwanje made a rolling growl that sounded like a purr on steroids, and then he bounded up to me.

Beside me, Dreyson tensed, fingers tightening around my arm.

Mwanje the Leopard seemed to grin at me and opened his mouth very wide. Indeed, I could fit my entire head in there.

"A mint wouldn't hurt," I told him, patting his snout.

"Remember, don't eat anything here," Detective Davis called. "No matter how delicious or annoying they are. That includes Claire."

Mwanje chuffed and went back to stand by her.

"I'm steady now," I said.

Dreyson released my arm, more energy crackling around him.

Sofia was finally upright, no longer looking sick.

A white stone path led out of the circle. Dreyson and Mwanje took point.

Detective Davis held a glass bottle in one hand, walking between Remington and me.

Mrs. Bancroft-Owens and Samuel brought up the rear, with Sofia bookended between them.

The trees shifted then, the wind rushing past us as taller growths formed a perimeter around us, leaves blotting out the light.

Detective Davis scowled and marched to the front, where thick trunks blocked the path. Uncorking the bottle, she poured it onto the roots.

Something screamed, somewhere between a bird and a pissed-off cat, and the trees rustled as they shifted again, getting off the path.

"Are we supposed to damage things?" Remington asked out of the corner of his mouth.

"I know the rules, and I know when they've been broken. So if this damn haint-twisted hawthorn wants to block the path because it's gone and forgotten where its roots belong, and more importantly, it's forgotten its own covenant, well, then it gets what it deserves," Detective Davis said sharply. "A reminder."

The nearby trees shrunk back at her words, now leaning slightly away from the path. Detective Davis was normally a congenial woman. It was surreal to see her bullying trees.

Dreyson chuckled.

Mwanje flexed his paws, like he intended to use the trunks as big scratching posts.

And so we walked on the path. A couple roots rose up between steps, trying to trip us. One coiled around Remington's cane, but Detective Davis reached for a bottle and then suddenly the knobby wooden tendril was gone.

"Forests," she muttered. "Doesn't matter where, they all use the same tricks."

Branches leaned too close, but Dreyson brandished his axe, a tongue of flame dancing along the edge of the blade, and that cleared them out fast. He glanced over his shoulder at me, a smug look on his face.

"Show-off," I mouthed.

We were only a few minutes down the path when we heard a child crying from the forest.

"Mom! Mom! Is that you?" it said in Innis' voice.

Sofia flinched.

"Mom! You came! How did you get here? I was so scared!" A shadowy figure appeared behind some trees. It peered at us with Innis' face, but the body was a blobby mass. "Aren't you happy to see me?"

Sofia closed her eyes, shuddering as Samuel put one hand on her shoulder.

"That isn't your child," Mrs. Bancroft-Owens said.

"I know," Sofia exhaled.

"That's not fair, Mom," it said, with a good approximation of Innis' speech. "Just because I'm not your blood child doesn't mean I'm not yours. Or are you planning to give me up? Are you going to demand your real child back instead? How could you?" The thing began to sob and shuffled back into the forest.

Sofia started to reach for it, and then clenched her fist, turning her gaze back to the path. "I'm fine," she said tightly. "I know it's not them. That thing is just toying with us."

"That thing's an asshole," I muttered.

"Behave," Detective Davis said. "We're guests in this land. So we have to put up with their bad manners for a spell, even if it is just some old booger borrowing faces."

"Booger?" I giggled, suddenly seven years old again.

Detective Davis scowled at me. "It's a word for the unclean things that—"

"I know, I'm not laughing at you, but 'booger'? The word is just funny."

"If you're a child," Detective Davis said archly.

"It's like calling it a 'fartknocker,'" Remington piped up with a chuckle.

"Or Mr. Poopypants," I said.

Detective Davis gave an exasperated sigh. "That thing wants to eat you and wear your skin like a costume."

"Absolutely horrifying, a total booger," I agreed, shouldering my rifle. Because something was moving along the path up ahead.

"Unca?" A little cherub-cheeked toddler in a pink onesie appeared on the path. Her dark hair bounced in a spritely palm-tree. She reached out, her voice squeaky. "Unca!"

I looked around, unsure of which of these men it was talking to.

Samuel and Remington looked unbothered.

Mwanje stood on the path, the fur on his spine bristling.

"Unca!" she said happily, and then screamed as something pulled her into the brush, snapping branches and dragging her deeper into the woods. "Unca!"

Mwanje jerked forward, but stopped himself from leaving the path.

Bloodcurdling childish screams came from farther away, abruptly cutting off. Then bones crunched, followed by a wet sound, like organs slipping out of a body.

Mwanje growled, obviously displeased by the thing mimicking his niece.

Detective Davis cleared her throat. "If it can't feed on your flesh, it'll feed on your discomfort."

"Yeah, it's a real booger," Remington said, mustering a weak smile. "Makes sense. Don't give it a scary name. It'd like that."

Detective Davis nodded. "He gets it." She gave me a look.

I shrugged. "Booger" was a funny word. That thing wasn't funny at all.

We continued down the path through a clearing. It was warmer here, the forest alive with birds, animals, and worse things. Bright flowers bloomed everywhere, with little winged creatures, humanoid and not, flitting between the leaves. Even brighter mushrooms sprouted along the bases of the trees. Swathes of moss dangled from reaching branches.

In the distance, A man's voice called for help. It sounded almost like the lieutenant, but too faint to identify. Remington grimaced, but proceeded to ignore it, and it faded quickly enough.

And then a woman stumbled out of the trees. She was battered and bruised, her chestnut hair matted and bloody, her blue eyes wide with panic. Her pretty face set wrong, because that bastard had beaten her so badly.

Oh, I remembered exactly how Ivy Beaumont looked that night.

"I'm getting tired of this," I said, glancing at Detective Davis.

She just sighed. "Stay on the path."

It came to the side of the road, reaching for me. "Thank God you're here! He's going to kill me," it said in her panicked voice, the words forming clearly, unlike how she sounded that night.

"How aware is it? And how much is it lifting from my memories?" I asked.

"It's mimicking. Don't know if they have real thoughts," Detective Davis said. "Easier for them to steal yours. It's just a booger trick."

I chuckled at that. "I got a booger trick too." I touched my nose.

Remington gave a loud sputtering, like he had been trying to hold it in.

It didn't like that laugh, because suddenly it changed again, and I knew this form too. All the SIU detectives did.

She was naked, waifish, and covered in blood. She looked exactly how I remembered, dying in that terrible place where I found her.

"Are you here to help?" it asked me. "Will you save me?" She stared at me hopefully, those bruised eyes free of malicious intelligence. It held the same tired relief, vacillating between sorrow and resignation. "Will I see the sun again?"

Mwanje growled.

"Three times is enough," Detective Davis told me, because she was there that day too. "Don't kill it. Stay on the path."

I stopped, even as it limped to catch up with us.

"You're good," I told it. "But you're not really selling these performances. Let me help you out. See, the girl whose shape you wear, she didn't move like that." I raised my rifle and fired a shot into its thigh. At this range, the sights were just fine.

It screamed and toppled to the ground wailing in a guttural voice.

"That's better. You're more in character now. She couldn't walk," I said, voice bright with exaggerated cheer. "He cut her tendons, among other things, so no, she did not see the sun again. She died down there in the miserable dark." I leaned closer. "Would you like me to show you how?"

The thing sobbed and began to crawl away, bleeding black ooze on the flowers.

I slung the rifle over my shoulder and walked briskly back to Detective Davis, ignoring the side-eyed looks. Let them think the compounded stress of fresh Fey air was getting to me.

"You good?" Remington asked after a few minutes.

"My booger trick is better," I whispered. "It has real boogers."

Dreyson watched me, like he knew how close I'd come to just killing that thing, despite the warnings.

Remington patted my shoulder. "Talk shit, get hit," he said out of the corner of his mouth.

"Play stupid games, win stupid prizes," I said, still not feeling good about seeing her crawl off like that. It wasn't truly her, but now I was stuck with that image, and well, that was my own fault.

We walked in silence for awhile.

The forest tried to mislead us. The path would shift, disappearing into tall grass or diverging into false trails. But Detective Davis wasn't easily led. She kept us on the right track, checking stones, touching tree trunks, marking the direction of the wind and the palace that manifested in the distance.

The sky grew darker now, likely due to the geography, because allegedly, the sun did not set in the Spring domain. This land was more desolate: black volcanic sands, rings of eerie glowing fungus, and the bleached bones of massive creatures that I could not identify. I sort of hoped they were dinosaurs, but they were probably something worse.

And then the path wound back into the woods, where a bloodied teenager stood by the road waiting for us, his limbs mangled.

Dreyson stopped. "Hellcat," he rasped, voice raw.

"Yes, Warp Warrior?"

Beside me, Detective Davis choked.

"If that thing opens its mouth, shoot it again," he enunciated, though his teeth were clenched and his scalding hot rage turned the words raspy.

"My pleasure," I said, raising the rifle.

The thing that looked like a teenager backed up.

"Then I'll set it on fire and it won't bother anyone ever again," he said, not taking his eyes off the retreating figure.

"I can still shoot it."

It moved faster, like it heard me, fading from view. Who was that boy? His dead friend Gregory?

Dreyson chuckled, favoring me with a feral grin. "I appreciate it."

"Anytime," I said with a wink.

Dreyson's smile widened. "Careful," he said, raising one finger to his lips. Then he turned back around.

I felt Detective Davis' scowl before I saw it.

"You better not be offering to shoot people for him *anytime*," she said.

"No, just boogers," I said, offended by the assumption.

Remington chuckled. "Shooting boogers at someone on the playground still means something."

"That you both need to grow up," Detective Davis growled.

Someone's hard stare drilled into my back. I glanced over my shoulder to see Samuel watching me. He flashed me a charming smile that lit up his face, turning it from respectable to handsome.

I smiled back and turned around.

What was that about? Was he jealous? If so, it was less about me and more about Dreyson. It seemed like every insecure man who walked into a room had to compare himself with Dreyson, and I kept wandering into the crossfire.

We walked till my feet hurt, but I could not keep track of time here. And it didn't matter, because it did not pass the same way on our side of the divide. I wasn't tired, but Remington was having some trouble. I didn't say anything, because he didn't complain. But I noticed, and so did Detective Davis.

"We should take a breather here," she said. "I need to reinforce the wards." She began to fiddle with the charms on her belt.

Dreyson and Mwanje stopped, surveying our surroundings. The trees were starting to thin, and in the distance that castle loomed larger.

Sofia crouched down on the path, resting her head between her knees. Mrs. Bancroft-Owens stood beside her, mouth pinched in a frown.

Remington leaned on his cane, stretching his bad leg.

Behind us, someone screamed.

I spun, rifle raised, to see Samuel being dragged into the brush by his legs as he struggled to unsheathe his sword. I drew the dagger, couldn't risk shooting with Samuel in the way.

Dreyson leapt forward, swinging his axe and barely missing Samuel.

"Be careful!" Samuel shouted, before he disappeared into the bushes.

Dreyson took off after him. Instantly, the obsidian dagger in my hand vanished. I looked around, then at the empty sheath, and lifted the rifle. Shouts echoed in the distance, branches snapping, fire roaring. I started after them.

"They're professionals," Remington said, grabbing my arm to keep me from crossing into the tree line.

Nodding, I bit my lip and dug through my charms.

The forest went silent.

Mrs. Bancroft-Owens looked at her watch, glowering at the forest.

"Do you want to step off the path?" Detective Davis asked, uncorking a bottle.

"Give them another minute." Mrs. Bancroft-Owens sounded bored.

Branches snapped under heavy footfalls. Something moved through the brush toward us. I aimed my rifle, knowing there was a chance that the next thing to emerge would not be Samuel or Dreyson. Or worse, it might be just a part of them.

A bloody Dreyson stalked out from between the trees, Samuel limping close behind him. The battlemage sat down on the path, sucking down deep lungfuls of air, a wild look on his face.

I crouched in front of him, keeping one eye on the trees. "Are you hurt?"

"I'm fine," he spat, glaring over his shoulder at the forest like he was about to go back in. "It got away." He held the dagger, ichor dripping from the obsidian.

"Do not drop your guard," Mrs. Bancroft-Owens said icily, her voice echoing. "Carelessness will get you killed."

Samuel flinched.

Dreyson turned that harsh stare on her.

"Thought they weren't supposed to touch us on the path," Samuel said angrily.

"If it comes back, it won't be escaping again," Dreyson said.

Detective Davis nodded. "We stayed on the path. They're the ones stirring up trouble. If you want to blow the devil down, that's your choice."

Dreyson solemnly offered the knife to me. "I need you to be careful," he said gruffly.

"I'll do my best," I said, opening my hand.

Dreyson exhaled slowly, the tension not leaving his shoulders. His fingers brushed against mine as he returned the knife.

"That's a cool trick. How'd you do it?"

"Magic," he said with a wan smile, letting go of my hand so he could draw his axe and take point again.

Just past the tree line, the shadows flickered, something moving in the brush.

We continued in silence, that shining white domed palace growing closer with each step. I did not miss the fact that Dreyson could have summoned his knife back at any point after he loaned it to me. That was something to think about.

Interlude III

THE CROW KNIGHT cocked his head to the side, as if someone were speaking to him. He sighed, shaking his head.

"Fann," he said.

The girl appeared in the doorway.

"I need to go. The situation is about to become…more complicated. Take them somewhere safe." He gestured to Innis.

The girl stared at him. "What do you mean?"

"We have unwanted guests," he said, shaking his head.

"How could that happen?"

"How indeed." The Crow Knight smiled sardonically. "I doubt it's a coincidence that I found that woman by the Autumn Archives right after I helped you sneak back into your quarters."

She stiffened, her eyes getting very big.

"Fann," he said quietly. "That's your business. But keep them safe. The Bloody Bones already have their scent."

Fann nodded. "I understand."

Innis sat there, watching them both.

"Go on, then," the Crow Knight told them. "And if you see Claire before I do, tell her, no hard feelings." And then he disappeared.

"Come on," Fann said, beckoning impatiently. "If we're careful, we might be able to watch."

Chapter 23
The Princess Is in This Castle

笑里藏刀 Trad. 笑裡藏刀-xiào lǐ cáng dāo – Literally: hide a dagger in a smile, this is both an idiom and the tenth of the Thirty Six Stratagems. There are so many colorful proverbs about deception. I don't know if that's a cultural thing or my personal bias. Obviously, this one is telling you to be charming and friendly to get close to someone. Not to hide your dagger in your mouth. Cool trick if you can do it, though.

— From the Very Personal Journals of FYG

THE MONSTERS ATTACKED as soon as we set foot on the palace grounds, long before we had a chance to announce ourselves. They were expecting us. But I did not see any guards in the raiment of the Spring Court. No one issued any warnings or asked any questions. As soon as we approached the entrance, the creatures swarmed us.

They were not sidhe, not even humanoid. There were a dozen shadowy hellhounds, built like reptilian draft horses, a trio of even larger greenish-black kelpies with smoke pouring from their nostrils, seaweed tangled in their manes, and a blood red draconic lindwyrm the size of a city bus. It was not a pretty aquatic creature with delicate scales and billowing fins; it had tiny forelimbs, no wings, and a row of sharp spines along its back. Its skull was too big for its slug-like body, and a thick mane of scales covered its neck. It looked like a cursed tadpole, vicious, spermatic, and upsettingly top-heavy.

Ahead, Mwanje leapt onto a kelpie's back, the last place you were supposed to be, as they plunged their riders into the water so they could drown and eat them. But he sunk his massive jaws into the creature's neck, tearing out a portion of its spine. He crushed those bones, roared over the body, and dove at the nearest hellhound.

Dreyson started to laugh, and it was not a happy sound. He swung that axe, and suddenly it was alight with orange flames, blade sizzling as he began to cut a swathe through the hounds.

Detective Davis' witch bottles lit up, absorbing the curses aimed at us. She took out another bottle and tossed it at a pair of hounds. The glass burst on the stone. A smoky figure appeared, almost human-shaped but lacking clear features. And then the hellhounds began to shriek and writhe.

Remington and I provided suppressing fire. It was hard to cover Mwanje. He was far faster than he had any right to be, bouncing back and forth, running up walls, and leaping down onto his prey.

Dreyson was a lot more predictable. He went after the lindwyrm, because of course he would. My rifle wasn't going to pierce that hide. Instead, I targeted the smaller beasts. I focused fire on a smoldering hellhound that broke through our defensive line and headed straight for Detective Davis. The bullets burst on impact, cratering its hide but not bringing it down.

"I got it!" Laughing, Remington stepped up and spun his shotgun. Just as the beast opened its mouth to take a bite out of him, he pulled the trigger, blasting its throat out its skull with enchanted shot.

The thing went down hard, nearly crashing into him as momentum carried its corpse across the courtyard.

"Cutting things a little close, aren't you?" Mrs. Bancroft-Owens asked him archly.

Remington gave her a sharp smile. "Shotguns are most effective at close range, ma'am."

If I'd known we were going to be monster-hunting, I would have asked for a higher caliber rifle.

Samuel stuck to Sofia, his rapier in one hand. He moved gracefully, neatly piercing a kelpie through the eye with that elegant weapon, while deftly keeping Sofia between himself and Mrs. Bancroft-Owens. He used magic too, but I couldn't shoot and pay attention to him.

He was different from Dreyson, who tore through everything that came at him. The lindwyrm spewed a sickly brown liquid that fouled the air. Still laughing, Dreyson threw himself sideways, rolling through blood and ichor as he circled the beast. He was fast too, slamming that burning blade through the monster's back, crushing spines, scales, and bones.

The lindwyrm shrieked furiously, spinning and spitting poison.

Dreyson just moved with it, laughing as he hacked away at the monster with an unnatural fury. He was a whirlwind of flashing metal and white-hot flames. I couldn't look away. It should have been terrifying, but I was exhilarated.

"Losing control is unbecoming," Samuel said loudly. "It's a reflection of a troubled mind."

I ignored him, centering my sights on the lindwyrm's buggy left eye. It was not moving very fast, so I lined up the shot, staring very hard at the veiny blood-red orb the size of my fist. Between breaths, I pulled the trigger.

The lindwyrm screamed as its left eyeball burst. It rolled to one side, nearly crushing Dreyson.

"Sorry!" I yelled.

The lindwyrm wailed louder.

Dreyson glanced my way, mouth open in incredulity. He looked at the thrashing monster, then back at me. Shaking his head, he grinned and went back to cutting through the lindwyrm's thick hide.

Wait, I took out the *left* eye. He was missing that too. Oh no, was that insensitive?

To my left, something snarled and lunged, the motion catching my attention.

Cursing my distraction, I spun, firing my rifle as a hellhound bore down on me. The shot went wild, and it bowled into me, sending me crashing into the dirt. I rolled across the ground, the rifle clutched flat against my chest. The shredded body of a kelpie halted my spin, and I ended up on my side, trying to pick myself off the ground as the hellhound caught up to me, its massive slavering jaws quivering over my shoulder. Jerking the gun upward, I fired again, the monster screeching as the bullets hit.

Bits of smoke and ooze leaked from its wounded chest, but it growled at me, opening its bear-trap-like jaws as it lunged again. I jammed the rifle against the roof of its open mouth and pulled the trigger.

Its entire body spasmed, jaws closing around the barrel. I rolled onto my back, wedging one foot under its chin and trying to pull the gun free. When that didn't work, I kicked it, with no real effect, and fired again.

The creature shuddered as a massive flaming axe bisected its body. The front half toppled forward, and I had to roll sideways to avoid getting caught under it. I now had weird sulfurous fluids all over my clothes. Gross.

Dreyson stood over me, blood smearing his face, his flaming axe in hand. He leaned over, grabbed a fistful of my jacket, and lifted me to my feet.

"Interesting maneuver," he said, grinning at me.

"I uh, didn't mean to almost drop that thing on you," I said sheepishly. "And the target choice was purely opportunistic." I gripped his arm to steady myself.

He just chuckled. "It was a good shot. No, I was talking about how you got *underneath* the monster."

I squinted at him. "Tactical choice. I was aiming for the soft underbelly. I don't always have to be on top."

Dreyson's smile widened, and he let me go. He looked me over. "Are you hurt?"

"Nope," I said, and knelt down to pry the hellhound's jaws open to free my gun. I checked the barrel for damage. It was trapped in the space between the creature's teeth, not in the actual bite zone. It looked undamaged. "You?"

"Nothing major," he said.

"Going to be sore tomorrow, though," I said. "But that's how you know you had fun."

Dreyson's eyebrows went up. "You get into fights often?"

"No— actually yes," I said, reloading my gun. "But I wasn't just talking about fights."

"I didn't think you were," Dreyson said, shaking his head with a smile.

I chuckled, looking around. The monsters were mostly dead, but I was wide awake, adrenaline still pounding through my body. Few things were so primitively satisfying as standing over one's dead enemies, drunk on the knowledge that they attempted murder and failed miserably.

I glanced back to see Mwanje chewing on the spasming lindwyrm's head. Around us were the smoking, oozing remains of fairytale monsters. The courtyard was also charred and battered, with lindwyrm acid dissolving some of the landscaping.

"Are those good to eat?" I asked, watching Mwanje gnaw on chunks of lindwyrm face. He did that sometimes, but never with anything sentient, so I wasn't surprised, or even disappointed, just concerned. It wasn't like I could call a big cat vet from the Spring Court.

Dreyson crossed his arms. "They're supposed to have useful properties."

"But should he be eating it?" I asked.

"No idea." Dreyson shrugged. "Does he normally do that?"

"Sometimes," Detective Davis sighed, kicking aside a dead hellhound. "He gets hungry, often. Shapeshifter metabolisms. He should be fine – he's accepted no one's hospitality and he's like her." She gestured at me. "They're gluttons, and they'll eat anything."

I eyed the lindwyrm. Would I eat that? Maybe. Definitely, if Valeria made it into tacos.

Dreyson headed over to the lindwyrm and bent over it, examining the body.

I looked around. Remington stood over a twitching hellhound with his shotgun and gave it a coup de grace.

Samuel wiped off his rapier, smiling pleasantly as he worked. Sofia watched him with disgust. Had he said something tone-deaf to her too?

Mrs. Bancroft-Owens surveyed the carnage, looking slightly irritated. "I find his Vernal Highness' standards of hospitality to be slipping. This would not have happened with his consort present."

"Savage," I said.

"Don't sass her," Detective Davis sighed.

"I'm not! I'm admiring her," I said. "I want to be like her when I grow up!"

Detective Davis gave me a long-suffering look.

"OK, like her" — I lowered my voice — "*but more fun.*"

Detective Davis shook her head.

We regrouped on the path, marching toward the palace entrance. The building was majestic, shiny, and mostly indescribable because it was never the same when I looked at it. Made of smooth white stone, with occasional veins of color and sinuous lines; the style stayed consistent, but the pieces shifted. A spiraling seashell of a tower simply materialized, and then in a blink, was replaced by a domed hall, the shell tower now even farther away. I couldn't tell if pieces were actually moving, or if it was be-spelled to look a certain way and the fairy ointment affected that illusion.

We ascended a hillside of stairs toward the entrance. As we drew closer, the parts of the image stopped moving. Lining the entryway was a curved colonnade, flowering vines blooming along each of the intricately carved stone pillars. Pools of water rippled on either side of the walkway, large shadows moving beneath the surface. We gave them a wide berth. The entrance was a gracefully tapered arch, with fine gold-and-green latticework forming a gate. It was shut.

Mrs. Bancroft-Owens stepped up to the front. "I am here because of the oaths sworn and sealed in blood. I am here because of the treaties made in the Alluvian plane. I am here to give you a chance to redeem your bond. Honor your vow!"

It wasn't pithy like "open sesame," but just like that, the gates swung open.

We entered a massive white stone hall, where the top half opened up into a starry nebula, much like the Shadow Dunes. Maybe I had trouble seeing this place from the outside because it wasn't just one place. Maybe it was an intersection of planes, possibly in constant motion, a Schrodinger's dream of Escher sketches.

I was so entranced by the metaphysics that I almost missed the welcoming party. He was just a shadow, flitting across the walls, almost too fast to see, but I remembered how he moved.

"Look out!" I shouted.

A twisting blur lunged at Mrs. Bancroft-Owens.

Dreyson was already between them, sparks flying as his axe struck that sword.

The Crow Knight laughed. "There you are, Warp Warrior! Not hiding behind your woman anymore?"

"I can't help that you weren't smart enough to track me down on your own," Dreyson said, teeth bared.

"I expected you to do a better job protecting her, but then given how our last meeting went, maybe I was expecting too much."

Oh, that bastard went there. I leveled my gun at the Crow Knight, keeping him in my sights.

Dreyson swung his axe, flames bursting along the edge of the blade, his lips pulled back in a snarl. The Crow Knight danced around him, sword whipping through the air, faster than I could see, but barely grazing Dreyson. The battleaxe orbited Dreyson, seeming to hover in the space between the two men, Dreyson nearly blurring alongside the Crow Knight.

Laughing, the Crow Knight threw something, and as Samuel spun his rapier, a throwing knife clanged to the ground in front of Mrs. Bancroft-Owens. Swearing, he launched himself into the fray.

Mrs. Bancroft-Owens glowered, real anger sparking on her face.

"Is that him?" Sofia asked.

"Yup," I said.

She cursed under her breath.

"Yup," I agreed, not taking my eye off him, the gun an extension of my arm and my will. They were moving around the hall very quickly, taking a shot would risk friendly fire, but if I had the opportunity…

"He's too fast," Sofia said.

Samuel tried to keep up with the Crow Knight's footwork, but he could barely parry the strikes. Dreyson, meanwhile, met him blow for blow, throwing him off-balance.

"You really were holding back." The Crow Knight sounded delighted.

"A mistake," Dreyson said. "Should have finished you that night."

"I agree," the Crow Knight purred and looked right at me. "The three of us could have found a much more satisfying way to conclude the evening."

My finger rested on the trigger. I almost took the shot at his insufferable face. But then another shadow beast lunged for Mrs. Bancroft-Owens. Bipedal and cloaked in darkness, with long ripping claws; as much as I tried, I could not bring its form into focus. It shifted between smoke, scales, and mirrors. And then suddenly, it had a washed-out version of *my face* on a too skinny, clawed body, and I knew exactly what that fucker was.

I swung my rifle to the right and fired directly into its head. It was very weird to shoot a version of myself in the face, but to be fair, it was a piss-poor copy and an affront to the original.

"Fuck you, I look way better than that!" I shouted.

It spasmed, losing hold of its shape. It was bonier now, the skin a deep blue shade, the form only vaguely humanoid.

Bones and ichor splattered Mrs. Bancroft-Owens' proper suit. She glanced over at me, her expression hard.

"Sorry, ma'am," I called back sheepishly.

She just raised one hand, and the liquid rose off the fabric into the air and then dissolved to dust. The thing began to screech as she closed her fist, the body crumbling into powder.

A finger bone dropped to the ground, a strip of bloody rag tied around it. And then Mrs. Bancroft-Owens crushed it under her heel.

"That is like the thing that killed the Soltanis," Sofia said, breathing hard. "The thing that tried to lure in Innis."

"Yup," I said, looking around.

Dreyson was still occupied with the Crow Knight. He and Samuel both bled from numerous slashes.

Vines began to crawl toward us. Many plants twisted around the pillars. Mwanje stuck with Detective Davis, who threw some kind of dust at the encroaching vines. Mrs. Bancroft-Owens seethed with energy. Was it safe to leave Sofia with her?

"You weren't invited to this conversation." The Crow Knight kicked Samuel in the stomach and raised his sword to finish him.

Dreyson dropped his axe, fire in his palms. He struck the Crow Knight's right arm, throwing off his thrust and saving Samuel from impalement.

"Switch me," I yelled to Samuel, gesturing to Sofia. I slung the rifle over my back and drew the revolver, shoving it in my jacket pocket.

He hesitated, glaring at the Crow Knight.

"*Claire,*" the Crow Knight said my name with real delight. He even had the audacity to laugh. "I know you want another round with me, but I made an agreement, darling. You need to sit this one out. I just have to borrow your man for a bit. But if you ask nicely, I won't hurt him too badly."

I was going to kill him. Once my hands stopped shaking in rage.

More vines crawled across the stone floor toward us.

I marched toward the Crow Knight.

"We're switching now!" I snapped at Samuel.

He blinked at me, and then he drew back, nodding.

Dreyson chuckled.

"So commanding," the Crow Knight simpered, giving me that infuriating lazy smile, even as he dodged Dreyson's attacks. "Go on, then, ask me for his life, darling. I know for a fact that you can be *very convincing.*"

That fucker. I smiled back, and maybe it felt more like that other thing's imitation of my expression: too wide, all teeth. I wasn't fast enough to stab him. I wasn't strong enough to do real damage when I hit him. I wasn't even going to try.

I still raised Dreyson's knife in my left hand, the one that he successfully took from me the last two times we met. Now that I knew Dreyson could summon it, I wasn't worried about losing it to him.

The Crow Knight gave a condescending chuckle. "You're adorable, Claire."

"Come and get it, Crowfucker."

He could not resist; he was here in a blink, one hand around my left wrist, the other on my waist like we were dancing. Plucking the knife from my hand as we moved, he spun me between him and Dreyson. He had the knife and my body between him and the others. He was exactly where I wanted him.

My right hand slipped into my pocket, and I shot him then, firing through my jacket. It blew a hole in the material, ruining it, but it was worth it to see him stagger backward into the wall, shock on his face, his sword clattering to the ground. Blood seeped from his bicep. I only hit his sword arm. What a shame, I was aiming elsewhere.

"Where's Innis?" I demanded, leveling the gun at his face, my finger on the trigger. Dreyson appeared at my back.

"They are unharmed, like I promised," the Crow Knight gasped, touching his wound. "You shot me." He flinched, then dropped to the ground. "There's something *nasty* in this bullet. Cursed?" He stared down at his arm in disbelief. "You actually shot me."

"And I'll shoot you again for ruining my jacket, you bird-molesting, child-swiping, arrogant ass—"

"We're here for the children," Dreyson said, gently tucking the knife into the sheath on my right hip. He had no trouble taking it back. His hand did not wander, but it was still distracting to have him so close.

The Crow Knight stared. "You shot me."

"He's still stupid. I'll shoot him again," I said, cocking back the hammer with my thumb. He was fast, but I trusted that Dreyson would be able to cover me.

"The changelings we rescued are unharmed—" he began.

"Rescued? I recognized that cheap face-forging nightmare! That thing killed a lot of people, including changelings!"

The Crow Knight winced. "The situation is complicated. We are under orders from different masters. I took the children to save them from the Bloody Bones. The Bloody Bones were…disposing of evidence."

"Uh-huh," I said. "You were both tampering with evidence, and that *evidence* happened to be children."

"I wasn't killing them." The Crow Knight straightened up, sounding offended. "Don't lump me in the same category as them." His gauntlet crept toward the sword on the ground.

Dreyson moved then, his axe swung low, in a perfectly controlled arc, hovering right along the Crow Knight's throat. "I wouldn't," he said, shaking his head.

"Where are my children?" Sofia snarled over my shoulder. "What did you do with them?"

"They are unharmed. *Both of them.* Call for an audience in the throne room. The *Lares* knows the way," the Crow Knight said, holding very still. He exhaled slowly. "I cannot stop you now." He gave me a wry smile. "So what now, Claire? Are you going to kill me? Or are you leaving that dirty work to your man?"

"He's all yours," Dreyson told me, not moving the axe. "Whatever you want. Just say the word."

The Crow Knight sat on the ground, back to the stone wall, shoulders slumped, one edge of Dreyson's massive axe held along his neck. He stared up at me, that stylized helm still covering his eyes, a crooked smile on his face.

I leveled the gun at him.

He sighed wistfully, his smile tinged with regret. If he had any tricks up his armored sleeves, now was the time to pull them. But he slumped there, blood dripping onto the floor, all the fight gone out of him. Whatever was in those bullets was potent. I could finish this with just one shot.

Or with one twitch of Dreyson's axe, it would be done. I wouldn't even have to waste a bullet. He was spent and helpless. It wouldn't be hard at all. He nearly strangled me last night. He broke into my house. He kidnapped Innis and other kids.

But he avoided killing me. He distracted Mandragora that night in the Shadow Dunes. I wanted to shoot him again, yes. My finger traced the trigger. I wouldn't regret killing him in combat. But I didn't want to murder him while he was helpless. That didn't feel right, even if his crimes and his attitude pissed me off.

"Fuck," I muttered, lowering the gun, shaking my head.

"Would you like me to do it?" Dreyson asked calmly.

"Do what you want with him," I said with a growl. "I don't kill pathetic *helpless* prisoners."

I expected Dreyson to make it quick. He stood there for a moment, narrowed his eye, and then lowered his axe.

"So you both want to spare me?" The Crow Knight's smile lit up. "Can it be that my charms have persuaded you—"

"You get your measure of grace for two reasons. She's still alive, despite your orders," Dreyson said, "and the incident with Mandragora. That's it. The scales are balanced. Cross us again and you won't find us so merciful."

"Are you done yet?" Detective Davis asked.

I turned, to see everyone else watching impatiently. While I was busy baiting the Crow Knight, Samuel and Mwanje slew something that had been person-shaped, but was now a mass of rotting vegetation.

"Kill him or don't. We need to keep moving!" Remington called out, trailing behind Mrs. Bancroft-Owens. She knew where she was going; she and Samuel were already walking ahead with Sofia.

Mwanje cocked his head at me, chirped, and pointedly looked away. I knew what he was thinking. He wouldn't blame me for killing the Crow Knight in the Courts. He would just shake his head and say, "The asshole had it coming. Not our jurisdiction, not our problem."

"Claire." The Crow Knight carefully sheathed his sword. "I want to ap—"

"I don't care. My neck hurts. You suck. Stay the fuck away from me. I will shoot you again if you annoy me," I said, marching off to join Remington.

The Crow Knight laughed softly. "I'm going to follow. I promise I won't cause any trouble for you."

Dreyson was silent.

"Don't be jealous that she likes me a little. I like both of you a lot. None of that business was personal." He said it loud enough for me to hear clearly.

I gripped the revolver. It was not too late to shoot him again.

"You think she spared you because she likes you?" Dreyson asked, his voice echoing in the hall.

"Yes," the Crow Knight said indignantly.

Dreyson actually laughed. "She isn't planning to kill you because you don't matter. We came here for the kids, not some unresolved issues with a preening peacock of a man."

Wait, what? I was so planning to kill him. I was going to stuff my next throw pillow with his stupid armor feathers. If I ran out of ammo, I could beat him to death with one of Detective Davis' witch bottles. Or Remington's cane. Or Samuel's stupid hard head. If Dreyson thought he could speak for me—

"You don't mean that!" the Crow Knight cried in dismay.

Oh. Being considered unimportant would bother him more. Dreyson had the correct idea.

"You did the right thing," Detective Davis told me as I holstered my revolver and switched back to my rifle.

"But it's going to bite me in the ass. I already know it," I muttered. Doing the right thing often did.

"Maybe, maybe not," she said. "But killing someone in cold blood has grave consequences too. I'd rather that you were less trigger-happy. Everyone here is prepared to smack that one down if he sneezes funny."

"Me? Trigger-happy?" I pressed one hand over my heart.

She gave me a very unimpressed look. "Claire, do you know how many things you've shot today?"

I began to count. I knew how many rounds I fired. How many connected? "Just shot, right? Not killed?"

"Come on," Detective Davis sighed, like I missed the point.

Mwanje chuffed softly beside her. At least someone thought I was funny.

We followed Mrs. Bancroft-Owens through the stone halls. Dreyson caught up to me, the Crow Knight limping behind us, but I didn't turn around.

"You OK?" I asked him.

"Just a couple cuts, nothing serious," he said with a straight face. "You?"

"Taking oodles of psychic damage for not putting him down when I could have," I muttered. "Maybe I should just shoot him again, just one more time, for peace of mind."

"No, you shouldn't," Detective Davis called over her shoulder.

I sighed, rolling my eyes.

"There's always later," Dreyson told me.

Somewhat placated, I walked with him down the curving halls of the palace of the Vernal Lord. The ceiling shifted, sometimes a nebulous galaxy, sometimes a brilliant sun, sometimes a moonlit sky. It would have been a scenic stroll if we weren't watching for ambushes the entire time.

The hall opened into a throne room the size of a football field.

The throne sat on a dais, shaped from the merging of two living white trees, the branches heavy with fragrant blue blossoms. A stream ran along the dais and down the center of the room, ending in a central pool. More stone pillars, covered in blue, green, and violet vines, bordered the edge of the room. The ceiling was another sunscape, bright clouds glimmering with a golden aura.

A familiar dark-skinned man sat on the throne, gazing at us solemnly. Golden flowers bloomed on his diadem, and his pale green diaphanous robes glowed with their own light.

"This conduct is most unbecoming of you, Lordship," Mrs. Bancroft-Owens said, stepping in front of the throne, Samuel and Sofia beside her.

"You barge into my hall and—"

"Don't waste more of my time with feeble posturing," Mrs. Bancroft-Owens said coldly, her voice echoing in the chamber. "We both know why I am here and why you were so desperate to stop me: I am here because of the Alluvian Treaties. I am here because the Courts have broken their vows. I am here to name you oath-breaker and to demand the restoration of the children you stole."

"You—" the Vernal Lord stood, looking around the room.

"Give me back my children!" Sofia snarled. "Both of them!"

The Vernal Lord stiffened when he saw her, and he sighed. If he was the Lord of the Court, where was everyone else? Did he send everyone else away? Or were we just awaiting another ambush?

"Where is everyone?" I whispered.

"He did not want witnesses," Dreyson said softly in my ear.

Because Mrs. Bancroft-Owens was naming him an "oath-breaker."

"You are...Innis' adoptive mother, then," the Vernal Lord studied her thoughtfully. "Which child—"

"Both, if they will have me," she said. "Because unlike some people, I'm not a monster who would abandon their child and then tear them from the only home they've ever known!"

The Vernal Lord's eyes widened.

"You took them, you will return them. As per the Alluvian Treaties, custody agreements can be arranged, once the children are safe outside of your control," Mrs. Bancroft-Owens said. "Reparations will also be demanded. And there is the small act of your broken oath, Lordship." Mrs. Bancroft-Owens enunciated each word with striking politeness.

The Vernal Lord laughed bitterly. "You punish me for saving them, Harriet."

"I'm holding you accountable for your violation of the treaties," Mrs. Bancroft-Owens said coldly. "I am aware that your counterpart was involved, and was behind the slew of changeling murders in the city. Those deaths are on you both. Instead of coming to me to work something out, you *let* it happen rather than reveal your own involvement. So don't pretend that you cared about the well-being of those children, Lordship. It's too late for that."

"We only took children who were slated to die young," the Vernal Lord raised his chin. "We saved them."

"Impossible to verify now," Mrs. Bancroft-Owens said. "Especially given the advancements in medicine, healing, and malg-tech over the past decade. Don't throw *humanitarian* reasons at me, not after all these years, and not when you're in direct violation of your oath."

"We would have done it overtly if *your* counterpart did not murder everyone involved in the Foxglove Pact. You can't blame us for—"

"For violating your oath? Oh, I can. And Ketch didn't get everyone." Mrs. Bancroft-Owens tilted her head to the side primly. "Your use of HerbAway to surreptitiously select candidates was not lost on us. You never had any intention of asking for help or coming clean. Stop trying to lay this at our doorstep. This was a choice you and your counterpart made. Now there are consequences, Oath-breaker."

The Vernal Lord stiffened, like he was in pain.

"You harmed us, Oath-breaker. You never tried to make amends. And it is too late now. Your Court will not suffer you to sit on the throne, not without proper reparations."

The Vernal Lord rose from his seat, wobbling slightly. He held his head, and then removed the diadem.

"A dozen of the human children remain. And we have eighteen changelings," he said through clenched teeth. "Give them a choice."

"Of course," Mrs. Bancroft-Owens said. "I'm not you."

He flinched. "But you're just as ruthless."

"You forced my hand." Mrs. Bancroft-Owens seemed to loom, even if she was the shortest person in attendance.

The Vernal Lord sat down on the ground of the dais, his breathing labored. "Corwin."

The Crow Knight limped past us to the wasting Vernal Lord.

"I ask that you handle this final responsibility," the Vernal Lord said softly. "I have already granted the boon."

The Crow Knight inclined his head. "Then it will be done."

"Thank you," the Vernal Lord said with some difficulty.

The Crow Knight bowed.

And then something swirled into existence on the other side of the stream.

She was beautiful, sharp and spidery, with long flame-colored hair and dark eyes, her skin moonlight pale, her misty dress formed of silk and shadows that seemed to swallow the light. At her side were a dozen shaded creatures, and they turned in unison to look at us. One cackled, and suddenly it wore my face. The others took up the call and shifted into the sickly greenish-tinged mimicries of me. Some of them were more accurate than others, but they were all disturbing.

"One of you is more than enough," Remington said, patting my shoulder.

"I don't like this." I scowled, looking away from the Bloody Bones sluagh. That single one in the entry hall went down way too easily. Of course there were more, and of course they shared stolen faces. I had no way of knowing which one was the original nightmare monster, and it didn't matter.

"Don't like this—" they began to parrot, in variations of my voice.

"Silence," the woman glowered, her voice raspy like the rustle of dried leaves, and suddenly the sluagh returned to their faceless shapes, a wiggling mass of darkness on the stone.

"You cannot sit on two—" the former Vernal Lord began.

"You have no power here now," the Autumnal Lady said, leaning over him. "Who will stop me?"

Mrs. Bancroft-Owens shifted, eyes widening in alarm.

"You also broke—"

"Shhh," she said. "Your sacrifice will be remembered, for a little while." And then she plunged her hand into his chest, tearing out his golden heart and eating it in three bloody bites. His body fell backward, his blood pouring into the stream.

Chapter 24
Unification

移花接木-Yí huā jiē mù — To graft flowers onto a tree. In modern times, the application is really cool. Unfortunately, this is another one of those skulduggery idioms, and it means to use the grafting technique to trick someone into thinking a tree trunk is more valuable than it is. But plenty of fruiting trees are the result of grafting now.

When I think about how this applies to certain substitutions, I don't blame the branch or the root. I blame the asshole performing tree surgery.

— From the Very Personal Journals of FYG

THE CROW KNIGHT immediately vanished from sight.

The air pressure dropped. The sky overhead darkened to a violet glow. The vines on the pillars turned a brilliant shade of red. The petals on the throne dropped off, leaving bare branches. Cold wind began to lash through the room, a cyclone building around a nexus that was the fallen Vernal Lord's body.

Detective Davis held up a glowing bottle, her braids blowing in the gale. Remington stood with her, one arm over his face. Mwanje crouched down beside her.

Samuel had one arm around Sofia, also shielding her. Mrs. Bancroft-Owens stood straight, bearing witness, seemingly unbothered by the growing storm.

"Cover your eyes," Dreyson shouted as he braced me against his chest, the whirlwind spinning faster. My ears popped as a shielding ward went up. I held on tight as the stinging winds tore at us. I wanted to look, but Dreyson put himself between me and the eye of the storm.

Faster faster faster. That power pulsed, the remnant surging out of control.

Someone was screaming. It wasn't me.

And then the matrix of energy burst. The sound was deafening. The winds stopped.

Very slowly, Dreyson let go of me, glancing over his shoulder at the dais.

The Autumnal Lady sat on a silver throne, red flowers blooming along the borders. The sky overhead returned to its golden glow. But the vines remained red. There was no sign of the Vernal Lord's body or the sluagh.

Our party was still on their feet. Mrs. Bancroft-Owens looked unruffled. Remington glanced back at me, eyebrows raised.

I shrugged.

"I am grateful to you for handling him for me, Harriet," the Autumnal Lady laughed, her voice deep. "I could have never ascended two thrones if he was at full power. But you caught him out. You laid him low for his sins."

"Sins that you share," Mrs. Bancroft-Owen said sharply.

"Alas, what proof do you have?" the Autumnal Lady asked. "He already admitted his own fault. You bore witness to the throne's rejection. But it accepted me, so I am here merely to pick up the pieces and usher in a stronger era of prosperity for the sidhe of both courts."

"I suppose congratulations are in order." Mrs. Bancroft-Owens gritted her teeth, a flash of anger on her face. She meant to negotiate for a lot more concessions, but the Autumnal Lady swooped in and stole both that opportunity and the throne. Fuck.

"The king is dead. Long live the queen." The Autumnal Lady beamed. "Have no fear, Harriet. I have no desire to keep those failed children. They can go where they please. The Treaties stand. Now where is that slippery Crow Knight?"

No one answered.

"His faithful, foolish hound till the end," she sighed. "No matter. He can swear fealty to me or he can suffer the consequences. I care not." The Queen leaned on one elbow, staring at us. "You may enter now."

"Hey!" a familiar voice shouted, running into the hall from a doorway that was not there a minute ago.

"Innis?" Sofia raised her head.

"Mom!" Innis blinked. They were still in their jeans and sweatshirt from last night. "Mom, what are you doing here?" It was not something wearing Innis' shape. It was really the kid.

Sofia ran forward, pulling Innis to her with a sob. Behind them was another child, familiar but not identical. She could have been Innis' sister. She wore a gray tunic, and she regarded me.

"I know you," she said in a soft voice, and I remembered the child from the hall, the one who guided me to the archives from the Shadow Dunes.

"Your sibling has probably said a few things about me," I said carefully, not sure how much was safe to reveal.

She smiled awkwardly at me.

"You're... *Dios mio*," Sofia sighed, looking at the other child.

"We decided that you can call me 'Xana,'" the stolen child said. "To avoid confusion."

"Xana," Sofia breathed. She opened her arms.

Xana looked at her thoughtfully but stood back.

"Or if you're not comfortable with a hug, maybe a handshake, a high five, or a fist-bump?" Sofia asked.

Xana stepped forward and offered her hand, staring very hard as Sofia gently shook it.

"Please, come home with us," Sofia said. "I don't know how much time your father has, but...you should see him at least once. I would love for you to stay with us, to get to know you. I want you to come back with us. But I won't try to force you."

To my surprise, Xana glanced at the Autumnal Lady.

"As per the Treaties, the changeling children are free to stay or go," the Autumnal Lady said, sounding bored. But she watched Xana with sharp eyes.

"I would ask for leave to visit my family, Your Highness," Xana said, curtsying gracefully.

"Granted," the Autumnal Lady said.

Mrs. Bancroft-Owens frowned.

"Interview them, Harriet. See who wishes to stay and who wishes to go. Do your due diligence. We have the time. I know how much you *love* children."

Mrs. Bancroft-Owens stared sourly at the queen.

Dreyson chuckled softly.

A door opened to another chamber.

"The rest of them are assembled for your inspection," the queen said. "Take your too-human ones and be gone. I have work to do." She paused. "Though it was lovely seeing you again, Harriet. We really should do this more often."

"Indeed, the trend for regicide might grow popular."

The Autumnal Lady smiled thinly.

We followed Mrs. Bancroft-Owens to the next room, aware that we were being observed.

Reluctantly, Mrs. Bancroft-Owens began interviewing the children. Detective Davis and Remington went to help, Mwanje sticking close to them. Dreyson and Samuel began to confer about logistics.

"I'm sorry, Claire," Innis told me, tugging on my arm.

"I told you to run, multiple times," I said as they hugged me.

"I couldn't let him kill you and Mom." They made puppy eyes at me, and even though I wanted to yell at them, there really was no point. It wouldn't change anything, and I was tired.

"There is no guarantee he would have killed us," I said, giving them a look.

"The Crow Knight was *definitely* supposed to kill you," Xana said, very matter-of-fact. "I heard that the Vernal Lord figured out that you saw something that you should not have."

I narrowed my eyes. "Really? I wonder what that might be."

"They say the Crow Knight found you near the Autumn Archives. Then you were involved with this business, so they thought you knew too much," Xana said gravely. "At least, that's what I heard."

"You hear a lot," I said, eyeing her. How much did she repeat, and to whom? She looked like a little girl, but those eyes were knowing, shrewd even. Maybe she could not have survived the Courts otherwise.

"We need to get tacos again," Innis told me. "Xana has never had tacos."

"Well shit," I said, rubbing the back of my neck. "We do need to get tacos, if you're ever allowed around me again."

Innis just laughed, like I was joking.

But Xana watched me with those solemn eyes, and I wasn't sure how to think of her. She seemed old beyond her years, but she was the same age as Innis. For her part, Xana stood with her newfound family, answered their questions, and tried to be civil.

More than half of the changeling children wanted to come back. Unsurprisingly, there were a few who showed no desire to return at all. A dozen human children survived the Courts. Most of them were willing to visit, though they were cagey about committing to their "real" families.

"These children would probably do better meeting their biological families with supervised contact," Dreyson said.

Mrs. Bancroft-Owens grimaced. "We don't have the facilities—"

"How else are you going to protect them from Ketch and screen their families for suitability?" Dreyson asked.

Mrs. Bancroft-Owens' nostrils flared. "I don't need the Wergeld's head of Arcane Security to tell me how to handle family reunifications."

Samuel blanched.

"If you don't have the manpower, I can always ask Salvatore—"

"That will *not* be necessary," Mrs. Bancroft-Owens said. "I will oversee it."

Dreyson raised a brow.

"The Meteora has the appropriate facilities," she said, referencing a local hotel. It was nice, not luxury accommodations but cozy. "Dr. Erasmus is available to continue his work with the remnants of the Foxglove Pact. And I suppose it is past time to hire more social workers."

"Salvatore can always appeal to the Archdiocese. They have resources for—"

"Stop trying to bring him and the Holy See into this," Mrs. Bancroft-Owens said sharply. "You should know better—"

"I'm trying to help," Dreyson said. "We all know how much you like children." His voice was calm, his delivery was grave, and his intent was absolutely acerbic. He was yanking her chain in a professional manner. I liked that about him.

Samuel covered his mouth, clearly trying to hide his amusement.

Mrs. Bancroft-Owens glowered at him, pointed toward the opposite side of the room, and got out her phone.

Chuckling, Dreyson walked away from her.

We did not have to take the long way back. The queen simply opened a gate and sent us to the stone fairy circle in the woods, with about twenty more kids, human and changeling, than we had before. It was still daylight, and when Remington checked his phone, we were only gone for an hour.

There was a charter bus with attendants and a black Rolls Royce waiting when we got to the parking lot. Samuel and Mrs. Bancroft-Owens took the Rolls. The children hesitantly filed onto the charter bus.

"Would you mind coming with us to see Leonard?" Sofia asked.

"Please?" Innis asked, looking up at Dreyson beseechingly.

He nodded. "If that's what you want."

"Claire?" Innis asked.

"Sure," I said.

Xana was silent, looking around the parking lot suspiciously. She saw bits and pieces of this realm, but claimed she never actually left the Courts.

The ride was quiet. Remington, Dreyson, the Wilder-Ramos family, and myself took one vehicle. The detectives left to make their own reports.

Sofia rode in the front, glancing back every few minutes to check that the kids were both in the middle row.

Dreyson and I sat in the back.

"The Crow Knight asked a lot of questions about you, Claire. And he wanted to know all about Dreyson too," Innis said.

I rolled my eyes. "He's a menace."

"What did you tell him?" Dreyson asked.

"That I'm a kid and I don't know much." Innis smirked. "But obviously Claire doesn't like creeps who treat her badly."

"He's not a creep," Xana said. She turned to look at me earnestly. "He really isn't."

"I'm glad he doesn't hurt children," was all I said, because I didn't want to argue with her.

"Most well-adjusted people don't appreciate threats mixed with romantic overtures," Dreyson said. "That is not acceptable behavior."

Xana frowned. "Wait, was he trying to *court* you?"

I sighed, rubbing my forehead. "No."

"Yes," Innis said at the same time. "He definitely likes her."

My eyeballs twitched.

"I see," Xana said, eyeing me thoughtfully, her gaze drifting to Dreyson.

"What do you know?" Innis whispered. "Tell me."

"Later," Xana hissed.

And then both kids looked back at me and started to giggle.

I sighed.

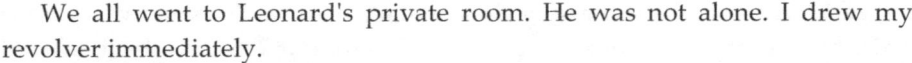

We all went to Leonard's private room. He was not alone. I drew my revolver immediately.

"Claire, *please*." The Crow Knight held up one hand. He sat in a chair by the bed, a little girl with brown skin and rust-colored braids, maybe a kindergartner, asleep in his lap. "You'll wake her, and she's so obnoxious."

"What is going on?" Sofia hissed.

"Innis, clever, clever Innis, demanded a boon." The Crow Knight chuckled. "And I am here to fulfill the bargain. After all, they wanted *both* their parents restored to good health. I've done what I can for your husband. He will live."

Sofia inhaled sharply.

"But?" Dreyson asked coolly.

"Much of my power came from the Vernal Lord," the Crow Knight said, "and he is dead. So there are limits to what I can do now. It took *forever* to get that nasty bullet out of my arm. Please don't shoot me again. It was thoroughly unpleasant."

I smiled sharply at him.

"Is that...?" Xana's eyes widened. "You took her!"

"For her own safety," the Crow Knight said. "But I am not equipped to raise a child in this world. You —" He looked at Sofia. "Are good parents. This child was recently orphaned. Her father asked me to find her a safe place. She...is not human, but I don't think that bothers you, does it?"

Sofia grimaced. "No. That detail isn't what bothers me."

"There are...benefits to housing her," the Crow Knight said. "Her presence would make your husband's recovery faster and better the fortunes of your household."

"And the Autumnal Lady?"

"I do not know how exactly she would dispose of a rival this young, but I do not wish to find out." The Crow Knight smiled. "Do you?"

"You have a lot of nerve," Sofia snarled.

"Nerve is not something I am lacking, no." He smiled with false modesty.

"This is something I would have to discuss with my children and my husband," Sofia said coolly. "I don't know how you expect to keep this a secret from Mrs. Bancroft-Owens."

"I don't," the Crow Knight said. "I expect the *Lares* to be very excited about this opportunity. Just like I expect that you would have a big problem seeing a small, helpless child exploited by such ruthless people. I, of course, would be available to help guide Innis, Xana, and this one in fields that you and your husband may lack expertise in."

"He is very good at magic," Xana said.

I groaned, belatedly realizing that she might be the Crow Knight's biggest fan.

"And sneaking," Innis said, giving him a dirty look.

"I am a man of many talents." The Crow Knight smiled. "I must go make more arrangements." He placed the girl in the chair and covered her in a silky green blanket. "Whatever you choose, your husband will heal faster if she stays close for a few days." He then vanished.

Sofia gave a groan of exasperation. "Leonard, what have you gotten us into?"

"I'm sorry?" Leonard murmured. "Didn't mean to..." He grunted and slowly opened his eyes.

"That doesn't fix a dam —" She stopped, and then she shrieked, throwing her arms around him as Innis ran up and hugged them both.

"Dad, Dad, we got her back! Dad!" Innis shouted.

"Oh my God," Leonard hugged his wife, mumbling apologies into her shoulder as she cry-laughed.

A nurse rushed in, his eyes wide as he took in the scene. He was a young man with a mop of blonde curls and a round face. "Please stay put! Dr. Jackson is on her way."

He hovered nearby, clearly unsure of what to do in the case of a simultaneous miraculous recovery and an impromptu family reunion. That was fair; maybe etiquette books covered this sort of thing, but who had time for that?

Xana stood back as she watched them flail and cry into an embrace. There was a bleak sort of confusion on her face. She did not know how to react.

"They're good people," Dreyson said quietly. "It will get easier, if you give them a chance."

Xana blinked up at us.

"They are happy that you're here. But you don't have to feel close to them right away. I know they're strangers to you," Remington said. "Building relationships takes time."

And in this case, probably a lot of therapy.

Xana nodded slowly, walked over to Leonard, and very formally offered him her hand to shake.

Paler and skinnier than before, he sat up and stared at her with wide-eyed delight. "You look so much like your mother," he wheezed. "What's your favorite color? What do you like to do? What's your favorite meal? I want to know everything-"

"We have...a lot to talk about," Sofia said, glancing at the sleeping child in the chair.

"Let's give them some privacy," Remington said, patting my shoulder.

I nodded, and we stepped into the hall.

Dreyson was silent. "I need to get back to the guildhall and check in. Will you be all right?" He glanced down at me.

"Yeah," I said, already planning to keep some of the enchanted ammo. It was time to price getting my own guns warded properly. It was complicated and expensive as hell, but if the Crow Knight was going to be around more, I needed to be prepared.

Dreyson nodded. "I'll be in touch."

"I'll be planning another murder," I said.

Dreyson smiled. "Try not to kill him in front of the children." Then he was gone.

"It's annoying how easily he does that," Remington said after a moment.

"No, what's annoying is that he doesn't double over in agony afterward." I rubbed the back of my neck, my fingers catching on the bandage.

Remington gave me a sympathetic smile. We stood in the hall while Remington checked his phone.

"Boss lady on her way?" I asked.

"Yeah," Remington said. "Can't tell much from the text, except that she's in a hurry and that we should stay here and be vigilant." He tucked his phone into his pocket, his amusement fading.

"Do you think—?"

"Yeah," he said grimly.

My hand rested on the hilt of the knife.

I peeked into the room. Leonard had one arm around his wife with Innis tucked between them.

The nurse, though, was on the far side of the room now.

Xana stood between him and the princess, her eyes very big, the fear apparent. She knew something was wrong. She just didn't know how wrong.

"Here," he said, his voice low and sickly sweet. "Let me help you with that—"

Xana backed up, trying to push the princess farther behind her.

I lunged forward, grabbing his arm and yanking him away from her.

He snarled. "You!" The man's face twisted in fury. "Do not interf—"

There was a click as Remington held his revolver to the nurse's head. "That's enough, Ketch."

I felt a familiar twinge of energy, and I knew that incapacitating pain would follow.

And then the Vernal Princess awoke, looked around, and began to wail, a real ear-splitting scream.

I clapped my hands over my ears, even as Xana hugged the child and began murmuring to her, trying to soothe her, the sound tapering off.

Even Ketch flinched, that power dissipating. "You can't keep that thing," he snarled. "You think you're good progressive parents, but those aren't truly your children! One of them is a cuckoo, and the other is corrupted beyond your ability to salvage. You're better off starting over. I would be doing you a favor!"

I had the knife out, looking for the cuts in his arm. I did not want to kill the nurse. He was an innocent bystander.

"Just give me that thing," Ketch growled, that voice too raspy and vicious to be coming from the young nurse, "and I will consider sparing your treacherous spawn—"

"Xana, sweetheart, please cover the little one's ears. She doesn't need to hear this," Sofia said, putting Xana and the Vernal Princess behind her.

To my surprise, Xana obeyed. But the Vernal Princess watched Ketch with eerie focus, her brown eyes wide and outraged.

"You need to leave me and my children alone," Sofia said.

"They're not *yours*, you stupid bitch!" Ketch shrieked. "You're just the bleeding host to a bunch of ungrateful parasitic—"

"That's motherhood," Sofia said wryly. She crossed her arms. "You're still not touching these kids."

"You can't stop—"

"That's enough, Jack."

I glanced over to see Mrs. Bancroft-Owens standing in the doorway. "Possessing Paean Hills staff *and* threatening children? That's low, even for you."

The nurse sucked in a sharp breath. "Back off, Harriet."

"I think not. You clearly can't be trusted to be rational about this matter. Now release the boy, and we'll talk about this later."

"That thing cannot stay—"

"You don't get to decide that." Mrs. Bancroft-Owens gave a triumphant smile. "Now get out of him, before I let them cut you out."

The nurse shot her a look of pure hatred, before snarling and then slumping against Remington.

"Put the gun down, Thomas," Mrs. Bancroft-Owens said. "He's gone."

Remington spun the gun back and holstered it. Sometimes I forgot how *fast* he was. We set the nurse down on the ground.

Mrs. Bancroft-Owens eyed the knife in my hand, before turning to Sofia. "I understand that you have been asked to take on another mouth to feed. It would be in everyone's best interest if you accepted. I am authorized to extend provisional aid to your household, should you be inclined to foster this unfortunate child."

"Do you have security that can handle Ketch?" Sofia asked.

"Arrangements will be made, and he'll see reason. Or he'll be replaced," Mrs. Bancroft-Owens said coolly. "I realize your family is still recovering from this series of shocks. My people are making preparations. I expect to speak with you in a few days about your situation. Can you keep the child till then?"

Sofia took a deep breath, glancing over at the Vernal Princess, who was staring very hard at Mrs. Bancroft-Owens. "Yes. I can do that much."

"Splendid." Mrs. Bancroft-Owens nodded stiffly. "Samuel will accompany you today. I can put you up in the Meteora while we do a sweep of your home."

Samuel leaned in the doorway, his gaze flicking from the Vernal Princess to Xana to Innis. He did not look particularly excited.

Sofia nodded tersely.

"Claire, are you going to come too?" Innis asked, squirming out from behind their mother.

"I'm beat," I said, the exhaustion starting to weigh on me.

"But you'll visit, right?" Innis asked.

"Sure," I said with a yawn.

Innis dashed forward and gave me a squeeze that actually lifted me off the ground.

I blinked and patted their back. Was that normal?

"I'll message you later," Innis whispered. "We have *a lot* to talk about."

I laughed. "OK."

"I am glad you stopped him," Xana said almost shyly as she peeked out from behind Sofia.

"Me too," I said.

Leonard gave us a sheepish smile. The Vernal Princess just continued to solemnly stare at Mrs. Bancroft-Owens. The little kid had good instincts: the *Lares* was the most dangerous person in the room.

I disentangled myself from Innis, and we waved as we headed out of the hospital room. Mrs. Bancroft-Owens and Samuel could handle this.

I couldn't relax till we were in the elevator, though.

Remington leaned against the wall. "I need a nap and food."

"Yeah, me too." I yawned. "You know, we haven't seen Boyle for awhile. We should visit his restaurant."

"Oh, that sounds good too. Let's go there for dinner," Remington said as we headed back down to the car.

Chapter 25
It Begins and Ends with Coffee

Addendum to Case 13-XI-2622: Cross-reference with Changelings, the Foxglove Pact, the Courts, the Crow Knight

Any questions regarding Changelings, including identities, health concerns, and custodial arrangements, should be forwarded to Dr. Roger Erasmus. This is out of our hands now, folks. Let's hope it stays that way.

— *SIU Police Reports: Blackout Files*

"Put that down. Don't stick your finger in there. Eubha, if I've told you once, I've told you a dozen times, strangling people is not an appropriate way to show affection. I don't care what they taught you in the Courts." Dr. Erasmus, still Fleance in my head, was a tiny nucleus of order in a chaotic hotel conference room. After over two weeks of dropping by the Meteora, I was used to the constant stream of noise, running children, and weird surprises.

I still expected to see Dr. Erasmus in a lab coat or a suit, but he wore khaki cargo shorts, a T-shirt, and most notably, a worn olive drab fishing vest with many, many pockets. He was clean-shaven, his thin face framed by big round glasses, gray hair in a ponytail.

About thirty children congregated in small groups around the large and now very cluttered hotel conference hall. Some families—including the Wilder-Ramos clan—were there, talking with nurses, Samuel, and other specialists. Mrs. Bancroft-Owens was notably absent.

"You know, Rogue," Dr. Erasmus said, when he caught sight of me. "I don't think this is actually safer than living incognito in the Sticks."

"If you want to fake your death again, I'm not going to stop you," I said with a shrug. "Just warn me so I can duck babysitting duty."

"But I was going to leave it all to you," he said.

I winced.

"Honestly, making Claire babysit will backfire," Remington said.

"Really?" Dr. Erasmus stroked his chin. "According to some of my admittedly biased subjects, you are an exemplary, if unorthodox, babysitter. Mrs. Bancroft-Owens said I could turn to you if I needed any assistance." He gave me a smug little grin.

"No one will ever find your body, Dr. Hide-and-Seek Champion," I told him cheerfully.

Dr. Erasmus squinted at me, like he knew I was probably joking but couldn't be completely sure. "Anyway, I know you wanted some updates. The Wilder-Ramos family needs more security measures enacted. I keep seeing jackbooted thugs lingering on the outskirts of the hotel grounds. Nothing too blatant yet, but I don't want to be caught unawares." His gaze hardened, lip curling. "Mrs. Bancroft-Owens says he won't try anything now."

"After getting so decisively trounced, maybe he's sitting at home eating a carton of ice cream and watching old rom-coms." I shrugged.

Dr. Erasmus snorted.

"The merc he puppeted is out too," Remington said.

I had no contact with Ketch. Naomi already gave her testimony, and no charges were being filed, though I wasn't sure if she would keep her position in the Wergeld.

"The Wilder-Ramos family needs more attention," Samuel said, tapping Dr. Erasmus' shoulder. "Hello, Claire, it's nice to see you," he said, giving me a pleasant smile. He was wearing a navy-blue suit, looking like a responsible adult with the bare minimum personality.

"Hi," I said, mustering a smile that felt at least 73 percent insincere. I saw him last at the office a week ago, with a phone video of Mrs. Bancroft-Owens informing Commissioner Porter that he had two weeks to get his affairs in order. Because "she was tired of him hobbling her Special Investigations Unit, and if he didn't retire quietly, things would go poorly for him. And it would be even worse if he decided to cross the Giles girl again." It was cathartic to see Porter turn that shade of purple.

Samuel then casually asked me to dinner. I gave an "Oh I'm so busy, but maybe later," answer because an outright "no" would probably just get him to push harder.

"Looks like the kids need some intervention," Remington said, nudging me and gesturing to the table where Innis and Xana bickered while Leonard tried to mediate. Sofia sat beside him, reading a book to "Bridget," the child's eyebrows knitting together as she made the effort to stay focused on the story time.

"Oh, yeah, I should run interference. During their last argument, Xana apparently cursed Innis with temporary blindness for a day." I knew, because the kid texted me constantly. That day, they called me to complain. But in spite of that traumatic incident, Innis both loved and hated their "new sisters" in unpredictable waves. Xana was clever, but also weird and moody. They weren't sharing a room, which went a long way toward helping them adapt. But "Bridget" was a spoiled brat and made Innis realize that they *never* wanted kids.

I headed over to their table, not giving Samuel a chance to respond.

Innis saw me first, their face brightening for a moment, before they scowled at Xana. "I don't want to talk to you anymore. Hi, Claire!"

Xana glowered at us both.

"Whoa, what did I walk into?" I asked, holding up both hands.

"Movie night negotiations," Leonard said with a crooked smile. "You know, we can do a double feature, guys. You each pick a film. Next week, it'll be someone else's turn."

Innis crossed their arms, not looking convinced. "But I'm sick of —"

"Claire, would you like to come over?" Leonard asked.

"Sorry, I'm meeting some people after this," I said, and it wasn't even a lie.

"Another time, then?" he asked.

"Sure, what do you want me to bring?" I asked Leonard. "We're going to need tons of popcorn."

"We should order pizza," Innis said.

"I don't know if we can find organic unprocessed pizzas, but we can do homemade ones," Leonard said hesitantly, looking at Xana and Bridget. The kids returning from the Courts needed extra time to adjust to the new environment, including dietary changes. Bridget required even more caution.

"Homemade is good too," they said. "That way we can pick our own toppings."

"What kind of toppings?" Xana asked.

"Oh, whatever you feel like, pepperoni, sausage, ham, pineapple, olives, anchovies, peppers, onions, mushrooms," Innis said, hostility forgotten when they got another opportunity to educate their new siblings.

Xana's eyes got bigger and rounder, the longer her sibling droned on.

"Sofia, do you have a moment?" Dr. Erasmus asked.

She nodded, handing off Bridget and the book to Leonard.

The four of us stepped aside. The noise around us faded to a muted roar as Dr. Erasmus activated a sound-dampening spell.

"Should keep the little eavesdroppers from hearing too much," he said. "First, we retained thirteen changelings out of the eighteen survivors, and brought back nine of the dozen surviving human children." That was twenty-two out of fifty kids. Not great. "Given my records, the ratio of sidhe changelings is much lower than expected."

"They killed the sidhe?" Remington asked.

"One," Dr. Erasmus said. "They likely put more effort into retaining the sidhe children, given their privileged position within the Courts. The human children all exhibit a talent for magic, even if they have no family history of it. Obviously, being raised in the Courts affected this. But that's secondary to the neglect and abuse these kids endured."

"We're in family therapy already," Sofia said. "Mr. Dreyson recommended a very good trauma specialist for the kids."

"Excellent," Dr. Erasmus said, hands clasped in front of him. "The human children who returned have a surviving changeling counterpart. I don't think that's a coincidence, but it's too early to make any concrete judgments." He rubbed his chin. "Bridget is another issue entirely."

"Mrs. Bancroft-Owens offered us very generous incentives to keep her," Sofia said carefully. "I am growing fond of her, and Leonard is enamored. But we are not equipped to handle her magic."

"Is her *other guardian* providing aid?" Dr. Erasmus asked.

I grimaced.

"The Crow Knight comes around," Sofia said hesitantly, avoiding my gaze. "He is helping us maintain a united front. I cannot complain about his current conduct, but Innis detests him, and there are residual...issues."

I looked away, trying to keep my thoughts to myself. The Crow Knight's budding relationship with the Wilder-Ramos family was news to me, though not a complete surprise. Since he was not a supporter of the Autumnal Lady, he was staying in the city, which was an uncommon choice for the Fey. I was taking extra precautions.

"The changelings have power dampeners built into their protective glamour, though some of the ones who returned from the Courts are having trouble maintaining their 'human' forms. You might consider one for Bridget," Dr. Erasmus said. "She is royalty and full sidhe, so it won't be foolproof. You need dampeners for Xana. Innis isn't quite as advanced as Xana in magic, but that could change with age." Dr. Erasmus rubbed the back of his neck. "I'm not sure what branch of Fey Innis' biological parents are. But they are not sidhe. Some of the colloquially named 'lesser Fey' were included in the project. I'd guess some variant of kobold, based on their abilities, but I don't know."

Sofia frowned. "Do you suspect that they are a danger to themselves or others?"

"There are Fey who are innately...disruptive. But it is unlikely that any of those were chosen as candidates for the Foxglove Pact."

"I don't get it," I said, looking around the room. "They put in all this work, ruined all these lives, and for what? To kill off nearly a quarter of the changelings? To treat all these kids poorly? It's cruel, unnecessary, and just...wasteful."

"I know, but it didn't start out like this. It certainly wasn't meant to go this way. The Fey are not wired to be good parents. They live too long, and their reproductive maturity comes much later in life, often after centuries. Many of them are too predatory or solitary to make good caregivers. There are exceptions, of course, but that was a problem they themselves acknowledged at the beginning of the project."

"So they know that they're unsuitable, and that giving up their kids might be the kindest thing they can do?" Remington asked.

Dr. Erasmus nodded. "Maybe. But the Vernal Lady was so optimistic." He glanced at Bridget. "And we trusted her husband. We shouldn't have, but…" He sighed. "Still, twenty-five healthy Fey children in only one year. They hadn't seen numbers like that in centuries. It was meant to be the revitalization of their species. I suppose it's only fitting that they ruined it for themselves."

"I'm not sure I follow," Remington said.

"Do you know why we called it the Foxglove Pact?" Dr. Erasmus asked.

"Digitalis is pretty and extremely poisonous," I said. "It's a medicine and a *medicine*. The folklore claims foxes or Fey use the blossoms in sneaky ways. So I figure it's part poetry, part threat."

Dr. Erasmus chuckled. "Good guess, but no, that's not what Maria had in mind." His gaze softened for a moment. "Just because the Fey aren't naturally good parents does not mean that they are indifferent toward their children. In the Victorian language of the flowers, foxglove means 'I am ambitious for you, not myself.' It's uncharacteristically selfless, but I like to think that some of the Fey really believe that." He smiled wistfully.

"That's why they gave them up, isn't it?" Sofia asked, her gaze misty. "They were selfish, immoral, and didn't care who else they hurt, all in the name of giving their children a better future. I hate it, but it's not so hard to understand."

"Yeah," Remington said. "But imagine how much better this could have turned out if they did things right."

Sofia flinched.

"It's not over yet," Dr. Erasmus said with a small smile. "If the Fey can't manifest that sentiment for these children, there are still plenty of us who can."

"Are you sure that you want me here?" Ivy asked for the third time, as we sipped our coffees on the patio of the cafe. She wore a gorgeous angora sweater in a bland shade of beige, yet it still looked really good on her.

"You were just going to track my location and call me every fifteen minutes anyway," I said. "I figured this would worry you less. At least this way, you get to have a latte too."

After my visit to the Meteora, I came straight here.

Ivy lowered her sunglasses, brushing back her chestnut curls and giving me a sharp look. "How many people did you upset in the last couple weeks?"

"I don't know," I said with a shrug. "In my defense, some have *forgiven* me and others are dead." I grinned.

Mwanje shared some interesting news with me. Officer Hartford disappeared, but *someone* anonymously mailed an incriminating package of documents to Detective Davis. Among the papers was a flash drive with an audio recording of Hartford confessing that he tried to arrange an accident for Dreyson and me, at the behest of Commissioner Porter. But now nobody had any idea where he was.

Mwanje watched me so carefully when he told me this story. I had theories, but I didn't actually know what happened. Maybe Porter tied up a loose end. Maybe Ketch didn't like failures. Maybe Hartford got wise and ran for it.

It wasn't my job to figure it out.

Mwanje was relieved to know that I was telling the truth, so he didn't question me too closely. He didn't need to; he probably had the same suspicions I did.

Apparently that handsy bastard, Officer Ryan, died in his squad car while we were in the Courts. A single stray bullet caught him in the temple. No leads, no suspects, no eye witnesses.

That one, I had no idea about. But I wasn't too broken up about it.

With them both gone, there was no investigation. I was still counting this as a win.

"So you shot the guy who broke in, but he's still running around?" Ivy asked, giving me a look.

"There's always later," I grumbled.

"You think he'll be coming around?" she asked.

"I don't know. We fixed the wards. If he bothers you, I'll kill him," I said with a smile. I didn't need an excuse.

"Claire, that is both extremely sweet and worrisome." Ivy shook her head in exasperation.

I grinned, even as a large shadow fell across our table.

Ivy stiffened.

I glanced up at Dreyson. He wore a tight black T-shirt and jeans and carried a white box in one hand.

"Hey," I said. "Dreyson, this is my friend Ivy. Ivy, this is Dreyson."

Dreyson politely extended his free hand. "A pleasure to finally meet you."

Ivy blinked, and then the uncertainty evaporated. She tossed her head, shook off the nerves, and eagerly took his hand while dialing up her smile to incandescent. "Dreyson! I've heard so much about you from Claire!" She hit him with her best socialite, life of the party charm-beam.

Dreyson only raised a brow, his cheeks turning pink. "Should I be worried?" he asked as he sat down.

Ivy laughed.

Dreyson set the box on the table. "I thought you might like to try this."

Inside was a beautiful round layer cake, covered in white frosting and little curls of white chocolate and lemon rind.

"It's the limoncello cake from Sal's," he said. "It's my favorite."

"Don't you only eat healthy?" I asked, eyeing the cake.

"When I'm *working* a serious job," he said dryly. "I can relax now."

"Only a little," I said. "She's a lawyer and I'm me. We're very dangerous."

"I am aware." Dreyson chuckled. "I'm going to get some tea. Would you like anything?"

"More coffee," I said. "Cream and sugar please!"

"No thanks," Ivy said, giving him an angelic smile. We watched him go into the cafe. "Oh my God," Ivy said out of the corner of her mouth. "Claire, he's a giant."

"Be nice."

"I am. That man is built like a demigod. Look at him, those shoulders, those *arms*. There's so much, I didn't get to finish looking," Ivy said, grinning widely at me. "If he's packing what I think he's got, he's going to break you in half, you lucky girl."

I choked on my coffee. "Damnit, Ivy!"

She grinned at me. "And he brought you a cake." She glanced at it. "An expensive cake." She leaned in, nudging me with her elbow. "His favorite."

"And if he doesn't hurry back, I'm going to eat it all," I said happily.

"Do you want me to disappear?" she asked.

"No, stay for cake at least," I said.

Dreyson returned soon, carrying two cups. He sat back down and opened the box. He brought a plastic cake server, disposable plates, and forks.

I sipped my coffee. It wasn't as sweet as I liked it, but with the cake, it didn't need to be.

"He came prepared," Ivy said, giving me an approving look.

"It's a requirement of my job," Dreyson said, cutting the cake very neatly. The slices were identical. He set the first one in front of me, one for Ivy, and then himself.

I happily took a bite. The cake was light and lemony, the creamy frosting blending beautifully with the fragrant citrus flavor.

"Oh, that's exquisite," Ivy said. "This is from Sal's?"

"Yes," Dreyson said, looking at me with a small smile. "Do you like it?"

My slice was half gone. Dreyson had good taste in sweets. I grinned at him, blotting at my mouth with a napkin. "I don't know, I might need to have another slice."

"I thought you might say that," he said, looking amused.

"Very wise of you to bring a whole cake," I said.

"That does look lovely," a man said from the table beside ours.

I froze, because I recognized that voice. I slowly turned my head to look at him, one hand slipping down to my purse.

Dreyson's expression went flat.

Ivy straightened up, also reaching into her purse.

"Are you going to invite me to share a slice?" The Crow Knight sipped a drink. He was out of the iconic armor, instead clad in a neat narrow-legged black suit and waistcoat over a black collared shirt, with gloves and a silver tie clip. He had numerous rings in his rounded ears, and his long reddish-brown hair fell in unruly waves around his face. He must have cut his hair—I didn't see any sign of the braid. He had a pointed, elegant face with sharp cheekbones. He was prettier than I expected, with dark brown eyes, a slender straight nose, and full lips.

"If he tries to take a slice, I will shoot him," I said.

"Is that—" Ivy began.

"I'm Corwin," the Crow Knight said, flashing a bright smile like some kind of pop star. "I would offer a warmer greeting, but I don't want Claire to shoot me again."

Ivy's smile was sharp. "Claire's not the only one you have to worry about."

The Crow Knight's smile widened. "Claire, you know such interesting people."

To my surprise, Dreyson served up a slice of cake, rose, and set it in front of the Crow Knight.

"I understand if you can't afford to buy yourself something nice. It must be very hard. So here, have a slice of cake and be on your way. I'd hate to see you arrested for vagrancy." He turned his back on the man and sat down.

The Crow Knight stiffened, his eyes widening at Dreyson's insult. "Dreyson—" He breathed, sounding wounded.

Dreyson gave me that crooked smile. "I gave you cake. You can leave now. That was the bargain. You understand bargains."

"You two are so clever *and* vicious," the Crow Knight said, picking up his cake with a forlorn sigh. "You've bested me, then. I do hate to impose, so I will be on my way. With only this small confection to ease my broken heart." He drifted off to the sidewalk, walking away slowly, looking back at us mournfully, the wind ruffling his hair.

"You know, if you feed him, he'll only come back," I said, after he disappeared around a corner.

"Unfortunately, I don't think we'll be rid of him for some time," Dreyson said. "But I'd rather he didn't bother either of you today. That seemed the fastest way to get rid of him without making a scene."

"I still could've shot him," I said, patting my bag.

"Have some more cake," Dreyson said, shaking his head and offering me a second slice.

I grinned at him and accepted it. "What kind of bargain are you trying to drive now?"

Dreyson leaned back in his chair. "The cake is freely given. I would not dream of trying to reuse the same trick on you."

"It would work," Ivy said, laughing softly.

"I know, but I'm not trying to chase her away," Dreyson said, and took a bite of cake.

ABOUT SEN ZHANG

SEN ZHANG is outnumbered by her dogs, generally outgunned by her cat overlord, and skews outlandish on the best of days. She enjoys reading, cooking, and naps. You can find her at senzhang.net.

If you've enjoyed this book, please consider leaving a review for the author on Amazon and other book retailer sites. Actually, it would be great to leave them for any book you've enjoyed. Authors truly appreciate it.

Made in United States
Cleveland, OH
20 July 2025

18543410R10166